HO
THE H

Roopam Kapoor is a senior officer in customs and indirect taxes. He did his graduation and post-graduation in English Literature from Delhi University. After joining the civil services, he worked in various positions, including anti-smuggling formations and tax enforcement wings. Having worked in the border areas of India's west coast, he has closely observed the rise and fall of organized criminal gangs in the 1990s. He is also a keen trekker and photographer. This is his debut novel.

श्रेयान्स्वधर्मो विगुणः परधर्मात्स्वनुष्ठितात् ।

It is far better to live your own destiny and
perform your own duties imperfectly than to live
an imitation of someone else's life with perfection.

—Bhagavad Gita, Chapter 18, Verse 47

I have seen the moment of my greatness flicker,
And I have seen the eternal Footman hold my coat, and snicker,
And in short, I was afraid.

—T.S. Eliot, *The Love Song of J. Alfred Prufrock*

HOUR OF THE HOUNDS

ROOPAM KAPOOR

Published by
Rupa Publications India Pvt. Ltd 2023
7/16, Ansari Road, Daryaganj
New Delhi 110002

Sales centres:
Bengaluru Chennai
Hyderabad Jaipur Kathmandu
Kolkata Mumbai Prayagraj

P-ISBN: 978-93-5520-514-8
E-ISBN: 978-93-5520-515-5

First impression 2023

10 9 8 7 6 5 4 3 2 1

Printed in India

Contents

Prologue

Six men huddled closely inside the small wheelhouse of the boat, trying to find space where there was none. Six scared men who stared at their skipper with looks ranging from fear to hope as he hunched over the boat wheel trying to navigate them out of a difficult situation. In normal times, the wheelhouse could accommodate four people with difficulty. But these were not normal times, at least not for the seven men on the boat. Small boats were not supposed to venture out to sea during monsoons. Monsoons in the Indian Ocean were never kind to small boats, and now the sailors were experiencing its fury as their boat was mercilessly tossed about by the raging storm.

The sailors were not scared of the storm. Two of them had been braving the incessant rain just a short while ago, standing on the prow of the boat, guiding the skipper to their destination. That was before the firing had started. Now, the noise of the howling wind and the crack of breaking waves was being periodically shattered by the boom of the 30 mm gun of the Coast Guard ship that had been chasing their boat for the past six hours. By now the men on the boat knew that the cannon shells were not likely to get them. Visibility was poor due to the heavy rain and the two-metre swells were making it further difficult for the Coast Guard gunner to judge the distance accurately. They were more scared of the staccato of 12.7 mm machine guns whose bullets were intermittently sweeping the sea. Some of the bullets had thudded into the hull a few minutes back, forcing their captain to take the risk of sailing closer to the shore.

So far, their twenty-metre-long boat had been able to evade the ninety-metre-long Coast Guard ship successfully due to the skilful manoeuvring of their skipper. His tall frame was hunched over the wheel, as he peered through the blinding rain, eyes furtively scanning the sea to spot the next big wave that may capsize his boat. His bony hands spun the boat wheel desperately, more by instinct than design, trying to keep the little boat afloat while evading the Coast Guard ship.

The skipper was the only Indian on board, and the six Pakistani sailors marvelled at his knowledge of the Indian coastline. He seemed to know intimately not just the coast, but every jutting, every sandbar, every shelter on this part of the sea. He was now sailing dangerously close to the shore, and at times the sailors felt that they were bound to smash upon the rocks. But then, incredibly, there would be open sea again, and their skipper would take advantage of the opening to crest another swell, providing them with precious moments of invisibility from the Coast Guard's ship. The skipper knew that he could not escape his pursuers in open sea. Their boat was bigger and faster, and he could neither run, nor hide, from them in the open sea. So, he sailed close to the shore, where the waves were higher, but where his skill gave them a slim chance to escape.

The Pakistanis rued the day when they had agreed to this trip. Their regular dhow had been incapacitated by an engine failure at Fujirah, and they had been approached by an agent to sail on a vessel smuggling silver to India. It was supposed to be a quick trip, and the money was good. The agent hinted that the vessel was sailing for Salim—and one did not slight Salim if you wanted to sail safely on the gulf of Yemen or the African coast. The Lion of Dubai was known to be generous, but he was also notorious for his short temper. The bodies that occasionally floated ashore along the Persian Gulf bore ample testament of how Salim treated his adversaries. The lure of payment—one lakh rupees each—and the chance to work for the legendary Salim were strong additional incentives for the voyage. They now regretted their decision. Salim was apparently not as powerful as he was made out to be. Why would the Indian Coast

Guard be chasing his consignment if he was all powerful? So, they hoped that the skipper would be able to dodge the Coast Guard's ship. Otherwise, they would be incarcerated in an Indian prison for a long time, maybe as smugglers, but more likely as spies.

The skipper had no time to think about the past. He was concentrating on manoeuvring the boat, digging deep into his memory to picture the coast as he remembered it. He had encountered the Coast Guard ship at the mouth of Dighi creek, just a kilometre before the jetty where he was supposed to hand over the contraband silver to the local agents. They were blocking the creek, and he had instinctively known that they were waiting for him. He had, without thinking, turned his little boat towards the sea, refusing to halt when they had hailed him. He had been trying to evade the Coast Guard ship since then. He was sure that he had passed Murud Janjira some time back, and sensed that the coast of Shrivardhan was not far. He remembered that there was a cove out there somewhere. There was a sandbar that blocked its entrance, leaving just thirty feet of channel for the boats to sail in. In this weather, he would need more than skill to sail the 25-feet-wide boat into the cove. He prayed. Prayed for his safety, to see his two wives and children again, and for the safety of the cargo he was carrying. The crew did not find a place in his prayers.

The sea gods finally seemed to smile upon the skipper and his crew. They guided his boat into the cove just as an extra spell of heavy rain had brought down the visibility to all but zero. He was confident that the radars on the Coast Guard's ship would not have been able to distinguish his boat from the rocks. So he, along with the others, waited with bated breath. They saw the Coast Guard ship turning slowly towards the open sea. The sound of intermittent firing faded, but they could still hear the 30 mm cannon booming once in a while. They now realized that the Coast Guard gunner had been firing blind.

They waited for four hours, and when they knew it was safe, sailed out of the cove. The captain did not need to look at the map to know that he was near Shrivardhan. He was now, as per the backup plan, required to sail to Mangalore, where he was to wait fourteen nautical miles out from Kapu lighthouse for the fishing boat that would smuggle their cargo to shore.

Two, three days more and I can be home free, he thought.

The exhilaration of escaping death made him forget that skill was not the only thing that helped you survive. There was also fate.

1

The Blundering Nincompoop

Approximately One Month Earlier

'So, you are now going to chase smugglers?' said Kanwar, looking at Prakash over the pile of files stacked on his desk. He had just been told of the ferocious firing Prakash had received from Salunkhe, the Collector of Customs at Pune, who had, somewhere in the middle of his fifteen-minute diatribe, also announced that Prakash was being transferred to Dapoli, a rural hamlet on the Konkan coast of Maharashtra, and headquarters of a Customs formation dedicated to check smuggling of contraband along the west coast of India.

'Come on, it's not so bad,' Kanwar said, looking at Prakash's morose expression. 'Yes, you will miss all your friends and will not get to eat butter chicken or dal makhni, and there will be no parties… but look at the positive side, you will be James Bond incarnate to your friends. Of course, you will have to write letters to tell them about your exploits. The communication systems at Dapoli are rather primitive.'

Prakash stared at Kanwar, the man who, along with Salunkhe, usually decided the destiny of Customs officers in Pune. They moved them like pieces on a chessboard. Use this guy to defend, this one to attack, and let's sacrifice this one to the wilderness. He decided not to respond to Kanwar's baiting.

'It's okay, sir. I can live without the butter chicken and the friends, but a third transfer within two months of starting a career? What am I doing wrong?'

Kanwar looked at Prakash. His lean 5'8" frame, with the mop of striking black hair falling over his forehead, and the perpetual twinkle in the grey eyes that he just could not cloud when he was carelessly listening to the homilies spouted by his seniors, often reminded Kanwar of his younger self. He smiled.

'Think about your past actions, imagine what had gone wrong during any of the actions done and then think about what you have not done...and then think about what could have gone right if you had done that, and then think where did you maintain the status quo, and think what could have happened if the status quo had changed. Hidden among those acts done, not done and the status quos is the mistake that has landed you in Dapoli.'

That was deep, thought Prakash, *but I would need to be stoned before I could make sense of that*. He knew he would not be able to get anything more out of Kanwar. So he decided to change tacks.

'The Collector also called me a blundering nincompoop,' Prakash said, in a tone he thought would lighten the mood.

That elicited a guffaw from Kanwar. He leaned back on his chair, giving Prakash a look mixed with wonder and speculation.

'Two months in service, three transfers already and an epitaph that is going to stick to you for the rest of your career in the Indian Revenue Service. You will never ever be able to live down that you were called a "nincompoop" by Salunkhe, the respected Collector of Pune.' Continuing in a jovial tone, he said, 'You English-literature types...you should know that the word comes from the Latin phrase *non compos mentis*, meaning not of sound mind. How are you ever going to live it down?' He guffawed again in genuine mirth.

Prakash could not help himself. Muttering under his breath, he said,'Over here things are falling apart, the centre cannot hold, anarchy has been set loose on planet earth, the blood-dimmed tide is loosed...and he thinks of explaining the etymology of the word "nincompoop" to me.'

'What was that?' said Kanwar sharply. 'You think I can't recognize Yeats' writing even when you just quote fragments? As I have told you countless times before, being sarcastic is not going to get you anywhere.'

'I wasn't being sarcastic,' said Prakash with a beatific smile. 'I was just checking whether you had fallen so far down while being in service so as to forget your own literature background.'

This time the wonder was clear in Kanwar's look. He stared at Prakash for a long time.

'So, you really aren't going to let anything detract you from your style of working? This transfer doesn't faze you at all,' he stated, half questioningly.

Prakash did not reply.

Kanwar softened after a brief pause. 'Come to my house in the evening. I should at least give you a drink before dispatching you to Dapoli. And maybe beat the Romantics out of your head. Don't expect a Black Label. You sainik school types do not merit anything more than a rum. Eight. Sharp.'

'Yes, sir,' replied Prakash. He was relieved that their relationship had not been substantially affected by the course of events. Kanwar would not have invited him only to snub him. There was still hope that he may be able to understand the intricacies of the bureaucracy he had accidently landed himself in.

◆

'Goodbye Pune, at least for now,' said Prakash to himself as he packed all his belongings, which consisted of two suitcases—one for his clothes, the other for his books. He suddenly realized that he had no friends in Pune to say goodbyes to, and to bid farewell to Pune, he nostalgically walked down to his favourite bookstore on the corner of the street and bought the latest Tom Clancy novel. He then added *The Secret Pilgrim* by Le Carré as a going-away present for himself. Then, in that depressive mood, buying *Paradise Lost* was the automatic choice.

'Let's see if Dapoli is hell or purgatory,' he muttered to himself. He looked around to check if he needed to buy something else, and looking at the vast display of cartoon video cassettes, bought the latest edition of Looney Tunes for Kanwar's daughter. 'Goodbye bookshop,' he muttered as he walked out of the door.

◆

Kanwar was playing with his four-year-old daughter when Prakash came in. Prakash gifted her the Looney Tunes video cassette and Kanwar, inserting the cassette in the player for her to watch, poured two large pegs of his favourite brew, Johnny Walker Black Label.

'So…angry or disappointed?' Kanwar asked as he handed Prakash his drink.

'More frustrated actually, sir,' Prakash replied. 'Primarily because one does not know the reason behind these transfers.' He hoped that Kanwar would take the hint.

Kanwar pondered and then said, 'And I am not going to tell you. You need to learn the nuances of bureaucratic functioning before you plunge headlong into taking action. There are consequences, and the softer you tread, the easier it is to avoid pitfalls. You need to learn from your mistakes.'

'But how can I?' retorted Prakash, 'If I don't know what they are.'

'And in bureaucracy, no one is ever going to tell you,' Kanwar said. 'So, do what you think is right and keep marching on. The only thing I can advise you is…don't disturb the status quo very much.'

'Hah! The Collector said much the same thing. He said that he was transferring me before I did too much damage to the system in Pune. But I don't even know what am I supposed to do in Dapoli, and maybe I will end up making a bigger faux pas over there,' Prakash said.

Kanwar, instead of replying, got up to tuck his daughter into bed. She waved a sleepy goodbye to Prakash. Kanwar poured another drink for Prakash as he seemed to settle down for a long evening.

'You will make mistakes there. Certainly. Just make sure they don't get you killed there.'

'Killed!' exclaimed Prakash. 'I thought that senior officers don't get killed.'

'That is because not enough of them are in the field. Smugglers don't know the distinction between senior and junior officers. Knowing you, you will be on the front, leading the charge. Just keep one thing in mind. Don't trust anybody when you are in the field. And when I say *anybody*, that includes your colleagues, your subordinates, me…even your parents.'

'You, and my parents!'

'You never know when someone is under threat,' said Kanwar, getting up to insert another cassette in the video player. His back was stiff as he said, 'How do you know that someone speaking to you does not have a gun pointed at his head? Remember, even your shadow leaves you when it's dark. If you can't trust even your shadow in times of trouble, how can you trust anyone else?'

The TV flickered briefly before settling to show a leading comedian entertaining guests at a birthday party.

'Watch this. It may help you understand why you shouldn't trust anybody,' said Kanwar.

This is weird, thought Prakash. *Watch a birthday party!*

The camera panned to show some minor politicians, a few businessmen, and then focused on a leading film star who was talking animatedly to a stocky man with a bushy moustache, who seemed to be listening carelessly as he caressed the bare thigh of a beautiful girl sitting next to him.

Kanwar paused the video.

'Recognize them?' asked Kanwar.

'One of the guys is a top film star. The other, I think, is Salim—the gangster? I'm not sure. And the girl, I don't know,' Prakash replied.

'The girl is a nobody,' replied Kanwar, not knowing just how wrong he was. 'But I want you to learn about Salim. This is his birthday party, and note the guest list. Politicians, film stars, even businessmen. This party shows the extent of his hold over Bombay and the west coast. His syndicate smuggles the maximum quantity of gold and silver into India, and it is his boys whom you will encounter on the Konkan coast,' Kanwar let the cassette play for a while and then paused it again. In the video, two flamboyantly dressed people were locked deep in conversation with a sheikh. One was tall and lean, had a pockmarked face, and was wearing an open-neck printed shirt, bell bottoms and a lascivious expression. The other was stocky, sporting a moustache rivalling Salim's and an intense expression.

'Rangeela and Master, the two brothers who seem to be controlling the Konkan coast for Salim now. This cassette showed for the first time that they have moved up in the underworld, nearly into Salim's inner coterie. Master loves killing. It is surprising that Salim let a killer move up the hierarchy. Nobody should trust killers. They are cowards. But now, Master has gained power, and you should be wary of him.'

Kanwar let the cassette play on, briefing Prakash on some faces, commenting on the film stars present in the party, drawing Prakash's attention towards Salim's family, pointing out the politicians at the party, adding an anecdote or two about each person and generally giving him a feel of the underworld. The cassette lasted for about an hour and a half, and when it had played out, Kanwar poured Prakash another drink.

'Dapoli is a small hamlet on the Konkan coast, midway between Alibag and Ratnagiri. You are now responsible for approximately two hundred and fifty kilometres of the west coast. Small beaches scattered along the coastline are used by smugglers to offload their illegal cargo. These smugglers also use the four major creeks at Bankot, Dabhol, Jaigarh and Devgarh, which flow in from the sea right up to the foothills of the Western Ghats, with nearly thirty kilometres of navigable waters, for smuggling. Smuggling is not just a vocation for the people on the coast, it's a passion. You have seen just a glimpse of the people who support Salim. Your job is to counter him, and *saam, daam, dand* or *bhed* will not be sufficient. You will need more than that in your arsenal of stratagems.'

Before Prakash could answer, Kanwar got up and said, rather abruptly, 'Finish your drink. This is what you get from a military school guy,' he said, pointing to himself. 'Getting that cassette was an intelligence coup. Let's see if you sainik school types can pull off something like that. Prove yourself. There are two kinds of people in the world—those who chase, and those who are chased. Anyone can run behind another. Life truly starts when you are the one being chased.'

The evening ended as inconclusively for Prakash as it had started, with a cryptic dialogue.

2

The First Interregnum

8 August 1991

Prakash was excited, and frustrated. He couldn't suppress the rage of range of emotions surging through him, and there was no one he could share them with. Dapoli was frustrating that way. The telephones rarely worked, and it had been ages since he had talked to any of his friends. And he missed sharing his life with them. It had dawned on him, over the last month, that of all his friends, he missed talking to Shelley the most. Shelley, who, while helping a bumbling, diffident, small-town boy navigate the libertine atmosphere of Delhi University, had become his smoking and drinking partner. Shelley, who would look him straight in the eye and tell him that he was a fool. Shelley, who could look right through his subterfuges. He used to share everything with her, and now, as he was passing through the most tumultuous period of his young life, he couldn't talk to her!

What the hell, he thought as he hunted desperately for some decent paper, and more importantly, a decent pen to write with, *If the phones don't work, there is always a letter I can write. Let me surprise her.*

◆

Dear Shelley,

Sorry for the lack of phone calls. This place really has a primitive phone system—just a shade better than the matchbox-and-string phones we used to play with in our childhood, and so I have been forced to resort to the forgotten art of letter writing. Preserve this. This is an epochal moment and my letter may become as famous as Hunt's letter to Shelley.

Let me try and help you imagine this place, purportedly the *Kala Pani* of bureaucracy, that proverbial exile where you don't get to drink the sweet water of Ganga. A forgotten place with poor communication systems, no parties and no exotic food. A village with population of just about a thousand people who should be content with fishing, farming and fucking, but still hope for some signs of development. Like a primary health centre, a college, maybe even a movie hall. I think people everywhere are waiting eternally for Godot.

But I still love this place. You should come here once. It's that idyllic sylvan retreat that the romantics have talked of. Nature, that eternal force, seems to guide all actions over here. Even travelling is via old-modes—boats and a few motorcycles. I, of course, jar the harmony by travelling in a car, but I think the broken windows of the car make up for the aberration. That, and the fact that my driver is an unmitigated arrogant SOB. He was caustic when I asked him about the car's air-conditioning. 'Why do you need air conditioning, sahib? The fads you big city-wallahs have. Enjoy the clean air; this broken window ensures you breathe fresh air,' he said. This is the only point on which the two of us seem to agree—the pleasure of breathing fresh air.

I am out in the fresh air a lot, mostly chasing the bad guys. Customs offices over here are replete with motorcycles, jeeps and boats—all to chase down the elusive smugglers. I use all of them freely, taking one or the other vehicle out at the slightest pretext, flying over mostly empty roads. Gone are the days when we were chased by police in Delhi while jumping red lights. In fact, the police call me for help now.

They called me two days back from as far away as a hundred kilometres, telling me that I needed to investigate some firing at sea, and I said to myself, *Police! Turning to me for action!* But I responded. Promptly! Drove a hundred kilometres in torrential rain, myself, alone, in that car with broken windows. I lost my way, not once, but twice! The fearless rider of the bylanes of Delhi managed to lose his way on a road with no turns! Don't view me with contempt. It is still a new place for me. And I did reach that place, Bankot, in less than three hours. And do you know what my driver did in those three hours? He tried to convince the police to register a report for a stolen office car! Thankfully, others noticed that a rifle was also missing, and then later on, discovered that even I was missing, and guessed, rightly so, that I must have taken the car and the rifle. Please note the sequence here. While locating missing things, in terms of priority, for government officers, guys come last!

So, following some deft reasoning by my officers, I was not booked for the theft of a government car, which I tell you, would have been petty malfeasance as compared to the things that do happen here. I say petty because while I was being reported for stealing a government car, I seized silver worth ₹6.5 crore. That's right! Six and a half crore! That is sixty-five million for you America returned types, which is quite a princely sum when you think that our bun-omelettes at the Jai Singh Dhaba used to cost us only sixty-five paisa. Yes! You can now call me the new Bond. After all, I too am chasing the bad guys over land and sea. Just not in an Aston Martin, but a broken down Ambassador. I think Bond gets the girls because of the Aston Martin. I can't think of any other reason why I haven't landed any so far. And don't say that I am not as good-looking as Roger Moore.

Am I rambling and rambling without having smoked a joint? That's what happens with me; 'eternally the seeker, so eternally the speaker,' as Lalitha ma'am used to say for me in college. But to come back to my ramblings, as I said, I lost my way twice, and I reached Bankot only in the afternoon to find a bunch of worried people from Customs, police and even the village headman. I couldn't imagine what they expected of me. After all, I was just the greenhorn, wet behind the ears freshie.

But I now understand that bureaucracy tends to push decisions to the top in a crisis. 'I had informed sahib,' as they say. Me. A sahib! You don't say! But isn't that what I am supposed to be? Be a Burra Sahib to the boot. All of them looked so relieved that I had finally arrived that I had to perforce be in charge of the events from that moment. They were rightly worried. Apparently, there had been some heavy firing going on at sea, probably even canon-fire. And at their level, they really could not have decided what to do. So, I had to lead them, which, you know, I am loath to do. But in this case, I led my troops to the coast. I did not know what else to do, as there was little chance of sailing into the sea amid such torrential rain.

You should experience the rain in Konkan. It's not like those two-hour showers in Delhi that leads to flooded streets and traffic jams. The rain, once it starts here, lasts for hours and sometimes, even days, and life may pause for a while, but it doesn't stop. Of course, the fishing boats are not allowed to sail during the monsoon. They're hauled up on the beaches, which protects the fishermen from monsoon storms, and gives time to fishes to procreate. And that is why you should not eat fish during May, June, July and August—the months that do not have the letter 'R' in it. These are the months when fishes fuck, and it's impolite to catch someone in the act. Over here they say that gives bad luck.

Do you remember how we used to believe in luck? Cross our fingers and all that. Remember how they played the CSNY song for the tie-breaker question during the Rendevouz quiz—and who except me listened to CSNY in the mid-80s! That was also the only time you kissed me. Well, something like that happened over here too. There was a solitary boat tied at the jetty, manned by three fishermen who had been out in the sea when the firing had started. As they hurriedly told their tale, we learned that the shots had sounded like they had come from big guns, very close to them. And although they hadn't seen anybody, they gestured to the north to indicate that the firing was possibly happening at the Bombay side of the coast. The sound kept closing in on them all the time they were in the sea. Scared, they had returned to the shore with the meagre catch of fish they had managed.

I, the landlubber, had never ever even sailed, let alone sail the sea in stormy weather. But if fishermen could sail in such weather, how hard could it be, I wondered. After all, I am just twenty-five and fit. I lit a cigarette (still the Gold Flake Honey Dew, not the 555 you guys teased that I would smoke after joining Customs) and asked them if they were willing to sail again, hoping they would say no.

I had underestimated the influence a government official could command in these regions. They promptly agreed in Marathi, saying—in rough translation—'If the bada sahab will order us, then yes.'

Now it was my face, my ego and what-not on the line. I couldn't back out now, could I? After all, there were six pairs of eyes watching my reaction. There were two possible options. First, I could have said that the firing has stopped, and we have all proved to be good citizens and conscientious officers, and let's go back now that we know that all is fine with the world. And the second, let's go into the sea and check it out. Have I ever refused a dare? So we boarded the fishing boat, carrying just two antiquated rifles and two revolvers to face the big guns. You were right! I never think before acting, but then, where is the fun in calculating the odds? The rush comes when you win against the odds.

That was my first foray into the sea. I have to admit that I was afraid, but fear along with that concomitant rush of adrenaline was, like always, exhilarating. The sea was rough, but not as bad as I was told it could be. I missed the cigarettes—the combination of sea spray and rain soaked all of them. I am smarter now. I have a plastic pouch to keep my cigarettes, just like the one we used to keep the grass in. And I have also bought a windproof cigarette lighter.

We didn't have to sail far. Less than a kilometre into the open sea, and just after fifteen minutes of expert sailing by the seasoned fishermen, we spotted a boat floundering dangerously in the rough sea. Everybody was excited, but also fearful. Were these the guys who were firing? Were they armed? Were they carrying explosives? The fishermen were sure that they had never seen this boat before, but they thought it was a Mangalore-manufactured boat. The fact that it was an Indian boat, and that it had a faulty engine, gave me some heart. Smugglers, or terrorists, would not use sub-standard boats, I felt. Little did I know!

This was no chase à la James Bond, but it will go down in history as my first encounter with the underworld. It was not very exciting; these guys, particularly the six Pakistanis, looked so beaten down that it was hard to believe that they were smuggling silver into India. Silver is banned for import into India; something to do with conserving precious foreign exchange. You would know better. After all, you are the MBA kind. But even you MBA types would not have studied the economics behind these country boats. They transport all kinds of things. Onions, goats, spices and cement from India to the Middle East; and then foodstuff from there to Africa. They make lakhs from legal trade, and millions from smuggling. This time, the owner was hoping to make millions, carrying contraband silver in the large hold. Silver—moulded as bricks, 350 of them, each weighing 30 kg, wrapped in gunny bags that had a handle attached on the top, presumably to make them easier to carry.

Seizing this cargo also gave me a shot at working on another intelligence craft—interrogation. You threaten, cajole, look for contradictions, lead the conversation, and even use physical violence. I may have gone a little overboard as I was rankled by the idea that these guys thought of me as such a small fry, so much so that they had started smuggling soon after I had been posted. It hurt my ego. But then, these guys are the small fry. I really need to go after the big guns. Like that don, Salim Bhai, who owned this consignment. I can draw some solace from the fact that the consignment was supposed to be smuggled through a place called 'Dighi creek', which falls outside my jurisdiction, but apparently, our elite agency, RI, knew about it and were lying in wait for them with a big Coast Guard ship. These guys ran. I don't mean literally *ran* ran, but I mean that they tried to escape their pursuers. Their puny boat, made by uneducated carpenters who know nothing about the displacement principles of Archimedes or Bernoulli's theorem of flowing liquids, was able to dodge the large ship of the Coast Guard, with all its fancy radars and dopplers and fast speed, by sailing close to the coast where, due to shallow waters, the big Coast Guard ship dared not venture. The guys would have actually managed to get away had their engine not failed. But then, I guess, fate had other designs on them.

It is exciting to be the leader of a team that seizes silver worth ₹6.5 crore and 150 watches of Rado and Kolber. What's your preference among watches—Rado or Kolber? I can now get you one, cheap, from the Customs shop. And don't you dare call me cheap, just because I can't afford to gift you one. I have always treated you to the best hash. Of course I can't smoke any here, even if you are around. Need all my wits around me. After all, Salim is the big, bad wolf and one is not supposed to mess with him. The office is abuzz with what is going to happen next. But can he be more than human? If RI and the Coast Guard can think of taking him on, I too can. And now I have already faced one of his henchmen, John. Seemed like a normal person to me, not a sociopath or a psychopath. He was a little scared of going to jail for the first time. Was boasting a lot. The reaction of a scared man, I guess.

Does that seizure, in any way, redeem me in your eyes, Shelley? Do you still think that I am wasting my life being a bureaucrat? Imagine how much good the government can do with six and a half crore rupees.

After experiencing life here, I realize there are only three professions that can change lives more than the bureaucrats. Politicians, godmen, and of course, writers. I am not cut out to be a politician; too much hard work. We all saw how much your Dad works as a Member of Parliament. I am simply not cut out to be a people's man. I shoot first and reason later. Godman would be an interesting craft. But then, the beard. It always gives me the rashes. That leaves the writer in me, which you always said is struggling to come out. Well, maybe, one day, he will come out.

Till then,
Bol Bum! Ciao!
Prakash

P.S. Are you missing my recitations? Let me give you one of *veer ras*:

O young Lochinvar is come out of the West,
Through all the wide Border his steed was the best;
And save his good broadsword he weapons had none,
He rode all unarm'd, and he rode all alone.

P.P.S. I forgot you wouldn't know what 'RI' is. That's one of the really elite organizations that does nothing but catch smugglers.

3

Dawn of Comprehension

Dapoli: A Tea

'Have you read this?' Prakash asked Lal, his most trusted Superintendent, over their morning tea as he read a newspaper report stating that the silver-smuggling on the coast had the blessings of the highest echelons of Customs. Lal, with a military school background, had become Prakash's confidant over the last couple of months. Although junior to Prakash in the hierarchy, he had more field experience, and with his sardonic sense of humour and a sensible, everyday approach to work, he efficiently countered Prakash's ebullience and inexperience.

'A seizure of more than six and a half crore rupees is bound to create a buzz. Forget about it,' Lal replied staidly.

'Forget about it!' exclaimed Prakash. 'They are imputing complicity. We cannot just let it go.'

'So deny it,' Lal replied calmly. 'But you can't, because at your level, you are not authorized to give statements to the press. You have to prepare a press release, which needs to be sent to Pune for clearance. The bosses will take time to discuss and deliberate it. By the time it is released, the release will be responding to stale news and will unnecessarily rake up the allegations all over again. Some articles are best filed and forgotten, sir.'

Prakash contemplated the candid assessment. What Lal had stated was true, but for Prakash, the universe was governed by cosmic truths that were fundamental for life. Honour and chivalry were two such cosmic truths that were vital for the existence of his universe, and an unsubstantiated underhand attack unbalanced the harmony of his natural world.

'Then I am going to call up this reporter and give him a piece of my mind,' Prakash said to Lal.

'Hmm…and what if he counters by asking you to comment on the rumour that Mahendra had met John, the landing agent?'

John, a bearded Goan giant based out of Bombay, had been identified as the landing agent with the help of inputs from the RI. Landing agents ensured that contraband goods were offloaded in India, loaded on to trucks containing specially prepared cavities to conceal them, and then escorted to Bombay, the major market for bullion, safely, without any interference from Customs or police. Landing agents would bribe, cajole, threaten or even entrap to achieve their goals. They were powerful individuals who, having worked long years in the shadowy world of smugglers, had deep-rooted contacts in law enforcement agencies. But in this case, Prakash had persisted. John was finally arrested on a tip off after a dramatic car chase in Savantwadi, close to the Maharashtra–Goa border, when he was trying to escape to his hideout somewhere close to Mapusa in Goa.

'Why should Mahendra, our inspector, meet John?' exclaimed Prakash, shock written all over his face. 'And why didn't you tell me?' He remembered Kanwar's advice. *Don't trust anybody.*

'As it was not necessary,' Lal said nonchalantly. 'Just like you don't mention that you smoke hashish when you go to Pune.'

'What?' Prakash nearly half jumped out of his chair. He would have fallen if the sturdy chair had not been designed for much more stolid characters than him. 'What…where…how?' He mumbled and then composed himself. 'That's scurrilous, Lal!' he said sharply. 'You should not make irresponsible statements like that.'

'And you, sir, should not sit in the official car smelling of hash and sex, even after meeting your girlfriend,' retorted Lal. 'You are no longer a college student, and they will always be waiting to take you down. They are watching you and they will pounce at every infraction, every indiscretion and every hint of you not adhering to the established norms.'

Who are they? Prakash wondered. He was convinced that his girlfriends and his smoking had nothing to do with his work.

'It's my personal life. Who are "they", or *you*, to track it, let alone comment on it.' said Prakash weakly.

'Ditch that myth, sir,' Lal said in a tone that would have earned him a sharp rebuke from any other officer senior in rank. 'You are an assistant collector now, and a lot of money rides on what you do. The silver you caught was worth six and a half crore rupees, and nobody would have blamed you if you would not have sailed the stormy seas to apprehend it. Nobody expected you to risk your life, but here victories last only till the first failure. So if you don't have a death wish, be like Caesar's wife. And why do you have to do it anyway, smoke hash when it's illegal?'

'It's been illegal for only three fucking years, Lal! And it has been in use for centuries, just like liquor. I only smoke it in periods of lull, when I have nothing to do, or when I am happy. Certainly never when I am working. By the way, it's less addictive than these,' he said, pointing to his cigarettes.

'Is that so,' Lal sounded surprised. 'But perception matters. Anything out of the ordinary, any hint of illegality, any violation of conventions is looked askance in your current job, and it's better that you conform.'

'Conform with what, Lal?' Prakash was riled. 'Moribund ideas? Morality is relative, and what may be wrong today may be right tomorrow. Or what was right a few years back may be wrong now. Am I supposed to change my life every time mores change?'

'Yes, if you want to pursue this career,' Lal replied.

Prakash intently listened to Lal. He found in Lal a bard of

bureaucratic wrangling who recited anecdotes full of meaningful lessons. In the short period of two months that they had spent together, they had developed a camaraderie that transcended their difference in rank or the gap in their age. In this case, however, he couldn't help but be acerbic. He had no intention of conforming. He decided to change the topic.

'I think it would be more productive for you to watch that new mistress of Salim's—Shabnam. She seems to have some influence over Salim, and maybe keeping a watch on her can lead to something,' Prakash said sarcastically.

Lal was surprised. He wondered where Prakash had obtained this information. As per his assessment, as yet Prakash did not have the intelligence networks to know about Salim's inner circles.

'How do you know that?' he asked. The surprise was evident in his tone.

'Don't ask me what I know. Find out more about her. Watch her movies. She is an unknown starlet for now, but looks really intelligent. If Salim is expecting another bimbo, he is in for a surprise,' said Prakash before shifting to the other point raised by Lal. 'And by the way, it was nothing—going into the sea, I mean—after all, there were reports of firing at sea and the police contacted us. What else could I have done?'

'You could have, following the same time-tested traditions under which the police officer passed the buck to you, composed a non-committal wireless message to all your formations across the coast. "Police has reported firing at sea. Stop. All formations to be at full alert. Stop. Special patrolling parties to be organized for next forty-eight hours at Mandangarh, Khed, Chiplun and Jaigarh. Stop." That's what is expected of you—not rushing out driving the official car all alone, carrying a rifle without informing anybody.'

Prakash pondered over the advise for a while but shook himself free of it. He had no intention to walk the time treaded path of Lal.

He intended on charting a different course. 'What is the story of Mahendra meeting John?' he queried.

'They are old friends. Mahendra is a frequent visitor of Blue Waters, Colaba, the cabaret joint owned by John and he claims that John is his informer.'

'Is he?'

'Maybe, maybe not. Nothing is certain in this world of big money. Sometimes the cat chases the mouse, but it's often the other way around,' Lal replied cryptically. 'And don't forget, Mahendra has his own connections with senior officers. So if the reporter wants to make analogies, it would be difficult to counter them.'

It took a moment for Prakash to register the thread of conversation.

'Oh no. I am not going to let him get away with insinuating corruption within the department. We will look into it ourselves if needed, nobody else will,' Prakash said indignantly, ending the conversation abruptly. Lal knew well not to argue once Prakash had made up his mind. He prayed silently, hoping that Prakash would let the matter rest there.

Chiplun: Lunch, same day

According to the 'Ratnagiri Gazette', the seizure of silver at Bankot was only the second seizure along the Konkan coast in the past three years. This in itself was not significant and the people would soon forget it. But they noticed other subtle changes in the workings of Customs. Customs boats on the sea were a little bit more visible. There were more Customs vehicles patrolling the rural roads. There was an aggressiveness the landing agents had not seen before. The three main landing agents of the area—Betal, Bansode and Parkar—met to take stock of the situation. The crackdown on smuggling was hurting and strategies needed to be revisited.

They had not faced this kind of situation for a few years. Salim's rise as the undisputed kingpin of the underworld had ensured their security. Before Salim had consolidated his hold over the world of crime, the area had been the home of internecine rivalries among various landing agents. They would work with any syndicate for a cut, and if they felt their grip over the area slipping, they would become informers for the government to cut their rivals down to size. Those were the heydays of the government departments when they could play one agent against the other. But everything changed after Salim's ascendancy. The landing agents were forced to bury their hatchets and work exclusively for Salim. Those who didn't listen were buried along with the hatchet. Salim's childhood friends slowly gained prominence in the underworld. Among the old landing agents, only Betal, who enjoyed the patronage of the incumbent minister for the region, survived. Now, there were no rivalries. Salim provided work for everybody, and everybody had started earning more. Greed and fear ensured loyalty to Salim, and his power kept growing.

Betal, the oldest operative among them, initiated the conversation. He, as a legal front, owned some of the biggest chicken farms on the coast, and his poultry trucks, prominently displaying the company logo, enjoyed a free run between Devgarh and Bombay. Besides transporting poultry the trucks also carried, sometimes, gold or silver in cleverly concealed compartments. They were never checked. Everyone knew the consequences of stopping Betal's poultry trucks. He had never lost a consignment, and was one of the most sought-after landing agents in the Konkan region. But even he now worked exclusively for Salim. He had not moved out of his farmhouse for more than a year, preferring the company of his chickens more than humans, and his presence in the meeting signified the grave crisis they were facing.

'This is unacceptable. Consignments are supposed to land without interference from Customs.'

Bansode, the portly ex-driver of Customs whose services had been terminated because of his close ties with Salim, picked up the refrain. 'If this keeps happening, how can we calculate our profits? How is it that we do not know the patrolling programme of the Customs officers? What are our informants in Customs doing?'

The Parkar brothers, who commanded respect as they were rumoured to be related to Salim, had been affected the most by the seizure. They owned a majority of the mango orchards in Mandangarh and controlled the Bankot creek, where Prakash had seized the silver. Yet they remained silent, knowing that the decision would finally be taken by the two brothers, Rangeela and Master, who had come from Bombay for the meeting. Rangeela, the younger of the two, was named so because of his colourful lifestyle. He fell in love with a new woman after every major event—whether a successful landing, buying a new property, or ruthlessly eliminating a rival. Master, the elder, had earned his nickname after he had killed three people with the finely honed blade of the Rampuri knife, which he carried concealed in his socks.

'Let's kill him and the others will fall in line,' Master said. 'The living would listen even to whispered threats after a death.'

'I already warned him not to wander around on his motorcycle,' Bansode said, continuing on that thread. 'I said that some truck may accidentally run him over.'

'Is that when he pulled out the revolver?' Parkar asked sarcastically. He believed that violence should be the last resort, and buying people off was better. 'This guy is a little *yeda.* I hear he was beaten on the head a lot when he was young. As a result, his brain is a little soft. Has somebody tried to reason with him?'

'Reason with him! This is the Lion's coast!' Master flared. 'He controls it. Even the tides need his permission to rise and ebb. Anybody who lives over here has to listen to him and to us. He either falls in line—or he takes the highway or the sea out of here.'

'This guy is a bachelor. He may acquiesce if I send him a starlet or two over the weekend,' Rangeela said while sipping at his Black Label.

'It won't work. I hear he gets his sex in Pune, so he must have his own settings,' Bansode replied.

'A solution must be found,' the elder Parkar said. 'All of us know what we are losing. I know he can't seize our consignments; he will never get the information. But the fear he is spreading is affecting all of us. I did fifty landings last year. They are down to two since this new boy has joined. The officers on our payroll are worried, their take also has been shrinking. Even then they are advising me to bide the time.'

'My landings are down to zero,' Bansode said. 'This guy somehow takes it personally that I was a driver with Customs. He seems to think that I am a traitor. This boy has some funny notions about loyalty. Why doesn't he understand that people like us, who are not that rich, can't afford to be loyal? I will be loyal when I am rich.'

'Maybe the Minister can get him transferred,' Rangeela said, looking at Betal.

Betal was the least affected of the lot. While he had his chicken farms in Jaigarh, he also owned mango orchards in Alibag. Whenever there was trouble brewing in one area, he would shift his operations to the other location.

'Let me talk to him. But isn't it a small matter to go right up to the Minister? Strategies can be reworked, payments can be increased, secrecy can be tightened. It's just been a couple of months. Let's wait a while,' he said reasonably.

The others looked unconvinced.

'I am going to kill him,' repeated Master.

They spent some more time deliberating on the subject, but could not arrive at a conclusion. Finally, they decided to let Salim take the final call on the desired course of action. Underworld gangs, it seemed, weren't much better than the bureaucracy when it came to taking decisions.

Dubai: Dinner, same day

The man who was to decide Prakash's fate was born to a policeman as Salim Suleiman. However, he was now known as Salim *Shaikh,* aka the Lion of Dubai, and was the undisputed sultan of the underworld of the western coast of India. He was no shaikh, but his mannerisms had earned him that legend. 'He is a shaikh, and all shaikhs lose their bearings in his presence,' said his boys. For them, Sailm Shaikh was the man who set the style statement for the underworld.

He was just sixteen when he had first forayed into the underworld. He started by providing local youth as labourers for unloading of contraband cargo of textiles and electronic goods smuggled through the Konkan coast. The landing agents of the area soon realized that their cargo would be pilfered by locals, or even seized by the Customs, if Salim's boys were not hired. Young Salim had learnt the art of forging and maintaining mutually beneficial partnerships with law enforcement agencies early in his life.

His birthplace, a small village in Konkan, was never going to limit him. Like all ambitious men, he wanted to be in Bombay, the biggest, baddest, richest and most glamourous city of India. But he did not want to be just another boy who was heading to Bombay with dreams, and nothing else. He planned well, sending two or three boys every month from his village to seek employment at Bombay docks, infiltrating the established gangs operating there. Their families at home were paid a second salary, a reminder that their boys were still on the rolls of Salim Bhai and owed their loyalties to him. The price of betrayal, they knew, could be terrible. Very early on, Salim had learned that everyone was for sale at the right price, or the right amount of coercion. Greed or fear, or greed *and* fear. That became his motto. People, he realized, would succumb to either, or both.

His army was ready when he left his home to come to Bombay—a hundred foot soldiers in the docks who were ready to do his bidding, and a couple of violent wannabes, ready for violence at the right price. All of them reporting to Hanif, his childhood friend. The takeover of the city was not smooth. There were killings, and he himself had a couple of close shaves. And then there was that bloody day in the month of December in 1981 when his boys went on a killing spree, murdering seventeen of their opponents in a single month. Salim had turned twenty-five that month.

The elders intervened. Peace was restored by dividing the areas of operation among all the gangs. Salim, being the most vicious of them all now, got an extra share of profits from the docks. That was all he wanted. To gain a foothold in Bombay, the gateway to India. After all, he had big plans for the city that controlled the country's economy. He wanted to rule Bollywood, fix cricket matches, and control horse races. Wherever there was glamour, he wanted to be there. He was already talking to politicians to change rules so that imports could be restricted. This would give his smuggling syndicate a boost. Anything that could not be imported would be smuggled.

All was going on well till he was challenged, this time by an upstart from the rural heartland of Uttar Pradesh. He could deal with the south Indians, he understood their psyche; even the Punjabis, they were so open. But he could never understand the Bhaiyas. They seemed to have a death wish, and they had that peculiar view of the world where relationships came before money. They also had the backing of the innumerable number of bureaucrats hailing from the Hindi heartlands. Neither greed nor fear worked. He was forced to kill the challenger with his own hands to ensure that a clear message was sent to his rivals, but this time no one stood by him. He had to flee to Dubai in 1985 when he realized that his arrest was imminent. Despite his formidable reputation, the Bhaiyas would have killed him in jail.

In Dubai, the genius in him turned adversity into opportunity. Free from the pressure of law enforcement agencies, and comfortably ensconced in a city-state that had no extradition treaty with India, he set about setting up the largest and the best smuggling networks that the world had seen so far, using his organizational skills to create an operational consortium that was a one-point solution for all illegal activities, initially on the Western coast of India, but steadily expanding to other parts of the world. He was soon recognized as a man with vision, style and generosity. His benevolence to the boys in his gang was unmatched. He would send a Rado as a gift on the birthday of a lowly foot soldier, or his brother would come carrying a television set on the wedding of another. There was always a throng of favour-seekers at his Dubai bungalow, and he rarely turned his back on his people. He cared for his people and they gave him their undying loyalty.

Tonight, there were just three of them. Salim, Shabnam and Hanif. They shared the mutton soup and salad that Shabnam, his starlet girlfriend, had been forcing him to eat in a futile effort to make him shed some weight. Salim believed that he did not need to lose any.

'I am thirty-five now, darling. I need a little flesh on my body. You youngsters will have nothing to hold on to if I lose these love handles,' he often said. Shabnam would smile and persist. She liked his good looks, and there was no harm in looking better.

'So, the consignment for Dighi was the only one we lost in the last two months?' Salim asked Hanif.

'Yes, but it was meant to be lost to RI, not to some upstart. We couldn't have told those sailors that they were supposed to lose that one. So they ran. It was a new Assistant Collector at Dapoli, Prakash, who intercepted them. He took a boat out by himself. Whoever thought that anybody in Customs at Dapoli would venture out into the sea in torrential rain! The sailors told the lawyer we sent that in another half an hour, the engine could have been repaired and they would have sailed for Mangalore,' Hanif replied.

'And John?' Salim asked.

'Caught on a tip-off by RI and handed over to Prakash. RI wanted to salvage something positive out of the disaster. They are red-faced over the fiasco, and it was prudent to give them some small victory of sorts. I gave them John without asking you.'

Hanif was possibly the only one who could do something like that. Decide on a course of action, if it ever came to that, without consulting Salim. People close to them knew that while Salim ran the consortium, Hanif was the one who kept it together. His uncharitable enemies called him 'Hanif Kutta', Salim's faithful dog. The truth was that Salim trusted him, implicitly. Hanif could, it was rumoured, with his disproportionately widespread nostrils set in a square face, smell out any conspiracy against their gang; some said that he knew everything that was happening in Bombay not because of his eyes or ears, but because of his nose.

'It's all right,' said Salim. 'John was flying too high anyway. He was taking decisions beyond his mandate. Last month, he forced Manoj Bhai to give a role to Sitara without even clearing it through me first.'

Shabnam looked up speculatively while sipping at her soup. Sitara was not her competitor, she was just a bit player in the Indian film industry. But in the cut-throat competition for roles among struggling actors, any space ceded to a competitor was an opportunity lost.

Salim noticed the speculative look. They had met six months after he had first watched her in a C grade movie, a bit role where she was raped and murdered. Even though it was a small role, she caught his eye. He had loved her short, snub, slightly upturned nose, her wide-set angelic eyes, her smooth skin. It took her six months to agree to share his bed, and surprisingly, they were still together after two long years. *Maybe,* he thought, *it was because she never bitched to him about her competitors, never pestered him to push a producer for a role, and treated him more as a man than a benefactor.* She knew that she could be a star, but you needed a godfather to be successful in the big bad world of Bollywood. Salim could be that backer, but she was too proud to request him.

'Hey, what are you thinking?' Salim asked affectionately. 'Sitara is a nobody, an upstart. She is no competition for you.'

'I know,' replied Shabnam. 'But it hurts that she is on screen more than I am.'

'I am saving you for the big one, darling,' Salim said, this time with a sense of proprietary pride. 'Kabadiwala is going to announce you as the lead in his multi-crore project on Sunday. Casting you against the genius. No less. So pack your bags to be in Bombay for the launch party. And then, come back. We have so many things scheduled here as well. After all, you'll be coming back as the new star on the Bollywood firmament.'

The announcement necessitated a response and Shabnam was up to it. She produced a gasp, the same gasp that had made her famous, that had sent a million men, all watching her from the front benches of cinema theatres, to bed, dreaming of her gasping for them. She rose with calculated speed, made sure that the chair fell, and threw her arms around Salim and covered his face with kisses.

'Oh, thank you, darling. With the genius…a film by Kabadiwala. That's a dream come true.'

She had just been catapulted into the top league. Her decision to risk being called the 'plaything of Salim' for nearly two years had paid off, and if she delivered, the snickers behind her back would die. She wouldn't be the bimbo any longer, she would be the star.

What a bimbo! thought Hanif, looking at her flushed face as she straightened her chair and sat down, too excited to eat any more. He had negotiated the financing of the new film and had opposed Salim's proposal for getting the lead role for Shabnam. He felt that casting Shabnam in such a big budget film would be risky, and they were, after all, businessmen. Why risk their investment? He had once quoted the age old adage 'Don't wear your heart on the sleeve when you go to work' to Salim. But Salim never listened. He wanted his mistresses to be stars, or a star to be his mistress. He mixed glamour with business. Hanif could never understand why their men kept on marrying the prostitutes they visited, or why they bought houses for their mistresses, or why even Salim kept insisting for more roles for his actress friends. Hanif viewed these relationships as transactions—you do the business, pay the girl and get it over with. He couldn't understand this infatuation with the women, not even when Salim tried to explain to him, 'Hanif Bhai, they have given a part of their life to us. Should we not also give something back?'

Hanif shook himself free of his thoughts, getting the topic back to business at hand.

'We may have to sacrifice another consignment to the intelligence guys. They may be running short of their targets,' Hanif said.

'Hmm… We will see,' replied Salim.

'Okay, but decide soon. And what do we do with Prakash? If he remains adamant that we cannot operate in his area, then we have to shift our businesses from three or four landing spots. That will really dent our reputation.'

'Let's wait and see, Hanif Bhai. In any case, the Alibag route is safe now. Rangeela met the Customs officers over there and they have agreed to our terms. Let's shift the major part of our operations there. Ask Betal to shift to Alibag for some time until we decide what to do with this young blood, Prakash. You're sure he rebuffed Rangeela's offers?'

'Yes. And now, Master is riled up and wants to kill him. He wanted my go ahead. I told him to wait for a while.'

Shabnam listened desultorily as Salim replied carelessly. 'Master always wants to kill on the slightest provocation. Let him take his own decisions. Don't stop him. Maybe it will send out a message.'

'I thought that these were just minor skirmishes that do not affect us financially...'

'What's to be done will be done,' Salim said cryptically.

'Mukul Sheth had sent the accounts for the last month. Will you like to go over them now?'

'No, Hanif Bhai. Let Shabnam go tomorrow. We will sit after that. For tonight, let us celebrate her success,' Salim replied, ending the dinner that was to change the course of all their lives irreversibly.

4

End of the Beginning

'I am bored,' Prakash said morosely to Lal over their second cup of tea. It was a lovely morning early in February. The green foliage that had covered the Konkan hills after the monsoon had faded into golden yellows. The grass had grown tall, often encroaching upon the roads. The moss on the hilly rocks had dried and fallen off, and the hills, bare of other vegetation, proudly displayed the green mangoes, called kairi by local farmers, which, as the heat built up, were ripening faster than they normally would. The plucking of the new crop of mangoes would start within the fortnight, but the locals would see none of the harvest. The first pickings of these Devgarh Alphonso mangoes were reserved for Dubai, followed by the second flush being transported to Bombay to cater to the insatiable demand for hapus by Bombayites, and then, only after the rich had satiated themselves with the Konkan mangoes, would the local populace be allowed to have their pick from the leftovers. The local economy was dependant on fishing, mangoes, poultry farming and smuggling—in that order. It was an idyllic retreat, but after six months of patrolling the coast Prakash was getting impatient and restless. The novelty of the sea was wearing off. He had learnt how the fishermen spotted a shoal, had spotted and sailed with dolphins, experienced a storm on the sea and had, once, spotted a lost baby whale. The sea still had a lot to offer, but now he longed for some meaningful work.

'But you are doing such a great job over here,' Lal said.

'What is the great job that I am doing?' retorted Prakash. 'For two months after we seized the silver, I did not move out of office, fearing that Salim's men may come and loot it just like they did in Jamnagar. I, who had eschewed violence after college, slept with a revolver under my pillow! And what do I have to show for it? Zilch!'

'But you did get that commendation letter for the seizure,' Lal stated, trying to assuage a visibly upset Prakash.

'Oh, stuff that commendation letter. Was that letter worth having to be a tourist guide for so many guests of senior officers, all wanting a picture of me standing next to the ten tonnes of silver? As if I was a hero of the Masai tribe who had shown them a lion during their safari. Shit, Lal! I never gave the Civil Services Examination for this. I thought I would be bringing change.'

'You have brought change. Smuggling is down on our coast. Even Betal has shifted base to Alibag. And Rangeela and Master have not been seen around for so long. Earlier they were operating here with impunity. Our method of placing patrolling parties at the last moment has rattled them. They are worried, and that's the change you have brought.'

'I know,' replied Prakash, slightly mollified. He leaned back on the chair and said, 'But you know it's not enough. I feel as if I am caught in a time warp, repeating my actions over and over...again and again. It's like the kaalchakra is making me live the same day over and over. Wake up, have tea, come to office, check the newspaper, talk to somebody, anybody, have lunch, sleep, wake up, send patrolling parties, take out the car or the motorcycle, check if the patrolling parties are in place, check a few landing spots, sleep. And repeat.'

'What did you expect?' Lal asked softly. 'Bureaucracy doesn't want innovation, it wants continuity. Innovation is reserved for scientists and dreamers. You are supposed to follow the set protocols, maybe tweak them a little, but not substantively change them. You are doing what is expected of you.'

Prakash understood what Lal was saying was probably true but his intrinsic heretic nature was still kicking inside him. He also knew that Lal, while overtly criticizing him for being a heretic, secretly hoped that he would be the harbinger of change. Prakash mentally cursed the selectors of the Civil Services Examination for flunking Lal. *Those selectors were not so wise after all*, he thought. Lal would have been a brilliant administrator. And now, maybe he was treating Prakash as his protégé.

'Nah, I am not doing what is expected of me. I should be busting some gangs. Maybe arresting Salim, maybe making a change that would stop these gangs altogether, I don't know,' Prakash said, throwing his hands up agitatedly.

'Who is making any impact?' Lal said a little more forcefully. He was exasperated by Prakash's unrealistic visions. 'Has anything been done by anyone in the past decade that has made a whit of difference in the lives of the people? Shake out of it, sir. It's a job, just another job, only with a few extra responsibilities and a little more visibility. But this job does not make you a messiah.'

Prakash, surprised by Lal's outburst, looked at him speculatively. He pondered over what Lal had said.

'You know, there is sense in what you say. I was discussing this with Rajiv ji, the SDM at Chiplun, and he too said that the hopes of the people have been broken so many times that people now aspire only to survive. According to him, nothing changes. His predecessors had been supplying drinking water through tankers during the summer season for years, and he is still doing the same. The same areas are flooded during the monsoon, even after forty years of independence. The more we talk of change, the more things remain the same. According to him, bureaucracy was created to temper down the hopes and aspirations of the people so that revolutions could be avoided, and see, how well we have functioned. People are happy with one road, a hundred trees and a tanker of water.'

Lal smiled. 'Wise man, the SDM.'

'He said something else that I didn't understand,' continued

Prakash. 'He said that bureaucracy survives by giving hope to the bureaucrats. I am still not able to understand what he meant by that.'

'Think over that, sir. I won't explain,' Lal said. 'But he is certainly wise for the years of service he has put in.'

'But these cryptic dialogues don't solve my problem. I am still bored, and sometimes that boredom borders on frustration. I am through with this phase, Lal. There is nothing more I can do here. I want out! I want to be in a place where I don't have to travel 300 km for sex, or some company for a drink…some place where I can play loud music, or just play billiards.'

'So do something about it instead of just moaning,' replied Lal mercilessly.

'And what do you suggest I should do?' Prakash asked, sardonically.

'Project yourself. Show the seniors that your dedication and commitment can be effective elsewhere too. Get the new boss to visit here to see the great work you have done. Organize a fabulous dinner, throw in a sea ride for his family. Show the Collector what an all-rounder you are,' Lal said enthusiastically.

'So, I am now also required to be the handmaiden and chef to the boss and his children,' Prakash added caustically.

'Oh no, let me be the handmaiden, you just be the *maître d'*,' Lal said with an uncharacteristic guffaw. But then, seeing the serious look on Prakash's face, he continued, 'You sit 200 km away from your bosses. They don't know you, don't know about your capabilities. How are you going to let them know about your aspirations, your ideas? What the eye doesn't see, what the ear doesn't hear, the mind doesn't comprehend.'

'My work speaks for itself. Why do I have to market myself?' Prakash said, his natural reticence coming to fore.

'You are one of fifteen for him. What makes you special unless you tell him about your achievements? Why should he single you out? Even a mother does not feed a child unless he cries. It's he who cries the loudest, who gets the most milk.' Lal quoted an oft-repeated Hindi proverb.

Prakash pondered over the statement. 'Okay, so I cry,' he said. 'But if I am going to cry, let me be the most beautiful baby. Let's go full monty. Let us give him a great dinner, and for that, let me invite him in person.'

◆

It was easy to convince the Collector. He jumped at the idea of spending a few days outside the drudgery of office. The visit was scheduled to be a two-day affair, on 14 and 15 February, which could be extended over the weekend. Wireless messages flashed across the coast to various Customs stations:

From: Leopard, Dapoli (Camp at Pune)

To: Rabbit, Dapoli

Date: 07/02/1992

Rpt: Rabbit, Ratnagiri; Rabbit, Chiplun; Rabbit, Khed

'Tiger shall be visiting Dapoli, Khed and Ratnagiri on 14th and 15th of February. Stop. The tentative programme is as follows. Departure Pune 0630 hrs on 14th February. Stop. Arrival Mahabaleshwar 0830–0845 hrs. Stop. Inspection of Mahabaleshwar wireless station. Stop. Departure Mahabaleshwar 1100 hrs. Stop. Arrival Khed 1300 hrs. Stop. Inspection of Khed RCP. Stop. Arrival Dapoli 1500 hrs. Stop. Inspection of Dapoli Customs. Stop. Departure Dapoli for NACE Guest House for night halt. Stop. Detailed programme for 15th shall follow. Stop. All stations to remain at full alert till the departure of tiger. Stop.'

And then, Prakash went to invite Kanwar to accompany the Collector to Dapoli. 'I need your guidance, sir,' he said. 'This is a first for me.'

'Do it yourself,' Kanwar replied mercilessly. 'I am not going to travel 200 km to hold your hand.' But Kanwar agreed to a dinner with Prakash's friends in Pune. 'After all, I should know the people in your life,' he said, thus affirming the special bond between them.

Prakash loved throwing parties, and this one was impeccably curated. He invited a brigadier and his wife (a senior from the Sainik School), the local superintendent of police (a senior of Prakash's from Hindu College) and Shelley.

Kwality, the premier restaurant in East Street, owed their license to the Cantonment Board and, with the Brigadier dining in and a slight nudge from the local police coming in, they made sure the group was given the best seats, that the food was cooked to perfection and that the DJ came to their table to ask for their choice of music. With the bartender ensuring a continuous flow of spirits of appropriate vintage, the conversation flowed smoothly, from anecdotes of school to college to the foibles of bureaucrats. Prakash was either a kid or a friend to them. They knew that Kanwar could have a hand in shaping Prakash's career and the Brigadier periodically dropped hints of the military–sainik school caucus. Kanwar watched Shelley and Prakash indulgently and wondered if they had a relationship beyond friendship. Prakash knew that he had won the first battle when Kanwar, while leaving, happily said, 'Why are you wasting your time in Dapoli? You should be here in Pune.'

Next day Prakash stopped at Kayani Bakery for some shrewsbury and ginger biscuits, and picked up some of the last of the strawberry crop from Mahableshwar on his way back. He then carried this tribute when he went to invite the District Magistrate of Ratnagiri for a dinner with the Collector. The District Magistrate was the highest-ranking officer of the remote district, and being well aware of his status, he initially demurred and dithered, but finally agreed after persistent requests by Prakash. The attendance of the Senior Superintendent of Police was a given after the confirmation from the District Magistrate, and the quorum was completed with a famous local director of Marathi plays, who while otherwise based in Bombay, was convinced to take his bi-monthly holiday to his hometown to coincide with the visit of the Collector.

Lal proved true to his word. He was the foot soldier, the sergeant-in-command and the Quarter Master all at once. He chalked out the itinerary, worked out the arrangements and was everywhere at the same time. But Prakash lost his cool when Lal said, 'Sir, did you check if the toilets of the guest house were clean?'

'Lal, this is not my daughter's wedding. It's just the boss visiting for three fucking days. We can't spend ten days just preparing for this visit. We have a coast to protect,' yelled Prakash.

'This is bigger than your daughter's wedding. This trip could impact your career permanently. You have already pulled off a coup against your colleagues by being the first to host the new Collector. Now don't spoil it with some silly mistake,' Lal replied firmly.

'What can I do to spoil it?' asked Prakash.

'Anything. You can't guess and you can't pre-empt it. Maybe you will do something silly, maybe you won't, maybe you will be seen as not doing anything,' Lal said, sounding like Kanwar. 'Que sera sera. But the only thing that can be classified as a catastrophe would be if RI seizes a consignment of contraband in our jurisdiction that day.'

This worried Prakash. 'Is that possible?' It's already the 10th of February. If any consignment was to land on our coast, it should have left Dubai by now, and we have no such intelligence so far.'

'We are not infallible. Our intelligence framework is not foolproof and history says that whenever some top shot visits Bombay, RI makes a seizure. It won't hurt them to score some brownie points with our Collector too. After all, he is destined for greater things.'

'Now you have me worried,' Prakash said, his expression mirroring his concern. 'But tell me, how is it that RI manages to make a seizure virtually every time some top honcho is visiting Bombay?'

'You have to understand the logistics, sir,' replied Lal. 'Estimates say that we seize approximately 5 per cent of the total gold or silver smuggled into the country. I think we seize less than that.'

'Why so?'

'Simple finances, sir. The price of gold nowadays is around ₹4,200 per 10 grams, while in Dubai, it's approximately $115 an ounce. With the exchange rate at ₹26, and hawala rate of 4 per cent, the landed cost of smuggled gold is approximately ₹3,400, giving a margin of nearly 25 per cent on each consignment. So, even if the smugglers lose one out of ten consignments to the law enforcement agencies, they still get a return of 50 per cent over a couple of months. Customs seized approximately five tonnes of gold last year. A 5 per cent seizure statistics means that over a hundred tonnes of gold is being smuggled into the country. However, my sources in Dubai say that Dubai imported more than 160 tonnes of gold last year. Assuming that 10 tonnes is their local demand, the remaining 150 tonnes was destined for India. Add to that the gold being smuggled in from Singapore and Hong Kong and my calculations say we are seizing less than 3 per cent of the total gold being smuggled into the country.' Lal leaned back after this treatise.

Prakash was suitably impressed. He had also worked out the economics of gold smuggling but had not ever been able to express it as succinctly as Lal. 'So where are you leading, Lal?'

'If we have 150 tonnes of gold being smuggled into India, and the average consignment is 50–60 kg…'

'Why 50–60 kg?' asked Prakash, interrupting Lal's flow.

'Gold is smuggled in 10 tola bars, which means each biscuit weighs around 116 g. One jacket contains one hundred biscuits or

11.5 kg approximately. It's rare for more than a jacket to be smuggled from the airport, and seizures on the sea show an average of 50–60 kg of gold being carried in a consignment. I assume that nearly 20 per cent of the gold is smuggled through airports in small quantities, but that still leaves us with over 100 tonnes to be smuggled through the sea. Let's assume that each consignment is 100 kg, not 50 to 60 kg, which is then worth nearly ₹4 crore…'

Prakash listened with rapt attention as Lal expounded: '100 kg per consignment means that there are at least a thousand consignments of gold landing in India, and if the weight is less than that, then maybe 1,500 consignments every year. Add to it nearly 500 consignments of silver a year, and it means that nearly six landings of contraband goods are carried out on the west coast of India every day. We know of hardly twenty-five landing agents in India, and each of them is probably landing at least six consignments every month, and if they are assured safe passage, maybe two consignments a week. That's an income of nearly ₹1 crore per month. And don't forget, your monthly income is just about ₹3,000 a month.'

'Safe passage?' asked Prakash.

'Come on, sir. Don't be naïve,' retorted Lal. 'There are ten major customs formations on the west coast. How difficult is it to monitor two, three or even four landing agents by a formation? And then the competition is always ready to put you down. And now that the informers have also increased, what with the reward scheme for giving information about smuggling, isn't timing a seizure a possibility if you have nearly one landing a day in your jurisdiction?'

'But then why can't we, in Dapoli, make a seizure?'

'Because you work with different principles. You had two major operators in your jurisdiction, Rangeela and Master. You refused to meet them, so they don't feel secure over here. The landing agents of the area, the Parkars, Betal or Bansode, you keep them under constant surveillance. As I said, Customs may seize one out of thirty consignments smuggled through the sea. After all, it is a long coast. Do you think you are going to beat those odds?'

'So what can we do? How do we ensure that there is no smuggling during the Collector's visit?' Prakash said, sounding rather disheartened.

'Using analysis. You would be down south, visiting Dabhol, Anjanvel and Boria, with the Collector. The shore guard parties and the road checking parties will naturally be on full alert over there. It would be illogical for anyone to make an attempt at smuggling any contraband there. The possibility of landing, if any, is highest between Bankot and Harnai. Also, I know that Parkar is in Bankot, and Bansode was in his house in Dabhol until yesterday, so the landing agents are in place. I think I should be patrolling these northern areas from the 12th. I will publicly camp over there, make a lot of chatter on the wireless, and let it generally be known that we are on a look out for a possible landing in that region.'

'Will that be sufficient?' Prakash asked, somewhat relieved, but still not fully convinced.

'No. Additionally, a couple of my sources will wander around, looking for unknown entrants in the area, primarily RI officers. And all hotels on the highway have been instructed to inform me if any new face checks in—even if they are from the government.'

'We are going to watch RI officers?' exclaimed Prakash. 'I thought we were looking out for smugglers.'

'We watch everyone. Even the watchers,' Lal said in a ruthless tone. 'There are multiple objectives this time. First, there should not be any landing during the Collector's visit. Second, if there is a landing, we should catch the consignment. Third, if we are not able to intercept the consignment, RI should not be able to catch it. And last, even if a landing takes place, and it gets away, the Collector should not get a whiff of it before he reaches Pune.'

'We let the consignment go through rather than letting the RI catch it?' Prakash was aghast, his high opinion of Lal teetering on the brink of collapse. 'What do we do next, escort the consignment for the smugglers?'

'As we were taught in school, sir, loss of reputation is a fate worse than death,' said Lal.

'That is incorrect, Lal. The correct proverb was that loss of honour is a fate worse than death.'

'No, sir. I do believe I am correct. But leave that aside. More than a thousand contraband consignments get away every year anyway. What's one more to that statistic? But there cannot be a screw-up in this visit.'

Prakash pondered over it and decided not to interfere at this crucial stage. He didn't realize it at the time, but he had taken the first step towards unshackling himself of the ghosts of the Romantics. The ideals and the vision that he held would peel away, layer after layer, now that the first cut had been made.

'Is that all?' he asked.

'No. After this we do what everyone else does in these circumstances. Issue a fake alert over the coast,' Lal said with a conspiratorial smile.

'A fake alert!' Prakash said, shaken completely.

'Yes,' Lal said. 'Something like "Reliable intelligence indicates that a dhow, made in Mandvi, with blue cabin located at the rear, has sailed from Fujirah on the 7th of February, carrying either silver or gold. It is expected to land its consignment between 13th and 15th February between Alibag and Devgarh. All formations to be at full alert. Any developments may be intimated to Leopard Dapoli—that is you.'

'But there's no such intelligence at all,' exclaimed Prakash in a louder than usual tone.

'That's what you and I know. But this covers our asses perfectly. If any consignment is caught, we can say that the alert had already been issued and our formations were also on the lookout. Or else, as always, there is the fib that the alert forced them to go back because they feared the seizure.' Lal seemed to be enjoying himself tremendously while the furrows on Prakash's brow grew deeper. He nearly regretted agreeing to Lal's idea of calling the Collector for a visit to Konkan.

'Anything else?' he asked sarcastically.

'Yes, sir. I expect that at the first opportunity you will tell the Collector that you have an intelligence that a consignment of silver or gold is destined for our coast, and that all of us are working very hard to intercept it. Inform him that all our boats are out in the sea, patrolling diligently. We will make sure he sees one of them during the joyride. I'm sure it will thrill madam and the young boy, if not the boss himself.'

'Will he believe it?' Prakash asked doubtfully.

'Trust me, he will. A sense of adventure is a great leveller. He may enquire a little about your source and other superficial things, but if he is happy with the way he and his family are taken care of, everything should be fine.'

◆

The preparations, accordingly, progressed on two fronts. One front, which Prakash considered to be the farcical aspect, included lies, fawning and the social niceties. The other front was led by Lal and it aimed at ensuring that there were no gaps in coastal vigilance.

They were victorious on both fronts. The breakfast in Mahabaleshwar was apparently delectable as the Collector and his family enjoyed the strawberries and the fruit jellies along with the makai cutlets on the front lawns of the sprawling colonial bungalow, which was their office at Mahabaleshwar. The lunch at Dapoli, duly curated by the only luxury hotel of the area, offered the choicest local delicacies. At the first opportunity after lunch, sensing his gentle mood, Prakash apologized to the Collector for the thin attendance in office, explaining with a straight face that they had an intelligence of a possible landing and that they wanted to make sure that nothing slips through their net. The Collector was rather enthusiastic about the hunt. He even expressed a fleeting desire to be a part of it.

That desire was forgotten at dinner. The movie director, encouraged by the interest shown by the other guests, dropped his reservations and narrated hilarious personal anecdotes about the film stars he had worked with. The whisky, brought out by Prakash from his personal collection, turned out to be the real McCoy. The mangoes were the biggest and the best of the local crop, and the fresh sweet dishes made from them put everyone in a soporific state. By the end of dinner, the District Magistrate and the Superintendent of Police managed to paint Prakash as the new rising star of Indian bureaucracy. Prakash demurred, but to demonstrate his diligence, immediately after dinner excused himself, telling the Collector he would like to go and join the chase of purported smugglers.

◆

Prakash was vaguely aware that he had achieved more by hosting a dinner than he had through his six months of diligent work. But nothing in life is linear. The bump came early in the morning when Prakash reached the guest house at Chiplun to escort the Collector and his family to Boria, where they were to board the boat for the sea cruise. He found the Collector lounging in his pyjamas.

'Come, come, Prakash. Great dinner last night. You want a cup of tea?' the Collector offered affably.

Prakash's heart sank. The high tide that day was due for 10 a.m., and if they didn't board the vessel by 9 a.m., they would not be able to come back by 12.30 p.m., when the tide would have ebbed, and their large boat could not sail in shallow waters. The change was placing the whole plan of showing off the sea patrol in jeopardy.

'All of us were a little tired, so can we postpone the sailing for tomorrow? By the way, did you get any sleep last night?' the Collector asked solicitously.

'Sir…yes, sir,' stammered Prakash, at a loss of words at the sudden turn of events. 'I did get a little sleep, sir. Sure, sir, let me rearrange the schedule.' He took a deep breath to marshal his thoughts. The skipper and the crew of the boat would have to be asked to stand down. The guest house booking would have to be extended if the Collector wanted to go sailing the next day. The cook would have to be asked to stay back. The patrolling boats would have to continue sailing the sea. The Road Checking Parties and the Shore Guard Patrols would also have to be kept on alert for another day. An extended stay of the Collector was going to create logistical problems. Why couldn't the bosses appreciate that any change is not easy to manage? There was no one he could turn to. Lal was away, reachable only on the wireless, which he didn't want to use as he suspected that the smugglers had hacked their airwave frequencies.

He resolved the predicament by coming up with what he thought was an acceptable alternative.

'Sir, can we make a slight change in the programme? You relax during the day. And then, in the evening, we can drive to Dabhol to see the dolphins coming in with the tide. From Dabhol, we can sail to Boria. It would be strenuous for you and ma'am to sail tomorrow and drive again. The sea tires you more than you expect.'

The mention of dolphins clinched it. The plan was discussed and approved. An inspector was despatched to Boria to escort the vessel to Dabhol, and amidst all the activity, Prakash forgot to send the wireless intimating the change in Tiger's programme. There was some chatter on the repeater station at Mahabaleshwar about the changed programme of the Collector, but in the absence of any official messages, they maintained radio silence.

The evening won the war. The dolphins obliged by coming in throngs and frolicked in the backdrop of the early evening sun. The evening breeze was refreshing, and as they boarded the boat at 6 p.m., the wind died, making the sea as still as a lake. There was no rolling or pitching to upset anybody. Prakash showed off his knowledge of the coast, pointing out the various landmarks and light houses.

'You know, sir…Boria…where we are going…is the only lighthouse that flashes a red light. We should be there by 9 p.m. Hope it's not too late for you. The sea at night is very different, sir. Sadly, it's not a full moon, otherwise, the sea shimmers, sir. It's an esoteric experience. Oh, you've experienced it when you were an Assistant Collector, sir…' Prakash had been rambling and the last sentence effectively stopped him from making a fool of himself.

Luckily, at that point they spotted the CPC Hazrat Mahal, one of their patrol boats, coming in from the open sea. The patrol craft quickly pulled in alongside. Chauhan, the local inspector at Dabhol, nimbly jumped over the railing, smartly saluting the Collector with the customary *Jai Hind, sir*.

'What are you doing on this side at this hour?' Prakash asked him.

'A fishing trawler informed us of a suspicious boat lurking about twenty nautical miles off the Jaigarh coast. The fishermen were rather sure that it was a Kerala-made vessel. Even though it was not a Mandvi-type dhow, we decided to go and take a look.'

Chauhan, naturally, was not aware that the wireless was a fib issued just to keep them on their toes and to cover Prakash's ass if anything went wrong.

The Collector, however, seemed impressed. He even made a brief remark about the efficient way in which Prakash was running the organization.

'What happened?' asked Prakash.

'We scoured the sea for five or six hours, but couldn't find any big vessel, sir. There was one fishing trawler, but he was also not able to tell us anything. So we decided to return to Dabhol.'

'How long have you been sailing?' asked the Collector, feeling left out.

'Today is the third day, sir. So please excuse our appearances,' Chauhan replied. 'We returned as there is very little water left, otherwise we would have kept looking for the dhow. Sorry we couldn't spot it, sir.'

'Doesn't matter,' Prakash said, feeling a little guilty for sending them on a wild goose chase. But he pushed the guilt back. He would find a way to reward these guys. 'It's a big sea, we can't cover all of it; and our boats are often not as fast as the smuggler's, sir,' he explained to the Collector.

'Yes, I know. Good work by your team, Prakash. But we need to go now. It's getting late and we have to leave early tomorrow.'

'You come with us to Boria, Chauhan,' Prakash said as he signalled for the two boats to procced. 'In a singular act of bravery, Chauhan single-handedly made a seizure of 130 silver bricks at Harnai last year. He has some interesting tales to tell,' Prakash told the Collector.

The weather was cool and the stars slowly started to shimmer over the sea as the two boats made their way towards Boria. Chauhan, in his own hesitant and diffident manner, engaged the Collector's wife and their son. He talked about the boredom and the perils of anti-smuggling work, showed them the guns, explained the various parts of the boat and even encouraged the Collector's son to handle the navigational wheel for a short while. The Collector and Prakash, at the other end, discussed the forts of Shivaji on the Konkan coast.

'They are fascinating if you are a history buff. The design and the locations are ahead of their times, and the tactics he adopted against the Mughals and Adil Shah were so bewildering. No wonder the Mughals couldn't really make inroads into the Deccan.'

'At times it is good to be unpredictable as well as secretive,' the Collector said sagely.

They spotted the lighthouse at Boria around 9 p.m.

'There we are, another fifteen minutes. How did you like the sail, sir?'

'Good, good. Things have changed so much since we were young officers. The scale and the stakes of smuggling have changed so much. What do you feel about this job, Prakash?'

'It's monotonous, sir. Strenuous and challenging, but monotonous. You don't get many informers here. Bombay is different. There you have the bullion market where traders can tell you about the expected arrival of gold or silver. Most of the landing agents, the financiers, the boatmen are also based out of Bombay. You can cultivate some of them as informers. Here, there are only the landing agents and transporters, and they are unlikely to turn informers, even for a reward. We are trying to encourage villagers to inform the department about illegal activities, but they are scared of reprisals. So, we have developed a routine of surprise visits and intensive patrolling—more of a preventive action rather than one designed for seizures. Anybody can do it. It's basic intelligence and hard work. This is not a place for a direct recruit to work for too long, if I can take the liberty of saying so, sir,' Prakash said, taking the rare opportunity to voice his thoughts.

'You may be right, although it all seems so exciting. As youngsters, we were only catching textiles.'

'Yes, sir, it's exciting, but only when we are working on an intelligence. The kind of intelligence we got this time, it's rare for this region,' Prakash lied with a straight face.

Chauhan, who had joined them as the boat turned into the channel to enter Boria, concurred.

'What the—' Prakash checked himself before swearing in front of the Collector and his family. 'Chauhan, there is another boat coming in from the Jaigarh side. The guy has not even put on his navigational lights. He may reach the jetty before us. Just ask your guys to stop him so that we can dock first.'

The wireless crackled, and CPC Hazrat Mahal, which had been following them, broke formation to intercept the incoming boat, which had, meanwhile, halted on its own.

'This seems to be the same trawler we encountered off Jaigarh,' Chauhan said. 'He seems to have some luck, coming back so early. They must have hit a good shoal of fish.'

'Fish, sir, is not found equally all over the sea,' Prakash explained for the benefit of the Collector's family. 'They move in shoals, and if a fishing trawler finds a rich shoal, all the trawlers congregate there. They normally come back around 3 a.m. or 4 a.m. so that the fresh fish can reach the market by morning. What Chauhan means is that this fishing trawler was sailing alone and must have been lucky to strike a major shoal to have returned so early. If you have some time, would you like to show Arun how Customs rummages through the boats?'

The Collector hesitated, but the sixteen-year-old Arun was having the adventure of his young life.

'Yes, Bhaiya. Let's do that,' he said, his face beaming with excitement. 'We don't come here every day.'

That sealed the issue. CPC Hazrat Mahal signalled the trawler to enter the small bay that led to the jetty at Boria. Surprisingly, there was some resistance from the captain of the trawler.

'What is it?' asked Prakash.

'He says the strong currents due to high tide makes it risky for three boats to be so close together inside the bay. He is asking us to go ahead, saying that he will enter after we have left the bay so that the there is no damage to the boats,' Chauhan replied.

Prakash looked at the trawler lounging about a quarter of a mile away. The crew sat huddled on the deck, while the *tandel* and another man stood in the wheelhouse, involved in what seemed like a heated argument.

'Chauhan,' he said suddenly, 'where are his labourers to unload the fish? And where is the refrigerated truck to transport the fish to the market?'

The questions were duly relayed to the captain of the fishing trawler by the skipper of Hazrat Mahal, and the shouted reply came that the trawler had arrived early and the labourers and the transport truck would arrive only by midnight. The boatmen still sat slumped on the deck, listlessly, refusing to move to sail the boat.

The Collector was becoming impatient. Disappointment was writ large on Arun's face. Prakash was now looking like a nincompoop who could not force even simple fishermen to obey the diktat of Customs. He decided to stake it all.

'There is definitely something suspicious about this trawler refusing to move,' Prakash told Chauhan. 'Inexplicable. Let's get it rummaged thoroughly. Chauhan, pull them in. Sir, would you like to carry on to the guest house? We are going to take two or three hours. I will join you in the morning after interrogating these guys.'

The Collector, in the face of such an aggressive display, decided to stay back to see his men in action.

The trawler was towed by Hazrat Mahal and fastened, bow to stern, with their boat. While all the others jumped nimbly on to the other boat, the Collector and madam stayed back, sipping the hot tea the crew made for them.

'No fish?' queried Prakash to Chauhan as they boarded the boat, noting that the deck was dry and there was no smell of fresh fish.

'No, sir. We had bad luck today,' answered the captain of the boat. Prakash eyed Chauhan. The same person had just informed that their unloading crew would be arriving by midnight. He knew that the captain was lying, but remembering the presence of the Collector and his family, restrained himself from beating the truth out of him. Chauhan and his team, along with Arun, descended the cavernous hold of the boat, finding it empty. They searched the spacious corners with large searchlights, finding nothing. They then rummaged the wheelhouse again, without any results.

Prakash looked around, and noticed the two iron tanks of 1,000 litres each on the deck of the boat. They seemed incongruous on a fishing trawler. He gestured towards them with a questioning look, and the *tandel* answered moodily. 'One for diesel, one for drinking water.'

Prakash called Chauhan. 'How much water do fishing trawlers normally carry?'

'Depends on their plans, sir, but normally 200 litres. They need a clean deck to operate.'

'How much diesel are they carrying in the engine room?'

Chauhan checked, and found a 2,000-litre tank connected to the engine, sufficient to last four or five days of sailing. Prakash looked at the two tanks questioningly. Chauhan, getting the drift, opened both of them, shining the light into the depths.

'Full,' he said, disappointed.

'Should we check them?' Prakash said softly. 'If for nothing, then just to impress the Collector.'

Chauhan hesitated briefly, looked at the staff, and then, trying to retain his reputation as the braveheart who had single-handedly seized the silver consignment at Harnai, stripped to his underwear and jumped into the water tank. He came up half a minute later, holding a neatly stitched cloth bag with numerous pockets and threw it on the deck.

'Bet it's gold,' he shouted triumphantly.

Prakash picked it up, feeling the bars concealed in the cloth, as Chauhan dived in again, bringing out two more similarly packed bags, setting into chain a flurry of activity on the boats.

'Ninety-nine bars in each,' Prakash shouted exultantly.

The exultant team crowded on the boat. The Collector decided to stay back with them, while madam and Arun were convinced to leave for the guest house. The diesel tank was drained through the night to yield another two 'jackets', each containing ninety-nine bars, and the toughest of interrogations could not reveal the mystery of the empty hundredth pocket.

◆

'My first reaction was—shit, I'm fucked,' Prakash said to Lal a week later.

'Why? Weren't you excited? You should have been exultant. There was a seizure on your information,' Lal said laughingly.

'Excited? I was ready to shit my pants. An attempt at smuggling right at the time of Collector's visit. My first thought was that he would feel that our area is a hotbed of smuggling. But then, the excitement was contagious. The boss was so ecstatic that one couldn't spoil the party by saying that it was a chance seizure.'

'Yeah, you were wise to keep your mouth shut for once,' Lal said. 'This turned out to be our quickest and best investigation so far. The carriers were caught, the truck that was supposed to transport the bars was caught, Bansode, the landing agent, was caught, and he also confessed that he was working for Salim. This is the first FIR against Salim in Konkan.'

'There is only one downside,' Prakash said with a grimace. 'Now I have no hope of being transferred out of Dapoli. What with two seizures in six months, I am being projected as a super sleuth! I think I will now have to get married if I hope to have sex. I can't keep on visiting Pune for it.'

'Que sera sera,' Lal replied philosophically. 'You should at least be thankful that the fake alert built up your reputation.'

'Yes, the alert helped. Dubai confirmed that a vessel containing silver and gold had left from their ports and sources confirm the landing of some silver at Mangalore after transhipping the gold. Gandhi ji was wrong. Truth is not always the best option,' Prakash said. He continued sombrely, 'Why did you think he did that?'

'Who did what?' Lal asked.

'Salim. Why did he send the consignment while the Collector was visiting?

'Who knows…?'

'I will ask him when I arrest him,' Prakash said, only half-jokingly.

◆

'Why did you do it?' Hanif asked Salim. The three of them were in Dubai again. Salim, Hanif and Shabnam. Shabnam was glowing. The movie was progressing well and the first cuts had proved that she was a much better actor than anybody, except herself, had expected.

'Do what?' Salim asked as he caressed Shabnam's shoulders.

'Send that consignment for a landing at Boria. We had decided that we would be smuggling the whole consignment from Mangalore.'

'Oh, that! Bansode was desperate for some work to come his way. He had been without any work since that bastard Prakash had been posted there. He was losing his boys. So I thought I would give him a small job,' Salim said.

'And see where it got him—in jail. And he has already named you as the owner of the seized consignment. You are now named in the FIR. Was this prudent?' Hanif asked.

'Not the FIR, just another FIR,' Salim said carelessly. 'No, it was not prudent, but I also wanted to show that upstart puppy, Prakash, that he cannot control the coast. That coast belongs to us, Hanif Bhai, and we must do everything in our power to regain it. After all, I was born there and those are my people. I have to take care of them. And Prakash is simply unable to understand that.' He suddenly flared. 'The bastard had the guts to include my name in a FIR! Tell Master to finish him. After all, it's Master's business that is being affected the most by that chap. Tell him he can take any measures to get rid of him.'

'I am informed that he is likely to be transferred soon.'

'Kill him anyway. Stupid, stubborn and lucky. That is a dangerous combination. The cur has troubled us for too long.'

'Let him be, Salim Bhai. He will be in Pune soon. Poor guy has not even married yet. *Randwa mar jayega bechara*,' Hanif said.

'Remember our childhood, Hanif Bhai,' retorted Salim. 'Days when we wanted to be stars. Remember selling stolen mangoes in Mandangarh to buy cricket bats, hoping that we would play for India one day. We did not become movie stars or played cricket for India, Hanif Bhai, but we are stars now. The movie stars want to look like us. We decide which matches India will win. And we didn't reach here by being soft or by being disloyal to our friends. There is no need to go soft, Hanif Bhai, just because we are at the top. Now we have to make sure no one challenges us. Kill him.'

Salim could feel Shabnam stiffening as he spoke so carelessly about disposing Prakash. 'What's the matter?' he asked her.

Shabnam shook her head, but then could not resist asking. 'I thought that you never hurt government officers. After all, they are only doing their job.'

'Sometimes, some people have to be made examples of. A large number of overzealous government officers also create problems, even if they are just doing their jobs. They regularly get their pay. Nobody is going to remove them for not doing their job. Why can't they leave me alone?'

Shabnam did not reply. To her, this sounded like warped logic—government servants not doing their jobs since they were anyway going to be paid. To her, everybody should be paid for *working*, and not idling. And for once, she did not think that Salim was the cavalier daredevil she had always thought him to be. She was still lost in her world when Salim took her hand and placed it on his crotch.

'See what you do to me. I am so hot for you. All this talk of violence. It is so erotic when you are around. Let's go.'

He got up and Shabnam followed him dutifully.

'Make sure that you communicate the decision to Master,' he instructed Hanif as he left.

Hanif thought about it for a long time and then decided to leave it to Master. He would not press him to kill Prakash. But he also wouldn't stop Master. He decided that he would leave everything to luck—Prakash's luck.

Salim's instincts were right. And Hanif's were wrong. They should have killed the lucky nincompoop, Prakash. But he lived. To become the nemesis that Salim feared.

5

The New Fields

'You are looking rather dissatisfied with yourself,' Kanwar said to Prakash over the second drink of the evening. The two, mentor and mentee, had been getting together every other Friday at Kanwar's home ever since Prakash had been transferred to Pune a few months back. They discussed everything under the sun on those evenings.

'I don't know where I am headed,' replied Prakash. 'I just keep giving permissions, approving applications, filing appeals in courts. I thought I would be part of the nation's progress and not be just another regulator. Life seems so meaningless and the file work hardly lets me sleep.'

'Hardly sleeps because of files,' Kanwar said with a chuckle. 'I thought your two girlfriends were keeping you awake. Besides, I thought that you loved Pune.'

Despite the light-hearted comment, Kanwar looked closely at Prakash. There seemed to be some truth in what Prakash had said. His eyes were tired, there was a recent weariness in his attitude, and his acerbic comments about the homilies his seniors dispensed to him were missing. The new job was taking away his zest for life.

Kanwar's comments did not surprise Prakash. He was becoming used to the fact that people, including colleagues, watched the personal lives of bureaucrats intimately. So, he stoically accepted the fact that Kanwar knew that Prakash was dating two girls simultaneously.

'Those two are just casual friends,' he replied dismissively, trying to veer the conversation back to the topic at hand. 'And yes,

I love Pune. The city challenges you. I haven't come across a more dichotomous city—it is so staid and conservative, but then, it still lets Rajneeshites thrive in peace. You have temples galore, more than two hundred of them with two hundred years of history, and the world comes here to worship an individual, who calls himself Osho. The nationalist movement was deeply rooted over here and the most famous bakery here is still the German Bakery. It is supposed to be the retirement city for the Marathi clan, and outstation students outnumber those very retirees. I love discovering parts of this city. It's the ten or twelve hours that I spend in the office that are frustrating. Why do I have to sit in there just approving applications? Can't we do something more productive?'

'Like chasing Salim,' replied Kanwar, a smile on his lips. 'I can sense you are itching to get back into action. Even over here you tend to go after tax evaders instead of sticking to your routine tasks. But you have a long way to go. You are still not ready to fight the underworld. And that's why I backed the Collector when he thought of transferring you out of Dapoli. You were likely to hurt yourself there. You are still like that bull in a China shop that leaves too many flanks open. There is no guile in you. No stratagems to counter the moves of your opponents. You are a sitting duck for any enemy.'

'Oh no, you can't say that,' countered Prakash immediately. 'I have just booked some of the top industrialists for tax evasion and I am still surviving.'

'Surviving only because the Collector and I are covering the flanks left open by you,' Kanwar said with a tinge of exasperation. 'The first person you booked complained to the Prime Minister. You didn't even know that he was so well connected. And then there was that question in the parliament about your activities. If you were in the field chasing smugglers, that would have been like two bullets that could have ended your life. You still don't research your targets, and they *can* hit back at you. Remember, everyone who reaches the top is skilled and often ruthless.'

'I am neither afraid of complaints nor of bullets,' replied Prakash stubbornly.

'Well, you should be. They end accomplishments.'

'You, a military school alumnus, advising me to be scared!'

'No, just to be strategic.'

The conversation was not going anywhere and Prakash decided to cut the evening short.

'I should be going, sir. Shelley has decided to drag me to a party tomorrow and I may as well get my beauty sleep.'

'How is Shelley doing? Any progress?' Kanwar asked with a mischievous glint in his eye.

'We are just good friends, sir. We have been for a long time,' Prakash said.

'Oh yes, I know. You've said it often. But my question is—good friends for how long?'

'I am leaving, sir. Goodnight,' said Prakash, but Kanwar heard him muttering 'For too bloody long now' as he exited the door.

6

First Encounter of the Close Kind

21 November 1992. Saturday. It was to be a defining date in Prakash's life. Ironically, he had no inkling of it as he stood in Shelley's flat at Koregaon Park.

'Do you seriously intend to take me to the party on your motorcycle?' Shelley looked at him, thunderstruck.

Prakash looked at the nattily dressed Shelley. 'How could I have guessed that you were going to the party dressed like my grandmother?' he countered, sounding offended.

But Shelley did look stunning in the dress, he admitted to himself. She wore a light pink ghagra choli that had probably been in fashion some twenty years back. It had such intricate zardozi and chikankari work on it that the fabric was nearly invisible. It hugged her body, and with her hair loose, she looked like the princess that she truly was. Her 5'5" frame was just beginning to lose the natural thinness of the teenagers and the dress was tight at certain places. He knew that he could not point that out—except at the peril of his life. She was looking beautiful and, despite the anger, her large, kohl lined eyes could not cloud their inevitable mischievous glint. He guessed that her natural happy approach towards life was likely to keep her face fresh and charming even as she grew older.

'Do you expect me to be dressed like one of the tourists at the Rajneesh Ashram?' Shelley said, looking contemptuously at the blue shirt and grey trousers worn by Prakash. 'You will anyway not be allowed entry to the party. They will ask you to come through the back gate reserved for waiters. You could have, at the very least, worn a jacket, if not an achkan. I thought all bureaucrats wore them.'

'Not when they are posted in a hot state like Maharashtra or Tamil Nadu. And they won't dare to kick me out, not with a princess on my arm,' Prakash said, trying to make light of the situation. He was stating the truth, and normally, the statement would have earned him a mild admonishment. Shelley belonged to one of the minor royal families of Rajasthan, and her father was a Member of Parliament, which no one cared about back at college. After all, children of public leaders had to study somewhere; there were so many of them in India and so few good colleges. Hindu College was the best of them all anyway. It was only after he had joined the civil services that Prakash had realized the kind of clout political leaders wielded.

'Oh, don't be your obtuse self, Prakash. I expected you to come in your office car or something. And here you come, riding on your "Dick",' Shelley said, referring to Prakash's bike, which because of its number plate—starting with 'DIX'—had been famously known in college by that name.

'I don't have an office car. I have a jeep that has two front seats, and I can't go driving a jeep. It looks stupid,' Prakash replied. 'And an Assistant Collector on a motorcycle with a princess riding pillion generates more buzz and discussion than landing up staidly in a car,' he continued lightly. 'Come on, nobody knows either you or me over there. We are going to have some good booze, and complete a formality. After all, I will have to tap Firozewala at the end of the year to achieve my revenue targets. He is, after all, the biggest manufacturer of televisions in India.'

'They may not know you, but they know me. I have been in Pune for nearly a year now,' Shelley replied.

'Come on, these old foggies know you?'

The argument could have carried on, but Prakash knew that you could rarely budge Shelley once she had made up her mind. So he requested the office motor pool to send him a car, which arrived half an hour later—an ancient white Ambassador with peeling paint. They shared a joint while waiting for the car.

'I can't look high at the party,' Shelley said. 'I just need a pick me up.'

The driver was in a bad mood for Prakash had spoiled his Saturday evening, but he dropped his grouchy look after one look at Shelley. Prakash was awestruck when the driver opened the door for Shelley even on reaching the Firozewala residence at Bund Garden Road.

'Sir, the Collector and the Additional Collector are also here today,' he informed Prakash conspiratorially. The drivers invariably knew everything.

The party was in full swing by the time they entered. A popular Bollywood singer was singing his latest songs from a small stage at the centre of the huge lawn.

There must be at least three hundred people here, thought Prakash. *I am going to be lost.*

'Ah, there is Firozewala uncle!' Shelley said, virtually dragging Prakash through the crowd to meet Firozewala, who stood at the far corner of the lawn, away from the stage, accompanied by two other leading industrialists of Pune. 'Let's wish him and get over with the formalities. We can go dancing after.'

Prakash blanched. He had forgotten the mandatory dancing he had to do with Shelley at parties and he dreaded it in his new role.

'Hello, uncle. Happy Birthday,' chirped Shelley, standing up on her toes and kissing Firozewala on the cheek.

'Thanks, beta,' Firozewala said, visibly brightening up on seeing Shelley. 'How are you keeping? One doesn't see you very often.'

'You are a busy person, uncle. I can't just drop in unannounced anymore,' Shelley replied politely.

'Happy birthday, Mr Firozewala,' wished Prakash, taking

advantage of a minor gap in the conversation.

'Ah, the young Mr Prakash. Good of you to take some time off from office and come to a party. Your bosses are here as well,' Firozewala said airily, showing off a little.

'And this is from both of us. I hope it still is your favourite fragrance,' Shelley said, opening her big handbag and thrusting a beautifully packed crystal bottle of ittar to Firozewala. 'I had gone to Bhopal and remembered that you loved this.'

'Oh, nice of you to remember,' Firozewala said, and then continued, a little surprised, 'You two came together?'

'Yeah, we're friends and classmates from college,' Prakash replied, kicking himself mentally for not carrying a gift. He may be a government servant now, but he had been, since childhood, taught the basic etiquette of carrying a gift to a party. *Am I already taking the privileges of the bureaucracy for granted?* He pushed the thought back. He would think of it later. Shelley, meanwhile, was smoothening things over. 'Yeah, classmates, and long-time friends, uncle. The whole class made notes for him when he was studying for the Civil Services Examination.'

'Oh! He learnt to delegate his work from college days itself?' said Firozewala, jokingly. 'He is going to be a successful bureaucrat then. You know Harry and Shroff?' he said, turning to the other two men standing next to him.

'Who doesn't!' said Prakash. 'Shelley,' he said, introducing her to them.

'Daughter of an old friend. She belongs to the royal family of Chavad, and her father is now a Member of Parliament,' added Firozewala.

Somehow, that single sentence changed the way the gathering viewed them. They were no longer the young brash Assistant Collector, and his friend; they were now the young princess, daughter of an MP, and the upcoming bright bureaucrat. As they moved around, Prakash realized that Shelley knew most of the crowd, and he slowly started enjoying the party. Between the two of them, they almost knew everybody, and while Shelley was updated on the social gossip, Prakash knew about their financial misdeeds.

'That's Karsan Bhai there,' Shelley would say. 'The gutkha king. Let's go and say hello.'

'Let's not. We raided him last week and he paid ₹2 crore in back taxes,' Prakash countered. 'And his accountant told me he has taken a new mistress, just twenty-one years old. The dirty lecherous old man!'

'Oh, who isn't keeping one over here, a mistress that is,' Shelley said flippantly and dragged Prakash to meet Karsan Bhai.

Prakash spotted the Collector and Kanwar. He nudged Shelley and turned towards them. As Prakash walked towards the Collector, the fawning crowd surrounding the Collector melted away.

'None of the people here seem to like you,' whispered Shelley as they approached the duo. While the Collector was dressed formally in a three piece that would have been in fashion in the 1980s, Kanwar was in a bright blue printed shirt and black trousers, which made Prakash feel comfortable in his staid dress. He looked at Shelley, his eyes seemingly saying *See, I am dressed perfectly*, when Shelley greeted Kanwar.

'Sir, remember me? Shelley? We met at Kwality!'

There was a momentary silence as all of them digested the information. How could Shelley have known that bureaucrats never referred to a dinner where the boss had not been invited? Kanwar was the first to recover.

'Yeah, of course I remember you. How could one forget a pretty lady like you?' he said gallantly, and then, turning to the Collector, explained. 'Prakash hosted a dinner for his school and college friends, sir. He is from a sainik school and I am from a military school, so he invited me as well.'

'Oh, is that so?' replied the Collector, and the conversation shifted to schools and colleges. The Collector wanted to pick their brains regarding a college for his son. Prakash naturally expounded the merits of going to Hindu College. While enthusiastically agreeing with Prakash, Shelley kept fretting as she was missing the rest of the party.

'I saw you meeting Karsan Bhai,' the Collector said to Prakash shortly.

'Yes, sir. And Prakash asked him to pay ₹1 crore more on back taxes, sir, that too after Prakash had already made him pay ₹2 crore earlier,' quipped Shelley, lying with a straight face, and Prakash nearly laughed.

With the formalities over, Shelley now wanted to escape to the din of the party.

'So many filmstars Firoze ji has invited, sir,' she said dreamily. 'Paji and the action hero…and oh! there is young Isha as well. I know her!'

'Are you coming?' she asked Prakash. 'She's from our college!'

Prakash looked at the Collector, who nodded his permission, and they escaped back into the crowd, finding their way to Isha, who was looking a little lost. She jumped up on seeing Shelley, and they exchanged those airy kisses that Prakash found so irritating, the ones that seemed to say, 'Darling, don't let my lips touch your cheek, or else I will lose some lipstick, and you may lose some facial foundation.' When the ritual was over, Isha peered at Prakash, finding him irritatingly familiar but not able to place him.

'Oh, he is Prakash, my class, our college. The guy with the "Dick",' said Shelley. Apparently, Prakash's infamously named motorcycle 'Dick' was more famous than the rider himself, for Isha immediately said, 'Oh, Dick! I once went riding on it. You lent it to Kali. What are you doing here, Prakash?'

'He is making life tough for the businessmen over here,' a tall imposing figure said. Patankar, the machinery innovator of India, walked up to them with his wife. 'I believe you had a spat with my people last week,' he said, gently placing a hand on Shelley's shoulders as she bent to touch their feet. Apparently they were related. Patankar ji had some roots in the royal circles as well.

'Not a spat, Patankar ji. They were telling me that they had read the law and I pointed out that laws written in the book are meant not just to be read, but to be followed as well,' Prakash replied softly.

'And that point cost me a million rupees, besides delays in clearing goods from the factory,' said Patankar. 'How do you know this firebrand? And if you know him well, advise him to slow down,' he told Shelley in a good-natured manner.

The party was threatening to turn into shop talk and Prakash was on the verge of losing his patience. Shelley, well aware of the short fuse Prakash had, immediately shifted the topic to Isha when Firozewala walked up to them.

'Enjoying the party?' he asked Shelley. 'You should be here more often. I had promised your Dad that I would look after you while you are in Pune.'

'Terrific party, uncle. You know how to throw a good one,' replied Shelley. 'And see, I even ran into Isha after three years. She is also from our college.'

'This party seems to be a college get-together rather than my birthday party. Glad to see you all enjoying yourselves.' Firoze was too much of a gentleman to embarrass his guests. Politely, he moved on and turned towards Isha for some small talk. Prakash looked for a chance to escape. He had come here to give Shelley company and was not comfortable being the centre of attention, even if it was only because of Shelley.

'Isn't that Shabnam?' he asked Shelley, pointing to a forlorn figure sitting all by herself. He knew that it was indeed Shabnam. He had followed her in the filmy magazines, had watched the five movies where she had played minor roles, and read with interest the announcement about her casting by Kabadiwala. John, after his arrest, had been in that garrulous mood of a person who knows he is going to jail for a long time, and wanting to retain a shred of dignity in the free world, had boasted that they did not know his reach. That he had recently convinced Kabadiwala to cast a two bit actress called 'Shabnam' against the genius, because she was Salim's mistress, and did they think Salim, sitting in Dubai, could have managed it himself? He was the point man for Salim Bhai, and they will see how Salim Bhai will not let him waste his time in jail. 'You just see, I will be out in a couple of months,' he had stated a year ago. 'There are too many people backing me.'

'Shabnam, who is Shabnam? Was she in our college?' Shelley asked, still caught up in that thread of talk.

'No, silly,' chirped Isha, 'It's Shabnam! The girl who is doing that big Kabadiwala film against the genius. It should be releasing soon. The industry is raving about her.'

Firoze peered at the girl. 'Oh. Is that who she is? My secretary said that we had to invite her. She has a big release coming up and her producer wanted to expose her a little to the 'high society' crowd so that she could hold her own afterwards. But she seems to be an introvert. Anyone of you know her? No. Then come, let me introduce you all to her. She just may become a star someday.'

They all trooped down to the girl sitting alone.

'Firoze,' said Firozewala, introducing himself. 'You still have not wished me a happy birthday.'

'Oh, Firoze ji, I am so sorry. I came with Paji, and then Paji met all his friends, and he told me that he would introduce me to you, but then…' Shabnam said, rather clumsily. And then, impulsively, she stood on her toes, pecked Firoze on the cheek, and said 'Happy Birthday!'

Firoze raised his eyes. 'All is forgiven,' he said, looking around to check if any of the cameras had caught that peck, and finding none, was relieved and rushed away. Whether the others knew or not, he knew that Shabnam was Salim's girl and he had no intention of explaining to Salim what he was doing getting a kiss from Shabnam. 'These bloody molls,' he uttered under his breath as he excused himself from the group.

'Hi, I am Shelley,' Shelley said. She was enjoying the evening thoroughly and looked to take this forlorn-looking girl under her wing. 'And this is Isha and Prakash.'

'Big fan,' gushed Isha. 'I just entered the industry last year and all of us look up to you with a lot of respect. You have achieved so much in so little time.'

Is she acting, or does she really not know that Shabnam's role has been managed by Salim? wondered Prakash. He distantly watched the three of them talking, barely participating himself. Shelley was trying to put Shabnam at ease by getting her to talk about the film, decrying the stars who leave their escorts. The four of them now formed a separate group comprising of the struggler, the 'has been' struggler, the princess and the dunce—who, from all the reactions that he had gotten at this party, seemed to be damned again.

Prakash looked vacantly at Shabnam, and the first thing that struck him was her simplicity. *She couldn't be more than 5'3"*, he thought, a good five inches shorter than him. He looked at her feet and noticed that she was wearing flat-heeled sandals. *She could have easily added a couple of inches if she wanted,* he thought. She was wearing a cream-coloured churidar, which clung to her shapely legs, and an off-white, plain, tight-fitting kurti that fell just below her hips. A thin gold chain with a small diamond-studded Ganpati hung around her neck. The only sign of prosperity seemed to be the ladies' Omega watch she wore on her left hand. Not on her right hand, he noted. *Is she unconcerned because she is Salim's mistress, or is she so confident that she thought that she didn't need embellishments even for such a posh party?*

He noticed that she was thin. *Could not be more than 50 kg*, he thought. *Even I could snap her in two, and I think Salim is much bigger than I am. Is she scared of him?* He shook himself free of thoughts and looked at her face. The blunt cut, shoulder length hair that fringed her oval face must have been set by a professional hair designer to give her a waif-like look. She wore very little makeup, and yet looked more beautiful than Isha or Shelley. She had that peach-coloured skin with a natural reddish hue that seemed like the blush of the morning sun, which possibly darkened to a deep red every time somebody told a dirty joke. *The eyes... What about the eyes?* He stared at her as she was looking at Shelley. Large oval eyes on a heart-shaped face. He could detect a tinge of light brown. *But they were guileless! How could Salim's mistress have such guileless eyes?* he wondered.

He was just starting to compare her to Shelley when he heard his name being called, seemingly from afar, and then, Shelley suddenly shook his arm, breaking his reverie.

'Wake up silly, what's wrong with you? You haven't had so much to drink that you can't concentrate on three lovely girls. Or maybe it is because you don't have sufficient drinks inside you...' she said with a giggle. It was so odd to see Shelley giggle, he realized. He was more used to her guffaw than this lady-like titter.

'I think he is tongue-tied. I think he is a big fan of Shabnam here, and now that he is face to face with her, he doesn't know what to say,' chirped Isha. 'He was the one who spotted her from a mile away. I think he has been hit by "the thunderbolt",' she said, copying the famous dialogue from *The Godfather*.

Prakash felt Shabnam's gaze on him without even looking at her. And when he finally fixed his gaze on her, he was drawn towards the eyes again. The large, dewy, dark brown eyes, with flecks of light brown rimming the iris. They were the most expressive pair of eyes he had seen in a long time. Prakash was not sure whether it was pity or sympathy that he saw in her eyes. *It was certainly not contempt,* he thought. He was surprised. He thought all stars looked upon their fans with contempt. He saw Shabnam noticing him and her eyes clouded as she turned her back to Prakash to look at Shelley.

'Prakash, tongue-tied. Prakash, hit by a thunderbolt.' This time, Shelley's laughter was definitely louder. 'You don't know him, Isha. You were three years his junior and he never dated girls three years his junior. So you missed out on seeing him at parties and socials. There is nothing that can silence the brash, rash, rude, all-knowing Prakash. Neither then, nor now. And certainly, no girl can strike him with the thunderbolt. He wears the shield of responsibility and the armour of duty.'

'That was a bewildering monologue to introduce me,' said Prakash, smiling awkwardly, 'but Isha is right, madam. I am a big fan, and at the moment, more than a little intrigued by the celebrity sitting at the party alone,' he said to Shabnam.

'Who is the madam here?' screamed Shelley, momentarily forgetting the setting and then continued, mockingly. 'Madam ji, please explain to this nincompoop that there is life beyond government, and he can be put in the doghouse for insulting a charming and beautiful girl like you by calling her madam.'

'Oh, so you are in government?' Shabnam asked quietly.

'Government...no...he is beyond the government.' Shelley was now in full flow. 'He is an officer who refuses to act like a government officer. He believes that all laws are made to be followed, he feels that duty is something to be done diligently. He believes that putting one's life at risk is the job of a government officer.'

'Really, is that all?' Shabnam said in an amused tone.

'Shelley has a tendency to blow things out of proportion,' Prakash said softly. 'But can one let a little personal risk stop you? Look at the soldiers on the border.'

Shabnam looked at Prakash speculatively, and then replied, 'Those are noble thoughts, and I wish that everybody in the government followed that principle. But is that really the maxim by which bureaucrats work? I believe that the primary thing taught in bureaucracy is that safety comes first.'

Shelley could not let that opportunity slip. They had not been out of college long enough for her to not make fun of such an inviting sentence.

'Safety first,' she said. 'He is so careless that even in this era of AIDS, you would not find a rubber on him!'

'Shelley!' Prakash said softly.

'Yeah?' she replied.

'Shut up. You are embarrassing her. She isn't from our college,' Prakash said.

Turning to Shabnam, he added, 'We have to give Shelley here a long rope. She is, after all, her royal highness, a true blue-blooded princess.'

That seemed to pique Shabnam and Isha's interest. They tried to question Shelley about her royal heritage, but Shelley knew that Prakash was only using it to shift the focus away from himself.

'Oh, yes. But why are you diverting the topic? *Noblesse oblige* and all that, you bureaucrats are the new royalty. You owe more to society than me. Go and make the country proud. Go catch some more of Salim's consignments,' Shelley retorted.

Prakash had been staring at Shabnam, and he was sure he detected a flicker of surprise and shock cross her face at Shelley's latest revelation. She immediately covered it with a look of disinterest. Prakash was sure that there was an element of recognition in that surprise. *Does she know of me?* he wondered. *If so, how and why…?*

'Oh! You have been locking horns with Salim, the big don,' Shabnam said easily. 'Really? Or have you been impressing your friends with tall tales? Are you in the Bombay Police, because I have never read of anybody in Pune catching Salim's consignments.'

'Oh, he is in Customs,' Shelley said, replying instead of Prakash.

'He caught lots of gold and silver when he was posted in an obscure place called Dapoli.'

Isha, feeling left out, chipped in. 'Prakash, tell us a little about how Customs officers work, no.'

Nobody responded. Prakash kept looking at Shabnam, who said, 'Isn't Salim a dangerous man to take *panga* with? Are you not worried?'

'Prakash, worried? He is a sainik school type. They live with a death wish. You should have seen him doing those stunts on his "Dick", or on those dangerous mountaineering trips he undertakes.' Shelley was unstoppable.

'Dick,' said Shabnam as Prakash simultaneously said, 'you know a lot about Salim.'

'Sorry,' said Prakash, after a brief moment of silence. 'She meant my bike. It has a registration number which is pronounced as dicks. You seem to know Salim,' he asked, venturing into choppy waters.

'Who in the film industry doesn't know about Salim? He is like the afternoon sun, shining brightly in the sky. He is called "the lion" that has marked the world as his territory,' replied Shabnam.

'People don't pay obeisance to the afternoon sun, they hide from it. When you are blazing, people hide from you, and slowly, as everyone finds shelter, there is nobody left to admire the brightness. Forget others, the issue here is how well do you know him, madam?' retorted Prakash with a touch of temper, irritated by Shabnam's praise of Salim.

'She is right,' Shabnam said, seemingly unfazed by his question and pointing towards Shelley. 'Please call me Shabnam. Madam makes me sound so old, or maybe, the owner of a high-class brothel.'

Shelley and Isha laughed.

Prakash noticed that his question had been smoothly glossed over. He also noted that she was a little agitated, although she had managed to cover it up well. Only someone who was observing her closely could see the slight flush creeping in under her light makeup. She continued, and he noted a sharp edge in her tone as she said, 'You should remember that the sun has a journey to perform every day. Some pray to him in the morning, and some admire him in the evening, but unless he blazes, people will not appreciate his beauty in the morning and the evening. I meet so many people who seem to have met Salim, both from Bollywood and in the government. It is said that he is a government informer at very high levels. Do you know about it? Or are you too junior to know…?'

There was definitely a challenging note in the question.

'What I know is that he is a law breaker, and like all law breakers, he will have to face the consequences of his actions at some point of time.'

'What I hear is that he is a dangerous and a powerful man, and if I were you, Mr Prakash, I would be very careful. Times are different than what they used to be, and government servants are no more immune if they hurt the economic interests of people.'

'Is that a threat?' Prakash was riled and his notoriously aggressive nature seemed ready to burst out.

'Come on, Prakash.' Shelley took up the conversation again. 'Stop picking on the poor girl. She is just saying what other people in the party have also been telling you. That you are a pain in the ass. Why would she threaten you? You're just a glorified clerk with an overinflated sense of self importance! Ignore him, darling, and tell us more about this role that is supposed to be your big breakthrough.'

'Thanks, Shelley. I think I am rather unwanted here. Why don't you watch the movie when it is released next month, instead of hearing me gloat about myself now? You can decide how well I have done for yourself. Do give me a call when you are in Bombay. Anyway, I think the party is over for me. I can see Paji coming over and I have to return to Bombay with him,' she said, scribbling her number on a piece of paper from her diary, tearing it and handing it over to Shelley.

'You can do that too,' she said, addressing Prakash. 'Call me, that is. Maybe you will be slightly less stiff if you knew more about Bollywood and me. And, if that is not too much trouble, can I have your number too? Maybe I will call you if I am stopped by Customs sometime.'

'Here, I will give it to you,' Shelley said before Prakash could respond, taking her diary and writing down Prakash's number. 'And I am giving you my number too. If you are not able to get through to him, contact me. I can always tell you where to find him.'

Paji walked in at that moment, full of importance as the leading star of the industry. He shook hands with them, asked if they wanted an autograph, and disappointed when they replied that they had no paper or pen, took Shabnam by the hand and escorted her out.

'Who were those rustics?' they heard him ask Shabnam.

'Oh, some princess and her entourage. Didn't get the chance to learn much about them.' They heard her lie smoothly as she exited the party.

From the other end of the lawn, Kanwar had watched Prakash talking to Shabnam. He sighed. Prakash will never learn, he thought and returned to his discussion on tax structures with the group of tax consultants surrounding him.

7

A Dangerous Trip

'So what was your issue with Shabnam?' Shelley asked Prakash. The two of them were on their way to Dapoli. They always knew what Shelley was going to do once she had left to study at Duke, but Prakash joining the Indian Customs had come as a surprise to both of them. Shelley now wanted to know everything he had done in the years while she was away.

There was a tinge of deep blue and light orange on the horizon as they climbed the road over a small hill of the Western Ghats. They had planned for a leisurely breakfast at Ambaghat, and then roll into Ratnagiri before lunch for a long cruise on one of the Customs boats. Prakash hoped to board the craft by 3 p.m. so that they could enjoy the afternoon, the late afternoon, the evening and the night at sea. It was a waxing crescent moon; Shelley would miss the glory of the full moon shining brightly on the sea, but this was the only free weekend both of them could manage.

'What was what with Shabnam?' asked Prakash, genuinely puzzled by the question.

'You were positively hostile to her. I have rarely seen you this hostile with any stranger, and certainly never to a girl,' Shelley said. 'If looks could kill, she would be dead. If stares could interrogate, she would be in pain. You were non-communicative and dangerous. You haven't met her before, have you? You seemed to know a lot about her.'

Prakash thought about an appropriate response to Shelley's query. *How much should I tell her? Everything*, he decided immediately. *You don't keep things from your friends*, he thought.

'She is Salim's mistress, and Salim, according to my sources, is threatening producers to get her roles. Seeing her at the party was a shock, and you were right, I would have loved to interrogate her, but it's no longer my job.'

'What! You don't say…' squealed Shelley. 'We met a real-life moll, and you didn't even give me a hint? What a missed opportunity!'

Shelley spoke again after a while. 'But she looked so lonely, and was so reluctant to talk about herself. Probably being the mistress of a don secludes one. And she is so young to look so forlorn. I bet she is younger than us. Can't be more than twenty-five.'

'Her first movie came out in 1988, and I know she finished college before coming to Bombay. Give or take a couple of years before landing the first bit role, so I would place her in our age group, maybe a year older or younger. And she has to be taciturn. Gangster's molls can't be advertising themselves. But what does it matter, we are not going to meet her again.'

'You might be surprised. That exchange of numbers was not for my benefit. She was assessing you while you were getting all worked up. Don't underestimate that girl. It takes guts to survive in the badlands, and she may just be regretting it.'

'Isn't it a bit too late to regret it after landing a role with the genius in a big budget film,' Prakash said sardonically.

'We all need a little help, a little nudge, a little push, for the world to recognize our potential and talent,' Shelley said reasonably.

'Yup. Dr Faustus also needed the nudge from the Devil for realizing his full potential, remember?' Recalling the lines of Dr Faustus in the play, Prakash said,

> *For the vain pleasure of four-and-twenty years hath Faustus lost eternal joy and felicity.*

He then continued, 'If she wants her two bits of fame, and then be consigned to hell, I am not here to redeem her.'

'Why not? Faustus had so many chances to repent but he renounced them every time,' said Shelley. 'Remember what the good angel had said in the end,

> *O Faustus, if thou hadst given ear to me,*
> *Innumerable joys had follow'd thee!*

'I think she was looking at you as her good angel.'

'Me, a redeemer!' Prakash scoffed. 'The devil's acolyte is to be the redeemer.'

'You are no devil's acolyte, Prakash,' Shelley said gently. 'You are the ultimate conformist, the man who moves by the rule book, who will look not just down the lane and up the street, but also over his shoulder if he decides to break any rules. You help people, and that girl, if she ever turns away from her path, has decided to come to you. You are easy to read, anybody can see through your bravado in two minutes, for you have not learnt to deceive.'

Prakash glanced at Shelley who was curled up comfortably on the large seat of the Sierra, at peace with herself and the universe. They rode in silence for a while, each lost in their own thoughts, till they stopped at a roadside stall at Ambaghat for breakfast.

'Do you miss it?' Shelley asked over their breakfast of kanda bhajiya, vada pav and strongly brewed, sugary tea. The tea stall overlooked a green valley with a small waterfall that, even so long after the monsoons, still had a steady flow. It provided the perfect backdrop for an intimate conversation.

'Miss what?' Prakash asked.

'The excitement, the thrill of the chase, the blood rush when you catch somebody, maybe the glory.'

'Why do you ask?' Prakash wondered.

'There is a sense of impatience in you, a tinge of excitement that is trying to burst out as you near Ratnagiri,' she said.

She knows me so well that she scares me, he thought. *I hope she never becomes my enemy.*

'When I joined Customs, I thought my job would be all outdoors, exciting pursuits over sea or road, like in the various spy thrillers you read. I never expected I would be doing drab file work sitting in a room. Yes, I love the outdoors. But India is changing, liberalizing its economy, and these smuggling syndicates, which seem so glamourous at the moment, will turn evil to survive. A new underworld may emerge, one dealing with drugs, arms, maybe human trafficking. Then there will be a bitter fight between them and the law enforcement agencies. I don't know if I am capable of fighting that kind of evil. So I am out.' He replied moodily.

Shelley pondered and then nodded. 'So, this is actually going to be just a nostalgia trip? I hope we have a good time.'

'Yup. This trip is just for sharing a part of my life with you. Shabnam and Salim are the past, not the future.'

They would both be proved wrong shortly.

8

Best Laid Plans of Dons and Men

They boarded the patrol craft at 3 p.m. sharp. Prakash heard the wireless crackle, 'Leopard Prakash from Pune and Leopard Ratnagiri have boarded *Tarini*. Moving out now.'

'Acknowledged. Keeping a lookout. Over and out,' the wireless operator at the Mahabaleshwar wireless repeater station said.

'Why announce me?' Prakash asked 'Bear', the young Assistant Collector at Ratnagiri—so called because of his short, cute appearance. He reminded everyone of 'Yogi Bear'.

'There is an unconfirmed intelligence about a silver consignment having left Fujirah. The coast is on alert. So, we are logging the location and movement of all officers,' Bear said. 'There are teams everywhere.'

'But wouldn't it be better to maintain radio silence? You know smugglers monitor our frequencies whenever a landing is expected,' Prakash countered.

'Policy of prevention. A murder prevented is better than a murderer caught. If they know we are at sea and decide to abort, so be it. I am no glory hunter,' said Bear.

Prakash looked at him. *Is the contagion spreading?* he wondered. Government looked at the number and value of seizures as a measure of the efficiency of officers. Seizures were tangible, prevention was hypothetical. He wondered if he would be where he was today without those two seizures, however accidental they might have been. He would have been just another unknown soldier. And here, a youngster starting his career could so confidently state that he was no glory hunter.

He shook himself out of the reverie. The weather was nice and the beer had put everyone in a more genial mood.

'Why are you here?' asked Bear.

'Showing Shelley a good time. Why?'

'There is a rumour going around that you are here to catch that consignment we just talked of. And there is another team from Pune, which I am not supposed to know about, sitting at Bankot.'

'Oh shit. Is that so? You should have told me. I wouldn't have come.'

'I thought of it, then decided that with so much patrolling, nobody is likely to land the consignment. And…' he added with a rueful smile, 'I don't get good company here very often.'

'Salim's?' Prakash had already begun to investigate.

'He refuses to entertain me with his company,' Bear said with a laugh. 'The consignment is supposed to be his, but there is only a slim chance that his men will try the landing with this much of overt patrolling. Who is she?' he asked, gesturing towards Shelley.

'A college friend,' replied Prakash.

'What does she do?'

'Ask her. She tried explaining, but I couldn't really understand. Some new-fangled business concept.'

They walked up to Shelley, who was just finishing her third beer of the day and had a glassy look on her face.

'The sea, the sun, the wind and Heineken,' she said dreamily. 'How could you leave it all and move to Pune?' she asked Prakash.

'Because you moved to Pune,' Prakash said mockingly. 'The city would have been in shambles if there was nobody to handle you. Bear here wants to know what you do.'

'Why does he want to know?' Shelley asked aggressively, and then, suddenly realizing that she was among friends here, continued in a softer tone. 'I am sorry. I am just so tired of explaining to people what I am trying to do. It's something that is just making inroads in India. It's called Business Process Outsourcing.'

'I know,' replied Bear. 'American Express is just starting it in India for their offices in Asia.'

Shelley looked at Bear with new interest. 'MBA?' she asked.

'IIMA.'

'Duke', said Shelley.

They struck off well after that. Prakash left the two of them to discuss the emergence of the new business environment. He watched Shelley's dusky, not too slim, 5'5" tall frame animatedly expressing her ideas to the short, stocky frame of Bear. Prakash stood at the bow, looking at the froth being churned in the calm sea, wondering if there was violence lurking below the foam. The boat slowly approached Boria.

'This is where he seized the gold,' Bear pointed out to Shelley, both of them joining Prakash, intruding on his solitude.

'I have heard that story,' she replied. They watched the sun turn into a great red ball as it sank over the horizon and then stared at infinity as the various hues of the sky surrendered their brilliance to darkness. The night was now lit just by the stars, and they listened to the various sounds of the sea. The splash of a wave, the call of a dolphin, the metals clanking on a boat somewhere far away. An hour later, the boat slipped into its anchor at the Customs outpost at the mouth of Dabhol creek. They disembarked, ready for their journey to Dapoli.

'Leopard Pune and Leopard Ratnagiri docking at Dabhol at 2015 hours,' the skipper announced diligently to the wireless station.

'I will join you guys for breakfast tomorrow morning,' Bear said as Prakash and Shelley left to navigate the meandering route to Dapoli. 'I would like to patrol a few more sensitive points.'

The night was dark, but the crescent moon and the stars wanly illuminated the hills surrounding the road, creating mysterious shadows. Half an hour later, they checked into the Agricultural

University Guest House at Dapoli for the night.

Shelley walked into Prakash's room a short while later, looking scrubbed and fresh, wearing white harem pants and a pink t-shirt, carrying two cans of Heinekens that she had pinched while alighting from the boat. She lobbed one across to Prakash as she curled up on the bed.

'I can't imagine you would let go of all this for a drab life in Pune,' she said.

Prakash looked at her. 'Can one be on a perpetual holiday? Go through life like it's a series of events without meaning? It is what this life is. Unconnected events that have no relationship with each other whatsoever. I cannot spend my life indefinitely sailing the sea trying to catch contraband without making any progression. Where would it lead me?'

'Well, it's so good to hear about progression from you,' Shelley said sarcastically. 'You forgot our motto so soon after joining the job. Life, baby, is a lark, and should be lived so till you lose it.'

'I disagree now,' retorted Prakash. 'Life, as Shelley said in his ode *To a Skylark*, is meant to soar higher still and higher…from the earth…like a cloud of fire…'

'I am in no mood to listen to the philosophies of poets who couldn't decide if they wanted to live or die,' Shelley said while gulping down her beer, and stood up to leave.

Prakash looked at her hopefully. 'You just said life is to be lived.'

Shelley threw up her hands in mock exasperation. 'When are you going to get it into your thick head that you are not going to get it from me? I do believe you have two hands and, as far as I am concerned, you only need one.'

'But what's wrong with me? We have been friends since '83, since you put an awkward, shy, blundering guy fresh out of the hostel of an all-boy's school at ease in the libertine atmosphere of Delhi University. We have been drunk together at parties, doped out at rock concerts and communed in the beauty of watching Bolshoi ballet.'

'And in the interim, you learned the art of taking girls to bed. How many of them? Five…six during college?' retorted Shelley.

'What can I do when you repeatedly refuse to sleep with me? But then, as I have always said—you say "Yes", and you will be the last girl I sleep with.'

'Aw, how sweet,' Shelley said sarcastically. 'I am not a dreamy-eyed debutante to be impressed with such dialogues. But,' she continued, a little more seriously this time, 'have you ever thought that we possibly lasted together so long because there is no sex involved. We are like two chaddi buddies, who know each other's secrets, weaknesses, likings, habits and tolerate all of them. Maybe sex will make us lovers, and lovers do finally drift apart, especially if they fall in love at the age of nineteen.'

Prakash knew she would not be convinced, and with a resigned shrug, an exaggerated disappointed look and an obscene gesture (which Shelley laughed at), he again resorted to reciting the ode *To a Skylark* to express his feelings,

What thou art we know not;
What is most like thee?

Shelley gave him an exasperated look and left the room.

◆

Lal came early next morning to take them to Harnai, where Shelley wanted to see the famed fish market. Bear joined them, looking fresh despite what Prakash knew must have been an all-night sea patrol.

'The Fisherman's wharf in San Francisco is such a big tourist draw, why can't something like that be replicated in India? The firangs would love this disorderly auction,' Shelley said to Bear.

Lal and Prakash sat on a rock and sipped at a cup of tea as Bear and Shelley enthusiastically discussed the esoteric possibility of converting Dapoli into a tourist attraction.

'How do you find Pune, sir?' Lal asked.

'Different work, but deep down, everything is the same. There too nobody wants to pay taxes. They too want to get rich quick. What's the difference between them and these smugglers, Lal?'

'Oh, there is. Don't paint them with the same brush. Smugglers are a different breed altogether. Tax evasion partly has to do with high tax rates. How much do tax evaders gain—10, 20, 30 per cent on their turnover? The syndicates look for that kind of return on a monthly, if not weekly, basis. And they are ready to cajole, threaten and kill for that kind of money. Just look at the havoc Master and Rangeela are wrecking in Alibag.'

'Why, what's happening?' Prakash asked.

'He is keeping a tight vigil here,' Lal said, pointing at Bear. 'So, Rangeela and Master decided to shift their operations to Alibag. They killed a couple of guys there to establish their hegemony. A minor gang war has erupted. Master is using his famous blade freely, and Rangeela has even used some bombs. Officers are being threatened or lured, and they don't know whom to look for directions. They tried to intimidate the new officers here too, minor threats aimed at demoralizing. None have succumbed because the boss is holding firm, but Master is turning more aggressive after his intimidation worked in Alibag.'

Prakash listened intently.

'Hopefully all of this will reduce. The new policies could dramatically affect the economics of smuggling and these syndicates, starved of funds, will then collapse under their own weight.'

'I don't agree, sir,' replied Lal. 'If the smuggling of gold and silver does stop, a more vicious underworld may emerge, one dealing in drugs, kidnapping, extortion and even arms. These syndicates have a hold over the finances of Bombay and Gujarat, and they will not let go of their appetite for quick profits without a fight.'

'There are already reports of Salim extending his smuggling operations to Africa, mainly South Africa, Mozambique and Nigeria.' Lal continued. 'There are already whispers of country crafts from India smuggling drugs to Africa.'

Lal looked at Shelley and Bear walking towards them. He admired Shelley's happy, carefree walk as she waved at them.

'You have a good friend in that lady,' Lal said. 'I hope you know what you are doing. You do have a tendency of being overtly brash at times. Be careful, be gentle.'

Prakash wondered what Lal meant by that, and then, after considering both the possibilities, laughed, a dry laugh this time. 'I never expected *you* to tell me to be careful. I still would go with Dylan Thomas when he says, *Do not go gentle into that good night… Rage, rage against the dying of the light.*'

'You do have a penchant for citing the wrong lines at the wrong time,' Lal chided Prakash, 'That's a poem about death, and nobody needs to talk of death now.'

'You never can tell,' said Prakash.

They parted with a firm handshake as Shelley and Bear came back, their eyes sparkling with visions of change. *Maybe there is hope*, thought Prakash, *everything is possible, especially if the not-so-young people can also dream.*

◆

They left Dapoli late in the evening, hoping to reach Pune by midnight. The promised late evening walk in the strawberry fields of Mahabaleshwar was forgotten after the sumptuous treat of kokum sherbet, sol kadi and malvani mutton.

'There is so much to explore in India,' Shelley said languidly, sprawled lazily on the front seat as they crossed Khed and started the sharp ascent of the Western Ghats for Mahabaleshwar.

'I agree. Told you it would be a good trip.' Prakash could not resist gloating a little. 'Now sit back and enjoy the Ghats till the lights last. Dinner at Mahabaleshwar?'

'Nah, who wants to eat stale food after the feast we have just had.'

'Then we will stop for a cup of tea at the office. You should see our wireless repeater station. It's unique, and very few government organizations have something as advanced.'

Singh, the Assistant Director in charge of Customs communications on the west coast, was waiting for them. He enthusiastically explained the intricacies of the wireless system to Shelley, patiently detailing the difference between very high frequency and ultra-high frequency, VHF and UHF, the range at which different communication systems could communicate and how communications could be kept secure.

'Where is Leopard Ratnagiri?' Prakash asked him.

'Sir, he left from Dabhol about half an hour back,' replied Singh.

'Heading for Ratnagiri?'

'I doubt it, sir. His rabbit informed me that they filled 500 litres of diesel from Dabhol.'

'Five hundred litres is good enough for another forty-eight hours of patrolling. Let's give him a moral boost,' Prakash said impulsively. 'Give me the mic, Singh sahab.'

Singh would never give the mic to anybody else on his duty, but he and Prakash had worked closely for a very long time, and Prakash had put his safety in Singh's hands so often that he could not say no. But nobody, neither Singh, nor Shelley, not even Prakash, had expected what happened next. Prakash, breaking all the established norms of secure communication, called in.

'Hey, Leopard Ratnagiri.'

The speaker crackled after a short pause, carrying Bear's voice over the airwaves.

'Leopard Ratnagiri here, over.'

'Don't let them go. Catch them and shake them.'

Thankfully, Singh switched off the system immediately and Shelley's wild Indian whoop was not heard over the airwaves.

◆

<u>TOP SECRET</u>

Transcript of the Interview of Sh. Prakash, Asst. Collector, Pune on 1st December, 1992, Tuesday.

Present: Collector, Deputy Collector (Preventive). Questions asked by D.C(P).

Note: No audio recording of this interview is available.

Q. Did you visit Ratnagiri, Dabhol and Dapoli region on the 28th and 29th of November, 1992?
A: Yes.

Q: Were your controlling officers informed of this trip?
A: Yes.

Q: Was this information given in writing?
A: No.

Q: Were you aware that a surveillance team from headquarters was camping at Bankot?
A: Yes.

Q: How did you learn of this?
A: I was informed of it by Asst. Collector, Ratnagiri.

Q: How did he know?
A: You would have to ask him that.

Q: Were you aware that there was a vessel with 250 silver bricks headed for Bankot?
A: No. But if there was a vessel intended for Bankot, with the

headquarters team so hopelessly exposed, they would have diverted the consignment to the alternate landing spot.

Q: Did you try to warn the vessel through the unauthorized use of wireless at 2134 hrs on 29th November, 1992?
A: Me? Warn the vessel? I would not answer any further questions. You may decide on the next course of action without my input.
Interview concluded at 1545 hrs. To be resumed at 1030 hrs on 2nd December, 1992.

◆

TOP SECRET
2nd December, 1992

I have just received a confidential note from Additional Director General, RI, that a landing of 250 bricks of silver was planned by Master, landing agent of Salim, at Dabhol creek. However, the landing was aborted as there was overt movement of Customs personnel on the Dabhol creek, and the vessel was asked to wait at deep sea by Salim till a safe place for landing the contraband could be found.

No further action to be taken on this interview without my prior clearance.

Sd/-
(Collector, Pune)

◆

<u>TOP SECRET</u>

3rd December, 1992

I have been informed that the consignment in question was intercepted by Pakistani smuggler, Dawood Jatt, and was destroyed or looted by him. The matter is closed.

Sd/-

(Collector, Pune)

9

Friends and Enemies

There were two separate interviews over the incident, neither of which were ever made public. The first was among the Collector, one D.L. Sharma and Prakash. Prakash knew that Sharma was an Additional Collector in their department, but knew little beyond that.

'You have been saved by the skin of your teeth in this case,' opened the Collector. 'Do you know how many rules you broke over the weekend?'

'Yes, sir,' replied Prakash, duly chastised, but then added, 'The Deputy Collector had no business imputing motives to my actions.'

'That time is over,' interjected Sharma. 'You were wrong to take a friend, a woman, on the departmental boat when you knew there was an operation being conducted. You were also wrong when you used the wireless without proper authorization.'

Prakash remained silent. Sharma continued, 'Your wireless stunt was a stroke of luck. What we now know is that the landing was supposed to happen at Dabhol, and the news about it being destined for Bankot was a red herring floated by Salim's henchmen to divert our attention. Your headquarters team fell for it—hook, line and sinker.'

'Headquarters team is full of idiots, sir,' said Prakash.

'You were no less of a nincompoop. Wandering around unannounced in sensitive areas,' flared Sharma. However, he calmed almost immediately. Lowering his voice, he said, 'In any case, Salim's men and Master thought that you had travelled from Pune with confidential information and that they were exposed. They aborted the landing and the new Pakistani gangs took advantage of their uncertainty. You have a reputation in that region, Prakash.'

'Is that a compliment, sir? I thought I behaved like a nincompoop,' Prakash replied sulkily.

'I don't know what you are—nincompoop, efficient, or just plain lucky. But because of you, Salim has lost face thrice, and more so this time because his consignment was looted or destroyed by his rivals who are trying to muscle into his territory. I would be very careful if I were you. He is a dangerous man.'

'Thanks for the advice, sir,' replied the blundering nincompoop.

'It is not just advice. We hear that a supari has been floated for your name by Master. It seems to have Salim's blessings. We just don't know who is going to pick it up.'

'How much, sir? Just interested in knowing.'

'Will you ever get serious, Prakash!' The Collector spoke out in astonishment. 'This is your life that is being discussed!' Sharma looked at Prakash, gave a wry smile, and said, 'One lakh rupees.'

'That's all?' exclaimed Prakash. 'He doesn't seem to hold me in high regard.'

'That's true,' Sharma said. 'He thinks you are plain lucky, as do we, so far. But to put things in perspective, ₹1 lakh is equal to twenty months of pay for you, that is, 20 months of pay of a person who has cleared the Civil Services Examination. Imagine how much it would be for a fresh boy out of Azamgarh.'

Prakash let the new piece of information sink in. 'Thank you for the warning, sir. I will try and watch my back.'

◆

The genesis of the warning was a discussion that had taken place at Salim's bungalow in Dubai.

'Prakash again?' Salim asked Hanif.

'Yes, but it seems that he was there just for fun with his girlfriend. Master and his men panicked unnecessarily,' replied Hanif.

'What does this gaandu have on us? Why does he keep stumbling onto my consignments? I have now lost three consignments to him. That must be a record. Nobody has ever made me lose three consignments without my nod.'

'This happens sometimes in business, Bhai,' replied Hanif reasonably.

'Not in my business.' Salim flared. 'Because of this chutiya, I have now lost a consignment to those Pakistani Agencywalla. They have been putting pressure on me to help them. I don't want to, I will never be able to go back to India if I work with them, and that *tediya* was telling me that he will broker some deal to beat the murder rap. Even those R&AW guys were saying that if I cooperate, something can be worked out. But this loss, this has made me lose a lot of face. Why did we not kill that gaandu?'

'Because he was transferred to Pune,' reminded Hanif. 'Master was just waiting for an opportunity, but then it stopped being a priority after his transfer to Pune.'

'Hanif Bhai, you are slipping in your old age. If you had pushed Master to kill him then, we would have saved three crore and our reputation.'

'Profit and loss are in the hands of Allah, Bhai. We are just agents doing His work. If not Prakash, maybe somebody else could have stumbled upon this consignment,' Hanif said philosophically.

'Do it, Hanif Bhai,' Salim said, ending the discussion. 'Tell Master to end this boy's tale.'

◆

Prakash got a call to meet D.L. Sharma at his house in Bombay on a Friday evening.

'Who is he?' Prakash asked Kanwar a day before leaving for

Bombay, hoping to know more about the person before meeting him.

'He is a legend in the intelligence world,' replied Kanwar. 'Been around for nearly fourteen years now. Made his bones in RI, where he decided to junk the intelligence manual and devise his own craft. Everybody looked askance at his activities. But then, he started intercepting Salim's consignments, slowly chipping away at his increasing clout, damaging his reputation. He was soon transferred out of RI to Bombay to be part of a shadow government organization—but knowledge about that is way above your pay scale. Salim's power grew once he was out. Some say that Salim had a say in his transfer. But it is all speculation.'

'Why do you think he came to my defence before the Collector?' Prakash asked.

'Why does Sharma do anything that he does? One can only wonder,' Kanwar replied. 'Just be thankful that he is on your side. He makes a bad enemy, as Salim learned at considerable financial cost.'

'Why do you think he has called me to his house?' Prakash was persistent, apprehension clear in his voice.

'Why don't you go and find out. After all he has been standing up for you, so far.'

◆

Prakash felt the tap on his shoulder as he alighted at Dadar bus stop. He turned to face a burly man who introduced himself as Sharma's driver. Prakash was quickly whisked to a flat in Matunga. Sharma, all 5'6" of him, was waiting in a grey pair of shorts and a white t-shirt.

He is thin, even emaciated, Prakash thought. *And he has dark circles under his eyes that I had not noticed inside the Collector's chambers*. The eyes burnt with the fervour of the devout.

'Beer?' he asked Prakash, without waiting for any perfunctory greetings.

'If you are having some,' Prakash replied courteously.

'Of course. What else is to be done during the lull except recourse to some form of addiction?' Sharma replied serenely, pouring two Heineken's into glasses. Prakash, who as a bachelor was more used to drinking directly from the can or the bottle, cradled the glass uncomfortably.

'Master is going to try and get you soon,' Sharma said abruptly. 'You better take some protective measures.'

'Let him try, sir. I am not scared,' Prakash said.

'Don't be stupid, Prakash. This is not going to be an honourable fight—a hand-to-hand combat or a staring contest. This could be a truck running over you while you're crossing the street, or a shooter firing at the back of your head when you are not looking.'

'Then I can't do anything anyway, sir,' replied Prakash, only a little chastised.

'Oh yes, you can. Get out on the street. You are now known as someone who has seized three consignments that Salim was trying to smuggle. Exploit that advantage. Build a myth around yourself. Let the boys come to you. To the person who has bested Salim thrice. The disgruntled need a symbol to believe that retribution is possible. Be that symbol against Salim, or maybe against the whole underworld. And then somebody will whisper to you when and how Salim's men are going to attack.'

Prakash remained silent. He was not convinced that it was possible to infiltrate the underworld, especially not to the extent that one could have access to their minutest plans. His experience in Dapoli had been dismal. Nobody was even ready to talk about Salim, let alone help him against the underworld don. *But there must be something to what Sharma sir is saying*, he thought, else he would not have called him all the way to Bombay for a meeting.

Sharma seemed to read his mind. 'You're the youngest officer ever to have a bounty on your head at Salim's behest. The question is whether Salim is after you because he thinks that there's more to you than meets the eye, or are you just the means to send a message? I hope that the former is true, otherwise I have wasted my time.'

Prakash finally decided to respond.

'I am out, sir. I am not in a posting where I am supposed to chase Salim, or for that matter, any of the other underworld gangs. I can now go after only white-collar crimes.'

Sharma fixed his penetrating gaze on Prakash. 'If that was the case, Salim would not be after you. Myths transcend postings. Once you have faced the underworld, you will always be a part of it. You can never leave it behind. Don't ever dismantle your networks. You never know when they will be useful. Your Sujata and, who is that other girl—' he continued without waiting for a response, '—they are good distractions. Everybody needs distractions. But then, keep your objectives clear.'

Prakash was surprised by the amount of knowledge Sharma had on him, but he managed to maintain a poker face.

'Anyway, my job is done,' the thin man said suddenly. 'There is something big about to happen, and I am not able to lay my finger on what that thing is. Do let me know if you hear something. And stay safe. Don't die a meaningless death.'

The meeting ended as abruptly as it had started.

10

The Beginning of the Final Interregnum

Prakash survived, but only because others died. Just three days after Salim had reiterated his orders to kill Prakash, and two days after Prakash's meeting with Sharma, kar sevaks demolished Babri Masjid in Ayodhya on 6 December 1992. As expected, the demolition led to widespread riots across India, particularly in Bombay, where a large number of people were killed between December and January.

Prakash was surprised by the mob fury in Bombay. He had expected that the wastelands of Uttar Pradesh and Bihar, where people wore religion on their bodies, would react violently. But he saw, with morbid fascination, violence erupt not just in the commercial capital of the country, but also in other prosperous cities across India. Bombay was an inferno of burnt bodies and buildings. Surat, the diamond city, blazed, and even Karnataka, a developed state with a high literacy rate, was engulfed in flames.

Everyone in Pune, including Prakash, Shelley, Kanwar and the Collector, watched and read about the violence all round them. They waited with bated breath for when it would singe them. Incredibly, Punekars remained calm. The students, the retired people, the farmers, the Rajneeshites, the workers, none of them believed that the demolition of a structure was worth the loss of life. For two months, there was little work to be done. Everyone only discussed the fatalities across the country and to praise the maturity of Punekars.

During one of those dark hours, Prakash sat in Shelley's expansive flat at Pune, staring glumly at the slowly burning hash joint. Shelley took another long drag, wet the burning end with her spittle to slow the pace and passed it to Prakash.

'This is shit stuff. Last year's crop, on the verge of going stale,' commented Prakash.

'Everything has gone to shit nowadays.' Shelley replied with the kind of deep philosophical insight that only a high can generate. 'The hash, the people, the world. The only good thing about the last two months is that you are still alive.'

'Yeah, and that your business is getting more enquiries because Pune was not affected by the violence,' retorted Prakash.

'You are just jealous that I am going to be a rich girl, but are you comparing your life to my money? That's cheap even by your standards. How can you equate the two, Prakash? How can you be so flippant to compare your life to my money? My money is infinitely more important any day,' Shelley continued, now ruminatively. 'When will the world realize that life, good life, with all its attendant pleasures provided by money, can bring highs that the opium of religion can never provide?'

'If the world can be flippant enough to link thousands of lives to the demolition of a structure, I should also henceforth measure my life against money,' Prakash said bitterly, reflecting the morbid mood that had settled over him. Meaningless loss of lives always affected Prakash deeply. 'People were always difficult to understand, now it's becoming impossible to even comprehend them. How can they give or take life for something that does not concern them? Why are they in such a hurry to die. They will die anyway. As Eliot said, *...who were living are now dying, with a little patience.*'

'Don't be so morbid, Prakash,' Shelley said impatiently, struggling to salvage something out of a grim night. 'Wars, plagues, diseases and murders most foul have happened throughout human history, and still we live and thrive. The world has not reached a stage to quote *The Waste Land*, I hope, as yet.'

'Why can't we learn from the animal world? Why can't we just be happy with eating, shitting and sex?' Prakash carried on, not even listening to Shelley. 'Why do humans have to create symbols, the flags, the tilaks, the skull caps? Why do they wake up in the morning and say, "Hey, I am going to kill somebody today?" Why can't they just say, "Hey I am awake, and I am going to have a good shit?" Isn't a good shit a greater pleasure than murder?'

Apparently, the shitty hash was better than he imagined, Shelley thought, *he is repeating himself.*

'We have all discussed this since college, Prakash...since the riots in 1984,' she said gently. This gloom was not going to be lifted easily. 'And I will again say what I used to say then. Don't carry the world on your shoulders. Messiahs die and leave behind a legacy for their followers to die for.'

The arguments flowed through the night, continuing till early in the morning. The fresh air helped the mood. Prakash walked down, called for an auto, and went to Sujata to try and fuck his morbidity away. He did not yet know that worse was still to come.

◆

While in Pune Prakash and Shelley mourned the pointless loss of life, in Dubai Salim looked angrily at the package of broken bangles lying on the table. There were three that day, and he had already received more than fifty such packages since the Bombay riots.

'Why are these being sent to me?' He asked Hanif.

'You are the Lion of Dubai, Bhai. A lot of boys have lost someone they know in the riots. They have been dominating the neighbourhood in your name for too long and now they are scared and angry, Bhai. They are looking at you to lead their vengeance,' Hanif said.

'So, they send me bangles,' replied Salim.

'I think these packages have not been sent by the boys but by the Paki Agencywallahs. They want to rile you. They have been looking for a chance to foment trouble in India, and this is the perfect opportunity. Our boys are angry, and they are ready to listen to anybody who says they can help avenge them. For once, they are even ready to listen to these Paki agents. But even the Paki agency knows that they can't conduct a big operation in Bombay without your help, and so the Pakis are trying to instigate you to join them. You will have to make a decision soon. The boys are restive. They want revenge.'

'Let it die down, Hanif Bhai. Tell the boys to bide their time. All this killing is bad for business. We make money, good money, so that these boys lead good lives, not lose their lives. This fight is a fight based on emotion, not reason.'

Hanif looked speculatively at Salim. He knew Salim was not religious. He had not even added the title of Haji before his name. Even his close associates did not know if he was a namazi. In the liberal environment of Dubai, he was known to drink in private, and sometimes even in public. He preferred to be called Bhai, and he viewed himself as a businessman, one who took advantage of the restrictions of the law. His closest associates were Muslims, but there were Hindus, Christians, Muslims, Parsis at all levels in their gang. Taking sides could be counter-productive.

Hanif was not so liberal. While Salim would bed a girl after killing a rival, Hanif went to the masjid. His father had always taken pride in the fact that his son would be the first at the masjid when the azaan was called, five times a day. He was a namazi, a Haji, a non-drinker, and he had been taught that while jihad may not be waged on the weak and the defenceless, the killing of non-believers in response to their aggression was mandated by the religion.

The boys knew him as their protector. After all, they prayed together, celebrated their festivals together, mourned the deaths in their community together. Everybody was loyal to Salim, but some boys were more loyal to Hanif because he was religious. And though he too had moved to Dubai, these boys still obeyed his commands first. They were all his boys, and some of them were now dead, and so, Hanif knew what he had to do.

'Bhai, how can these boys think of making money when they are grieving? These Pakistani agency guys will keep inciting our boys. The desire for revenge is a strong emotion. Those Pakis, that Jatt fellow, and that kutta, Suleiman, they are already approaching our boys in Pydhonie and Bhendi Bazaar, telling them that you don't have the guts to fight for them and that our boys will be more prosperous than ever before if they were to work with them instead. They are offering good money. Thirty of our boys have already visited Pakistan in the last month to meet Suleiman. Even if we lose three or four of our trusted fellows, the information leaks can affect our operations.'

Salim was listening carefully. There was truth in what Hanif said. Secrecy was of paramount importance in their business. There was no rebuilding a lost reputation or getting back a lost lieutenant. *Everything was going on so fine*, he thought. *Why did people have to take to the streets?*

'What do they want?' he asked.

'I don't know, Bhai, but there is no harm in meeting them once.'

'Okay, let's listen to them. Tomorrow. How can it get any worse than this?' said Salim.

He too did not know how wrong he was.

◆

Nobody knows what happened in that meeting between the Pakistani agency, the Pakistani smugglers and Salim, or what prompted Salim to finally join hands with them. Everything is speculation. Maybe Suleiman gave Salim a list of gang members who were ready to leave if there was no retaliation for the December riots. Maybe the Pakis, with the backing of their agency, threatened to intercept and destroy all his consignments. After all, the routes taken by his boats passed close to Pakistani borders. Some even said that the agency offered him a piece of their profits from their lucrative drug smuggling routes, although his gang members always maintained that Salim Bhai never dealt with drugs. Nobody ever talked of Hanif's role, and he too always maintained a stoic silence. But sometime in January, a message went out that Bhai was planning something big, and the rewards were enormous. The networks were operationalized, the money was distributed and the consignment, bigger than they ever expected, landed on the Shrivardhan coast, to be taken to unknown destinations and to be delivered to unknown people. It was only whispered among the chosen few that Bhai had brought massive quantities of 'sabun' into the country.

11

The Final Interregnum (continued)

The blasts that shook Bombay on 12 March 1993 did not significantly change the lives of common people. The poor remained poor, the middle class continued to move in the grooves that they had settled into and the rich, well, they kept on getting richer. Lives changed only for those who had links with the underworld during those times—the cricketers, the stars and the producers of Bollywood, politicians and bureaucrats. For the rest, it was just an obituary for the anonymous, and there were precious few requiems sung.

Nobody except the perpetrators had anticipated the blasts, but the perpetrators too had not anticipated the aftermath of the blasts. As the reality sank in, people realized the capacity of the underworld gangs to wreck mayhem on such a vast scale on the financial capital of the country, and every segment of the society joined hands to condemn them. And to hunt them down. Salim had anticipated the backlash, but he had calculated that his friendship with the politicians, the long-term relationships with the policemen, the connections with Bollywood and the reports by pliable journalists would combine to ensure that the event, like others in the past, would not even sully his image in the eyes of the people, let alone link him to the blasts. But in this case, the mistakes were a little too obvious, and the investigations a little too thorough.

Salim had grossly miscalculated. Before the blasts, the dons were just a masala topic for most people. They were vaguely aware of their existence, just like they were aware of the dalliances of film stars. But the blasts killed their neighbours, their relatives, somebody they knew, somebody who toiled for their livelihoods, just like they did. People were outraged. And they wanted punishment for those who had committed the act. This time, the bangles were sent by real people, to their local representatives, their councillors, the members of the legislative assembly, their minister. The politicians stopped picking up their phones when Salim called.

The policemen had also lost a few of their colleagues in the riots, and the force was baying for blood. The name of the Bombay Police as one of the most efficient forces in the world had been tarnished, and they were out to redeem themselves. But by the time they had regrouped, most of the culprits, who had already gauged the public mood, had fled the country, along with their families. So, the police rounded up everybody and anybody who had the remotest link to the underworld. Tales of torture leaked out, and gang members went deeper underground. Salim started losing his hold over his favourite city.

◆

There was only one thing that Salim had calculated correctly. His gang had people from all religions, and as the news that Salim had relied only on the Muslim gang members to give effect to the blasts came out, a religious backlash emanated. His gang split up on communal lines. His gamble that the lure of the lucre would keep the gang united failed. The Hindus broke rank first, stating that they would not work with an anti-national, a man who worked with Pakistanis. The Christians and the Parsis exited next, saying that they couldn't work with an anti-national who was a fundamentalist. Salim fretted, threatened, cajoled, but nothing seemed to work. Half of his top men had to escape within a week of the blasts, leaving Bombay for safer shores, and most of them denounced Salim when they saw his power waning. The low-level street soldiers left for their villages, and those with longer history sheets, for Nepal. The rumour was that the Bombay police was shooting at the kneecaps of those involved in the bomb blasts. Nobody even remotely connected with Salim wanted to be in Bombay. He had lost control and needed to do something quickly.

Hanif remained stoic as their world crumbled around them. He had made his peace with Allah.

◆

Shabnam had watched the mayhem unfold with horrified fascination. She was not totally unaware of the conspiracy. Sitara had visited her towards the end of February. She had, after the arrest of John, moved on to live with Javed, who was quickly moving up the underworld hierarchy.

'Are you planning to leave the country?' Sitara had asked anxiously.

'Why?' Shabnam asked, surprised by the question.

Sitara looked at her searchingly, looking for some sign of deception, some hint that she was hiding something from her.

'Salim Bhai has not warned you?' she asked.

'Warned me about what, Sitara?' Shabnam was irritated. She didn't like anyone referring to her relationship with Salim so casually, and Sitara was not even close to her. In fact, for her, Sitara was a nobody.

'He does not trust you.' The tone was partly questioning, partly wondering, but there was a vicarious satisfaction in Sitara's voice. Her paramour trusted her more.

'They are planning something big. These Hindus will come to know the full might of Salim Bhai and Javed. Javed asked me to accompany him to Malaysia. I am not sure what I will do there. So, I thought I would ask you if you were leaving the country too.'

Something big. The phrase had stuck with Shabnam, and she thought that she would ask Salim. But, with her now hectic schedule, she could not meet him. The movie with the genius had hit the screens in December, and despite the violence in different parts of the country, or probably because of that, it was a superhit. Shabnam had arrived. She was a star, and this time, with or without the backing of Salim, producers were ready to sign her.

When the blasts hit Bombay, she guessed what Sitara was talking about. She knew, before the police and the public did, that the blasts had been triggered by Salim and Javed. She prepared herself for the early morning knock that she knew would come soon. To her surprise, she was never questioned by the police. She thought long and hard about it and couldn't come up with any explanation. Eventually she just accepted it as her luck as she saw a number of her co-stars being questioned for their association with the gangs. Some were even arrested. Some left the country thinking that their benefactors would soon regain power, not realizing that a paradigm shift had taken place in Bombay's power structure. Salim would no more be there to protect them.

Shabnam did not need a new benefactor. Her life with Salim had been a surreal adventure, one which she thought she was sharing with a glamourous, powerful businessman who relished breaking rules. A modern-day Robin Hood. For the two years she had been with Salim, she had been, in various measures, ignored, feared or at times, even insulted, by her compatriots. But she had carried on, hoping that Salim was truly the generous man she saw during her visits to Dubai. She had reasoned that the order to kill Prakash was an exception, and that Salim was not a mindless killer. But the blasts shattered the image that her imagination had created. However hard she reasoned, she could not arrive at a justification for anything that was happening around her. And now, she was angry, angry at the loss of life, angry at being ignored, angry, she admitted briefly, for not being trusted!

She desultorily received the congratulatory call on the success of the film, and listlessly heard the new offers, until she realized that there was no phone call coming from her lover to say that he was not the architect of the bomb blasts. She slowly reconciled herself to the fact that Salim could actually be the person behind the bomb blasts, and she wondered what to do next. *Can I sleep again with a man who has the blood of so many innocents on his hands?* she brooded. And then, Sitara also died. Sitara's death shattered her, but she had not survived so far by crumbling at every catastrophe. She decided to shake herself free of the memories and went back to work.

◆

After the initial rage had subsided, Prakash came back to work with renewed zeal. This time there were no refugee camps to work in, no blood donation camps to be organized and in any case, he was now no more a nineteen-year-old fire brand organizing marches and protests. *Fat difference in the world they had made*, he reasoned. *Whatever you do, people will go out and kill each other senselessly once every decade.* And so, he threw himself into the job with an unexpected vigour.

Apparently, he had not learnt his lessons from his transfer to Dapoli.

'You should collect taxes like a honeybee collects nectar from the flower. She takes her fill, but the flower also survives,' the Collector had advised him solicitously when he had joined Pune. He had heard the phrase during his training, but now, on the job, he realized that every time the honeybee settled on the flower, the flower trembled and screamed that it was a violation of its rights. The honeybee, in his experience, was supposed to buzz, but not to settle on the flower to draw any nectar. He was now facing increasing complaints of harassment and intimidation as he went about collecting taxes scrupulously, and the bosses were again getting irritated by the constant phone calls being received by them to rein him in.

But he had learnt something else at Dapoli. The art of organizing dinners. He now, at monthly intervals, organized the best dinners the collectorate at Pune had ever seen. He just needed an excuse—welcoming a colleague back after his wedding, the colourful festival of Holi, birthday of the Collector. Pune's officers were experiencing an avalanche of good food and bonhomie that they had never ever seen before.

So he was given a long leash, more because of his flair for organizing parties rather than the fact that, as Kanwar put it, he happened to stumble upon and catch some tax evaders.

'When will you learn?' said an irritated Collector on a late March afternoon. 'You can't just go barging into the managing director's office alleging tax evasion. After all, they have a turnover of more than a thousand crore.'

'Yes, sir,' Prakash said, sounding duly chastised. That was another art he had recently imbibed from Kanwar. Not to ever contradict the boss.

'Did you have any evidence?' Collector asked.

'No, sir, but there was a discrepancy in his balance sheet, and I thought he would be able to explain it. After all, he has done his MBA from Berkeley.'

'You could have asked the staff! Why did you have to go directly to the managing director? Now he has complained that you are spoiling his image in the eyes of his buyers. Were you able to find anything wrong?' the Collector said, munching on his favourite snack, the Mahabaleshwar chana, and sounding, in his own mind at least, extremely reasonable. Belatedly, he realized his mistake and offered the chana to Kanwar, who was brightening the room with his parrot green t-shirt and bright blue jeans. He delicately picked four of them out and popped one into his mouth. None was offered to Prakash.

'Not yet, sir, but we are still investigating,' replied Prakash in a subdued voice.

'So you should have gone there after you were sure.' The Collector then asked Kanwar. 'Did he tell you before he ventured there?'

'No sir,' Kanwar said sanctimoniously. 'I would have guided him appropriately if he had.'

'See. You should take guidance from your seniors sometimes. You are running like a bull in a China shop. It's not that we are not answerable for our actions,' the Collector said piously, possibly quoting the scriptures.

The buzzer interrupted Prakash's inquisition.

'What?' barked the Collector, and then listening, said, 'Okay, send him in.'

'Ajay ji is here. He must be really irritated to have come all the way here. What do I tell him now? You explain this nincompoop's actions to him. I am washing my hands off this episode,' the Collector said to Kanwar.

Ajay ji trooped in, followed by his chartered accountant, his vice president of finance and the manager who looked after his taxes.

'I will not be taking too much of your time,' he said to the Collector. 'I know you are a busy man.'

Everyone knew that this was just an opening gambit, and of course, he was duly convinced to have a cup of tea.

'It is good that young Prakash is also here,' Ajay ji said as he graciously accepted the Collector's offer of some Mahabaleshwar chana. 'Very healthy, this chana. Doesn't add to your weight and keeps your cholesterol in check. Pannikar, we should also keep some of these in our office,' he told his vice president. 'Send somebody to Mahabaleshwar tomorrow to get some fresh ones and get some for Collector sahab also.'

The Collector, duly gratified by his wise choice, said, 'About this visit by Prakash, I have looked into the matter…'

'Oh yes,' interrupted Ajay ji. 'I was rather surprised by his visit, and I guess I was somewhat disturbed also. After all, we are honest taxpayers. And like the honest taxpayers that we are,' he said, putting special emphasis on the word honest, 'I asked my people to look at the figures again.'

He paused for the effect. 'I think they made some mistakes and they have recalculated it. They feel that they have paid three crore rupees less. I really shouted at them. We have already paid those three crore now. They will calculate it again and tell me if any more tax is to be paid.'

There was a brief silence in the room as Ajay ji concluded his rather long explanation. Prakash noted that Ajay ji had come out smelling like roses after this whole saga. He was the conscientious owner taking his errant employees to task for the wrong tax payment. Nobody talked of tax evasion.

'Is it okay, Prakash?' the Collector asked, his voice a little bit more authoritative now.

'Yes, sir,' Prakash said meekly. There was no point of rubbing it in at this point. He would score brownie points at the right time.

'Kanwar ji, you now take charge of this case. Please make sure that the correct tax is paid,' the Collector said. Then he dismissed both Prakash and Kanwar.

12

The Final Interregnum (concluded)

'So what's that, the sixth one so far?' Shelley asked Prakash over drinks during the weekend, referring to the evasion case booked by Prakash against Ajay ji. They had decided to lay off hash till the new crop of Himachal hash filtered down in May, and were instead consuming copious amounts of alcohol.

'Yup.'

'You are becoming quite the sleuth! Your bosses must be pleased.'

'Nah, my bosses say I am just plain lucky, and where I am not lucky, it's their guidance that leads me to success,' Prakash said wryly.

Shelley gave one of her characteristic guffaws. 'You should do an MBA. Only then you will shed the stupid principles of modesty, duty, etc. that have been drilled into you by that crazy Sainik School. You need to learn, like all successful people, to pass your failures on to others and claim their successes as yours. That's the cardinal principle of getting ahead, whether in the government or out of it. Stop letting others take the credit for your achievements.'

She continued, this time in a more serious tone, 'Don't you feel bad about it? This constant undermining of your efforts, the usurping of your success?'

Prakash pondered only momentarily. 'Nah, I think this works fine for me. I deliver, they claim credit, and then leave me alone. No heartburn, no competition, no rivalries. It helps me lead a peaceful life. Look at Sharma sir. Lived for the world, had huge achievements, made a name for himself and, what did it get him in the government? Success that elicited petty comments from his colleagues, a dogmatic devotion to duty that bred enemies in the underworld, a nearly broken marriage and four bullets.'

'What? Sharma sir has been shot!" exclaimed Shelley.

'Not just shot, shot dead. Just a month after the bomb blasts. You were in the US during that time.'

'Terrible news,' said Shelley. 'Where does the needle of suspicion point?'

'Rumours say Salim,' Prakash said morosely. 'And I am here, stuck in a place from where I have no chance of chasing his killer.'

'You do miss the thrill of the chase,' Shelley noted sympathetically. 'But then, as Sharma sir told you, you never ever truly get out. You will get Salim some day. Keep sniffing like the pernicious hound that you are.'

'Fat chance,' replied Prakash. 'Do you have any idea about the organization that Salim heads. He has at least two thousand foot soldiers on his monthly payroll. Then there are at least thirty known sharp shooters spreading fear, all of whom owe their allegiance exclusively to his gang. And then there are the landing agents, transporters, boatmen. You name them, everyone who wants to be part of the underworld wants to work for Salim. Also, he still enjoys the backing of some politicians whom he had helped in the past. They are not too keen to displease a person whose organization has a turnover of more than five thousand crore. And, as Shabnam hinted, he hedges his bets by working, at times, as a freelancer for the intelligence agencies. Keeps them in good humour. And you are telling me that I will have a chance to avenge Sharma sir's death!'

'Wow. I was wrong. You don't need an MBA degree. That was one of the best SWOT analysis I've ever heard,' Shelley said lightly, and then continued, trying to keep the conversation light, 'But you are persistent. See you've never ever stopped chasing me. And some lives are intertwined. You are bound to get a chance to avenge Sharma sir's death. It's in your karma. After all, he tried to save your life, even though you had met him just twice.'

She continued softly. 'Why do guys like him and you join the bureaucracy? You don't have a love for power, have no desire to showcase your achievements and yet you are ready to sacrifice your life, and more importantly, your freedom—and still slave, often on meaningless tasks, over twelve hours a day.'

'That's par for the course. You work for fourteen hours a day, most of our friends in the private sector work over the weekend too, and yet, they do not get membership of the Royal Western Turf Club at the age of twenty-seven.'

'But you work those twelve hours for 4,200 rupees a month, and then, whenever you rub people the wrong way, you get transferred.'

'Yeah, that is a major drawback, but not for me. I get to see the country for free and "suck the nectar out of the flowers of every region delicately."' He said, making a parody of the Collector's homily on tax collection.

'Thank God this sucking has only been limited to Pune so far, and that too, off just Sujata and Savitha. Do you have a fetish for girls whose name starts with an 'S'? Does it have to do something with the phonetics in the bed?' Shelley said sardonically.

'Gentlemen never tell,' replied Prakash with a laugh, and then continued seriously. 'I was not going to say so, but this nectar sucking may be spreading to other regions soon.'

'What!' exclaimed Shelley. 'What are you saying?'

'I got a call from Salunkhe, you remember, the guy who posted me to Dapoli. He asked me if I was willing to work in RI.'

'RI, where? Bombay?'

'As if!' Prakash scoffed. 'Bombay is only for the truly privileged. In any case, nobody would like to let a bull free in the biggest china market of the country.'

'Then where?'

'Jamnagar!'

'That backwater in a dry state?' Shelley exclaimed. 'You will die of boredom.'

'I haven't accepted the offer yet. Can't even think of dumping all of you here and leaving for an exotic, end of the earth place like Jamnagar. But I think I am going to be sent there, whether I like it or not. I may be proving a bit too stubborn for people in Pune. Although,' he continued, 'I don't mind being posted to Jamnagar. What with some of the biggest criminals coming from that area, it would be a great learning experience. Sharma sir honed his intelligence skills there. And then, Lal was telling me that Salim has shifted a part of his operations to the Kutch.'

'I knew you missed Dapoli and Salim. You do have a death wish!' screamed Shelley in delight, lightening the atmosphere. 'You just love playing a cowboy. Whom do you impersonate in your dreams, Charles Bronson or Clint Eastwood?'

'Oh, come on, it's not as if they are going to post me there tomorrow, and remember, there is no love lost between me and RI.'

◆

The posting order did not come the next day, not even the next week, but it did come, and in the month of June, Prakash was posted to Jamnagar.

'Guess I won't be seeing you for a long time now. I am going to miss our weekend sessions,' Prakash said over the curling smoke of their second joint of the night. The new crop of hash had hit the market and Shelley guaranteed the freshness of the new tola she had scored.

'Don't bet on that. I have just received a proposal from an Ahmedabad-based pharmaceutical company to manage their data backend. We may just open up an office in Ahmedabad, and I will visit the city often in the initial phase of the onboarding.'

'Wow, that is great news! What is it, your third office?'

'Fourth. We also opened a satellite office with two people in Hyderabad last week.'

'That's cool,' Prakash said. 'It would be great if I can see you even once a month. I guess I will have to score the hash in Gujarat.'

13

Packed Bags

A farewell dinner was held for Prakash, when Kanwar, true to his generous nature, presented Prakash a bottle of Blue Label.

'He is, after all, going to a dry state. It will be some time before he finds a bootlegger. This will, till it lasts, remind him of the good times he had in Pune,' Kanwar said as part of his farewell speech.

The Collector was more forthcoming. 'I never expected him to do so well. After all, he is so careless in his attitude. He never even carried a notepad when I called him.'

Other Assistant Collectors, more conscientious than Prakash, who carried a notepad and a pen—to note down the instructions given by the boss—looked smug.

'But then, I guess some people are lucky. His performance has, by far, been the best among Assistant Collectors in the past decade. And, as I told him earlier, he is being kicked upstairs for his performance. I think he will continue to do better. There is less file work and more field work in RI, and Prakash, for one, is not cut out for file work.'

Prakash winced at the words, but he could not dispute them. He was developing a reputation in the department as a 'Preventive Man', a guy cut out for the field and not the files. And bureaucracy had not been able to reduce his love for the outdoors.

The advice poured in along with the liquor. Kanwar cornered him first.

'The Collector may be a good administrator, but he has always been a file pusher.' Kanwar said in one of his uncharacteristic, uncharitable moments. 'He has never been, nor will ever be, able to appreciate the thrill of field work. We, from the military school, relish the outdoors more than being cooped up in an office. You are going to enjoy this stint. After all, you will have a vast area of the country to cover—the whole of Saurashtra and Kutch. I was in RI in Gujarat, and all our activities were concentrated in that region alone.'

'Is that so, sir?' Prakash said. Kanwar rarely talked about his stint in RI.

'Yes.' Kanwar said as Prakash handed him his third large drink of the evening. 'There is a lot of drug smuggling from the Saurashtra coast. Bhavnagar, Porbandar, Veraval, so many minor ports, all of them controlled by the underworld. And as befits a progressive state, a lady gangster has taken over the underworld in Porbandar. You know, the Godmother?'

'Yes, sir,' Prakash said. 'Lal told me.'

'Good man, Lal,' Kanwar said. 'Is he joining you in Jamnagar?'

'I asked him to. He is not very sure at the moment.'

'You will need somebody you can rely on.' Kanwar advised. 'You can't be everywhere at once. It's a vast area. Kutch border is increasingly being used by the heroin smugglers of Pakistan, even though they still prefer the Rajasthan border. With Salim cosying up with the Pakistanis, narco-terrorism is soon going to be the new buzzword.'

'Is Salim active in that region?' Prakash couldn't resist asking.

'You and Salim,' Kanwar sighed dramatically. 'No, he is not. Gujarat has its own homegrown underworld dons who dominate the smuggling circuits as well. They handle some of Salim's consignments, but there are none of Salim's men as such in Gujarat. There has been a crackdown on the underworld after the bomb blasts, and the Gujarati Muslim gangs are facing a lot of heat.'

'Muslim gangs? Are there others too?'

Kanwar looked with wonder at Prakash. 'Who are they sending into the lion's mouth? A kid, a *bachcha?* Read and talk to people before you go there. Learn about the Darbars, the Kutchis, the Rabaris. Learn their history. It's a fascinating place you are going to, the wild west of the country. There is no law there, just a race to reap rewards.'

'Tough posting, sir?' he queried.

'What are you worried about? You are a sainik school guy. You can handle any posting. Just think of it as the magic of life and dive in it for the experience.' Kanwar was definitely high. 'Look at Jamnagar. A small town located in the middle of the geographical formation on the western coast of India that looks like a magic lamp.' Kanwar was becoming lyrical now. 'Or if you look too closely, maybe it looks like the open mouth of a lion. It depends with which perspective you look at it—hoping for a magical ride with history, prosperity and natural beauty, or despair about being in a land where crime is a way of life and breaking law is a matter of pride.'

Prakash wondered if they were talking too loudly, looked around the room to see if they were being stared at, and found the Collector beckoning him.

He left Kanwar and walked up to him.

'What was Kanwar talking about?' Collector asked as an ice-breaker.

'About his stint in Gujarat,' Prakash said.

'You have been dumped in a useless posting,' Collector said, taking a diametrically opposite view. 'It will be such a waste of time. You should have headed to a desk job in the ministry in Delhi. You would have done well over there.'

Prakash wondered at the comment, especially since the Collector had just said that he had little aptitude to deal with files, and what was a posting in the ministry if not pushing files day in and day out? If he was going to have a sixteen-hour work day, he preferred spending those hours out in the field, rather than being cooped up in a small room in a corner of a labyrinthine maze.

'What will you do over there? You don't know the languages. Yes, languages. Even I know that there are at least three languages, and at least ten dialects spoken there. How will you develop informers without knowing their language? I tell you, these guys have no brains, posting somebody who is not a local in an intelligence posting. They should have given you at least a three-month crash course on the languages before asking you to join.'

Three months to learn languages! Won't I be transferred out in a couple of years? Prakash wondered. *I am already on my fourth posting in less than two years of job.*

'And you are such a junior officer. You don't have sufficient experience. What are you going to do in RI?' Collector continued, 'Anyway, if nothing, at least you will enjoy the area. You know, Saurashtra had nearly 220 princely states, and as you already have friends from princely families, you will have lots of friends there. Wear lots of colourful clothes and do a lot of garba,' making an attempt at humour.

'Yes sir,' Prakash replied dutifully.

'And get married? You can't find many girlfriends there,' the Collector said as a parting shot, leaving Prakash wondering if everyone in Pune knew about his affairs.

◆

Lal picked Prakash as he bid farewell to the others at the party.

'How bad was it?' he asked lightly, knowing fully well how Prakash hated farewells.

'Wasn't too bad, Lal. Kanwar, today of all times, decided to talk about Gujarat's smugglers, and his stint in Gujarat RI. I should have picked his brains earlier.'

'You would not have been able to pick his brains. Nobody talks about the specifics when it comes to their stint in RI, not even to another RI man. He would probably have just told you to concentrate on developing informers in Salaya in Jamnagar and Mandvi in Kutch. Most of the country boats sailing to Dubai and Africa are built over there and there are these cavity makers, these truly creative guys who make undetectable cavities in vessels to carry contraband goods. They are in demand with all the smugglers. They are virtual encyclopaedias of the smuggling world. The past, present and the likely future, they know it all. And then, the best seamen and *tandels* in the country come from these two villages. Get some of them to work for you, for fear or for favour.'

'The Collector says that as I can't speak their language, I can't get any intelligence.' The jitters of a new job were surfacing slowly.

'Bullshit.' Lal was vehement. He continued softly. 'He hasn't ever worked in Preventive, sir. What would he know? The world of intelligence understands only three languages. Greed, guts and fear. Use them effectively and there is no language barrier.'

Prakash nodded, but was still not convinced.

'They will test your guts. Do remember that you have a bounty on your head. Some Johnny-come-lately may decide to pick up that supari if he can contact Salim or Master, which, of course, is unlikely at the moment. However, it would be wise to be careful.'

'Thanks for the boost in confidence, Lal,' said Prakash sarcastically. 'Now I have one less thing to worry about.'

'Keep your chin up, sir. You are now an RI man, and they normally think twice before taking a hit at any RI man. It's bad for business. All the intelligence agencies will get together to hunt down the culprits. And Salim anyway is insecure. He is shifting locations even within Dubai. Master has absconded and will be lying low for a while. I don't think that you are, at least for now, important enough for them to expose their location to some petty, wannabe shooter. Be careful, but don't be paranoid. And, if my wife agrees to move from Pune to a smaller town like Jamnagar, I will join you soon.'

'That would certainly be a boost, Lal,' Prakash said, this time sincerely.

'I will come and see you off tomorrow. I doubt anyone else will come,' Lal said, writing a minor epitaph for Prakash's stint in Pune.

14
A New Game

His first stop was Ahmedabad, the regional headquarters of RI. On a Sunday evening, in the absence of a direct train from Pune to Ahmedabad, Prakash left by road for Bombay to take the Saurashtra Mail, looking forlornly at the passing familiar industrial belts of Pimpri-Chinchwad, Talegaon and Lonavala. He would miss the chicken 65 and kanda bhajias at Tony da Dhaba, the rains of Lonavala and the weekend treks to Khandala. He wondered if he had done the right thing by choosing this life of constant transfers, where he lost the company of friends periodically and had to move into unfamiliar flats. Would a peaceful existence in one city, the luxury of familiar faces and places and comfort of a fixed routine have been better?

The only thing Prakash had experienced about Gujarat was Gujarati food. He had first tried it when he had landed in Bharuch as a member of a trekking team trying to trek all along the Narmada. He still remembered the Annapurna restaurant in Bharuch, where he had paid a princely sum of five rupees in 1983 for an unlimited eight-course meal. He had loved the Gujarati kadhi sweetened with jaggery, the dal cooked with a pinch of sugar, the slightly sweet potato curry and assorted fried farsan. He and the other seven trekkers had subsequently kept the memories of the forty-five-day trek alive through their monthly dinners at a small place serving Gujarati thalis on Rajniwas Marg in Delhi.

Now he was going to combat in Gujarat without knowing its culture or language. His brother had told him that Gujaratis didn't like doing business with north Indians, and it seemed that his brother was right. His research showed that there were no flights from Jamnagar to Delhi—only to Bombay—and even Ahmedabad had more flights to Bombay than to Delhi. In fact, there were more flights to London than to Delhi. It seemed that the world, except for north India, was an oyster for the Gujaratis. What was he letting himself, a north Indian, into?

Saurashtra Mail reached Ahmedabad a little late, and he was quickly whisked to the RI office in the waiting Gypsy and dumped into a small, stark, windowless room at the back of the office. He looked at the ubiquitous white towel and the Lifebuoy soap in the wash basin, and a barely clean toilet.

'Welcome to Ahmedabad,' he said to himself, loudly.

Singh, his boss, reached office sharp at 10.30 a.m. and summoned Prakash immediately.

'Ah, Prakash! You are here, finally,' he said, pumping Prakash's hand jovially. Prakash's enquiries had yielded little information about Singh, and he tried to assess the man now. He looked around the room to see if it would reveal something about him. A large road map of Gujarat dominated one of the walls, and Prakash wondered if Singh ever used it, or was it merely one of those relics found in government rooms, a legacy of the predecessor. The room was bare of any other wall furnishings; the table was spartan and the chairs uncomfortable. The inevitable sofa was missing, but he noticed an ante room. There was a bed, a dining table and a refrigerator in that room. This was a room unlike any other bureaucrat's rooms he had seen. He would have to find out more about Singh.

'Has the family come with you?' Singh asked the inevitable question.

'Not yet married, sir,' Prakash replied with a smile.

'That is bad, man. How will you manage for food in a place like Jamnagar?' he said immediately, shaking his head, concerned.

Prakash wondered why he immediately associated marriage with food, and not sex or company. He had a cook in Pune who used to cook for him twice a week, and he was sure he would find someone to cook for him at Jamnagar as well. But he didn't have anyone to visit him twice a week for sex. He wondered if he should tell Singh about his problem, but remembering that he was a bureaucrat now, dropped it with a smile.

'I will manage, sir. I think there will be too much travelling to do in any case.'

'Yes, that, of course, will be the case. You know, you have an area of more than 100,000 sq. km in your jurisdiction, more than 500 km of land border with Pakistan and 600 km of coastline with more than fifty landing spots. And just six officers.'

It seemed like Singh was rather keen to elaborate on this theme.

'How does one manage such a vast jurisdiction with just six officers?' Prakash asked helpfully.

'Be the boss,' Singh said with a laugh. 'You are no longer a field officer with specified tasks. You can now choose what you want to do. Whether you want to collect intelligence about smugglers, fraudsters or even your colleagues. There is no compulsion to act. We only act when we are after truly big fish. Else we compile dossiers or ask our counterparts in the field to act.'

'So no routine work, sir?' Prakash asked.

'None,' replied Singh. 'But use the extra time to learn your area well. Research the operators in your area, and don't run after every Tom, Dick and Harry. Go after the big guns; we have to maintain our reputation of being the elite. And above all, travel a lot. Lots of people will be watching you—travelling will make you visible,' Singh said a little too smugly for Prakash's taste.

'Be the elite and travel.' Prakash could not resist. 'It looks like I am becoming part of the jet-setting crowd.'

'What was that?' Singh asked suspiciously.

'Nothing, sir,' Prakash replied, kicking himself mentally for not being able to keep his mouth shut. 'Just talking to myself. I end up doing it a lot since I live alone.'

Singh stared at him. 'I have been told that you are irreverent. And also rash. I was told that you are too young and inexperienced for RI. But you are here now, and I have to live with it. We have a sensitive job here, Prakash. I hope you keep that in mind while working with me. Don't muddy the waters too much.'

So there was the same everyman bureaucrat's conservatism beneath that genial exterior, thought Prakash. *I hope there is a spine of steel as well.*

Outwardly he said, 'I have to learn a lot from you, sir.'

'Oh, I am always available for you. Just give me a call anytime. And read the dossiers. We have some good background material on everyone.'

Prakash could not resist asking. 'Even on Salim, sir?'

'Ah, Salim,' Singh said, leaning back a little on his chair and looking at Prakash speculatively. 'What is this between Salim and you? What have you done to rile him up so much that he is ready to pay supari for you?'

This irritated Prakash. Not just the question, but also the smugness, the sense of genteel superiority being conveyed by Singh. He controlled himself.

'I think you should instead ask what he did. I was just doing my job, while he was smuggling contraband and, over that, killing a lot of people. I am fighting not to become just another statistic, another dead person, added to Salim's account,' Prakash said, but then, realizing there was no reason to antagonize Singh, continued hurriedly. 'But how did you know about the supari? I don't think that it is known to everybody.'

'*We* are RI. *We* know *everything*. It's our job to know everything,' said Singh. He then continued on a more serious tone, 'My experience is that personal vendettas bring more grief than satisfaction. Do your job, but any obsession with one person can seriously skew your perspective.'

'At the moment sir, I am just obsessed with my life,' Prakash replied lightly.

'Do that. Enjoy that life while you do your work. Salim is anyway not very active in your area. Your officers will be here by noon to escort you to Jamnagar. They wanted to come last night to receive you at the station, but I told them that you are a young guy, and that you can manage without them,' Singh said, leaving no doubts about who was calling the shots. 'Have some lunch with me before you leave, I will give you some North Indian lunch—dal, roti, some butter chicken. Don't know when you will get to eat some North Indian fare again.'

◆

Limbdi, Chotila, Rajkot, Dhrol and Jamnagar. He recalled the route from the map in Singh's room as the Gypsy quickly gobbled up miles over the smooth road. The driver, Manu Bhai, short and garrulous, with kohl in his eyes, kept asking all kinds of personal questions, while the senior officer, Chudasama, remained silent. Prakash couldn't decide if he was naturally reticent or if he was assessing the new boss. His eyes, the most confusing Prakash had ever seen, displayed nothing at all. The Gandhi spectacles further heightened the deadpan look of his thin face. The only expressive feature of his face was possibly the thin handlebar moustache, which he never twirled in public.

I have to work with him day in, day out, Prakash thought. *How will I ever survive the silence?*

Prakash would soon learn that beneath that deadpan look and silence lay a brain brimming with an encyclopaedic knowledge of the underworld and its operatives.

In Jamnagar, he was taken to Hotel Aram and settled into a comfortable room.

'How are we going to pay for it?' he asked Chudasma.

'We have operational funds,' Chudasma replied briefly.

His ingrained miserliness made him resist the idea of spending money on hotel accommodation. 'Can I not move to the circuit house? That would be cheaper.'

'Why do you want to expose your schedule to others, sir? The room is not in your name. This way nobody knows where you are staying, and nobody will be able to track your movements till you settle. You come with a reputation of being marked by Salim. Why expose yourself?'

Prakash remembered Lal telling him during the Collector's visit to Dapoli that he would be watching out for the movements of RI officers. *Will I also have to move stealthily*, he wondered, *or is it just the Salim contract that has these guys worried?* He decided to confront them.

'This Salim thing is turning out to be a headache. In Pune, nobody was aware that I was targeted by Salim. And I moved as I wanted to. Over here, you are the second person today who has referred to it. I don't even care about the fact that Salim is targeting me.'

'Even I am not worried about Salim. But it's our job to keep a watch on the activities of the underworld and smugglers. It's our job to hear stories. And people talk more if you are an enigma. The less they know about us, individually and as an organization, the more rumours they believe. The stories of our invincibility emerge from our ability to cover our failures and publicize our successes. We can't do that if people know everything about us.' The expression on Chudasama's face did not change at all while speaking. It was just another fact.

He continued, 'The boys working for the gangs go to Bombay for all their pleasures. They can't blow all their spare money over here.

We want to hear their stories from there, and not let them tell our stories. There is no harm in being cagey. It allows us to weave legends around ourselves, which reinforces the tales of our invincibility. And now that you have confirmed that there is a contract on your life, we will ensure that we know the killer before anyone else does.'

Prakash noticed that it did not seem to be an overconfident, belligerent claim. He wondered if he could trust that statement. 'As if I will sleep the better for it,' he muttered under his breath. But he continued to stay at the hotel until he shifted to a house of his own.

15

Coming up Trumps

The next few days were a blur of briefings, meetings and travel as Prakash tried to get a grip on his new job. There were no files, no fixed schedules, no approvals to be given and no reports to be sent. He was free to do as he liked, and he turned to his team to pull him out of the vacuum he was experiencing. He slowly learnt about them, all veterans, proven intelligence operatives, with years of experience behind them.

Chudasama in Jamnagar and Raijada in Bhuj were the senior operatives. Both tall, fit guys, sporting thick moustaches.

'What is with the handlebar moustache? Is it a RI thing over here, should I keep one too?' he asked lightly as the three of them shared drinks in Kandla a couple of months later.

Raijada laughed and even Chudasama let the faintest smile touch his lips.

'No, sir,' Raijada replied. 'We are Darbar Rajputs. More than 50 per cent Darbars keep an upturned moustache. It's a tradition.' And then he continued, with a little mischievous glint in his eye, 'You should also keep one instead of this drooping one that you have. Maybe the changed look will help you land a girl.'

His bachelor status was an enigma to everybody. Shortly after Prakash's arrival in Jamnagar, Chudasama had found him a small unfurnished third floor apartment on a quiet street. 'Safe place, sir,' he had stated conspiratorially. That meant that somebody would be watching it perpetually, and whatever little privacy he aspired to, was gone. They now expected a wife to make that house a home, and when no one turned up, the topic was first discussed in hushed tones, and then more openly.

He finally decided to put a stop to the discussion tonight. 'Raijada,' he said, 'I am twenty-seven with a price over my head.' They understood this immediately. Threats had to be constantly factored into their lives.

They took him under their wing, the youngster with a funny reputation and a death threat. They started him with meeting the other agencies like R&AW—the famed counter-intelligence wing with the best technology at their command, military intelligence, naval intelligence, the intelligence bureau, the local intelligence bureau and the police. He soon realized that the area was not just a hotbed of smuggling, but also of enemy infiltration. His perspective soon blurred, and he found himself talking of 'crossings', sending people across the border to spy, instead of just limiting himself to collecting intelligence on smuggling of gold, silver or narcotics. Commercial frauds took a backseat for him. The Bombay blasts were invariably discussed, and talk of tracking the perpetrators often dominated discussions. The death threat was discussed openly, never in hushed tones.

Everybody expected the youngster to take precautions. Instead, he insisted on travelling incessantly. To Salaya to see the country crafts manufactured there, Porbandar to learn about Godmother, Veraval to experience the way the smugglers used the porous coast to their advantage and Somnath just to take the blessings of God. He was fascinated by the salt pans in Kutch and Jamnagar, and often wandered there on moonlit nights, listening to music on his Walkman, revelling in the shimmering moonlight reflected off the water, surrounded by mounds of unrefined salt. That was where he often met the sailors to listen to stories of Gulf, Africa and their adventures at sea. His world was expanding. The travellers told tales of distant shores, and the sea brought in more than brine. It brought messages from afar that fed him knowledge of stratagems adopted by smuggling syndicates across international borders.

Alone, he explored the city that was said to have been born because of a dream. He found out what Kanwar had meant when he had stated that Jamnagar was a cauldron of cultures. The city was a mix of tradition and modernity. He explored the architecture by wrangling an invitation to Pratap Vilas Palace and then went to Darbargarh Palace to see the lifestyles of the royals. School loyalty took him to the Sainik School Balachadi, the counterpart of his school in Gujarat. He envied the cadets. They had a hostel with a sea view! The school was located at a place where children fleeing the Nazis had been given shelter when no one else was ready to accept them. It was now training children to be soldiers who would defend their country. His chest swelled with pride when he met the cadets. *We will still bring sanity to this world*, their sparkling eyes seemed to say. He recalled his own childhood, spent wearing a similar uniform, imbibing the principles that still governed his life—'knowledge, honour, courage and chivalry'. All to be practiced with the combination of strength, brains and wisdom.

He walked beside the corals in shallow waters, watching small octopuses scurrying in the clear sea of Pirotan Island, the only marine life sanctuary of the country. He was told that there was a bird sanctuary, and he wondered how birds survived in this parched land. But he visited it anyhow, and watched the seasonal lake and the shallows host a veritable trove of birds.

As he travelled the inhospitable terrain, he understood, not just learnt, but *understood*, the motivations behind smuggling. The reasons behind the loyalty among smugglers. And above all, why the land produced fiercely proud people.

He reserved visiting the most inhospitable region of the area, Kutch, and its largest city, Bhuj, for August, when the rains had subsided and the Rann of Kutch was clear of all tracks, ready to be experienced in its primal glory. On his way to Bhuj from Jamnagar, he admired the occasional rabari walking with their cattle or goats. The elaborate headgear, the frocked shirt and the blooming short pants tickled his imagination. *I would certainly wear that to one of the parties in Delhi. One day!* he thought.

'Why is our office based in Bhuj? Isn't Kandla the hub of commercial activity now?' he had asked Raijada.

'The transporters who carry the heroin smuggled from Pakistan to Bombay are based in Bhuj,' Raijada replied. Transporters, whether over land, water or air, were the backbone of smuggling syndicates, and the intelligence networks believed that keeping the transporters under watch was the easiest way to catch contraband.

'And how is the heroin carried from Pakistan to Bhuj?'

'Different ways,' replied Raijada. 'Sometimes on camels that just know the way to their home across the Rann, sometimes by men who need money and sometimes even by men who go to Pakistan to spy for intelligence agencies.'

Prakash was thunderstruck, but he then realized that even he had no control over his informers.

'You will see the routes that they take,' Raijada continued. 'We are going right up to the Pakistan border. But they don't ride in vehicles. And they risk their lives for meagre money.'

They left early in the morning. The weather was still hot, and the BSF guide was fretting about the discomfort sahib was going to face. Prakash overruled the objections, and the concern slowly turned into grudging admiration. 'Keep a lot of water, sir. You will need it,' the escort advised.

Chudasama and Raijada knew that, but besides the water, they also loaded their Gypsy with innumerable packs of mawa, the famed local sweet, and as much fresh vegetables they could carry before leaving for their foray in the desert.

'For our hosts, the jawans of BSF,' they replied on seeing his raised eyebrow. 'Fresh food is always welcome in these inhospitable locations.'

What followed were two of the most incredible days in Prakash's young life. He had felt puny before the vastness of the sea during his sails. He had experienced the majesty of the mountains in the Himalayas and had been hypnotized by the rage of the mountain rivers. He had been mesmerized by the colourful, carefree revelry of Holi. He had been in love, had experienced fear, joy, passion. But nothing in his life had prepared him for the Rann, for the unending spread of dazzling white sand, with no tree, no bush, not even a bump in the land to break the monotony of unending whiteness. There was no water to offer any succour. There were no waves to break the monotony, no stars to help him comprehend the numbers, no peaks to emphasize the heights. Just unending white sand, brightly reflecting the heat of the sun, as if there was no end to the journey. He imagined trees and water where there were none, hoping for something to be out there, anything. The sun beat on them mercilessly, and there seemed to be no saviour. The earth seemed to tell him, accept me as I am, be a part of me, else there is no hope for you.

They stayed for two days in the Rann, travelling only in the mornings, spending the hot afternoons in the underground bunkers of BSF. In the evening, the veterans and the guides told them stories of smugglers of India and of spies from Pakistan, and of legends of the force and their valour, of the brave men who had tackled the enemy riding their trusty camels. He learnt...

The trip over, they reached the hotel overlooking the Rudrani Lake. Monsoon had been kind that year, and the lake was filled to the brim. It was relaxing to see some water after experiencing the scorching, inhospitable desert. The intensity of the Rann of Kutch had been unsettling, and he was still disoriented, trying to assimilate the different facets of the experience.

A joint would possibly put things into perspective faster, he thought.

'I will take you to Kala Dungar and the Banni grasslands tomorrow,' Raijada said. 'You may not get a chance again. Have a look at the Kutchi wolves before you get busy.'

'Wolves!' Prakash exclaimed, his love for wild animals surfacing at the words.

'You didn't know…' replied Raijada in wonder. 'The temple at Kala Dungar has wolves that come in to feed every day.'

Prakash was awestruck. The trip warranted no discussion at all.

'I have to go back to Jamnagar,' Chudasama said. 'The BSF guys have given us some leads. Raijada and I will start working on them.'

'I will accompany him till Bhuj and come back tomorrow morning,' Raijada said.

'Do you want to leave tonight? You are anyway going to leave for Jamnagar tomorrow. Stay the night here, and let us leave together in the morning.'

Raijada looked at Chudasama, and they decided to share their dilemma with Prakash.

'Actually, this place is all booked for the lead stars of a film being shot in the Rann. We pulled rank, but the owner was ready to part with only one room. He is still going to get some flak from the filmi guys and he requested that we talk to these moneybags personally, but they seem to be late. So we will leave the owner to face the flak alone.'

Prakash was aghast. An argument ensued where he offered to vacate the room and accompany them to Bhuj, but they would have none of it from the youngster. 'Stay, sir. Relax. You never know when you will get such a lull in work again. The underworld is bound to regroup soon. So enjoy the sunrise at Rudrani while you can. Maybe you will also get a chance to have a drink with the stars. I am told that some big names are going to stay here. And what's done is done. The room is ours,' Raijada said.

'If anyone argues with you, just tell them that RI is conducting a sensitive operation in the area with the BSF and that their permission to shoot in the area is likely to be cancelled,' Chudasama added.

Prakash looked searchingly at Chudasama to see if he was joking but found the same inscrutable expression as always. Even Raijada's eyes lacked the mischievous glint that would have indicated that they were not serious. He wondered, and then decided not to question them further.

◆

A caravan of two SUVs and two pickup trucks arrived soon after Chudasama and Raijada had left. Five or six people tumbled out of the pickup trucks, and the film stars glided out of the SUVs and quickly walked into the cottages reserved for them. A portly guy, who seemed to be in charge, was soon approached by a lackey. The guy possibly explained the dilemma of the missing room to him. The owner appeared and an argument ensued; wild gesticulations could be seen, and then, just as it seemed that the situation would warrant Prakash's interference, the owner said something that seemed to cause some concern to the people surrounding him. They threw surreptitious glances at him, and then, after some persuasion from the owner, one of the women went and knocked on the door of one of the cottages occupied by the stars. One SUV, with three people packed into it, left shortly thereafter.

Prakash did not move during the whole show, preferring to sit and stare at nothingness. The stars were out, dancing in full force, and after experiencing the majestic beauty of earth in the Rann, he was happy witnessing the magic of the cosmos. A falling star streaked across the sky. He looked at the place where its descent ended and found hundreds ready to take its place. *Life mimics the universe*, he thought idly.

He looked at the sky while pouring himself another drink, checking whether he was still able to identify the constellations.

He had memorized a few before starting on the Narmada trek. Star gazing, a rudimentary knowledge of palmistry, the art of close dancing to 'Careless Whisper' and a supply of decent perfumes was necessary to be able to take a girl to bed in the hip 80s. Even the girls knew that. It was easier to show a girl the stars and move on if she said that she had no interest in astronomy. He realized that he could still show a girl Ursa Major, Orion's Belt, Canis Major, followed by most of the sun signs.

What am I doing here? he thought. *And when I am here, what am I doing with a glass of whisky, and that too alone? Oh, how the mighty have fallen. Oh, my kingdom for a joint of freshly rubbed hash. I can't even get high after experiencing life's high. I can't even have a fuck to consummate infinity.*

From the corner of his eye, he observed another chair being brought out. He contemplated if he should call it a night. After all, he was blatantly breaking the laws of a dry state. But then he decided to throw caution to the wind. In for a penny, in for a pound, he reasoned. He had already abused his power to grab the room, he might as well relish the night as much as he could.

The faint aroma of Poison, the popular perfume recently launched by Christian Dior, wafted over the gentle wind. It reminded him of Sujata. It was his last gift to her before he left Pune. *Why do we carry gifts only for the people with whom we have a superficial relationship, and carry none for the people for whom we care?* He wondered why he never carried any gifts for Shelley. *Would she even accept one if I took one from here? Possibly the black dress that Kutchi women wear. Why do they wear black? Were they not aware that black absorbs heat? But then, in the winter the temperature in Kutch often drops to zero. Maybe it helps then.*

Is the girl sitting there as majestic as the Kutchi women who carry themselves so proudly? he wondered. He looked across the dark pathway. Nobody else had come out. It was just the two of them.

Two silhouettes on a dark, starry night. The others seemed to have called it an early night. He sat awkwardly, wondering what to do next. His reverie had been broken by another person walking into a universe that he thought was his own for the night. He was intensely conscious of the other body that had intruded his communion. *What do I do?* he wondered. *Do I offer her a drink, or be the boorish bum and keep drinking alone? Will she consider me a pest or an admirer if I offer her a drink?* Chivalry, for Prakash, won again.

He walked up to her and said, 'I am sorry, madam, but I am drinking whisky out there. I hope you don't mind.'

Shit, that sounded so lame for an introduction, he thought immediately as the words came out of his mouth.

There was a momentary silence, and then Shabnam looked up at Prakash and said softly, 'Shelley was right, you do make the word madam sound so dirty.'

Prakash staggered, involuntarily taking a step back, peering intensely into the darkness to confirm her identity.

'Shabnam. What are you doing here?' he asked. He immediately realized he sounded aggressive.

'Planning to threaten you again,' she replied serenely.

This was turning out all wrong again, thought Prakash. He had wanted to meet this girl—this woman, he corrected himself mentally, to learn about Salim from her. She was his passport to Salim's little-known private world, and instead of being friendly to her, he had invariably managed to antagonize her. He needed to be his normal self, he thought, treat her as just another girl.

'Ah, I was drunk that day,' he said, hoping he sounded appropriately contrite. 'And when you are drunk, you dive deep.' Shit, he did it again. *Why does she have that effect on me?* he thought, feeling incoherent.

'I think that may not be the only day that you were drunk.' Shabnam sounded amused.

'Yup. No. Would you like to join me for a drink?' He continued lamely.

'Isn't that illegal over here?' Shabnam teased.

'Not for stars. Particularly when there are so many stars in the sky,' he said hurriedly. Receiving no response to what, even to him, sounded like a poor effort at humour, he continued, 'I have a government permit to possess, use and consume liquor for the preservation and maintenance of my health. But don't tell anyone this. My bosses anyway question my sanity. With this information, they will be certain that I am an addict. I am placing my future in your hands.'

Shabnam chuckled. 'How can one refuse an indigent person the maintenance of his health? But does your poor health permit you to carry my chair closer to yours? Or do I have to flex my muscles for that?'

Prakash, naturally, carried the chair.

'Genuine,' Shabnam said after the first sip of Black Label.

'You doubt a customs man of drinking spurious whisky?' Prakash sounded surprised.

'You would be surprised by what I experience in Bombay. Peter Scot in Black Label bottles, McDowell's No. 1 in Vat 69 bottles, Diplomat in bottles of Red Label. So it's a compliment to declare a whisky genuine,' Shabnam stated simply.

They had little to share, so they sat in silence, sipping slowly.

'I believe the movie with the genius was a hit,' Prakash said, trying to restart on a positive footing.

'Yup. You watched it?' Shabnam asked.

'Yes. You acted well,' Prakash stated in what he hoped sounded like a matter-of-fact tone.

'Yeah. I was lucky. I had a good role, and everybody liked the performance. I may even be nominated for a Filmfare award,' Shabnam stated like a star.

And get it as well, if Salim has his way, thought Prakash, and then shook the thought away. He was not going to think of Salim tonight.

'That would be great,' he said. 'You'd be a superstar then, and I can tell my grandchildren that I had drinks with superstar Shabnam, twice.'

'And your grandchildren will say, who, that droopy old woman? They will have their own superstars, Mr Prakash. Fame is transient, and when I am just a pale shadow of myself, people will say "There goes Shabnam. She flickered in the firmament for a while", and I would look at them, poignantly, hoping for two minutes of fame all over again. I don't seek fame, I seek work, and wish to be very good at the work I do.'

Prakash was surprised. He had placed Shabnam as the quintessential moll, a bimbo, currying favours to seek fame, which, as the stupid always thought, was eternal. She, instead, sounded more like him. He muttered,

Fame, like a wayward girl, will still be coy
To those who woo her with too slavish knees,
But makes surrender to some thoughtless boy.

'Keats. I read this one when I first entered the industry,' Shabnam said. 'My then roommate, a writer, told me to keep Keats by my bedside, said that he would keep me sane. But a bureaucrat quoting him! I thought bureaucrats were drab, rule-bound hounds, who sought their two minutes of fame in their work, which, by the way,' she added hurriedly, 'is probably their path of choice to have tales to tell their grandchildren.'

'Vestiges of studying English Literature from Hindu College, Delhi,' replied Prakash. 'Thought I would become a writer, and then, took the Civil Services Examination on a drunken bet with a friend. Flunked, and spent two years of my life to satisfy my ego that I could crack any exam. Nobody would allow me to not join once I cleared the exam. My family and friends thought I was skylarking, and being a bureaucrat was my last chance to make something of my life. Funny how life takes us to places we had no idea of landing in. What's your story?'

'Small town girl, big dreams. Won some awards in theatre while in college, fuelling my ambitions for acting. Decided to break out of the middle-class rut. Everybody thought that I was stupid to struggle in Bombay, chasing an elusive dream, when I could have easily married my rich cousin. I knew the day I left that I would not go back till I had succeeded. But I still have not been able to define success, and am not sure if it is the same as that of my family. I haven't visited my home for six years now. Life could have gone either way, but I got lucky in my choice of roommate in Bombay. She taught me to read beyond plays and scripts. She widened my horizon by taking me through a wide cross section of writings, from Faiz to Keats, from Shakespeare to Ghalib, from Premchand to Lawrence. They gave me some perspective at a time when I thought I would go mad in all those years of struggle, when I was out there hunting for small roles, trying to tag my career with some theatre group, trying to stave off the pawing of the casting agents. Art, in any form, I think, influences your life.'

Prakash felt comfortable talking to her. Her openness was disarming, and he found himself slowly empathizing with her struggles, even though she had smoothly skipped the part about Salim. Their soft voices in the silence of the darkness seemed to float into nothingness.

'I guess I can understand what you mean by sanity in a struggle. I saw your early films on the VCR. The small role of the cheerleader in *Cricket*, where you take off your t-shirt, baring your back. The raped girl in *Thirst*. Followed by the slightly longer roles of an alcoholic in *Chai*, and the hash smoking aspiring actress who is ready to sleep with anybody in *Joint*. You tried to bring intensity and meaning to those roles, even when they merited none. Literature does help you to push your limits further.'

'You seem to have seen all my movies.' Shabnam seemed thoughtful. 'What are you, a crazed fan?' Then the reality seemed to dawn on her.

'Salim,' she said, only half questioningly.

Prakash's silence seemed to answer her question.

'So this meeting was planned?' she was riled.

'No,' Prakash answered quickly. 'I didn't even know you would be here.'

'Even if you had known, you couldn't have guessed that I would come to sit outside tonight.' Shabnam reasoned with herself. 'You knew all along?' she queried. 'Even when we met in Pune?'

Prakash nodded.

'Therefore, the hostility.'

Prakash nodded again. 'Salim's men have been my nemesis for too long. They had been threatening me, trying to bribe me and failing in that, discredit me. There were at least two adverse newspaper articles that were prompted by them. Then I accidentally ran into the woman being promoted by him, and you represented everything that I was fighting. Things were so black and white then. Life was uncomplicated. Right was right, and wrong was wrong. I am just beginning to learn that there are shades of grey in life,' Prakash said tactfully, and then continued, 'But you are different than what I had imagined. You looked so forlorn and lost in Firozewala's party. And today, you still have no airs, no rude remarks about the room that has been so illegally occupied by a boorish government officer. Shelley told me I am wrong about you, but, at that time, Salim occupied too much of my universe to allow me to think rationally. I have probably grown since. I am learning to live with my enemies and I understand that people associated with evil may not themselves be evil.'

'Is that your convoluted attempt at an apology, or an attempt at a backhanded compliment? Or is it a blatant insult?' Shabnam asked seriously, but there was a twinkle of amusement in her tone.

Prakash mumbled something.

I like this guy, thought Shabnam. *He has no deceit in him.*

'That means you know about the other thing too?' Shabnam asked gently after what she thought was enough time for Prakash to ponder on his words.

'Know what other thing?' Prakash asked, confused.

'That Salim had asked Hanif to kill you.'

'Hanif? I thought he asked Master to get me killed? I know that he ordered it just after we met in Pune.'

'After we met in Pune! But he asked Hanif to kill you much before that. It was after you had caught his consignment at Boria. He felt that you were unlucky for him.'

'No, he ordered my death after the consignment meant for Dabhol was burnt by the Pakistani smugglers. That was the consignment that could not land because Shelley and I were in Ratnagiri after the Firozewala party,' Prakash retorted.

Shabnam thought hard, and then said, softly, 'You are living a charmed life, Prakash. You were ordered to be killed at least six months before that. Don't argue,' she said as Prakash opened his mouth to protest, 'I was there, I heard it all.'

Prakash was stunned into silence. In an irony of life, he was drinking with a person who was confirming that her lover had ordered his death. Till now, he had nursed a faint hope that Sharma sir was wrong, that he had heard the rumours from some low-level operatives, whispers that were spread as a scare to get him off Salim's back. After all, he had reasoned, in periods of hope, officers don't get killed for money.

Shabnam observed him closely. *He is not so brash, rash or bold as he is rumoured to be*, she thought.

'That means Salim asked Hanif to have me killed twice. I just never learnt of it the first time around. Thanks for telling me,' he told Shabnam. 'I owe you one. This clears up a lot of things. But why are you telling me this?'

'Like hell you do—owe me one, that is,' she said. He noticed that she used the colloquial slangs comfortably. *What is she doing with an uneducated boor like Salim?* he wondered. 'I wanted to warn you even at Pune. Why should Salim bump off a person for doing his job? You were not his enemy. Why should you be killed for doing something you are expected to do. I said this to Salim, but he is a difficult man to argue with. And then I met you and your friends, and I just couldn't allow this head with its impossible black mop of dishevelled hair to be chopped off.' She was trying to lighten the intensity of her tone. 'That is why I gave Shelley my number, to warn you, but you never called back.'

'Ah. That's why Shelley said that the exchange of numbers could be for my benefit. But then, she also turned against you once I told her that you were sleeping with the enemy. She never gave me the number. She got you right. I think I have lost my ability to read girls.'

'Did you ever have it?' Shabnam asked with a touch of sarcasm. 'The capacity to read girls, that is.'

'Oh, only till I was seven years old, or possibly till the count of seven, I forgot which one,' replied Prakash with a wry grin.

They went silent, relishing the quiet, and surprisingly, the comfort of each other's company in the ever-darkening night.

'Do you like astronomy?' Prakash asked after a while. 'Should I show you the constellations?'

'Shit, and the next thing you'll be doing is reading my lifeline and trying to press my mount of Venus and my mount of Jupiter. You were right, you lost touch with girls after the count of seven. I stopped boys from showing me the Ursa Major when I turned seventeen,' Shabnam said with a laugh, and Prakash joined her.

They were shocked by the loudness of their laughter, and looked guiltily at the other cottages, half expecting somebody to walk out and admonish them.

Nobody did, but they fell silent.

'So, smoke a peace pipe before we call it a night?' Prakash asked, offering Shabnam a cigarette.

Shabnam thought for a while as Prakash held out the pack.

'No,' she replied. 'Not these.' She then continued. 'But I have something that brings true peace on earth.' She dramatically pulled out two reefers from her clutch. Prakash looked at them in amazement.

'Are these what I think they are?'

'Don't tell me that you do not smoke. I caught a whiff on both yours and Shelley's breath in Pune. This is as good a bud as you can get. I have sampled it.'

'You smoke hash! I was not even sure that you smoked cigarettes.'

'Only when I have nothing to do, and on shootings at remote locations. You never know what shit liquor may be passed on to you by the producer. This, anyway, gives you a better appreciation of nature and solitude than liquor.' Her reply nearly echoed what Prakash had been thinking a while ago, 'But you, a bureaucrat, breaking the law?'

'I was doing that with liquor in a dry state anyway.' Prakash replied, but then added quickly, 'It's just a remnant of a world that is fast being left behind, and I am trying to hold on to the ashes of a past that seems like a mirage now.'

'Salim, or your other enemies, will exploit this information if they come to know of it.' Shabnam said, now seriously.

'That's what somebody else also said to me. But I don't smoke this indiscriminately. Just with friends. And I can't remember when I went to buy last.'

'So, you are a bummer,' Shabnam said with a devilish look, 'a scrooge.'

'No, just a true devotee,' Prakash said reverentially. 'A true follower will land up with his prasadam wherever he is. But we can't smoke it here, what if somebody comes out?'

'And we can't smoke in my room. My hairdresser, who was so unceremoniously evicted from the cottage to the tents, courtesy some big shot RI chap, will be back at six o'çlock in the morning and the residual scent is bound to cheese off the big director sahab.'

'And I can't think of taking you to a dark corner. That would be ungentlemanly,' Prakash gallantly said.

They stared at each other, none willing to state the unspoken fact. Finally, Prakash took the plunge.

'But you can come to my room. A friend's room is not restricted, and I promise I will be the perfect gentleman.'

'Give me a minute,' Shabnam said, jumping at the offer. 'And don't worry, I have been to too many rooms, alone, with a lot of men. I can handle myself. But friends, you sure?'

Prakash looked at her, and sensing the insecurity, extended his hand, offering his pinky finger. 'Pinky friends,' he said.

She smiled and linked his little finger with her own, and then held him by the palm of his hand for just that extra second, which tells you that they were now going to be more than friends.

◆

Shabnam arrived in his room in ten minutes. She had changed into loose jeans and a black t- shirt. Her long hair was tied loosely at the back and some of it fell over her shoulders, curling over her breasts. No bra, Prakash noticed as he followed the fall of her hair, and was surprised how erotic that simple fact seemed to him. He hastily shifted his gaze to her face, but not before Shabnam had noticed him. The black tee brought out her fair complexion, and even the slightly droopy eyes looked large set against her snub, short, girlish nose. He stared, locking a look with Shabnam. Both of them hastily averted their gaze, trying to look at nothing. *You are behaving like a star-struck seventeen-year-old kid,* both of them thought.

He had changed into a kurta-pyjama and hoped that Shabnam didn't notice that he was not wearing an underwear. She finally gave him a smile, puckered her lips in a funny grimace, and flopped down on the empty chair.

'It's just nine,' she said. 'Nights seem to be interminable in these rural areas. The others had gone off to sleep by eight, I think.'

'Or they are avoiding me. My guys apparently sent your unit a warning that the permission for their shoot would be cancelled if I was disturbed.'

'You can do that!' exclaimed Shabnam. 'I think they heard everything that we talked about, and we are soon going to be the talk of the town.' She said impishly as she fished out the joint and handed it over to Prakash.

'I doubt it. They will fear that they will be booked for espionage.' He laughed and proceeded to smell the hash, licked the joint once, and handed it back to Shabnam.

'Your privilege,' he stated, taking out the Dunhill Seaman's lighter to light the reefer.

Shabnam took a long drag and passed it to Prakash, who took a drag, held the joint to his head, repeated his chant—'Bol Bum'— and passed it back to Shabnam, letting the thick chemical-laced smoke rest in his lungs. They passed the joint to each other in silence.

'Man, this is good stuff,' commented Prakash, 'or is it because I was already high after three drinks.'

'No. I told you. This is some of the best. Supposed to be Malana cream. Cost me 200 bucks a tola.'

'Are you carrying a whole tola?' Prakash asked, greed obvious in his voice.

'Of course, silly,' Shabnam said with a giggle. 'I had a six-day shooting schedule. Would not like to be left high and dry.'

Prakash slid down from the chair on to the floor, leaned his head back and enjoyed the trip. Shabnam followed him soon after.

'I have a Walkman with two headphones. Do you want to listen to Santana?' he asked.

'Only if you have "Black Magic Woman".'

'You know, "Black Magic Woman" is not truly Santana,' Prakash said lazily.

'Who cares, it's great music,' replied Shabnam. Her voice seemed like it was floating across miles of desert to reach Prakash. *Either I am high,* he thought, *or she is. Her voice is reaching me quite slowly. Could she have kaleidoscopic eyes?* He opened his eyes to look at Shabnam, who was sitting lazily on the floor, eyes closed, soaking in the music.

He shook her gently by the hand.

'Open your eyes,' he said.

'I am not so high that I'd be unable to open my eyes,' she replied.

'No, open your eyes, just for a second, please.' He insisted.

She opened her eyes to look at him, faintly questioning.

'No, they are not kaleidoscopic, they are light brown,' he said, lying back and closing his eyes again.

Shabnam was high enough to make the connection with the famous Beatles song.

She tapped Prakash's hand. 'Open your eyes.'

'Yeah?'

'I need a newspaper taxi to take me across the lake to my room.'

'Nah, not yet. Not before I see the sun in your eyes.' he said, continuing with the refrain from 'Lucy in the Sky with Diamonds'. 'And we have still not smoked that second joint.'

'Are you sure you can handle it?' Shabnam asked.

'Are you challenging my capacity?' Prakash said. He had the inevitable defiant tone of a person high on drinks or drugs.

'No, just your sobriety,' replied Shabnam simply. The trip was too good to get into a chauvinistic challenge. She wanted to smoke, but the whole joint would have been too strong to smoke alone. *And*, she thought, *I am enjoying myself in this company. Who the hell wants to get high alone anyway?*

The combination of whisky and hash was taking its toll. Shabnam remembered that there was a saying that beer over whisky is always risky. 'Where is the saying about hash? I think I should create one.'

'Whiskey with hash, what a bash!' she said.

'I know. I've never done it before,' Prakash responded.

'Are you ready for the second one?'

They straightened up a little bit as Shabnam lit the second joint.

'Do you think the small mirrors in these Kutchi cottages are broken pieces of the looking glass tiles?' Prakash asked.

'No, these are broken bottle tops. They capture a reflection of the soul of the men in these mirrors,' Shabnam replied.

'From Keats to Santana to Beatles to Michael Jackson. Is there something she doesn't know?' Prakash muttered dreamily in his high, in what he thought was under his breath. 'Gawd, she is hot.'

'Of course, I am hot. Isn't that why you have an erection?' Shabnam said lazily as she took the burning reefer from his hand.

Prakash sat up a little straighter and watched her delicately wet her ring finger with her tongue and roll it around the tip of the burning cigarette.

That was so erotic, he thought.

'I am high,' he replied. 'A good high always gives me an erection.'

Shabnam passed the joint to him.

'Yeah, me too,' she said, pulling her lycra t-shirt against her breasts. 'See how erect and hard they are.' She pointed at her nipples.

Prakash was shocked even in his stupor. He focused on Shabnam with a little difficulty and passed the joint back after taking a small drag.

'And they get bigger and harder as I get higher. You want to see?' she asked.

He knew he was asking the wrong question, but he asked it anyway. His sense of propriety demanded it. 'Are you sure?'

'That they get harder? Of course, silly.' Shabnam pulled her t-shirt over her head, baring her breasts. 'See for yourself.' She took the last, deep drag of the joint. 'See, they got bigger with that drag.'

'Why me?' he asked, knowing that he was being stupid. He actually liked her, and one never looked a gift horse in the mouth.

'Because nobody else can sleep with me. They are all scared of Salim. But what can Salim do to you, kill you twice for sleeping with his mistress?' Shabnam laughed, only half seriously.

'That's as good a reason for me as any,' replied Prakash, pulling her close to him. They kissed passionately, their eyes open, slowly letting trust creep in their looks, which then transformed into desperate passion of the deprived. Both of them realized that they were suddenly free of the shadow of Salim that was holding them back. The freedom fuelled their pleasure, already intense because of the heightened sensitivity induced by hash.

◆

They couldn't sleep. High on happiness and hash, they explored each other. Lying in semi darkness, bodies entwined in a light embrace, their murmured voices revealed their fears, their aspirations, their victories and their losses. Words flew easily, about his anger on riots, her frustration at being rejected by casting agents repeatedly, the debt he owed to Sharma and the longing she felt for her parents. He skirted Shelley, and she did not mention Salim. The night passed quickly, and after a while they lay quiet, curled against each other, satiated.

◆

Shabnam tiptoed into her room just before the break of dawn. Sleep still eluded her, and a range of emotions was surging through her, muddling her thoughts. She had guessed that it was Prakash who had usurped her room. She knew he had been posted to Saurashtra, and when her hairdresser had informed her that one of the rooms had to be surrendered to some RI officer, she had faintly entertained the possibility that it was Prakash. Sitting out had been a deliberate act. She had noticed how caring he was to Shelley in Pune, and had wondered at his hostility towards her. Even in his stiff and distant behaviour, she could spot a diffident gentleman whom she found oddly charming, especially after all the ogling and propositions she received from the boors in Bombay. Sleeping with him certainly had not been on her agenda. However, somewhere between the first drink and the poetry, the forgotten feelings of passion had been reignited in her. The joint had been the first step—a stolen moment of complicity in breaking the law. A simple act that brought them closer. *The rest*, she thought, *was not to be analysed but savoured.* She surely would not mind sleeping with him again, she decided.

The morning was a blur of thoughts and sleepless dreams. Her hairdresser arrived at 6 a.m., took one look at her, and called the director, who insisted on calling for a doctor, which she successfully resisted as the nearest doctor, anyway, was at least sixty kilometres away. She shooed the hairdresser away to the shoot, popped a couple of pills to satisfy everyone's anxiety and pretended to sleep.

Prakash hardly slept at all. The events of the evening and the night were so surreal that he could not stop thinking over them. He walked out of the room at 7 a.m. and watched the sun rise over the waters of the Rudrani Lake. He periodically glanced towards Shabnam's room, wondering what she was doing or thinking. He went back to his room as the sun rose high over the horizon. Raijada came at 9 a.m., took one look at Prakash, looked meaningfully at the empty bottle of Black Label, and politely told him that he would send the driver later in the afternoon to pick him up. Prakash instead asked him to leave the Gypsy and said that he would drive it himself.

By 10 a.m., they were the only two people in the resort. Prakash did not know what to do next. He kept asking himself, 'Should I meet her? On what pretext?'

Shabnam was sure that she wanted to meet Prakash again, and so, around 11 a.m., she sent him a message through the resort owner.

Prakash hesitated for a moment outside her door, and then, taking a deep breath, walked in. She was sitting on the bed, wearing a night suit buttoned right up to her slender neck. *Had he left a few love bites there last night?* he wondered. He didn't know what to do in this sober state; everything had felt so right last night. Shabnam smiled, a smile as tentative as his pause at the door, and then he mustered the courage to walk up to her and give her a quick hug.

He sat on the side of the bed, waiting for her to say something. She no more looked the aggressive, confident woman from last night. Nestled in the crumpled bedcovers, she looked more like a vulnerable girl, unsure of what had happened. She looked at him with those light brown eyes and his heart went out to her.

'They are still not kaleidoscopic,' he said lightly.

Shabnam gave a wan smile. 'Yeah, but they are sparkling.'

'You know, with a wit like that, you should be a writer, not an actor.'

'Oh, shut up! It's my knowledge that always gets me into problems.'

'Yeah, mine too,' Prakash said seriously. 'I speak too much, and it invariably gets me into trouble.'

They sat in moody silence as the owner brought tea and gave them the sugary, deeply brewed beverage.

'What next?' Prakash asked.

'I shoot for five more days and go back to Bombay. You go back to Jamnagar whenever you want to. Out of sight, out of mind,' she replied.

'It will not be easy for me to put you out of my mind. After all,

I slept with the budding superstar—who is also the mistress of the guy trying to kill me.'

'That's true. I too won't be able to push you out of my mind until I know that you are dead. There is only one solace. I won't have to carry the guilt of your death. You already had invited it with your own actions,' she replied. Prakash saw a trace of last night's confident spirit.

'Oh, yes. But if Salim learns about this and orders your death, I will have to carry that burden,' Prakash said truthfully.

'There is that.'

'I can't protect you in Bombay,' he continued.

'I don't need your protection. I am very capable of taking care of myself. Don't be a bloody chauvinistic pig,' Shabnam said with a flash of rage. 'And you don't have to carry the guilt either. You are not the first guy I have slept with.'

She took a sip of her tea and then spoke slowly. 'I think there is a latent death wish among all of us who follow the Romantics. We just want to flare once, instead of being frustrated by obscurity.'

'When you are thinking of Keats,' said Prakash, 'do remember that he also said that melancholy has her home in the temple of delight. We touched a high of happiness last night, and now, at least I wonder if we can hit that pinnacle ever again. I don't know, but I will look forward to it with anticipation. Maybe we can reach that intensity that defines immortality.'

'Really?' Shabnam said, surprised by the invitation. She had wanted to make it to him. 'You felt connected too?'

'How can I not feel connected to a girl who carries Malana cream?' Prakash said lightly. 'And then gets an erection from it!' He added sleazily.

'Oh, shut up,' replied Shabnam. She thought for a while, and then said, 'We have a wrap-up schedule next month. I will try and route my journey through Jamnagar and stay a night there.'

'If both of us are alive by then,' Prakash said with a smile.

'There is that. Our chances improve if you don't ask me about Salim's activities,' said Shabnam. 'Including about his prowess in bed.'

Prakash could not resist laughing.

'Scout's honour,' he said. 'But can I at least ask if my dick is bigger than his?'

'No. After all he drives a Harley,' Shabnam replied with an impish smile, 'and he can do better stunts on it than you can on your Dick. Ground rule two. I will not be flaunted. I am not a trophy.' She continued.

'You forget that you *can't* be flaunted,' Prakash replied, relieved at her light-hearted repartee at his reference to "Dick". 'If you are, both of us may be killed. I too have a condition.'

'What?' Shabnam asked suspiciously.

'You will tell me if you get the slightest whiff of danger.'

'Done.'

Prakash got up from the chair, walked up to Shabnam, held out his little finger, and said, 'Pinky promise?'

◆

Shelley called Prakash a week later.

'You slept with the enemy's mistress, you dog! And you didn't even tell me. I am going to kill you! I told you that she is a lovely girl, but you turned me against her. And after that, you go and bed her! What a backstabber!' She screamed over the phone. She would have carried on but Prakash stopped her.

'Shelley, Shelley, listen,' and when she did not stop, he shouted. 'Shelley! Stop! Listen!'

That quietened her, and he asked. 'How did you know?'

'She called me, you bastard. You never even called, after everything I have done for you.'

She would have started her frenzied rant again but Prakash interrupted her.

'Why did she call?'

'She just wanted to know about my relationship with you. Poor girl was feeling miserable at the thought that she was probably stealing my boyfriend,' Shelley laughed mirthlessly.

'What did you tell her?' Prakash asked suspiciously. He knew Shelley could spin any yarn if she was excited.

'The truth,' replied Shelley.

'Whose version of the truth?'

'Plato's version of the truth, which else, you fool. I explained to her that there is always a truth that is bigger than what exists on this earth.'

'Shelley, tell me what you said,' Prakash said gently.

'That's what I am trying to do but you keep interrupting me. I told her everything is to be measured from the perspective of universal forms, and what we have cannot be understood in terms of these earthly pleasures.'

'Shelley, are you stoned?' Prakash asked impatiently.

'No. But I was when she called me. Surprisingly, she understood what I was saying and said that she was glad that we were not sleeping together. I had to really put her down then. How could she even imagine that a true-blue royal like me could sleep with hoi polloi like you?'

'Great. What else?'

'I had to, of course, tell her about Sujata, and Savitha, and…'

'You didn't!' Prakash nearly yelled.

'Of course, I had to. She is such a sweet girl. And it is not as if she herself is a virgin.'

'You said it, Shelley,' Prakash said ominously. 'She is not a virgin, and she is still sleeping with the enemy.'

There was silence on the other end. Then Shelley said, 'I hope I have not fucked up somebody's life.'

'I doubt it, but I thought I was the one with a loose tongue.'

'I was high…if that is any justification. And she sounded so friendly and familiar on the phone. It just felt right to tell her. Also she said that you have promised to see her again?'

'I hope your instincts are right. I would, of course, like to see her again. She was good, Shelley, one of the best. You would like her.'

'I hope so. I am coming to Ahmedabad next week. Will I see you?' she asked.

'Not sure. We are in the middle of an operation here.'

16

A Paean to the Past

The genesis of the operation, the one Prakash mentioned to Shelley over the phone, lay in events that had taken place more than a year ago. Just after Prakash had seized the gold at Boria, Salim, with his ear to the ground, had realized that despite the massive profits that they were making from smuggling gold and silver, diversification was necessary to hedge their bets. There would always be mavericks like Prakash who would interfere with business, and the Pakistanis were steadily spreading their influence. Paki agencywallahs were already in the business of white powder, and Salim did not want to compete with them.

Salim talked to the syndicate members, the financiers and the operatives. He needed to get into something new. One of the syndicate members told him about 'Mandrax', already being smuggled in dhows carrying foodstuff and medicines to Somalia, Kenya or Mozambique.

'What is it used for?' he asked one of the smugglers.

'Bhai, what can we say about Africa, I don't know,' the man replied. 'The Vaniya in Kenya who buys the spices asked me to carry these tablets from Bombay. He paid me one lakh rupees just to carry one bag.'

The syndicate member in Kenya knew the business. But he had never thought that Salim would venture into drugs.

'Bhai, there is huge demand. It is being used with hashish by child soldiers in Angola, Syria, Somalia and Sudan.' He informed with a tinge of distaste in his voice. 'They call it dagga. It relaxes the kids, Bhai, but when they are not drugged, they get irritated and aggressive, ready to kill anyone who crosses them. Very effective for getting these child soldiers to fight.'

'What about payment?' Salim asked, ignoring the disapproval in the tone of the syndicate member.

'They pay in diamonds, non-traceable diamonds.'

'How much can they consume?'

'At the right price, they are ready to buy up to twenty-five lakh tablets a month. And there is a market in South Africa that can also be tapped. It's easier to send money to Europe from South Africa, as easy as it is from Dubai.'

'Who manufactures it?' Salim asked Hanif.

Hanif came back with the reply in just a couple of hours.

'There are too many, Bhai. One of them, Bhatt, had even put some money with Qasim in the movie *Anna*. He came with Qasim to your birthday party also. Qasim says that he can immediately bring Bhatt to see you.'

'I don't want to meet Bhatt,' Salim said. 'Ask Qasim to talk to Bhatt. Ask if he can manufacture fifty lakh tablets of Mandrax for him. Let it look like Qasim's operation. I don't want this being linked to me. Let everything be in Qasim's name.'

His boys on the street did not know of it, but Salim had entered the illegal drug trade as early as 1992. It started with Qasim selling just the overseas rights for his new movie—the production cost of which was estimated to be three crore—for an unheard of sum of three crore. The rights had been bought by one of Salim's front companies in Dubai. That left the income from theatres, music rights and video rights as profit. Qasim immediately transferred ₹50 lakh to Bhatt as the final settlement of his share of profits as co-producer of his earlier movie *Anna*. Bhatt used the money to buy machinery to expand his medicine factory in the industrial area of Vapi.

The sample batch of one lakh tablets weighed just over 150 kg and was produced at a cost of ₹1.5 lakh. They were smuggled in the cavity of Al Kausarbi, a dhow that sailed from Navlakhi carrying cement clinker for Dubai, and then dates and other edible cargo from Dubai for Mombasa, where the 150 kg of Mandrax tablets were clandestinely removed from the cavity and transferred to a skiff that carried it to the shore. The consignment was immediately shipped in two jeeps to Somalia and Sudan, and the potency and quality of the tablets was approved by the warlords. They offered a payment of ten thousand carats of small rough diamonds for every ten lakh tablets. The second consignment was of five lakh tablets, which were concealed and smuggled in packets of dates. The packets containing tablets were not sealed properly, and on arrival, smelt like the dates. The warlords refused to pay the agreed amount in full.

The issue of transporting large quantities of drugs stymied the gang. They were used to smuggling consumer goods, gold and silver, contraband that was passed by Customs or Police without any compunction. But drugs were different. Nobody, except the incorrigibly corrupt officials, were ready to turn a blind eye. They were stuck with a capacity of ten lakh tablets a month and no way to transport them. There were simply not enough confidential carriers available without the street knowing that Salim Bhai had entered the drug trade.

The other businesses carried on as usual. Indians were buying more gold than ever, movies were doing well and Bombay was seeing a real estate boom. The competition to own land led to frequent clashes among rival builders, and the gangs were often asked to intervene, resulting in quick earnings. The sharpshooters from the hinterlands of Uttar Pradesh and Bihar were a dime a dozen, and the stories of those making it big in the underworld hierarchy ensured an unending supply of loyal troops.

Things were good then. Nobody had expected the Babri Masjid's demolition, or foreseen the riots on the horizon at that time.

So the production of ten lakh tablets a month, manufactured with a paltry investment of ₹50 lakh was not the foremost thing on Salim's mind. In any case, Hanif ensured that Al Kausarbi managed to smuggle two to three lakh tablets a month, which kept their operation alive. The diamonds kept accumulating in their locker in Portugal. It was a small operation, and Salim could not have guessed that such a small part of his operation, and Shabnam, were to prove his nemesis.

◆

Shabnam, at that time, did not know about Salim's flirtation with smuggling drugs. She had been with him for two years, after meeting him for the first time on his birthday in July 1990. He had pursued her with an unexpected vigour, but she had been unsure. It had taken Salim more than six months, and gifts worth at least twenty lakhs, before she went to bed with him.

Shabnam went to Salim fully aware. In her mind, she had one life to live, and there was no taboo, no shame, no inhibition that would hold her back from living it to the fullest. She was not so naïve, not anymore, as to not use her beauty to further her career. She had, so far, combined her innate intelligence with an intuitive canniness to traverse the jungle that was Bollywood, moving from one target to another, her goal clear in her sight. She wanted a platform to unveil the talent trapped in her, and if Salim could help her achieve that, well, he could have what he wanted. She had come to Salim knowing what he was, and then had stayed back, partly fascinated by his world, partly knowing that Salim could help her chase her dreams, and partly because she fell in love with his generous nature, his capability to take care of his people, his loyalty to his friends.

She became a monthly visitor at Salim's bungalow, sometimes staying for as long as a week, and she was not at all upset when somebody called her his moll. She was not offended by his coarse language and she did not flinch, as other girls had done, at the crude expletives Salim used in bed. *Everybody has a fetish, and this was his*, she had reasoned.

It was not easy being the mistress of one of the biggest underworld dons. She was viewed suspiciously and watched over constantly. Sometimes she felt that she was being watched even in Bombay. Hanif's boys seemed to be everywhere.

For Hanif, Shabnam was an enigma. She did not seem to be with Salim for money at all. She was not even in awe of Salim, although she seemed to like him. Sometimes she would look at Salim as if he were her ticket to the stairway that led to top billings in Bollywood. But at other times, she simply didn't seem to care. Hanif seemed to sense that behind those alluring eyes was a mind more incisive than the razor he carried hidden in his socks.

Shabnam, on her part, always maintained a respectful demeanour for Hanif. He was, after all, Salim's man Friday, the man who handled affairs as diverse as getting a builder shot in Bombay to deciding who could meet Salim and when. He always reminded her of the consigliere of the Godfather. Tall, thin and with the customary Haji beard, he had the inscrutable face that she had expected of Salim before meeting him. He had the broadest nose she had ever seen, nostrils flaring to reach the edge of his thin, wide mouth. His eyes, nose and mouth were in a straight line, giving his face a curious square shape. It was rumoured that these wide nostrils had bequeathed on him the power to sniff out traitors, which is how he had come to be known as Hanif kutta, the sniffer dog, though nobody alive would dare to call him that to his face. Legend had it that he had once, without reason, shot a passer-by on the busy Crawford street in Bombay, a person never ever seen before, one single person out of a thousand people, and it had subsequently been found out that the man had been recently recruited by the rival Dadi gang to kill Salim. Shabnam knew she would not survive if she crossed Hanif and she was appropriately respectful with him. There existed an uneasy truce between the two of them.

It was on a late Saturday afternoon in October 1992 that Shabnam became a part of the story that was to become folklore in intelligence circles as well as in the underworld. Salim and Shabnam had spent the afternoon in bed, where Shabnam had spent two hours fantasizing about the new house she would buy after her movie would be declared a hit. There was one for sale next to that ex-superstar's house in Bandra. A small one, but in Bandra nevertheless, with a clear view of the sea.

She would buy that red Ferrari too, the one whose poster hung in her room, that had a nude model spread over the car. The boys got off on the model, she on the car. Maybe, this time, she would be the girl spread out nude over it, not some unknown model.

That would be orgasmic, she thought, and a girl needs her fantasies to reach orgasm. Most men just didn't know how to make women come. Salim, at that time, was trying very hard to do just that, make her come. He thought he could achieve that by talking dirty.

'Squeeze that hard, baby, tighten that tight cunt of yours,' he said.

Then, 'Can you feel that deep, right up to your ass.'

Or, 'Open your eyes, girl. I want to see that cum oozing out of your eyes.'

Shabnam looked at him lovingly. He was a darling. She lifted her neck, and softly covered his face with kisses. She started to push her hips up to meet his thrusts, squeezing her hips as she did that. Salim came with a mild tremble in his stomach, which both of them felt.

They were sitting in the patio, smoking the ritual post coital cigarette, when Shabnam looked up to find Salim looking at her speculatively. She gave him one of her dreamy looks.

'You are tightly packed around that tight hole of yours. All muscle, no loose points,' he said after a while. 'Let's see if we can recreate you,' he said cryptically.

Shabnam wondered what he meant. Salim looked excited as he called Hanif, who came half an hour later. He walked in to find Shabnam sipping on some champagne, trying to convince a reluctant Salim to come with her to the souk for some shopping. However, Salim's mind was already on business, and he told the driver to bring the Mercedes around to take her away.

'Hanif Bhai,' he said, waving her away impatiently when Hanif walked in. 'How much stuff is lying in the factory at Vapi?'

Hanif looked meaningfully at Shabnam, and Salim, despite the look, continued, 'Oh, her. That's right, Hanif Bhai. She is tightly packed around a hole. Let us recreate that.'

Both Shabnam and Hanif were now staring at Salim, bewildered.

'I think she has led me to the perfect solution to move that stuff out to Africa. Just tell Qasim to be here.'

The servant came in to inform them that the car was waiting.

'You run, girl, and don't spend more than 10,000 dirhams. I don't want you to be stopped by Indian Customs again.'

She could see that he was all charged up, and hardly noticed her exit as he kept on explaining his idea animatedly to Hanif.

'The one thing Customs in Africa never questions is the import of machinery oil. So, we forge the perfect papers for the export of machine oil from Dubai to Ethiopia. Except that the oil will be stored in a tight, deep, vertical hole created in the barrel, right from top to bottom. We divide the barrel vertically, instead of doing it horizontally, which we normally do. And then we pack the rest of the barrel with Mandrax tablets. Voila! Victory! A tightly packed body around a tight, deep hole,' Salim said dreamily.

Hanif looked at him strangely. The idea was perfect, but then, what a warped way for it to be conceived. From the tight cunt of a muscled tramp to the mind of a gangster. 'Allah moves in mysterious ways,' he said.

The message was passed to Qasim, who consulted Bhatt. It was going to be difficult, but not impossible for his people to manufacture the barrels, he informed. First the barrel would need to be cut from the top, then a tubular hole would have to be created from the opening to the bottom, and then, after stacking the Mandrax packets in the body, the top would have to be welded perfectly, without leaving a mark, and done with expertise so that the flammable tablets did not catch fire. Then the oil would be poured in the tubular cavity. If the welding was perfect, it would not leak over to the other part of the barrel.

'At least two to three months,' he told Hanif, when asked about the time needed to pull this off. 'We have about fifty lakh tablets in the factory.'

'Make a large number of barrels. At least fifty. Ten thousand litres of machine oil looks like a credible import. Get them ready by January. It's time to move the tablets out of India.'

But the best laid plans of men, mice and dons are often defeated by bolts from the blue. The demolition of the Babri Masjid and the ensuing riots affected Gujarat as well, and the packing of the barrels could only be finished by February. They were transported to Porbandar, from where Al Billal was to carry them to Dubai, where a friendly officer was to make the documents that would state that the machine oil was of UAE origin, and meant for export to Mombasa.

The barrels moved out of the factory in February, but there was a setback on reaching Porbandar. There was nobody there to meet the trucks. The local agent, Suleiman, was dispatched to trace out Shreeram, the owner and *tandel* of Al Billal, and found him with Laxmi, whom he had been wooing for more than a year. She had finally agreed to marry him after the riots. Uncertainty of life apparently spawns a desire to copulate and procreate, as was extensively witnessed during the World Wars and the Vietnam War. Neither the threat to life nor the lure of money would deter Shreeram from his chosen path of love. He wanted to marry Laxmi and spend at least two months with her before sailing again, and by that time, monsoon would hit the Arabian Sea.

'I think I will sail again only after she is carrying my first child. No one else can touch her again,' he told Suleiman smugly.

The trucks had to be moved quickly from the industrial area at Bhavnagar where they had been parked. That place was too close to the area controlled by the Godmother, and she had not been taken into confidence. She would not like others trespassing on her territory, even if it was Salim. Suleiman called Hanif.

'What do we do, Hanif Bhai? This guy is simply not ready to budge and getting another trustworthy chap to sail at such short notice will be difficult. It will take at least a couple of months before I can call one of our trusted vessels back from their Africa run.'

'Did you offer more money to the *khalasis*? They could put some pressure on Shreeram.'

'Bhai, the guy has turned unpredictable. I don't think we should trust him anymore.'

'We have to keep it safe then.' Hanif thought for a while. 'Call Charak, that bootlegger smuggling liquor from Rajasthan into Gujarat. He owes me. He has a wadi in Junagadh Forest where he used to hide his liquor. Keep the barrels there, and let me know the location of the wadi, in case anything happens to him. Pay him what he asks.'

And so, through a bizarre conjunction of death and life, the barrels, conceived in a moment of sexual ecstasy, were consigned to a barren wadi in the wilderness.

17

The Toll of Bells

Chudasama had brought that wisp of information shortly after the conclusion of their Kutch visit.

'There is a transporter who normally arranges trucks for smugglers. He has been approached by one of the locals, now based in Dubai, to provide two trucks, probably for Salim.'

Prakash was stunned. Salim saga seemed to follow him wherever he went.

'Isn't Salim lying low after the bomb blasts? I thought he was hibernating.'

'He never stops. And at the moment, he needs money more than ever. Regular flow from extortion and smuggling has been interrupted. All the gangs are exploring new avenues.'

'What's the source of information?' Prakash asked.

'None. The transporter was unsure because there has been heightened vigil after the bomb blasts, and he sought the advice of a police sub-inspector. A constable, a habitual drinker who often sources his liquor from us, overheard them talking of a big don of Dubai requiring some trucks to move some chemicals.'

'So, an alcoholic constable hears about transport of some chemicals for a Dubai-based operative who seems to be working for some big don. Where is Salim in this? And what is the contraband?' Prakash was surprised. This seemed like a conversation that did not even merit filing in the intelligence logs.

Chudasama allowed himself the faintest of smiles.

'I assumed that the way Salim's consignments follow you,

this must also be Salim's.' He waited for Prakash to smile, which he dutifully did, and then continued, 'Batuk, the transporter, is suspecting Salim. He said so.'

Prakash was still not convinced about Salim being involved in the case.

'We can't go by his suspicions. And what is the consignment, after all?'

This time, Chudasama had a broader smile.

'You have changed in the past four months, sir,' he stated. 'You are more confident. You don't accept a statement at face value anymore, cross-question even us, and don't chase every lead anymore. You have worked hard to develop informants, without knowing how to. You travelled, and learnt a lot on those travels. But you have to remember, you have just spent four months here, and the trust of informants is rarely developed in such a short period. Trust, sir, is something that is given after considerable thought. In fact, even we start by not trusting anybody, including our colleagues.'

Where is this leading? wondered Prakash, but he decided to listen. After all, Chudasama was not one to engage in discourses.

'You have, however, despite your known inexperience, brought a lot of respect to our office here. All intelligence agencies acknowledge that the new assistant director, RI, that is you, means business, is dedicated and is backed by a competent team. We were always the best, but we lived in the shadows that we had created for ourselves, unsure if we had a role beyond what was laid down in the rule book. You seem unaware of the rule book, have no respect for jurisdiction and you brazenly walk in anywhere, unafraid of the consequences.'

'You mean, as the boss says, that I am brash and I don't know my limits,' Prakash said with a smile.

Chudasama returned the smile.

'Yes. The boss has been calling me, trying to convince me that as I am the more experienced intelligence operative, I should guide and convince you not to be overzealous. That stepping out of bounds often leads to problems. Raijada has also received similar calls.'

'And so, this is the counselling session?' Prakash asked.

'No,' replied Chudasama. 'Raijada and I discussed it. There may be a lot wrong with you. You are too trusting, for one. Second, you refuse to keep a low profile. Third, you venture into uncharted waters. But then, there are no manuals when it comes to intelligence agents, and you, since your arrival, have created a buzz that is leading a lot of people to us. The more the people trust us, the higher the flow of intelligence.'

Prakash waited for Chudasama to continue.

'The intelligence flow from informers has picked up in the recent past, as has inter agency cooperation. It's time to exploit these gains. You are under threat, and one can't live forever waiting for someone to strike you from the shadows. So, we have crafted a strategy to force Salim to play his hand.'

'To kill me, you mean,' Prakash said with a laugh.

'As I said when you joined, we would know when somebody picks up that contract. That now holds true more than ever. So, we are going to give Salim a lot to think about in the near future. He will, henceforth, be implicated as the prime accused in any case that we detect. Even if there is another mastermind, Salim will still be made a co-accused. This will be a clear message that we have declared a war against him. He will be forced to retaliate. He can't afford not to retaliate. He will lose face.'

Prakash laughed, a conspiratorial laugh that conveyed his concurrence.

'So you want to cut my life short by foisting false cases on Salim,' he said, with more appreciation than rancour. 'But there seems to be just some chemicals in this consignment. Will Salim be even remotely affected by it? He has much bigger cases to worry about.'

'Nobody manufactures chemicals here,' countered Chudasama.

'There is no hint of illegality,' Prakash retorted.

'But still the transporter is looking for security.'

They argued, more to bring clarity to their thoughts than anything else.

'What should we do?' Prakash asked, unable to reach a consensus on the desired course of the action.

'Let's run the source on Batuk,' Chudasama offered.

'It will take at least a couple of days for the permissions to come in,' Prakash mentioned.

'My guy in the telephone department will start the tap immediately if we show him the proposal.'

'Okay. What else?'

'We have to assume that if they are running an operation that requires two trucks, then it is big enough for them to run counter-surveillance. You and I have to launch an elaborate charade that convinces them that we are going about our daily routine. I am also placing Rathor on a twenty-four-hour watch over you, except when you are at the office.'

'Who is Rathor?' Prakash asked.

'The guy who has been keeping a watch on your house. You will meet him,' replied Chudasama.

'So, you are finally telling me that you had somebody keeping a watch on my house.' Prakash was riled up. He had vaguely expected something to the effect, especially since Chudasama had said that his house was safe. But then, he quickly calmed down. There would be time to take up the issue with Chudasama later.

'Okay, we run the tap on Batuk,' he said, coming back to the topic at hand. 'And we keep leaving and entering the office regularly, leave the home lights on. What else?'

'We need the Bhuj staff for backup immediately, sir. Batuk would not have started counter-surveillance yet. We need to take precautions that he does not see too much movement in the office when his trucks move. Raijada would anyway be needed.'

Prakash agreed, and two men from Bhuj landed the next day.

They waited, and nothing happened for three days. They waited, maybe, for nothing to happen.

◆

In Dubai, Salim was fretting. His organization, painstakingly built with blood, was still collapsing. He had, by now, accepted that the police, one of the cornerstones for the survival of his organization, had abandoned him. But he was surprised by the ferocity with which they had gone after his people. He couldn't understand that it was the vengeance of the betrayed. His people could not tolerate the heat. They all escaped, some via Nepal, others using the Burma route. That left a vacuum on the streets of Bombay. There was nobody to tell his boys what to do next. The boys started to look for other work. That stopped the flow of information from India.

The politicians stopped answering his calls. He had hoped that they would turn back to him once the furore had died down, once people forgot the blasts. Normal people always tried to forget all the bad things that happened to them. And after all, he was the one that provided politicians with men to crowd their rallies, to take their voters to the booth and to capture the booths. But now, he was being made a symbol of what was wrong with the country. His opponents would not allow the people to forget his misdeeds. They kept telling the people—go about your daily work, but vote out the people who let Salim flourish.

The last, and the unkindest cut of them all, was the split in the gang on religious lines. He reminded Hanif, virtually every day, that he had predicted this. And with every loss of a valuable lieutenant, there arrived a new wannabe who wanted to make his name and stake a claim to a part of Bombay, and he was powerless to enforce his writ.

Hanif was stoic. He had also underestimated the scale of the backlash. But he hoped that his God would reward him for avenging the death of his brothers and sisters. The loss of power pinched. He may have his reward in the afterlife, but he was alive now, and he missed the homage of fawning film stars, the deference of the money seekers, the obeisance of the people seeking favours and above all, the fear of death in the eyes of the people when he was angry. He was human, and he had not linked his fortunes to that of Salim for the pleasures of the afterworld. He rued pushing Salim to support the designs of the Pakistanis, but what was done was done, and there were still things to be done.

Salim was chafing that Monday morning. Nobody had called him over the weekend, no one had come to meet him and the film producers he had called were all inexplicably away. He had nothing to do on a Saturday and Sunday!

'Hanif Bhai,' he said for the umpteenth time. 'I told you we should not have gone with those Pakis. We are losing our watan.'

Hanif kept silent. He knew that no answer was going to satisfy Salim.

'And we are strained for money. I still owe the sheikhs,' Salim continued. 'No money has been received from India for the past six months. Even the Pakis have not given the hundred crore that were promised.'

Hanif knew that the Pakis were squeezing them. They wanted to use Salim's network in other countries to strengthen their smuggling channels for heroin. They had offered to pay them in heroin, but Salim had refused. It would mean setting up channels for the movement of heroin, and he didn't want to lose the little support that was still left by being labelled a heroin trafficker. Hanif wondered how long he would be able to hold out.

'The money can't be transferred from India, Bhai,' Hanif replied. 'The hawala routes from India to Dubai are temporarily choked. There are hundred million dollars lying in cash with Sheth, but no way to transfer it. The accounts in Europe are being watched closely by Interpol. Maybe another six months Bhai, things will be normal. Inshallah.'

'That's what you said a month back, and I am telling you, things will never be the same. Face it, Hanif Bhai, we were party to the killing of innocent people; their blood will always be on our hands. We are now the outcasts of the world, not the Robin Hoods of the yesteryears. That's our destiny, and let's try and make the best out of it. But at the moment, I need some money immediately. Even fifty crore will do. Should I try and transfer money from the Montenegro account?'

'Bhai, wait a couple of weeks. I think I should be able to move that consignment of Mandrax lying in Junagadh. I have talked to Abdullah, and he is ready to sail from Kasargod in a couple of weeks. And then, another couple of weeks for it to reach Africa. This time we will bring the diamonds straight to Dubai.'

'That's still a month away.'

'Bhai, I will work it out.'

'Any problems in moving the Junagadh consignment?' Salim asked.

'A little. We don't have a reliable transporter on that side, and the Bombay transporters are all under watch. I am using Miyanchacha's transporter, and he is taking some time to work out the logistics,' Hanif said.

'Does he know what he is transporting?'

'No Bhai. We are calling it chemicals, and I think he is assuming acetic anhydride. No need to make him privy to the details.'

'Tell Miyanchacha to ring him up tonight. Let's move fast.'

◆

The call from Dubai was logged at the electronic surveillance centre, also known as the source room, at 11.26 p.m. The caller was identified as Miyanchacha. It was a brief conversation, lasting only one minute and fifty-three seconds. Miyanchacha, after identifying himself, asked Batuk to send two trucks—with valid national permits—ultimately destined for Mangalore, to Baba Dham, the day after tomorrow. The drivers were to expect a 'Loola Glass' who would hand the driver a ten rupee note. The serial number was read out over the phone. The caller assured that the money would be good.

Pandey, manning the source room that night, immediately rang up Chudasama who, after a brief conversation, picked up Raijada and went to Prakash's house. The watcher at the end of the street signalled an 'all clear' to Chudasama, and once they were sure that Prakash's house was not under watch, they entered the building at 1 a.m.

They went to work immediately. The logistics were confounding. They were not sure where Baba Dham was. They did not have any details regarding the registration numbers of the trucks that would be going there, or who were the drivers handling this particular consignment. Simply put, they had nothing except a tentative time frame.

'Baba Dham', Prakash wrote on the white board.

'I think it's the temple at Junagadh, sir,' Raijada said.

Prakash looked at Chudasama questioningly. He thought for a while. 'Possible,' he replied. The response was written against 'Baba Dham' with a question mark.

'Where in Baba Dham?' asked Prakash.

'We will listen to the conversation in the morning again. But, if there is no reference of it in the phone conversation, then they normally meet at the octroi post,' Chudasama said.

'Who knows the outlay of the octroi checkpost?' Prakash asked. Apparently, none of them did.

He moved on.

'Resources? First point. Number of people?'

'We have, at the moment, Pandey, Patel, you and me from our

office in Jamnagar, and Raijada and Moin from the Bhuj office. One person needs to be left behind to monitor the electronic surveillance.'

'Let us leave two men. Electronic surveillance is important. Leave Patel and Moin. They can live in the office. I don't think that we need so many people in the field. After all, how long can the operation last,' Prakash said, making his first mistake.

'So a four-man team,' concurred Chudasama, 'and Chavda, the sepoy.'

'He will be an asset. Good hand with the rifle in case things get bad,' confirmed Raijada.

'And we can add Rathor, the autorickshaw driver who keeps a watch on your house. He is trustworthy, and has been under my wing for the past fifteen years. He can bring his motorcycle that will be an asset in the operation.'

'So, that makes it a six-people operation. I think it should be adequate. Vehicles?' asked Prakash.

'The office Gypsy cannot be used. It's marked. Let us engage one of our regular taxi drivers. Then there is Rathor's motorcycle. That's two vehicles with Jamnagar number plates. We need at least one car with a Rajkot registration number. Three vehicles with Jamnagar number plates moving together will look suspicious,' Chudasama said again.

'Patel's personal car is registered in Rajkot,' added Raijada.

'Let's take that,' Prakash decided and then asked, 'Weapons?'

'Chavda needs his rifle,' said Chudasama. 'So he should travel in Patel's car. Taxis are prone to more checks than private cars. Raijada and I will carry our .38s. What about you, sir?'

'Issue an office pistol for Pandey. We can share that,' Prakash said. He still did not trust himself with a gun. He had proven to be trigger-happy in the past.

With the logistics sorted out, they got down to planning the operation. The uncertainty about Baba Dham still haunted them.

'What if Baba Dham is a code and not the temple at Junagadh?' Prakash asked.

'We cannot follow the trucks from Jamnagar. They will abort the operation if we are spotted. I would prefer to reach the destination of the trucks before the trucks reach there, lie in wait, and spot this Loola Glass when he meets the drivers,' replied Chudasama.

'Who is this Loola Glass?' asked Prakash. 'Do you guys know of him?'

Chudasama glanced at Raijada, and then replied, 'We thought you would know of him. He is Salim's point man in Ahmedabad. He has a big farm outside Vatva where he runs a hotel. He was picked up by the police after the bomb blasts, but it was clear that he was not involved. A large number of witnesses vouched that he had not ventured out of the hotel for at least a couple of months before the bomb blasts. His involvement confirms that this is Salim's consignment, and that...' he added, '...Salim and your fate is intertwined.'

Prakash thought of Shabnam, and wondered if that was actually true. He gave Chudasama a wry smile. 'Why is he called Loola Glass?'

Raijada did the briefing this time. 'His name is Nippu and the farm was a gift from Salim when he lost his left arm after he was run over by a Customs vehicle in Daman, where he was trying to escape with ten jackets of gold. Now he drinks his liquor in copious quantities by holding the glass up by his teeth, although he still has the use of his right arm. That is why Loola Glass, the handicapped tumbler man. He was caught in 1988, came out of jail in 1990 and he has been out of our watch list since then. Salim must really be running short of operatives if he had to call Loola Glass out of retirement.'

'So what do we do? Can we not follow this Glass character?' queried Prakash.

'No. For one, we don't know his immediate location. He has

been dormant for so long that he is no longer on our radar. Secondly, he recognizes all of us. They will abort their mission immediately if he gets even the slightest whiff of us.'

They were stymied. Then Prakash ventured again. 'One thing is certain. They are going to Mangalore. If that is the case, can we not track them from the exit points of Jamnagar?'

The idea was discussed from all angles. There were two main exits from Jamnagar. One going to Rajkot, the other going to Okha. If the trucks had to go to Junagadh, they would have to pass through Dhrol. While one person would be deployed at Dhrol railway crossing, another team would keep a close watch on the Okha route. The Junagadh team would make a run for Okha if the trucks were spotted on that route. The surveillance on the road was anyway not expected to last long. The trucks had to move by morning of the day after next.

'Tomorrow,' said Prakash. 'It's already three now. But do we have any way to identify the trucks?'

Chudasama brought out a list with a flourish.

'These are the nineteen trucks that are controlled by Batuk. I know that three are being repaired, and two are on long-term contract with the contractors building the refinery. That leaves fourteen trucks that we must look out for. All of them, except one, have a Jamnagar registration, so we have to only remember the last two digits.'

There was consternation on Raijada's face as he said, 'That's twenty-eight numbers. I am bad at numbers. I can't even remember my girlfriend's phone number and am always worried that my wife will find it in my diary.'

Prakash smiled. They were accepting him slowly as an equal, and not an outsider who was going to boss over them. He still missed the easy banter he used to share with Lal, but this team was building an equally good rapport. *Perhaps if Lal could also join them, the team would be complete*, Prakash thought.

◆

They parted at 4 a.m., deciding to rest a while. They staggered into the office again around noon. Logistics were quickly worked out and Pandey left for Junagadh at 7 p.m. with Chavda. They carried precise instructions: Book a hotel having basement parking, near the octroi naka. Use a pseudonym. Park the car in the basement. Come to octroi naka at 3 p.m. next day, on foot, unarmed, to meet them. Patel's team was to watch the Okha route. They were to follow the trucks if that route was taken. 'Don't take precipitous action,' they were told. 'Just follow them and inform the Junagadh team about the route taken.'

Rathor left with the motorcycle at 5 a.m. the next day to keep watch for the trucks from the Dhrol crossing.

◆

The others left at 9 a.m. and crossed Dhrol an hour later. Rathor shook his head imperceptibly, indicating that the trucks had not been spotted as yet. They met up with Pandey and Chavda early in the afternoon. Chudasama and Raijada left for the hotel with them, leaving Prakash to reconnoitre the octroi naka. Prakash looked around. The octroi tax post was like thousands of others that dotted the entrance to towns across the country—mini commercial centres with small huts providing photocopying services and small tea shops where drivers and the tax collectors' agents milled.

Prakash wandered a little. A couple of agents had shown a faint interest in him when he had alighted from the car, hoping for another client, but his attire quickly dispelled their notions. Prakash was sporting a small rucksack over his collarless t-shirt and jeans, hoping to look like a young tourist.

Prakash supposed that he wouldn't be noticed unless he did something stupid. He occupied a bench at one of the tea shops, ordered the sugary, strongly flavoured beverage, opened a Ludlum novel and settled down to wait. As the sun touched the tall hills dominating the town, he prayed silently to all the gods residing on the hill for the success of the operation. What was this operation all about? They had discussed all possibilities, and still couldn't arrive at a conclusion. That had led to some problems at the time of getting the clearance from Singh, who could not understand the necessity of launching such a big operation without specifically knowing what, or whom, they were after.

'Are you sure that you are not chasing ghosts, Prakash?' he had asked. 'I hope it's not because of your personal enmity with Salim?'

'Sir, Loola Glass and two trucks, and a call from Dubai. There is something big in the works. We are in the middle of a lull anyway. There is no harm in chasing this,' he had replied.

Singh knew better than to try and dissuade a headstrong Prakash. But he would not let Prakash have a free run of the operation.

'Hundred hours,' Singh said. 'I am giving you a hundred hours to complete the operation. You cannot withdraw operatives from all units and expect me to wait for something to develop. After that, I want all of you back in your various offices. And name it Operation X,' he had said sarcastically. Prakash, now sitting alone, waited.

Rathor arrived with some good news soon.

'Two trucks from the list, 4917 and 7238, crossed Dhrol at 1 p.m. I left them after they had taken the turn for Junagadh. The drivers had stopped for lunch, so I think they should be here in an hour.'

Prakash's heartbeat quickened for a moment. He quickly glanced around, hoping to spot Loola. No limbless man anywhere. He waited.

True to Rathor's calculations, the trucks rolled in before sunset. The watchers had to now work in pairs. One of them would have to go to the hotel to alert the others whenever the trucks moved, while the other would have to follow the trucks. Chudasama and Raijada could not be the watchers. Their faces were too well known. That left four of them—Prakash, Pandey the IO, Chavda the sepoy and Rathor the autorickshaw driver. Thankfully, there were a number of tea stalls, which meant that they could spread out and watch without drawing any attention.

The first night, Chavda and Rathor took the taxi to the naka. After that they decided to continue watching in shifts of four hours, one team using the taxi, the other the car. The trucks did not move even the next day. They were in a fix. They were risking exposure by repeating shifts. Prakash regretted leaving behind Moin in the office.

Raijada offered to take the risk for the night saying, 'I am not well-known as Chudasama is in the Jamnagar smuggler circles. And it's night anyway. I will make sure that I remain in the shadows.'

Prakash, however, overruled the suggestion. He did not want any risks. Instead, he and Rathor took the taxi to the naka. The drivers were not sleeping in the trucks, he reported in the morning, as Pandey and Chavda replaced him again. The trucks seemed to be abandoned. Even the cleaners, who rarely, if ever, abandoned their trucks, were not visible. Prakash was getting fidgety.

They were running short on resources. And time. Sixty of the hundred hours were already over, and they were still in the waiting phase. They thought of calling for backup from Bhuj, but there was no time. And in any case, Singh may not agree. Instead, they decided to try a different approach. Two watchers, located at a distance from each other, to be replaced at different time intervals.

'Are you ready to shave your moustache, Raijada?' Prakash asked with a disarming laugh. Knowing that a Darbar prizes his moustache as much as his honour, he changed his own look instead. He shaved off his moustache, trimmed his eyebrows really close, donned a blue cap, packed a haversack and reached the spot riding the motorcycle. He commandeered a bench at one of the bigger tea shops, telling nobody in particular and everybody in general that he had rode in from Jamnagar, complaining about how bad the heat of Saurashtra was for a north Indian, smoking cigarettes, reading a novel. 'I am not going to venture out in this heat till the sun goes down. Then I'll drive to Gir,' he informed the dhaba owner, hoping that he had justified his presence. He was hiding in the open, confident that none would be able to identify him.

The two trucks Batuk had sent waited. The rest moved on after completing the octroi formalities. He wondered why nobody cared about the two trucks now parked for more than two days, and then realized that they were just as concealed in the open as he was.

The boy serving the tea periodically looked at the small pile of pinched cigarette stubs, but happy with the five-rupee tip, he let the guy with the motorcycle smoke his cigarettes peacefully. The dhaba owner looked over from the counter once or twice, but not finding any response he eventually decided to ignore him. Rathor arrived a little later, driving the taxi whose number plate had by now been replaced with a fake Junagadh registration, and parked at a distance. They waited.

◆

Loola Glass was impossible to miss. Five-feet-nothing, he was so thin he looked emaciated. The dishevelled hair and the two-day beard completed the picture of a habitual drunkard. He arrived at about 4 p.m. in one of the latest SUV. He got out, waited, and finding nobody in the trucks, moved on. He came back ten minutes later, and this time one of the drivers was waiting in the truck. Prakash realized that the drivers had been watching the trucks from unknown vantage points. He was relieved that none of them had ventured close to the trucks. Loola and the drivers talked briefly. The note was handed over, and they were ready to move. The trucks slowly followed the SUV through the crowded octroi post. They watched as another car joined the caravan. Prakash got on the motorcycle, went the other way, and stopped at some distance from the dhaba. Once he was sure that Rathor was following him, Prakash started following the trucks. They had waited for forty-eight hours for the trucks to move. It had been seventy-two hours since Singh had given Prakash the hundred hour deadline.

◆

During an intelligence operation, the best laid plans are often marred by bad decisions taken in the thick of action.

The caravan crawled through the crowded market. The SUV was leading the two trucks, which were being followed by the car. Prakash was close behind on the motorcycle, followed by Rathor in the taxi. Rathor had already phoned the teams to get ready. The SUV took the road towards Porbandar. There was little traffic in the evening and Prakash, once the route for the trucks was clear, signalled Rathor to bring the rest of the team from the hotel. About thirty kilometres into the drive, he started to wonder if Chudasama would guess that they would be moving so far ahead. That was when he realized his second mistake. He had not set up channels of communication for his team. They had not even decided upon a signal to inform each other of their tracks. They had never thought they would be so far apart. He hoped that the others would be following the route, trusting that he would find a way to communicate with them if something was amiss. *Why are we not issued pagers*? he raged. *Other elite intelligence agencies have them.*

There will be time for regrets and recriminations later. At the moment, he had to make sure not to lose sight of the trucks.

About thirty-five kilometres from Junagadh, just before Visavadar, the convoy turned right on a single-lane road. Prakash kept going straight on the highway and stopped when the trucks could not be seen anymore. He took out the map and traced the road with his finger. It seemed to lead into a thickly wooded part of Gir forest, and rejoined the highway about five kilometres ahead.

A meaningless road, possibly built to provide access to the farm of somebody rich and powerful, he thought. He wondered if the trucks had taken the road just to spot if they were being tailed. He decided to go ahead and wait at the other exit of the road. If the trucks came out and turned back towards Junagadh, then Rathor was bound to spot them. If they came out at the other exit, he would be able to follow them again.

The trucks did not come out from any exit. Rest of the team caught up with him half an hour later, and he explained the situation.

Chudasama was worried. 'They could have gone anywhere,' he said. 'It's best that we spot them before the night sets in. Pandey can start on the bike from the point where the trucks turned in, and the rest can enter from the other end. The taxi can wait over here with Chavda and Rathor.'

There was a sense of urgency in Chudasama's tone.

Prakash, however, chose the motorcycle again. 'In case they had spotted me on the bike, change of riders would fuel suspicion. None of us spotted that white car, and although I doubt that it had been there before, there is no reason to take chances,' he reasoned.

Prakash's heart thumped loudly as he entered the road as dusk set in. He could not tell if it was because of fear or anticipation. He rode slowly, like a tourist enjoying his outing in the forest. According to the map, the road was eleven kilometres long, just about a fifteen-minute drive.

We should be able to spot the trucks long before the night sets in, he thought.

The two groups soon crossed each other. Chudasama shook his head. They had not spotted the trucks! Prakash's heart sank. *I fucked up… Again!* In his very first operation with the new team.

How would I ever be able to live it down? For the moment, he had to put up a brave front.

'I would like to make another round. Did you see anybody? Or anything? Any counter surveillance?'

Nobody had spotted anything.

'Even then, we cannot take the chance of being spotted. I will go alone on the motorcycle and try to spot the tyre marks in case they went into the fields. They must have left some marks if they went in there,' he said, trying to reassure himself.

Chudasama looked significantly at the darkness falling in. They were in the lion's den, he possibly wanted to say.

'I will take fifteen minutes,' Prakash said. 'I will come out before it gets too dark.'

The motorcycle broke down five minutes later, and the surveillance team of the smugglers reached him hardly five minutes after that. A stocky man with a shotgun got out of an open jeep. Prakash kept fiddling with the bike, his heart thumping so loudly that he was sure the man walking towards him could hear it. He finally looked at the man when he did not move.

'I am an engineer from Jamnagar refinery,' he said in chaste Hindi, hoping to explain the Jamnagar registration of his bike. 'This map says that this road goes into the Gir, but there are no hotels here. And now my bike has broken down. Can you help?'

He only received a contemptuous look. The man tried to kick start the bike, but thankfully, it did not start. Another man got out of the jeep. This one sported an even burlier moustache than Raijada's. He looked over Prakash, and maybe because he seemed impossibly young and had no weapons on him, believed his story.

'It's getting dark,' the second man said as he got back into the jeep. 'Lions roam this area. We will see if we can send somebody, but don't depend on it. I advise that you drag your motorcycle on foot till the highway.'

Prakash wondered where Chudasama and others were. It would be catastrophic if they had decided to follow him out of loyalty. There was bound to be an exchange of fire. From afar, it would look as if he had been discovered and their operation had been blown. Would it have been better if he had followed them? Maybe even arrested and interrogated them on suspicion. Conflicting emotions swamped him. He missed Chudasama's experience. He decided to stay put. *We will, hopefully, get another chance*, he thought. He fiddled with the motorcycle, and realized that it was low on petrol. Opening the reserve cock, he exited the road.

Darkness set on the fields and shrouded the forest behind him.

◆

They were worried, but not yet defeated. The six men on the road had started with a whiff of intelligence, and now they knew that their hunch was correct. They also knew that the trucks were somewhere close by, and that the consignment was important enough to warrant a lookout.

Chudasama badgered him to describe the persons in the jeep in excruciating detail. 'Possibly Charak,' he said, after listening to him, 'and if he is involved, you were lucky. He is wanted for the murder of a policeman.'

'Have you studied every criminal in this area?' Prakash asked in wonder. 'Should I have followed them?'

'Only the big ones.' His inscrutable face neither reflected pride nor doubt. Like everything else with Chudasama, it was a fact. 'And it is good that you did not follow him. He is the most dangerous bootlegger of this area. Even the policemen don't mess with him. His involvement also means that whatever we are chasing is extremely valuable. He swims only with the whales.'

'What next? Do we continue our watch here?' Prakash asked them. He was, at the moment, full of self-doubt. However, he felt reassured looking at Chudasama and Raijada. They were the most seasoned intelligence operatives in the region. They had been part of countless operations and minor setbacks did not faze them. With these two beside him, there was always hope. They would know what to do.

'That would be inadvisable, sir.' It was Raijada who replied this time. His slow drawl was even more pronounced as he thought on his feet. 'We can easily be spotted over here. And they can keep the trucks concealed indefinitely. Their surveillance is likely to continue until the trucks actually depart, and our vehicles, waiting here, are like two black rocks on the white sands of Kutch. They can hide themselves forever if they spot us here. What we already know is that they are going to Mangalore, so they will have to take the Baroda highway. There are three ways to reach the highway from here—one of them is through an unpaved road of about eighty kilometres. It's doubtful that they will take that route. The other two routes meet the highway about eight kilometres apart at a town called Jetpur. It's better to place checkposts at those two exits.'

The decision was made, and they moved quickly. They identified the two exit points where the roads met the national highway, stationed the taxi at one exit and the car at the other. 'Here we go again,' Prakash murmured, as he and his team began the waiting.

◆

Every intelligence operative knows that the most difficult part of any operation is the waiting. Anything can go wrong while waiting. And now, they were back on the road, waiting, because of a bad call by Prakash. All of them hoped that the stars changing their positions during the night would change the tide of luck in their favour.

Time passed slowly for the four of them sitting separately at two junctions. At one junction, the taxi driver slept while Chavda sat like a vagabond on the road, peering at the trucks coming from

Junagadh. At the other junction, Rathor sat on the motorcycle at a cold drink stall, buying two hundred bottles of cola for a fictitious marriage party, which gave him a chance to look closely at every large vehicle. Chudasama, heading the team at one exit, and Raijada at the other, were calm, as if they knew the outcome of the operation in advance.

Prakash kept flitting between the two junctions. *It's like I have ants in my pants. I'm so jumpy,* he thought. *Is it because I lost the trucks? This will be discussed forever—the nincompoop lost the trucks, this waiting is interminable, time is being drawn out like a rusty sword from a scabbard. It's like the theory of relativity that they used to toss around in college. Time flies faster when you are sitting on a hot stove than when you are sitting in the lap of a pretty girl. Would time have passed faster if Shabnam had been here? Stop thinking of Shabnam! You are out here chasing Salim's consignment and yet you are thinking of his mistress!*

'What happens if they have taken the third route?' he asked Chudasama.

'That is unlikely, but then they would be lucky only for a couple of days. The drivers will have to call Batuk to update him and the surveillance team will pick up the conversation. In any case, now that we are in hot pursuit, we will chase them till Mangalore if we have to,' Chudasama replied calmly.

'And after that?' he asked, feeling slightly assured.

'That is what worries me. We don't know what they are carrying. Once we cross Saurashtra, we are out of our jurisdiction, and we will need to inform other units as well. What do we tell them? What are we chasing?'

'There is also that small matter of the hundred-hour deadline the boss has imposed,' Prakash said with a smile. 'Will he let another team join the chase if we cross that deadline?'

'We will cross that hurdle when we reach there,' Chudasma said.

'Should I go and take another round of the road where the trucks went in?' he wondered out loud.

'Wait, sir. This is the most difficult phase of any operation. Waiting. We already have a backup plan. Driving around is only going to reduce our available manpower. We are going to get them, at one place or another. Don't worry.' Chudasama was confidently soothing Prakash's nerves, and so he waited.

◆

Morning came slowly. The busy highway showed signs of slowing down as the truck drivers who had driven overnight stopped for morning ablutions and a cup of tea. A few early morning car drivers hit the highway. No one in the team had slept properly over the past three nights, and the early morning walkers looked curiously at the heavy lidded, dishevelled men and then, like people always do, walked on. The workers finishing their night shifts started to gather at the tea stall.

'This area is going to be buzzing with activity soon, sir. I think we have waited long enough. The trucks must have taken the dirt road. It's been more than twelve hours since they went into the wadi,' Chudasama said.

'I agree,' Prakash said. 'Let us have a cup of tea, and then I will go and call Raijada. We can plan the next course of action together.'

'Shall we meet at the hotel, sir?'

'No, let's first meet here. We have time till noon to check out from the hotel.'

Prakash's miserliness had manifested itself again.

◆

Two important words in the intelligence lexicon are *luck* and *patience*. The first is fickle, it can smile on either side. The other is confusing. It could be a virtue or a curse. Both, however, decided to side with

Prakash's team this time.

Prakash left after tea to bring Raijada's team, which kept all of them on the road for another hour. As he came back, he saw Loola Glass' SUV turning on the highway. He jumped up and down on the motorcycle, waving desperately to Chudasama, wondering why he was not intercepting it, forgetting that no one—except himself and Rathor—had seen the SUV before. *When am I going to learn that the minor details also need to be shared with the team!* Prakash kicked himself mentally for not sharing the number plate of the SUV with the others. Then he saw the trucks following the SUV, and as if in a surreal world, watched Chudasama get out of the car with his pistol in full sight, waving the truck down. He looked for the other truck and saw it rumbling to a stop behind the first one. Chavda was already pointing his rifle at the driver.

'Loola is getting away,' he shouted, pointing at the SUV. Loola peeped out of the SUV, taking in the scene, and then the SUV sped away

'Let him go, sir!' shouted Chudasama. 'We will find him.'

Prakash looked at the Kafkaesque scene in front of him. Two trucks parked in the middle of a street, one man pointing a revolver at one driver, another pointing a rifle at the other driver, a factory siren asking workers to report, and a gaggle of people passing by, just looking at them. Nobody questioned anything, nobody interfered. *How long can we brandish guns in the middle of a busy street?* he wondered.

◆

The trucks were loaded with sacks of wheat, and the drivers, after they had opened the back of their trucks, were belligerent. 'You could have killed us!' they said. 'Honest guys carrying wheat! Who are you anyway?'

Chudasama and Raijada rummaged the driver's cabins as Chavda and Pandey covered the drivers. The drivers produced documents for the transportation of sixteen tonnes of wheat to Mangalore. When nothing was found in the cabins, Rathor and Chavda started dumping the wheat bags on the road. A crowd of curious onlookers had now gathered around them. They seemed unconcerned about the rifle and the two revolvers being openly brandished by his team, and Prakash was astonished at their foolhardiness. They were not worried that they may soon be embroiled in a gun fight. He kept a wary eye on the onlookers, wondering if any of them were Salim's men.

Three layers deep, they found a few drums. The drivers, already worried when they had started unloading the wheat, now looked crestfallen. But then, they produced another set of documents for the transport of machine oil. The discovery of the barrels gave heart to the team. However, Prakash was now fidgety, remembering the attacks on Customs in Khambaliya where smugglers had run over two inspectors while fleeing with a truck loaded with contraband silver. He remembered Kanwar's advice, and decided to move to safety. They were vulnerable on this road, just the four of them effectively, in an area dominated by a bootlegger who was wanted for murder. He decided to make a dash for it and head for Jamnagar, irrespective of the consequences. 'Saving lives is more important. I will face the consequences if there is no contraband in the trucks,' he told his team. So they scrambled on to the vehicles. Prakash got into the taxi leading the caravan, and Chudasama and Raijada scrambled into Patel's car to guard the rear. Pandey and Chavda rode the trucks. The protesting drivers were threatened with dire consequences and they finally acquiesced. After all, they belonged to Jamnagar and were aware of RI's power.

Following Prakash's lead, the phalanx of vehicles ran a charge never seen before in the region. Police barricades were ignored, slow-moving vehicles ahead of them had to give way after constant honking by Prakash's taxi, and nobody was permitted to overtake their convoy. A couple of times Chavda hung out of the truck's door to scream profanities at vehicles that did not move out of the way. An angry, long line of honking motorists trailed the caravan impatiently as they crossed the octroi checkpost at Jamnagar. The policemen tried to stop them from entering a zone closed for heavy vehicles during the day, but were shouted down. Police wireless crackled, mentioning a possible hijacking and violence on Gondal road. But by the time the police could scramble their forces together, the trucks were safely parked outside the RI office.

◆

The drivers were sullen, and also aggressive. 'There is wheat in the trucks and barrels full of chemicals. There may be some mistake in the documents, but that was no reason to drag us a hundred kilometres away from our job,' they said.

'We have brought you home. You should be happy,' Raijada told them in a sarcastic tone. Their request to contact their families or the owner of the truck were turned down summarily. But the interrogation was failing miserably. The drivers stuck to the story. It seemed that they knew of the barrels, but little else beyond that.

It was already afternoon by the time they were able to unload all the sacks of wheat and the barrels from the trucks. Raijada could not stop his sneezing.

'I am allergic to hay, sir,' he said apologetically.

The wheat sacks contained what was expected—wheat. The barrels had black machine oil, and there was no apparent cavity dividing them. The rods pushed into the barrels had gone in all the way, suggesting that there was no partition inside them.

There was gloom in the office. The operation, with all its ups and downs, seemed to be headed for a disaster.

'I need to inform the boss,' Prakash said.

Chudasama nodded gloomily.

'It's inexplicable,' Prakash said. 'If everything is above board, what was the need for such secrecy? Why load the wheat, why identify each other through notes…and then the surveillance mounted by them? Was this a trial run for something truly valuable? Or did they change their plans at the last moment.'

'We need to interrogate these drivers more. Maybe we should have intercepted Loola as well when we had the chance,' Chudasama said. 'He could have told us.'

'*Double, double toil and trouble; fire burn and cauldron bubble,*' Prakash muttered, remembering the witches of *Macbeth* as Singh called him half an hour later.

'So you are back before the hundred-hour deadline. Any success?'

'Will brief you shortly, sir,' Prakash replied in a low voice.

'Have you guys, by any chance, been breaking police barricades?' he asked, carrying on without even listening to Prakash's response, expecting a natural denial.

'Why, sir? What happened?' Prakash tried to stall, knowing deep down that he was in for some heavy flak. Officers were supposed to be dignified and sombre, not running around the countryside screaming at police patrols who were doing their legitimate duty.

'I got a call from the DGP. He said that two vehicles, sandwiching two trucks, entered Jamnagar, and the people in the cars were waving guns. They also shouted that they are from the RI. He wanted to be sure that it was not us before sending out an alert. These are sensitive times, what with the bomb blasts in Bombay and all that.'

Oh shit, thought Prakash. *Terrorists.* He had forgotten to factor that in while planning his dash from Jetpur. At the time it had seemed like the perfect idea.

'Actually, sir, it was us…' he said hesitantly.

There was a pregnant pause at the other end, and then the phone exploded. Chudasama could hear the fragments. 'Too young… immature…what do I reply.' Prakash's feeble protests were being disregarded, particularly when he could not tell him what the trucks contained. *Singh is more worried about his loss of face than about the safety of his team*, Prakash realized. But then, Prakash thought fairly, *Singh could not know that their dash had been necessary to eliminate the possibility of violence in unknown territories.*

He was bracing for a long diatribe that would also, possibly, curtail his future scope of working in the RI when his driver Manu Bhai rushed in, all excited.

'The rod is not going sideways! There is something wrong in some of the barrels! They seem to be double walled,' he exclaimed loudly.

Prakash looked hopefully at his possible redeemer, a little bit of confidence restored.

'I will call you back, sir. You can please inform the DGP that we escorted two trucks from Jetpur to Jamnagar under threat of life.'

◆

The cavity so cleverly designed by Salim would have withstood normal, or even detailed, scrutiny by Customs. It certainly would not have been detected in any routine road check conducted by the transport or the octroi departments, or even by the police. However, it could not withstand a few hours of intense probe by a team of determined officers. Manu Bhai, with all his frustration of having been left out of the operation, was raring to go and play his part since the trucks had rolled in. Even after everyone had given up, he was still poking around the barrels. There were six hundred bags of wheat, he counted. And only fifty-two barrels. He kept saying 'Six hundred is not divisible by fifty-two'. Manu Bhai's illogical logic stumped Prakash. He could barely suppress his laughter when Manu Bhai explained the reason for his persistence.

Manu Bhai had kept probing, saying, 'Six hundred is not divisible by fifty-two.' He first tasted the machine oil to check if it was adulterated, but it was just that—machine oil. He had seen iron rods being pushed into the barrels and go right through. So he shook the barrels, but the weight seemed to be okay. He then opened all the barrels, one after other, exploring each for a false bottom. And then, somewhere on the thirtieth or the thirty-first barrel, the rod struck something as he was pulling it out. He probed diligently. There seemed to be a wall on one side. He rotated the rod. There seemed to be a chamber, skilfully partitioned from the rest of the barrel. He checked the other barrels and came up with the same result. There seemed to be a tubular compartment inside each barrel.

He decided to inform Prakash.

◆

'What do you mean you will call me back?' Singh was saying. 'What threat? What is in the trucks?'

'I will tell you, sir, after it's confirmed. I need another half an hour,' Prakash replied, disconnecting the call.

Singh, at the other end, stared incredulously at the phone. *I will skin Prakash alive if he screwed this up*, he thought. *Meanwhile, I will tell the DGP that there is a new boy who is prone to panic.*

◆

The excitement of finally discovering the secret of the barrels brought renewed hope to the tired team. Then, as the tools for opening the barrels were brought in, a word of caution came from Chudasama.

'Be careful,' he told everybody, 'it could also contain explosives.'

'It cannot be explosives. Not in these quantities,' said Prakash. But the seeds of doubt had been planted. What if these were leftover explosives from the bomb blasts that were now being disposed of? They debated if they should call police experts. But Prakash dithered. He had messed up too often in the operation, and was loathe to call any other agency in case another failure stared them in the face. He asked the boys to be extra careful. 'No jerks. No sparks. Open it gently. Treat the barrels as you treat your girlfriends,' he said in a poor attempt at humour. Nobody laughed.

They used a small chisel, without a hammer, to open the first barrel. It was like trying to cut frozen butter with a paper knife, and took full fifteen minutes before they could spot the polythene packets full of white tablets. This speeded up their task. Now they freely used the hammer as it became evident that there was no risk of explosion. The first packet was pulled out by Chudasama. He looked at the white tablets, marked with an inverted 'M' on one side and the Swastika on the other, and said, amazed, 'Mandrax!'

'Mandrax,' Prakash was bewildered. 'Mandrax from Junagadh?'

They had discussed all possible kinds of contraband likely to be carried, but even in their wildest imagination, they had not expected Mandrax. For one, there was not even a whiff of any intelligence of any laboratories in Saurashtra. And then, Salim in narcotics? That was the first time they had heard of it. As per intelligence reports, Salim had always shunned narcotics.

It was going to be a long haul of an investigation to establish that this consignment actually belongs to Salim, thought Prakash.

Barrel after barrel started to reveal their secret stash, all of them packed tightly with plastic bags of tablets.

'How much is it likely to be?' Prakash asked.

'We have weighed the first barrel, and it was nearly 100 kg. So far, we have opened twelve barrels, and all of them contain the tablets,' replied Raijada.

'God Almighty above! It's going to be nearly five tonnes of Mandrax,' he whispered in awe.

'Seems like it,' replied Chudasama, walking up to him. 'The biggest ever seizure of Mandrax tablets in India so far, sir. Maybe the highest in the world. You are lucky for the unit,' he said, pumping

Prakash's hand in a rare display of emotion.

Raijada came up and shook his hand with a twinkle in his eye. 'That clean shaven look, keep it for a while. It seems to work. Maybe it will land you a girl too.'

Chavda came out of the office, calling for Prakash. Singh was on the phone. He sounded irritated and was demanding to speak to Prakash immediately.

'You were supposed to get back to me in half an hour. You didn't call. Why are you shying away from calling me?' he demanded, anger palpable in his voice.

'Sorry, sir, but Chudasama and I were discussing where can we safely store approximately five tonnes of Mandrax tablets that were being transported in the trucks that we just escorted from Jetpur. I thought I would call you once the drugs—worth more than 500 crore in the international market—were secured.' Prakash was enjoying himself, underplaying one of the largest hauls of drugs in recent history.

'Five tonnes! Five thousand kilograms! Are you sure?' Singh, probably for the first time in his life, was at a loss for words.

'Give or take a thousand kilos, sir,' replied Prakash in his typical cavalier manner. 'I will call you back when I have the exact quantity...,' he said, '...and could you please tell DGP sir that a possible retaliation by Loola Glass, who escaped our net, prompted the rash dash?' He disconnected the phone before Singh could say anything, chuckling silently.

Less than four months, and a major successful operation, wondered Singh. *He had started without even knowing what was being smuggled. He had nearly blundered with the way he escorted the trucks. And now, possibly the largest ever interception of Mandrax in the world. What a bloody lucky nincompoop!*

18

The Aftermath

Dubai

Salim Muchchad fumed, and the anger turned into rage when it dawned on him that there were so few people who cared. He raged in his bungalow, with just Hanif there to listen to his rantings.

'What happened?' he asked after he had regained his composure.

'Loola could not tell us all the facts. But there were patrolling parties waiting for them near Rajkot. They knew about him too, but he was able to escape. The trucks have been taken to the Jamnagar office of RI.'

'Have they found the cavity?' he asked.

'No idea yet.'

'Can we buy them? Pay them twenty lakhs, fifty lakhs, maybe? Will they hush up the case?'

'We don't have many contacts on that side, Bhai. We just went there to keep the Mandrax off the Maharashtra coast, which, as you know, has been sensitive after the bomb blasts.' He did not know how to proceed further but knew that he had to. 'Loola was saying there is a new chap heading that unit, some guy called Prakash.' Hanif said it quickly, hoping that Salim would miss it, but then he saw Salim's body go rigid. He knew the connection had been made.

'Prakash. That idiot from Ratnagiri?' he asked in a cold voice.

'Maybe. I am trying to find out,' Hanif replied.

'Isn't he dead? I asked you to give a supari,' Salim said in an ominous tone.

'I told Rangeela,' he replied, 'but he had to lay low after the blasts.'

'And before that?' questioned Salim.

'I mentioned it to Master, but did not push it. Later, what with all the arrangements he had to make for landing the sabun and all the other guns and ammunition, he didn't follow up on it.'

Salim suppressed his anger. These were the few people who were helping him rebuild the network that had been destroyed in the aftermath of the bomb blasts. He could not break off with them too. But an example would have to be made. Soon, he promised himself.

'So a deal cannot be made?'

'If it is Prakash from Ratnagiri, I don't think so,' Hanif replied.

'Will they be able to link me to the consignment?'

'There is no possibility of that. You have been totally distanced from this. Everything is in Qasim's name.'

'I would hate to be implicated in a narcotics case. There is no bail. I will never be able to go back to India if that happens. I may be able to beat the rap for murder, even arms smuggling. But a case under the Narcotics Act. There is no getting out of that one, Hanif Bhai.'

'You will never be linked with this, Bhai,' Hanif said confidently. 'They won't be able to implicate even Qasim. The links have been broken at every stage. And I will ask Miyanchacha not to go to India. The transporter only knows that Miyanchacha had called him.'

Salim felt a little better. He still had money problems, but he would give his gold souk to the sheikhs as compensation. That would make him lose a lot of face in the eyes of the people he lived with, but at this stage it was inevitable. The seething anger against Prakash resurfaced.

'What about Loola?'

'He is flying to Nepal tonight. I am setting him up with Charulatha in Pokhara. He won't come back to India for at least a year.'

'Hanif Bhai, make sure Prakash is killed before he does any more damage,' he directed.

Hanif nodded.

'When is the route for funnelling money through Nepal opening?' Salim asked, shifting to the other aspects of his business.

◆

Bombay

The word on the street was that Salim Bhai was losing influence. Nobody knew the details, but there were rumours about an old loyalist who had been called out for handling a major consignment, which was, even then, lost to RI. The street also heard that the bounty on Prakash, an assistant director in RI, had gone up to ten peti.

As the news of the Mandrax seizure by the Jamnagar RI spread, the boys started to put two and two together. The whisper campaign by rival gangs grew louder—'Bhai has gone into drug smuggling', 'Bhai is in financial trouble' and 'Bhai has shaken hands with the devil'. The underworld was in a turmoil, turmoil that would churn out wolfsbane.

Salim had to do something big, something that would firmly re-establish his authority. People were defaulting on their payments, even legitimate payments. And he was losing the muscle power to enforce his writ and authority. He needed a high-profile target. The first victim of Salim's efforts to regain control over Bombay was Nazir, the person who had produced at least ten movies from Salim's money. The movies had been hits, and he had faithfully paid all the monies that were due to Salim Bhai. The movies had also established him as a canny producer, with a reputation for spotting good scripts. Directors and financiers flocked to him with money to produce movies for them now. He too believed that Salim had lost control and decided to produce his next movie without approaching Salim. And when Hanif called for the new girl, Abby, to be cast in the movie, he refused, saying, 'I have an obligation to my financiers, Bhai. Abby can't act at all. If you say so, I will cast Shabnam.' He was shot dead a week later by a rookie sharpshooter from Azamgarh who had been paid one peti for the hit. This was the beginning of a sequence of attacks on film personalities and builders ordered by Salim, all by unknown, new, wannabe gangsters. It shook Bombay for the next couple of years.

◆

The Intelligence World

There was near unanimity that the seizure of Mandrax had been an accident. The spies of old who had used Salim's resources for operations in distant lands stated indulgently that Bhai was too big to be affected by a small seizure, even if it was of narcotics. Prakash was anyway a nincompoop who didn't know his ass from his mouth. Why was he unnecessarily upsetting the apple cart? Didn't he know that the world ran on give and take? 'Just see, it will be business as usual soon with Bhai. The intelligence flow anyway will be better than ever now that there will be three or four powerful gangs. We can now prop up anybody, but if we help Bhai now, he will be obligated more than ever when he is back in business,' said one of the spies. The spies of the old still placed their faith on Salim.

They were proved to be way off in their assessment of both Prakash and Salim. Prakash and Chudasama, as they had already decided earlier, set about linking Salim with the consignment with a vengeance. And now that they knew the Mandrax actually belonged to Salim, they upped the ante. The truck owner was forced to state that Miyanchacha had told him over the phone that the consignment belonged to Salim. A charge sheet was promptly filed against Salim in the NDPS court. Hanif tried to explain to Salim that the evidence was not just circumstantial, but outrightly concocted and that the case would be thrown out in the first hearing, but in the later analysis, it was found that it was this seizure that ended Salim's chances of returning to India.

Salim, starved of money, turned bitter and started severing ties with his old patrons, which led to a drying up of intelligence flowing in from Salim's network. That probably led to a couple of major intelligence failures over the next couple of years.

◆

Prakash

People in Jamnagar did not know that Prakash was considered a nincompoop by his department. For them, the operation that led to the seizure of Mandrax could have been led only by a seasoned intelligence officer. Prakash became a minor celebrity. There were constant demands for interviews by the local newspapers. He tried to explain that it was a team that had succeeded and that the largest seizures of drugs always had a luck component. But these statements were interpreted as a sign of humility and made the press love him all the more. But try as they would, he would not let them print his photograph.

'Reserve it for the stars and the politicians,' he said.

The reporters laughed and eulogized him. They were having a field day, ruing the inaction of the police and applauding the heroism of the RI, especially the young guy who had decided to take on the mighty underworld. As it came out that Salim was involved in this consignment of drugs, the term 'narco-terrorism' was floated around, rather liberally.

Prakash wanted the news to die down.

He was being hounded for being successful and this threatened his cheerful and cavalier attitude towards life. The bosses anyway never liked his cheerful and devil-may-care attitude, and now the public also wanted to see a sober, intense and brave hero. The anti-hero within him was on the verge of being exterminated.

19

Towards Denouement

'So how does it feel to be a celebrity?' Kabir, the District Superintendent of Police, asked Prakash as they sat in Prakash's bachelor pad, sipping on a fast-depleting bottle of Swing, a fortnight after the now-famous seizure of Mandrax tablets.

'Terrible, sir,' Prakash replied. 'I am replying to phone calls half the time, explaining to journalists that case investigations do not progress on an hourly basis. And the bosses just can't understand why I am unable to arrest Loola and Charak.'

Kabir was his senior by three years and they had developed a liking for each other since their first meeting. Kabir was reputed to be honest and daring, and like Prakash, had scant respect for rules and established procedure. His policing techniques abandoned the standard protocols of the manuals. He would swing to extremes. On the one hand, he often abandoned the traditional tenets of a display of authority and would mingle with the crowds, trying to develop a rapport with people and, on the other hand, he had formed a small group of elite policemen who were rumoured to be killing criminals. 'Justice sometimes,' he had told Prakash, 'needs to be swift.'

He had been quick to understand Prakash's need to have a substantial supply of liquor. Liquor was a substitute for slush funds. In a convoluted barter, Prakash used to purchase six to eight bottles of scotch every month from the ships that called on Jamnagar port, and both the police and Customs turned a blind eye to it. He consumed two or three of them, turning the balance over to MI, who would give him six bottles of XXX rum or Officer's

Choice whisky for every bottle of scotch. When one of Prakash's men had been stopped by the police while carrying some scotch bottles from the port of Bedi, Prakash had gone to Kabir to explain his dilemma. Kabir had heard him out, and with Kabir's blessings, Prakash had soon become the favourite bootlegger in town for his informants, real or fake.

The local seafarers had soon learnt that they could carry juicy tales, true or false, about the vessels that were sailing to Middle East and Africa, or about the underworld in India or abroad, to Prakash for an easy bottle of rum. A video cassette that backed the tale could get them as much as four bottles, which was a small fortune in the dry state of Gujarat. There was a rush to meet Prakash at odd hours, and for the first two months, he entertained them all, hearing them out, questioning them, filtering out what he thought seemed improbable. He was the new kid on the block who wanted to learn about the neighbourhood before taking on the bullies. And he was ready to pay for knowledge about those bullies. A couple of months later, the storytellers realized that the days of telling tall tales were over, and the future lay in providing hard-core intelligence. There were those who still tried to take him for a ride. But when their stories did not check out, they would often find themselves being intercepted by the police for carrying illegal liquor.

The friendship between Kabir and Prakash grew. Prakash told him of the smaller events in the district and Kabir would keep him abreast on the bureaucratic wrangling within the state. Kabir's company also helped Prakash, a metropolitan child, develop a more holistic view of life in the smaller districts of India.

'They have a job to do, Prakash,' Kabir explained, responding to Prakash's moans about journalists. 'Most of them are small-time stringers, often paid a couple of hundred bucks for a story, and at the moment there is no bigger story than this seizure.'

'Yeah, I know that,' Prakash said ruefully. 'But these reporters refuse to give a true account of the seizure. Nobody is ready to believe that it was an accident. They are making me into a super sleuth, while it's you guys who really work hard to keep them safe.'

'That's true,' replied Kabir. 'The part about keeping people safe, that is. But it's not correct that it was an accidental seizure. A lot of operatives would have discarded the intelligence, deciding to chase other ghosts. You persevered at it. And that is what counts. How far have you gotten with linking Salim to it?'

'Officially, sir, the matter is under investigation. But,' Prakash said with a conspiratorial smile, 'between you and me, we have hit a dead end. The truck drivers don't know where the trucks were supposed to go. Loola Glass has gone underground, and we have no lead where the tablets were made. The statement extracted from the truck owner is the only evidence linking Salim to the consignment, and that too, frankly, was given under a bit of duress.'

Kabir took another sip of his whisky.

'What is this between you and Salim? I hear you guys go back a long way.'

Prakash grimaced. The tale was spreading like wildfire after the seizure, making everything seem personal.

'He took out a contract on my life, apparently twice.'

'And now you have seized another one of his consignments. Failure, particularly when experienced by the mighty, demands retribution. The bigger the failure, the more vicious is the vengeance. I hope you are aware that he will come after you again, this time with all guns blazing.'

'I am still alive,' Prakash replied with a flash, 'And now he is facing the heat. The first poems that were recited to us in Sainik School, where I studied, were *Jhansi ki Rani* and *The Charge of the Light Brigade*.' Prakash was feeling garrulous after two drinks, and standing up, recited loudly,

Boldly they rode and well,
Into the jaws of Death…

Kabir stared at him speculatively. 'So you are not as much of a nincompoop as your boss claims.'

'You know that too?' Prakash exclaimed. 'I am, of course, a nincompoop. After all, who else is transferred three times in his first three years of job and has a bounty placed on his head to boot?'

'Someone who is intensely enjoying his job,' countered Kabir, and then he continued a little more seriously. 'Let's try something to smoke Salim out.'

Prakash stared. 'Why, sir? Why are you joining this one-sided conflict?'

'How can I afford to lose my drinking partner?' Kabir replied in an irreverent tone. 'I am yet to listen to you reciting *Jhansi Ki Rani*. I can't let you die so soon.'

◆

There was a lull for a couple of weeks, and Prakash, easily bored, thought of fibbing to Singh about some investigation in Bombay so that he could sneak out and meet Shabnam, as promised. Then the lull shattered with a midnight ring of the telephone.

'We have shot dead a henchman of Salim's gang. He had come to kill you,' Kabir announced dramatically over the phone. 'If the reporters call you, you know nothing about it. You decide if this is the right time to officially announce that you are on his hit list.'

Kabir disconnected before Prakash could comprehend anything. His immediate response was to call up Chudasama who, despite the odd hour, was at Prakash's house in fifteen minutes, looking fresh as always.

'Do you ever sleep?' Prakash asked before narrating him the contents of the strange phone call.

'Stay put, sir,' Chudasama commanded Prakash. 'Rathor is outside, keeping watch. I will be back in a couple of hours.'

Chudasama was back before dawn.

'Police have shot dead two guys, not one. Ahir, a local extortionist and hitman, and Mishra, some hitman from Uttar Pradesh.'

'Ahir bought an AK-47 last week!' Prakash exclaimed.

'And he was shot dead soon after? When did you hear of this purchase?'

'About a couple of days back,' Prakash said, hiding the fact that he was the one who had informed Kabir about the purchase. 'I was going to include it in the dossiers at the end of the month. Who is this Mishra?'

'Somebody new to the area,' Chudasama replied. 'Kabir sir was gunning for Ahir. He had been threatening too many businessmen. Kabir sir's team raided their hideout yesterday morning, acting on a tip about the presence of an out-of-town gangster. Both of them were shot dead in an encounter about six hours back. Apparently, they were trying to escape. Nothing in the interrogation indicated that they had taken the contract to kill you, but all the reporters are being told that Mishra had joined hands with Ahir to kill you. The first reporter I called was already trying to trace you for a comment,' Chudasama briefed him succinctly.

'How were you able to find out so much in such a short time?' Prakash was amazed.

'Darbar loyalty, sir,' replied Chudasama in his usual matter-of-fact manner. 'There are Darbars in every wing of the police. We share information.'

'So, Kabir sir is feeding a fake narrative to reporters?'

'Seems like it, sir. But why is he bringing a spotlight on you now when you are already investigating Salim? This is bound to rile Salim up even more.' Chudasama sounded worried.

Prakash decided that it was time to share with Chudasama about

Kabir forcing Salim's hand. After all, Chudasama had always been intent on saving his life. His sole reservation in trusting Chudasama was the latter's propensity to be more loyal to the organization rather than to the individual. However, they had gotten closer after the Mandrax seizure, and Prakash hoped that Chudasama would not share all the actual facts with Singh.

Chudasama thought for a while after hearing the tale.

'Smoke Salim out. Not a perfect strategy. He is thinking along the same lines as us, but he will have to trust too many of his officers. Anyway, no harm done either. Maybe Salim will be forced to play his hand earlier than he had planned. We are now better placed to counter him with Kabir sahab also throwing in his lot with you.'

'You handle the reporters,' Prakash said with a tired yawn. 'I am going back to sleep. I will try to warn the boss regarding the impending storm before that.'

◆

Prakash tried, but he couldn't get through to Singh.

I now have a reason to avoid his calls, he thought. *I can always say that I was in hiding from a potential killer*. Prakash chuckled at the thought.

Singh was rather irritated when they spoke later in the afternoon. Singh hated headlines.

'Why do you have to be in the news so often?'

'Even I don't understand why the press makes such a hullabaloo about Salim trying to kill an assistant director,' Prakash replied, tongue in cheek. 'I am going to ask Kabir sir why he gave the news to the press. I would have stopped him and the press had I known about it earlier.'

'What kind of intelligence officer doesn't know when he is going to be in the news? And why can't you control the narrative?' Singh was not to be deterred by a little sarcasm. 'Can you imagine the kind of reports this news will entail? It is all right if police say that hitmen were hired to kill a film star, or a producer, even a businessman. But a bureaucrat. That is unheard of, Prakash!'

Prakash was irritated.

'More than a dozen officers have been killed in the past five years, sir. If it would have been known that they were under threat, they could have taken precautions, and then maybe they would have been alive.'

'Those deaths occurred in the heat of the moment,' Singh retorted.

'Did they? How do we know conclusively that those officers were not targeted?' Prakash countered.

The conversation was not going anywhere, and it threatened to sink into an acrimonious argument, so Prakash ended it by saying that he would be sending a report stating that the police were simply suspecting a plan to kill him, and the press had sensationalized the news. However, he would be taking all precautions.

Satisfied that the file would not show that there was a threat to life to one of his assistant directors, Singh finally told him to be careful.

◆

'Why did you do it?' he asked Kabir in the evening as he poured another drink for him. The journalists, not aware that Prakash was already under threat by Salim, had lapped up the theory that Salim had ordered the kill on Prakash to avenge the seizure of Mandrax, making Prakash an even bigger hero for them.

'You quoted *The Charge of the Light Brigade* to me, and so I charged,' he said lightly.

Kabir grew serious after noticing the unimpressed look on Prakash's face. 'Ahir had to be eliminated. He was trying to build a gang similar to that of the Godmother. I don't want that in Jamnagar.

You told me about his purchase, and I knew he was planning to kidnap Babu, who had refused to pay him one crore rupees. Mishra was here for that, to take Babu to Uttar Pradesh. Now, Ahir's death has set the ball rolling. Salim has to respond, unless he wants to look chicken,' Kabir said. 'Under normal circumstances, you would have been watching over your shoulder forever. Now, between you and me, we should be able to get advance warning if he plans anything in Jamnagar.'

Prakash wondered whether Salim would respond. He also wondered whether Kabir's response had been prompted by his desire for approbation. Trust, as a commodity in the world of intelligence, was always scarce. He decided to wait and watch. With all the activity, he forgot about his promised visit to Shabnam.

20
The Dance of the Damned

Shabnam called Prakash a couple of days later. 'You promised to come to Bombay,' she said softly, mild disapprobation evident in her tone.

Prakash was flustered. She had that effect on him. Set his heartbeat racing a little faster, leaving him with no way to counter her teasing questions.

'Something came up,' he blurted.

'Yeah, I know. The rabbit was chasing the big bad wolf. I thought you would be hiding in some hole. But you could have at least called me.'

He would tell her the next time they met that they couldn't talk openly on the phone, especially when she was a gangster's moll, and the person on the other end was on the hit list of that very gangster. He smiled at himself, mentally picturing the ridiculousness of the situation. That helped him respond.

'Deprivation deepens desire. So Bombay was postponed till the big bad wolf couldn't blow the house down.'

'I haven't heard that before.' Shabnam laughed. 'You still seem to have some of your wits about you.'

'I only lose them when I am around you.'

'Is that so? Okay. Let's check that. My wrap up shoot starts three days from tomorrow at Bhuj. I have managed to convince my director to let me fly through Jamnagar. I have booked the ticket for tomorrow. Will you pick me up or should I go to the hotel first?'

'Have you already booked a hotel?' asked Prakash.

'No. The producer was keen on turning it into some kind of a publicity trip, what with the film being shot in Bhuj. He said that he could even arrange a couple of press conferences—good publicity for the film in a small town. I was able to convince him that I would lose the mental frame for the shoot if I have to deal with crowds.'

'You want to stay with me?'

'Don't be silly. I can't afford a scandal at this stage.'

'Okay, I will book the hotel for you. And I will pick you up. Look for a blue Maruti with a Punjab registration number. Are you carrying some stuff?' He couldn't resist asking.

'Maybe,' she replied, then disconnected the call.

◆

She came out of the terminal after all the passengers had left, dressed as a student, making effective use of the art of makeup she must have learned at some acting school. She wore thick glasses, flat sensible sandals, had parted her hair into two plaits and had placed a small mole on the tip of the nose. A heavily underlined Physics textbook in her hand and an unfashionable backpack completed the transformation. Keeping to the character, her hair faintly smelt of coconut oil. He knew Rathor was out there somewhere, watching him, and he hoped that he was not enough of a movie buff to recognize Shabnam. He need not have worried about Rathor recognizing her. Even he had not recognized her while she was waiting for the crowd to thin.

'If you are going to park here for a long time, can you please explain the theory of relativity to me?' she said teasingly as she knocked on the window of the car.

'Yeah,' he replied. 'It felt like two hours waiting for you to come out of the terminal, although it was actually half an hour. Inexplicable, just as the actual theory of relativity. Welcome to the storehouse of PJs.' She pecked him lightly on the cheek after getting into the car.

'Hotel?' Prakash asked.

'With this look I think you can manage to sneak me into your house. You can always show me off as your cousin sister or something. I probably am looking like you,' she teased again.

Their banter continued as they drove down to his modest flat. Prakash eyed Rathor following him on his motorcycle, and then, as he took the turn for his house, watched him vanish into the narrow neighbouring lane.

'No bed, no chairs, no air conditioner,' commented Shabnam as she entered the house. 'Just an ash tray full of—' she picked up a stub and sniffed at it '—cigarettes.' She now had a semi-disgusted look on her face.

'Maybe you expected a four-poster bed with silk sheets and mirrors, hookahs and cushions with pictures of semi-nude nautch girls. That's a luxury possibly only you film stars enjoy. Where is my present?'

'Where is mine?' she countered.

'Guests are given gifts when they're leaving. Guests give theirs when they walk in.' Both of them noted how relaxed they felt in each other's company. Shabnam walked into the bathroom to take off her makeup and came out wearing a pair of boxers and a t-shirt, holding a pair of briefs by the tip of her manicured fingers.

'How can you wear this,' she said with a grimace as Prakash dived for that. 'This is as outdated as the loin cloth of mendicant sadhus.' She laughed, dodged Prakash's attempt at seizing the undergarment, and finding a wastepaper basket, threw them into it. She nestled on the mattress in the corner of the room and opened her Physics textbook. Prakash looked lost in his own apartment, trying to imagine what else, besides his underwear, he would have to hide.

'Voila, chemistry in physics!' she said, taking out a crumpled rolled joint from the book.

'Is that all?' Prakash looked disappointed.

'Were you looking forward to meeting me or to smoking hash?' She sounded offended. 'But anyway, I am more generous than you are,' she said while fishing out a block of gold-stamped hash. 'Two tolas of pure, certified Afghani cream. Thank God for the lax security in Indian airports. I can fly incognito and carry hash, and still throw tantrums at the security guys.'

They smoked and sex followed naturally. No awkwardness, no hesitation, no fumbling. *I can get used to this*, both of them thought.

'So you have managed to remain alive?' she said. It was late in the afternoon, and she was taking a drag out of their second joint of the day.

Prakash took the joint from her hand and passed on the stack of local newspapers to her. She glanced at the headlines, going pale, and then quickly scanned through the reports. She looked at him questioningly.

'All bollocks! These guys had to be eliminated and the District Superintendent of Police thought he could earn some brownie points out of that.'

'Is he stupid?' Shabnam raged, the high evaporating as she seethed with anger. 'Does he even realize the repercussions of something like this? Salim is bound to send sharpshooters now, just to save his reputation.'

'That's exactly what all of us are hoping for,' Prakash said. 'I am well protected here and maybe we can send a message across.'

'Send a message across! With you as the guinea pig?' she fumed. 'And you agreed with this glory hunter? Do you think that there will be just one killer coming for you? Killers are dime a dozen in Bombay, all with a desire to prove themselves to themselves. They will be lining up, one after another, to take the contract.'

'Frankly, I didn't have much of a choice. He decided it single-handedly. But in retrospect, I think he may be right somehow.'

'Somehow? I can't see how.' Shabnam was seething. 'You know

Salim got Nazir Bhai?'

'Who is Nazir Bhai?' he asked quizzically. 'Just as Bombay doesn't get news from these backwaters, we are a little ignorant about the happenings in the metropolis, particularly with so much happening over here itself.'

'Oh, you, your Mandrax and your death threats,' she said. 'Nazir Bhai was one of the biggest producers in Bollywood. He made his career with Salim's money. He was going to produce this one film on his own and Salim asked him to cast Abby.'

'Who's Abby?' Prakash asked.

'Just some floozie who thinks that cozying up to Salim during his bad times is a good idea. She can't act for nuts but wanted this role. Nazir Bhai refused. He even offered to cast me, but Salim wanted him to cast Abby. So he got him killed.'

'How do you know all this?' Prakash looked at her.

'From the horse's mouth. I ran into Nazir Bhai a couple of days before the murder. He offered me the role, but I couldn't have taken it when Salim wanted Abby. I am neither that brave, nor so disloyal. Hanif is telling everybody that they had the drop on Nazir Bhai. And Sitara is already dead.'

'Sitara?' Prakash interrupted her again.

'Javed's girlfriend. Javed, if you don't know, was one of the main people behind the bomb blasts, and Sitara had come to me to ask if she should leave for Malaysia with Javed. She didn't, but she must have known much more than what she told me. Javed was a blabbermouth. So maybe that got her killed.'

'Neither of you were ever questioned by the police?'

'Incredibly, I was not. I had very little chance of knowing about the bomb blasts. I was often with Salim, but I had not been to Dubai for at least a couple of months before the blasts, what with the shooting for the film. But Sitara was not questioned, and that was a surprise.'

'How did she die? Shot?'

'No. Her body was discovered in the sea. Police say that she was drunk and walked into the sea and just kept walking, probably losing her balance. It has been declared an accident, not even a suicide. Just after three days of "investigation"!' She was calm now, brooding. 'And now, maybe, it's my turn, particularly when he finds out that I have been sleeping with you. It is my hubris. I wanted to reside close to the stars, and then I co-habited with a man.'

Prakash wondered if her analogy was correct, but then hugged her a little more tightly.

'It's not your hubris, it's his,' he said. 'We will take him down. History shows that every man who thought that he was fate incarnate was conquered.' She looked so vulnerable sitting on the mattress that his heart went out to her. 'Want to go for a drive? We can sit in the salt pans and watch the sun set.'

'No,' she replied. 'I feel a fit of melancholy drooping in. Let us just binge on some music, some sad music, and read poetry. Do you have 'Tears in Heaven'? Just put on some Clapton. And where are the joints? Keep them rolling. Don't even think I am going to leave any for you. I need it for my shoot,' she said with some spirit.

They listened to music. Clapton, Santana, Dire Straits, all soulful, heart-rending music as they smoked. They lost track of time, comfortable in the silence of each other's company, when they were startled by a loud pounding on the door.

Prakash quickly took out his revolver from below the mattress, startling Shabnam. He checked if it was loaded, and signalled for Shabnam to move to the bathroom. He looked through the spyhole and was surprised to see Kabir and his gunman standing there. He quickly burnt a few mosquito killer mats and threw them around the room.

'What are you doing here, sir?' he asked, opening the door, but blocking the entrance.

'Where have you been? I have been trying to reach you for a couple of hours. Your office says that they don't know about your whereabouts. You are not picking up the phone? It's lucky that my PSI spotted Rathor, otherwise I was going to issue an APB.'

'You know about Rathor?' Prakash asked, surprised.

'Will you let me come in? Chheda, you wait,' he said, dismissing his bodyguard.

Prakash had to step aside as Kabir walked into the house. He looked at the burning mats, sniffed, and then said, 'Funny smell. I didn't think the mosquito menace was so bad here.'

'No, sir. Just precautionary steps,' he lied smoothly.

'We got the killers of D.L. Sharma,' Kabir was too excited to dwell over the smell. 'Ahir's boys, they finally broke down last night. Mishra's boss, one Sinha, had ordered the killing, and Mishra and some Dwivedi actually shot him. Mishra boasted to them. They say that Salim had ordered the killing as Sharma ji knew too much about the arms landing. He was helping the police arrest his gang members before they fled the country. Sinha and Dwivedi have been picked up from Varanasi and will reach here tomorrow under transit remand. It's circumstantial so far, but I am told that Sinha is ready to name Salim for the murder. He says that he is not going to save Salim anymore. Apparently, he hates drug smugglers. I want you there for interrogation. Salim's boys seem scared of you. They think of you as a shaman or something like that. The bomb blasts, Mandrax and now Sharma's murder, we are really going to cook Salim's goose. Pour me a drink, man. It's celebration time. And it would not have been possible if you would not have given me that tip about Ahir buying that AK-47. Foisting the charge of conspiring to murder you finally did the trick. Ahir's boys really cracked when they were told that they were being booked to murder you. They just kept repeating that they would not murder an officer, that it was all Mishra and his boss's planning. That only the UP goons can murder government officers. And that they were not Salim's men, although Mishra was. Where is that drink? And where are the high fives? What are you thinking?' Kabir was garrulous as he made himself comfortable on one of the mattresses in the drawing room.

Prakash was in a dilemma. Kabir seemed to be in an expansive mood. He was likely to settle in for a long session of drinking. He wondered what Shabnam must be thinking in the bathroom. He also wondered if he could get rid of Kabir without offending him. Caught in the horns of dilemma, he chose his colleague over his lover.

It helped that he felt more confident now that he knew that Kabir was riding with the angels. He would not have stated anything about implicating Salim in Sharma's murder if he was, in any way, linked with the underworld. Prakash decided to take a chance and introduce Shabnam to Kabir.

You can't, anyway, keep her locked in the bathroom for a couple of hours, he thought to himself.

It was an awkward introduction. Neither was aware of the other's relation to Prakash. Kabir looked at the girl dressed in boxers and a tee, and wondered what to say. Shabnam felt like she had been wronged. She was not here to meet Prakash's friends. It was left to Prakash to break the silence.

'Sir, meet Shabnam, a friend from Bombay. Mr Kabir, the District Superintendent of Police. He is responsible for all the news that you have been reading through the afternoon.' Prakash saw a trace of anger cross Shabnam's eyes, which she controlled immediately. 'He also caught the killers of Sharma sir today,' he added hurriedly. 'You know Sharma sir,' he asked, and she nodded imperceptibly. 'Apparently Salim had a hand in that too. And he couldn't wait to tell me, so he came over. The phone was off the hook.' He finished lamely.

'Pleasure meeting you, ma'am,' Kabir said like a true gentleman officer, and then continued, 'I think we have met somewhere, but I can't place you.' He waited, and when Shabnam did not reply, said, 'You have guests, Prakash. I will see you tomorrow when Sinha is there.'

'Stay,' Shabnam said softly. 'Prakash, I know, adored Sharma ji and it would be disgraceful if he doesn't have a drink with the person who caught his killer. I know that this would bring some closure to his angst about not being able to avenge the death of a man who had first warned him about the danger to his life.'

Kabir was mystified by this girl. He looked quizzically at Prakash. *Who is this girl who seems to know so much about you?* he seemed to ask. *A colleague, fiancée, friend…* Prakash maintained a stoic silence, leaving it to Shabnam to decide how she wanted to play this. Getting no answer, Kabir turned back to Shabnam.

'You sure I can stay ma'am? I can always come back another time,' he said.

'Of course, stay. But please call me Shabnam. Ma'am sounds like I'm the owner of a high-class brothel,' she said impishly, making things more complicated for Prakash, reminding him of Pune and Bhuj.

'You are Shabnam!' Kabir said suddenly, the profanity triggering some memory. 'The actress? I just kept thinking I had met you somewhere. We haven't met, have we?'

'No, Mr Kabir, we have not,' she said as she accepted a drink from Prakash. She lit two cigarettes and passed one over to Prakash. She was clearly baiting Prakash, challenging him to reveal their relationship, maybe head for a commitment and say that they were not just sex buddies.

'I hope you are okay with this?' she asked Kabir, gesturing with her cigarette.

'I am used to him smoking,' Kabir said, 'but...' He hesitated, but then failing to control himself blurted out, 'You are rumoured to be sleeping with Salim.'

'You will get used to it. He carries his tact beneath his knees.' Prakash said, trying to cover the inconsiderate remark.

'You weren't much better the first time we met either,' Shabnam said mercilessly. She was still waiting for Prakash to acknowledge their relationship. 'And yes, Mr Kabir, I am Salim's mistress.'

Kabir was flustered. Prakash could see all the signs of bewilderment on his face. He was possibly grappling with three possibilities. First, was Shabnam a spy for Salim? Second, was Shabnam an informer for Prakash? If so, what were the motivations that were prompting her to risk her life? And third, the most important of all, was Prakash mixed up with Salim, and if so, was Shabnam the go between for the two of them?

A year back, when Prakash still wore his devil-may-care attitude on his sleeve, he would have left Kabir to fight these invisible demons of doubt on his own. Not anymore. There were lives at stake. Salim had been wrecking mayhem all around him and he needed to build a force that could bring a semblance of sanity into the universe around him.

He realized, then, that his association with Shabnam and Kabir was changing him. They were exposing him to evil he had never known, and this knowledge threatened to influence his outlook on life. He shook himself free of these thoughts. For the moment, he had to tackle two of the three most important persons in his life.

'Shabnam has been sleeping with Salim,' he said, looking at Shabnam resolutely, 'and now we are also close friends.' Having acknowledged that, the rest came easy. 'And no, I am not concerned whether she has slept with Salim. And no, I have no dealings with Salim, and also, Shabnam is not my informer, and I am sure that she is not spying on me for Salim. It is the way of the world, but in that comic twist that fate often plays, we find ourselves kindred spirits.'

'That's what happens to him when he starts to get serious, he speaks in eighteenth century lingo,' Shabnam said with a mirthless laugh. 'Your world seems to be just as complicated and fearful as mine. All of us have to justify every action we take, everyone is viewed with suspicion. We can't even sleep with a person of our choice.'

She continued after a short pause, this time addressing Kabir specifically. 'Let me explain his logic from my perspective. Prakash is too insignificant, or was at least till he seized that Mandrax, for Salim to send his mistress to sleep with him. The loss of face would have been incalculable. So I can neither be spying on Prakash for Salim, nor be the go-between for Salim and Prakash. Prakash cannot be mixed up with Salim as too many boys on the street know there is a contract on him, and some of them may try to kill him just to ingratiate themselves with Salim. Salim can't tell everybody that the contract is a false flag.'

There was silence in the room as each of them considered the various possibilities. It was Shabnam who broke the silence again. Paradoxically, the conflicting worlds that they lived in shared similar ideas about relationships.

'Trust, in both our worlds, needs to be earned. Prakash trusted me, and funnily, it is I who may pay a price for it, maybe with my life. I did not put his life at risk, but you increased that risk without reason,' she gestured towards the newspapers.

'It's a net that I have cast. Risks have to be taken when you go after big fish,' Kabir flared. She had no business questioning his decisions. It never crossed his mind that he had not even consulted Prakash before taking a decision about his life.

'That's easy to say, but your net has too many broken knots. Salim has killed people even over perceived slights, and you have, with the newspaper articles, actually challenged him. He will now send a horde of small-time killers to kill Prakash. It would not be Salim who comes brandishing the gun, pulling the trigger. It will be some young boy from UP who wants to earn a couple of lakhs to buy a bracelet for his girlfriend in Orai. He will narrate the story of his valour as he screws her. And neither you, sir, nor Prakash here, would know him as he is anonymous today. Killing Prakash would be his road to fame, a road that the others too will be keen to follow, even if the first one on that path fails. I know how the underworld works, you don't,' Shabnam retorted.

'You think you know the underworld!' Kabir said in a slightly condescending tone.

'Oh no, sir. It is *you* who think that you know the underworld,' Shabnam's sarcasm was like a sharp knife slicing through their delusions. 'But you don't. I have slept with the topmost honcho of the underworld. I have seen the power that flows from those rooms from close quarters. I have seen the way gangs are formed, the way people are corrupted, the hope of a new entrant, the fear of the person out of favour, the humiliation of the supplicant. I have seen it all. And I have smiled at them, a smile that gave them hope, of having the ear of Bhai's mistress, for I shared the bed of the one who decided their fates. And then they came and whispered in my ears. I know the underworld, and I know it much better than you.'

The confidence in Shabnam's voice also had a trace of contempt for both of them.

The intensity in Shabnam's tone stunned both men in the room. Kabir was realizing, as Prakash had realized a few days earlier, that the frail-looking girl sitting with them was not just another dumb bimbo. Prakash tried to lighten the atmosphere. These discussions would never end, and life was to be lived in the interim. Shabnam had to leave the next morning, and Kabir had picked up Sharma sir's killers today. There was no room for bickering tonight. The doubts could be resolved later.

'Let's drop it, sir. Tonight is dedicated to the hope that Sharma sir's soul will finally rest in peace. And shoving another prick on Salim's side! He would be worried now,' said Prakash.

'Big deal,' Shabnam was not done. 'Salim would not be worried.

He would just come at you doubly charged. The contract for Sharma ji went for twenty-five lakhs. The bounty on you has already been increased to ten lakh, and I bet you didn't know shit about it.'

She had dropped another bomb shell on them.

Prakash remained unfazed. 'Ten lakh!' he exclaimed. 'When did that happen? My, oh my! Am I a star, or I am a star? Do you even get that much for a movie nowadays?'

'Oh, shut up,' Shabnam said, now with a wan smile. 'It's not a joke. Why are you never flustered?'

'We can't stop living because of threats, Shabnam. We decided that the last time.'

'Yes, but you have to take more precautions. With a hike in the bounty, and these news of killings and arrests, there are bound to be reprisals—and soon. Nothing may faze you, but I have a cowardly streak in me that refuses to let me live fully. I wish I could be as carefree as you are,' Shabnam said wistfully.

She paused, and Prakash could sense the internal struggle that she was experiencing. She seemed to be making up her mind about something. Finally, with a caustic tone, which seemed to be the result of her bitterness at the loss of a perceived peaceful era of her life, she said, 'And while you all are playing pin the tail on the donkey, trying to catch the people behind the smuggling of Mandrax while being blindfolded, look for Qasim Bhai.'

Prakash shot a glance at Kabir.

'Stuff it,' Shabnam said, still seething, 'he is either with you, and you and I trust him implicitly, or your goose is cooked anyway. Mine too along with yours. It wasn't my choice, or my intention, to run into him, but now that it has happened, I hope to God that it turns out for the good and I can trust him with some secrets. God knows, he has still not fully earned my trust. I have seen too many men turning once there is imminent danger to their families. But he has tipped his hand with the arrest of Sharma sir's killers, and I hope he continues to be on your side, because you are going to need all the help you can get.'

Kabir sensed that all of them were crossing some important milestones today, and that it was going to have a profound effect on their lives. Prakash was a totally different person in the company of Shabnam. Unsure, caring and even diffident. Shabnam too, beneath the bravado, seemed to be genuinely fond of Prakash. Here were two vulnerable people who were fighting what, for both of them, was an unequal battle, but probably due to each other's support, they refused to retreat. He didn't know where that war would take them, but he would like to be with them in it.

'And then you say that you have a cowardly streak in you,' Kabir said with a smile. 'I don't know many who would have taken a stand against Salim. You, cowardly! You are a good actor, Shabnam. You had me fooled easily.'

Shabnam smiled wanly.

'Who is Qasim?' Kabir asked, even as Prakash remained silent.

'That's what I say, babes in the woods, playing cops and detectives. That is why you big shots, the IRS and the IPS, and all those guys with the fancy three-letter abbreviations, are irrelevant in the bigger scheme of things. Your three letters are only a shade better than the four-letter words they use in the underworld. They depend for their survival and growth on the permanent guys, the Inspectors and the Havaldars, and those guys who are going to be permanently in Mumbai, not transferred every three years like you guys. What shit will you know in three years?'

Shabnam was still a little livid. 'Ask the inspector at the Juhu Police Station, and he will tell you that Qasim is a film producer known to be close to the underworld. But what even he can't tell you is that Salim used him to finance the Mandrax factory, which is somewhere in Vapi.'

If the news of the increased bounty on Prakash's head had fallen on them like the proverbial tonne of bricks, this information was a five-megaton nuclear bomb. All of them knew that any route for Shabnam to go back to her old life was closed now. Any relationship with her old world could now only be that of a double agent. There was no doubt in Kabir's mind where her loyalties lay.

'It's your field now,' Kabir said to Prakash.

'Why, are you not going to be part of the hunt for glory?' Shabnam asked. Kabir realized that she wasn't one to forgive anyone easily.

'Not when my friends are involved. I am here if you need me, but it's between Prakash and you now.'

He leaned back and watched as Prakash talked to her, cajoling at times, angry at others—pleading, affectionate and chivalrous at various stages. He was forgotten. He watched and envied the easy familiarity the two enjoyed. He hoped they lived long enough to enjoy that.

'So we pick up Qasim, and there is some guy called Bhatt we have to trace,' Prakash concluded.

'Need any help from me?' Kabir finally asked.

'No, sir, I am fine. I should be able to wrap this up within the week. It's going to be a challenge for you to hold the headlines with this Sinha guy.'

'When are you going back?' Kabir asked Shabnam.

'Tomorrow to Bhuj,' she replied.

'Should I get you dropped? Do you need security?'

'Not unless you want to simultaneously call Salim to inform him that I am sleeping with the enemy.' She was repeating, verbatim, the words Shelley had said to Prakash a while ago.

Are they so similar, and is that why Shelley liked Shabnam? Prakash thought.

'Shabnam arriving at Bhuj in a police car would be a dead giveaway,' Prakash told Kabir.

'Peace, I think. I do think a formal apology is in order, but I don't know how to go about it,' Kabir said with all sincerity.

'Smoke a peace pipe with us,' Shabnam said, looking at Prakash, as both of them burst into much-needed laughter.

'He is not like us,' Prakash replied. 'He doesn't even smoke cigarettes. He can't smoke a peace pipe with us.'

Shabnam walked up to Kabir, gave him a hug, and said, 'I am sorry. I am touchy, what with my world changing so fast. I never thought I would be seeing my friends murdered at the orders of the man I was sleeping with.'

'I think you people need some time to spend by yourselves. I will make sure that Rathor is removed from the watch.' Kabir said. He then asked Prakash, 'Are you sure she is safe?'

'She will reach Bhuj incognito tomorrow, sir, and even your best men won't be able to follow her,' Prakash told Kabir as he got up to leave.

'Can I confront these killers tomorrow about the fact that they were paid twenty-five lakhs to kill Sharma sir?' Kabir asked Shabnam before leaving.

'In for a penny, in for a pound,' replied Shabnam. 'The money was picked up from Sitara's flat by somebody called Pappu.'

◆

Shabnam left the next day disguised as a student again, packing ten bandhani sarees provided by Prakash.

'My return gift,' he said lightly. The son of an industrialist of Jamnagar, who thought that he was doing the assistant director of RI a favour by escorting his friend's sister, took one look at the girl, cursed his luck and kept silent till he dropped her at the hotel in Bhuj.

How can girls be so careless with their appearance? And that mole on the nose; she really needs to get that operated upon, he thought.

◆

Sinha and Dwivedi arrived at 1 a.m. on a flight from Bombay. Considering the inter-state implications of the murder, the case was soon to be transferred to a special team. However, before that, the accused had to be confronted by the confessors, so they were brought to Jamnagar. Kabir interrogated them personally.

In the press conference later that day, he dramatically announced that both of them had confessed to their role in the murder of Mr D.L. Sharma, and that they had revealed the location of the murder weapon. The investigations would be complete once the ballistics of the bullet were matched with the revolver. He also said, more as an afterthought, that they have also confessed that Sharma was killed at the behest of Salim. He kept silent about Pappu.

Prakash was present at the interrogation, without the press being aware of it, learning as much as he could about Salim's world. He made a formal appearance at the press conference the next day when the furore about Salim's involvement in the murder refused to die, and the press had started speculating about the similarities between Mr Sharma's murder and the impending threat on Prakash's life. Somebody leaked that Prakash had also interrogated the killer, and there were wild speculations about the role of RI in assisting the police in identifying the killers. Prakash refused to be drawn into the controversy, and just stated that it was satisfying when the killers of an ex-RI officer were apprehended, and that inter-agency co-operation was the need of the hour.

◆

'They finally confessed to everything when I told them about the twenty-five lakhs and Pappu,' Kabir told Prakash later. 'Shabnam seems to be really aware of the ins and outs of the underworld,' he said meaningfully.

Prakash refused to reply.

21

Conspirators

A couple of days later, after being sure that there were no whispers about Shabnam's visit to Jamnagar, Prakash called Shelley from one of the public booths.

'Hey, how is the setting up of your office in Ahmedabad coming up?' Prakash asked.

'Why the fuck are you concerned, you shithead! You keep up with your seizure of drugs and all that jazz and be careful enough to keep your sorry ass alive,' she replied. 'Leave the setting up of the office to me.'

'So you know.' He stated it more calmly than she had expected him to.

'Yup. Shabnam and I are becoming good pals. We end up talking at least twice a week. You have a winner on your hands, babe. Don't let her slip away easy.'

'And what do I do with her current paramour? He was already gunning for me. What will he do once he knows I am bedding his girl?'

'He will do what you used to do when you could not bed me!' Shelley said with a laugh. 'Shag. Or get another one.'

'That's there, but I still need to have a back-up friend if that doesn't happen.' Prakash said, joining the banter. He, then, continued seriously, 'I need you in Ahmedabad day after tomorrow.'

Shelley knew that tone. It brooked no argument.

'Lal will deliver your ticket today. You won't be able to get one at such short notice. Tell me a place where we can meet. We need to have a long talk.'

Shelley shared an address.

◆

They met at a semi-furnished office on the third floor of a newly constructed building in the upcoming area of Satellite in Ahmedabad. There was nobody around. Shelley, noticing the serious note in his voice over the phone, had ensured that they were alone.

'I have heard of the private sector moving towards paperless offices and manufacturing going just-in-time, but are you planning to have a human-less office?' he asked lightly as they entered a vacant chamber.

'Don't be silly. I still have tea for you, humans or no humans.'

'What, just tea?' Prakash teased.

'This is my office, not my home. Save your debauchery for home. In any case, you sounded so serious on the phone that I wanted to talk to a sober you,' Shelley said as she walked across to give Prakash a tight hug.

She pulled back, surprised. 'You feel tense…not your normal self.'

'Death threats do that to you, I guess,' Prakash replied tersely.

'You were under threat in Pune too, and that never stopped you from being carefree, or shooting your mouth off,' Shelley said. 'Are you sure it is not Shabnam?'

Prakash stared at Shelley, and then it dawned on him. Shelley was on the mark, again. He was concerned about Shabnam, concerned enough to lose his carefree attitude, after just three meetings!

Shelley was watching him brood. She continued.

'Nobody, and nobody, should be able to take away your freedom. Not just the freedom of taking your own decisions but also the freedom of thinking, the freedom to speak your mind or even the freedom to fall in love all over again. She knows what she is doing. She is no babe in the woods experiencing innocent love. She is a calculating actress, and maybe sleeping with you is part of those calculated moves,' Shelley said rather sternly.

'Yeah, I know. But after meeting her, my entire perspective seems to be shifting. Earlier, it was always hopeful. I felt that if anything bad were to happen, it would invariably be set right. Things were bound to get better. Now it seems that even when good things happen, there may be something bad on the horizon. She seems to have opened up a vista that shows the burnt-out vestiges of dead humanity, looking to destroy all joy for personal gain. Earlier, life used to beckon, saying, 'Come and experience me a little more.' But slowly, the voice in my head seems to be saying, 'Just survive.'

Shelley looked at him sympathetically.

'All of us remember that you have that propensity to bat for the underdog. Remember how you used to save the freshers from ragging? Craig and I used to have such a difficult time convincing you to live your own life, and not another's. Remember those lines from *Song of Myself* that used to be our motto in college?'

I exist as I am, that is enough,

If no other in the world be aware I sit content,

And if each and all be aware I sit content.

Then she continued. 'You never let us influence your life. How could you let Shabnam do it?'

Prakash smiled. 'I should talk to you more often. Maybe then I'll remember the good things more often and not lean too far over the precipice.'

Shelley embraced him tightly, holding him for a long time. It was a gesture that told him that she would always be there for him, conveying to him that all would be well in his journey.

She then pushed Prakash back, holding him still by the arms, and said in her normal banter, 'So tell me, why am I here? What was the urgency that prompted you to pull me to this dry state suddenly, without letting me even score for my quota? I hope it was not to listen to the sordid details of your sex life or the laments of your love life, because if it is, you are going to be kicked so hard that you won't be able to sit while going back to Jamnagar.'

'As if,' Prakash made a face. 'Listen to this.'

He sat down and explained the contours of his plan to Shelley. She listened intently, interrupting occasionally to clarify something. It took him half an hour to convince her.

'I personally think that you are taking this crusade a bit too far, or maybe your judgment is clouded by whatever Shabnam is telling you. Have you told her that you are planning to cash out a piece of information that she gave you?'

'Not yet. I am still not sure that she would openly join my crusade against Salim.'

'Despite her sharing so many details about Salim's operation!' Shelley was a little surprised to hear that from Prakash.

'Secrets shared in bedrooms, or in a heightened emotional state, does not mean loyalties have been shed or changed,' Prakash replied.

Shelley was silent for a moment, thinking. Her tone was serious when she finally spoke. 'You, my dear, are turning Machiavellian. Are you really sure you want to do this?'

Prakash nodded.

'It's your funeral then. Maybe mine too,' Shelley replied. 'But then, when we have done so many crazy things together already, why not do this as well? Let us have a go, and maybe, just maybe, there may be some good that may come out of it.' She paused. 'Shit, I am talking like you, talking about the good and all that shit. Next you will have me talking about objectives, outcomes and targets. I don't talk about that shit. I try to live in the present. I think I will have to maintain some decent distance from you. But till the time I achieve that, where is the silly paper that I have to sign? And if you are making me sign it, make sure that you and I remain alive long enough to cash in on it.'

22

Boy with No Name

Finding somebody to kill Prakash was not as easy as Shabnam thought. Hanif had contacted Miyanchacha again as he was a local. He was shocked when Miyanchacha informed him that no local goon was ready to take the contract.

'It's ten lakhs!' Hanif said.

'I know Bhai, but the boys say that Prakash is protected. He is being shadowed not just by his own people, but also by policemen. That Superintendent of Police, Kabir, has taken it on himself to protect Prakash, and you know, the boys are anyway afraid of RI.'

'So get a policeman to do the job.'

'Nobody local will do it, Bhai. They are all scared after Ahir was killed. You will have to look for an outsider.'

An outsider. Their gang had only a few loyal shooters left in Bombay, and he was loathe to use them. Those boys may be needed to counter the increasing influence of the breakaway factions in Bombay. *Was Prakash really so well protected?* he wondered. *Wasn't he just a lucky guy who kept stumbling upon their consignments? Why did Salim have to order his killing at this stage? They kept losing consignments, but he had never seen Salim in such a hurry to kill a government officer. Is it because he is losing control? Was it just another murder to send a message, like Nazir's?*

Like Salim, he too, of course, was still unaware that Shabnam had started sleeping with Prakash, or he would have gone about the task with much more conviction.

He thought about it, and then decided to call in a favour. He called Azim to hire a boy to kill Prakash.

◆

The boy watched the barren countryside pass from the three-tier compartment of Saurashtra Mail. He was born without a name in a small village in the similarly barren land of Bundelkhand. He already had two elder brothers, so there were no celebrations at his birth. As he was the youngest of the three brothers and two sisters, everybody just started calling him 'Chhotu'—the small one. Maybe the name affected his growth, and he remained small, growing only to five feet and three inches.

His parents were landless labourers, seasonal farm workers who travelled to Punjab in March every year to harvest the wheat crop. There they lived in makeshift camps on the edge of the fields where they worked, cooking food on makeshift stoves fired with foraged wood. In July, after transplanting paddy in the same fields, they came back to their village. For the rest of the year, they would hunt for odd jobs whenever they could get them. The money normally lasted till October, and the food cuts would start soon after the festival of Deepawali in November. Chhotu was perpetually underfed. He wondered why he had so many brothers and sisters if there was to be no food for all of them. Once he had mustered the courage to ask his mother who, having grown prematurely old under the pressure of arranging food for the whole family, replied, probably truthfully, that they expected that some of the kids would die before they grew up, but none did. The reality of death was learnt early. Death was a fact, and you accepted it, not as a metaphysical truth but as a vital part of existence.

Growing up, he watched his mother and sisters going to the forest to collect firewood while his father and brothers waited, often in vain, for someone to hire them to work as labourers in their fields.

He watched them struggle, perpetually hoping that hunger would not be a permanent part of their lives. He watched them failing to secure regular meals year after year.

He simmered. His parents and his brothers could not understand how he had turned out to be so, but unlike them, he resented the stoic acceptance of their semi-fed existence. As a young boy, with nothing else to do, he intently watched the farmers sling stones at the birds so that they would not settle on their fields to peck at the growing grains. He made one for himself, cajoling the bicycle repair shop owner to part with a small piece of rubber from a bicycle tube, promising to fetch water for him for a week from the well in return. He practised perpetually, perfecting the flight of the stone from his sling, experimenting with different stones till he realized that round stones had the most accurate flight, as well as the maximum range. Three days of visits to the dried riverbed near the village brought him a treasure trove of fifty smooth, round stones that fit his sling perfectly.

After a month of practice, he accompanied his mother to the forest when she went to collect firewood. His first visit yielded a partridge, brought down with a perfect shot on his fifth attempt. They had a feast that night, the bird shared between the four male members, and the women, who practised vegetarianism, getting a larger share of the sparse helping of lentils. There were frequent visits to the forest after that, although the rewards were few and far between. Sometimes partridge, and sometimes, if he was lucky, a quail. The feather in his cap was the rabbit he was able to maim on the first shot, chase it, secure a second hit and catch it while it was still alive. He cradled it in his arms, and then lovingly, looking into its pretty red eyes, broke its neck. He felt a strange satisfaction as the heart, which had been beating rapidly, slowly fell silent. He realized that he had relished the sound of stone hitting the body, the feeling of a living body dying slowly by the wound that had been inflicted by him, and he had stared lovingly into the rabbit's red eyes as life went out of them. He felt contented. He was all of nine years old at that time.

His poaching was discovered not long after, not because he made a mistake but because his brother boasted to his friends that they had a rabbit for dinner. He mentioned it in the wrong company, and the Thakurs of the village got to hear of the story. Traditionally, only the Thakurs were permitted to hunt in the forest. They organized a night hunt once every fortnight when a bunch of them would, in a show of power, descend on the forest on their tractors, and shoot anything that moved. Hunting in the forest by anybody else was sacrilege, a challenge to their authority. Chhotu and his family were hauled up before the village council, the offending sling was confiscated and the male members of the family were ordered to do one week of 'community service' without any pay. The 'community service', naturally, was to be done in the fields of the village headman. Chhotu saw their meagre food being rationed further that week.

A couple of weeks later, sharp iron pieces dug into the ground shredded two tyres of the village headman's tractor, causing considerable financial loss. Nobody suspected anything, and nobody noticed the slight swagger in Chhotu's walk when the mischief mongers were not caught.

He never went to school, and as he grew older he spent most of his time playing cricket. Everyone playing with him knew he hated losing. A fight was inevitable if he did not perform well, and the fight was rarely fair. There were no taboos for him. He fought to win. Now, everybody wanted Chhotu in their team. That at least ensured that they did not return home with a swollen lip, a bleeding arm or a blackened eye.

The swagger and the aggressiveness did not go unnoticed. In the barren land of Bundelkhand, there were two businesses: farming, and to protect the farmlands, guns. The aspirations and the pursuit of power by the oppressed spawned a flourishing industry of illegal guns called kattas. Some of the best country-made guns were manufactured in Bundelkhand. Manufacturing them was not difficult. Just mould a piece of pipe cut from a bicycle frame to make the barrel, fabricate the butt from iron plates, use the spring from the kerosene stove for the trigger and use a sharply honed nail as the hammer. These crude pistols would be sold for as little as five hundred rupees, but it gave the owner a confidence worth millions. Carrying a weapon was a status symbol, a sign of manliness, and few cared if it was legal.

Making guns was not difficult, and there were numerous gunmakers in the area. But delivery of the guns was not so easy. As most of the criminals were on police records, they preferred the deliveries to be made at their hideouts. The gunmakers soon discovered the advantage of using young boys. Dressed in school uniforms, they made the perfect delivery boys. They were paid twenty rupees for each delivery, more than their fathers earned after a hard day in the fields.

Chhotu, with his aggressive temperament and confidence, was soon spotted by the bicycle repairman who had given him the rubber for the sling. The shop owner also supplied bicycle frame pipes to make barrels for the guns. Chhotu was introduced to the local gunsmith, and at the age of twelve, he was making eight to ten deliveries a month, more during the festival and wedding season. He started to hang around the workshop all day, watching guns being made. He learned about the tensile strength of pipes, how to hone the trigger, how to check the strength of the stove spring that was to be used to fire the trigger, the range at which each of the guns was likely to be effective. By fourteen, he was a walking encyclopaedia on country-made guns of Orai, helping to forge some, earning as much as five hundred rupees a month. He saw hands injured by the firing of poorly made guns, bullets falling just 10 feet away as the bore was not properly forged, triggers misfiring. He heard stories of men who were shot when their guns misfired, and he decided that he would never ever own a poorly made gun.

In the workshops, he also heard stories of criminals who had made it big. Shamsu, who lived in Orai and ran an extortion racket earning ₹50,000 a month. Guddu, from Jalaun, who was the bodyguard of the local politician and got a cut from his kidnapping business. Pandit, who killed Thakur when he tried to bid for the scrap contracts of railways, and who had shot dead at least a dozen other rivals. They became his idols, people who had achieved prosperity through power that flowed from the barrel of the gun. He dreamt of being a part of the legends whose tales were told in the region.

At fifteen, he was confident enough to say goodbye to his family and move to Jhansi, recommended by the local gunsmith to the legendary gunmaker, Moinuddin. Veterans in crime used to say, '*Moin ka maal kabhi misfire nahin hota*.' He was part of the local lore in Jhansi. The master craftsman used stolen railway coach handles instead of bicycle pipes for the barrel, giving his guns more durability, range and accuracy. Machinery springs were used instead of stove springs, and firing pins were forged instead of using poor quality nails. He sold his guns only to the gangs of Bombay and Madhya Pradesh, charging ₹3,000 to ₹5,000 rupees per piece by guaranteeing that his guns would fire at least five quick shots. Chhotu forged a gun for himself despite Moins' objections.

'Dada, I am neither going to make guns all my life, nor be just a delivery man. I will buy land in my village, get my sisters married to teachers and have a girl to whom I will give a gold anklet as a present.'

He got his break when Moin chose him to deliver six guns to Azim Bhai in Bombay. The young, well-dressed, smooth-talking seventeen-year-old boy was less likely to be checked by the Railway Police than the tough-looking character that Azim Bhai had sent. Chhotu spent ₹500 from his savings to purchase the bullets for his gun, and left for Bombay, hoping that it would be his city of dreams as well.

He came expecting a city of lights, but was shocked by the dark, decaying buildings he saw as the train rolled into Bombay. There was a stink in the air, something he couldn't identify at that time, but later learnt emanated from the shit of millions of people defecating on the unused railway lines. The memories of rolling green hills that the train had passed through before entering Bombay were soon forgotten.

The crowds at Victoria Terminus staggered him, but thankfully he was quickly whisked away by another youth who escorted them to a black and yellow Fiat taxi. During his stay in Bombay, he learnt to like and respect the taxi drivers, who never haggled, rarely said no and loved to talk about their native villages. People came to Bombay from their villages with dreams, and they sought to live, not just survive, there.

I am here now, Chhotu thought, excited, *and soon, I will rule this city*.

◆

Azim Bhai's writ ran from Bandra to Andheri, the upcoming area in Bombay, where builders fought for every small piece of land and film producers sought police permission to shoot their dreams. He was searched before being allowed in Azim Bhai's presence, and the extra gun was recovered.

'What is this?' he was asked.

'Mine,' he answered.

He was slapped and beaten till he was able to convince them that the gun was unloaded and could not have been fired with so many people around Azim Bhai.

'Why are you carrying it?' Azim Bhai asked.

'It's a new city, Bhai,' he answered. 'One may need it.'

Azim Bhai examined the gun, marvelled at the craftsmanship and asked Chhotu to sell it to him.

'This is mine, Bhai. This will make my fortune in this city.'

Nobody laughed.

'Have you ever fired it?' he was asked.

'Never missed a target, Bhai,' he boasted.

'And what if the police catch you?'

'Never happened, Bhai. I dress well, and policemen only look at you twice if you give them either a scared or an aggressive look. I do neither. I am neither a ruffian nor a beggar. Who has the time to chase me?'

'He is a *chhaliya*, man,' Azim Bhai said with a guffaw. Azim, who had been given his share of breaks in life that had ensured he reached where he was now, could empathize with the boy's big dreams. And after all, the boy was from his region. 'Do you have a place to stay in Bombay?'

'I have a distant cousin in Mira Road…works with the builders.'

'That's too far. Put him up with the boys,' Azim Bhai said, giving him a five hundred rupee note. 'Here's a bonus. Go around Bombay.' The money was a fortune, more than what he normally earned in a month.

I am going to like this city, he thought.

The name Azim Bhai had given stuck. Everybody now called him Chhotu Chhaliya, the little chameleon, who could change colour according to his surroundings. He accumulated clothes, and spent money on looking good, not on prostitutes. He wanted a girlfriend, not a sex worker.

It was easy to enter the gang, but infinitely more difficult to gain their trust. He started by delivering some money, then collecting some. He brandished his gun for the first time in Bombay in December 1992 to threaten an aspiring muscleman belonging to another gang, hoping that the act would establish him in the gang. He had only recently been promoted to delivering extortion threats to builders when the Bombay riots happened. He kept away from violence, the Hindu member of a Muslim gang, and felt the vacuum in Bombay's underworld as his bosses and colleagues scattered. Those with money went to Thailand or Malaysia. The boys went back to their villages. He stayed put, knowing well that he had never been marked. And then, he quietly spread the word that there was still a boy with a gun in Bombay who was ready to shoot for the right price.

He was first approached by Suleiman in July. In a period when gunmen were difficult to come by, he was offered ten thousand rupees to shoot at a builder and miss. He did it perfectly, the builder could hear the bullet whiz past. On that single day he earned more than he had earned in his entire life. Other offers followed soon. Shoot at a builder to injure, not kill—twenty thousand rupees. Fire at the office of a film producer—twenty-five thousand rupees.

He became a master of disguise, changing his appearance often. A Muslim schoolboy with kohl in his eyes and a Quran in his hand sometimes, a drug addict at other times and once, he even dressed himself in a burqa, with shiny gold sandals to complete the illusion. He was not yet a Bhai, but he was not Chhotu anymore. He was Chhotu Chhaliya. And he could now be contacted only via a messaging service through a PCO, whose owner thought that he was a carrier for the unofficial courier firms working between Bombay and Gujarat.

He lost his virginity on what he believed was his eighteenth birthday. He celebrated it with a call girl, not one of those youngsters in Kamathipura, but a genuine Bandra girl who took a thousand rupees to spend a night with him in a posh hotel room, which also cost him 600 rupees a night. He went home to his village after that, travelling with the labourers going home for Deepawali. Unlike their sparse belongings, his suitcase was full of money and gold. He left fifty thousand rupees for his parents, promising to send more, asking them to buy land.

A message was waiting when he returned to Bombay. The PCO owner said that somebody had called offering him a job in Dubai. He would call again tonight.

'You are lucky, Chhotu. You can now work in Dubai. No need to keep working for this angadiya anymore.'

Azim Bhai had called personally, and there was no question of refusing. This would be his second kill. The first had also been arranged through Azim Bhai. He had killed a film producer, and for that he had been paid more than a lakh. He had used the money to put a deposit on a small tenement in Mahim. The contract was offered, accepted and the photo and address faxed from Dubai.

'Jamnagar!' He was surprised. He did not know the place, had no local support in the city and he had to kill a government officer over that. He was worried and called Azim Bhai to ask him for support. None was forthcoming. So he did the unthinkable. He asked for an advance of five lakh rupees, and a foreign revolver. Despite the displeasure at the other end, he refused to budge. The gun, a Smith & Wesson, and the money were delivered two days later. His brother came soon after and was given three lakh rupees, the rest going for paying another instalment for his one-room house.

'I will be home for Holi,' he told his brother. 'Find a match for our elder sister with this money, a government servant, a clerk in the court or a teacher. There will be more money at Holi. We will have a great time together this year, Bhai. Good times are coming for our family.'

Now, the boy looked at the passing countryside and dreamed. After this, he would never be called Chhotu Chhaliya again. He would be Chhaliya Bhai.

23

Rolling the Dice

'I hear that a film producer called Qasim financed the manufacturing of Mandrax,' Prakash told Chudasama.

Chudasama had, by now, stopped questioning Prakash on his information or his sources. 'Qasim has been involved in some unsavoury activities, but financing the Mandrax operation… That is a big leap for him,' he replied after some thought.

'You know him?' asked Prakash, surprised.

'I do not know him, but I know of him,' Chudasama said gently. 'He launders some of the extortion money for Salim. Produces small budget films from the extortion money, and sells the overseas rights of the films for huge amounts to Dubai or Africa-based companies. This money is then invested in properties in Bombay. He is also a small-time pimp, supplying minor actresses as bribes when Salim asks for it. A small dossier exists on him in the "accomplices" section.'

'Could he have financed the Mandrax operation?' Prakash asked.

'All his films have been financed by Salim. He can't say no to Salim.'

Prakash passed a paper to him. Chudasama read it. He looked up, surprised.

'An informant?' He queried, and then asked the inevitable question. 'How reliable?'

'Very,' replied Prakash.

'No information about the exact location of the factory. He just says Vapi.'

'That's all he knew. Is it possible that Qasim will crack quickly?

Apparently there are more drugs there.'

'Yeah, he says so,' Chudasama said, pointing to the paper. 'Any hint on Bhatt?'

'Yes. The guy shares credit as a producer in one of Qasim's films. They certainly have a link,' answered Prakash.

'Have you filed the information? Does the informer want a reward?'

'Yes,' answered Prakash.

'Then there is very little time. We will have to act now. Maybe as early as tomorrow.'

But luck had still not deserted the nincompoop. If they had struck the next day, Qasim could have resisted them.

Prakash and his team could not proceed to question Qasim the next day.

24

Scattered Deeds

'In retrospect,' Kabir told Prakash at a later date, 'you survived because you have developed your own craft of gaining people's trust. You have always had a reputation for hard work, patience, confidence, humility and above all, the capacity to stoically accept the events unfolding around you. But people did not know if you were capable. Your silence after the Mandrax seizure convinced the informers of two things—that you could act, and that you could be trusted.'

Chudasma had also noticed a change in Prakash. He was increasingly depending on other people, treating them as more important than himself. And people reciprocated, giving him their trust. In the case of some, Prakash did not just generate trust. He got something much more than trust. He got their loyalty.

Lal and Prakash had often discussed if it was actually trust that generates loyalty, or if it was the other way around. Lal always thought that trust came first, followed by loyalty. Loyalty needs more than just trust to exist, but there cannot be any loyalty without trust. Prakash felt that if one was loyal, then trust would be a natural corollary. Lal said that a dog trusts you, that is why it is loyal. Prakash countered by saying that people are loyal to their caste brethren without trusting them. It was an interminable debate, mostly inconclusive.

It may never be known whether Chedi was driven by trust or by loyalty, but he saved Prakash's life.

Nobody knew much about Chedi, except that at about the

age of thirty, he had come out of nowhere and bought the lodge located next to the bus stop at Jamnagar, and then, over the years, kept expanding it. His source of money had always been shrouded in mystery. Some said that he had bought the lodge from the reward money that he had received as an informant. Others said that in such a case, he would have been bumped off, and opined that some smugglers were in imminent danger of losing the consignment to RI, and they had sent Chedi to Customs to give information, thus salvaging 15 per cent of the money as reward from Customs. The stories invariably linked Chedi to the underworld. So, his lodge hosted most of the outstation *khalasis*, sailors and truck drivers during their stay in Jamnagar. He spent most of his time sitting in the room next to the reception, sipping tea and waiting for someone to join him in a game of chess.

It was rumoured that he was also a moneylender, and knew about the troubles of most of the people who stayed in the lodge. It was also believed that he was privy to most of the unsavoury activities going on in Saurashtra and beyond. People trusted Chedi, as he may, just may, if he was inclined to, help them out of a sticky situation one day.

Prakash had worked hard to cultivate Chedi, unsuccessfully, as an informer when he had just joined RI. After innumerable games of chess, which Prakash won with some difficulty, he stoically accepted that Chedi would never be an informer, not because it went against his principles but because it was against his business. He could not let it be said that the lodge was owned by a 'khabri', an informer. But respecting what Chedi had achieved, Prakash sometimes still stopped by at the lodge to play a game of chess with him.

Chedi, on his part, had easily seen through Prakash's attempts to recruit him as an informer, and dismissed him as another greenhorn wannabe. He was good for a few rounds of challenging chess, but he would always remain a second-rate intelligence operative, he decided.

Then, as Prakash's trips to the lodge became infrequent, he started to hear tales that forced him to revisit his assessment. The intelligence community seemed to be rallying behind Prakash. His obvious lack of expertise, instead of becoming a liability, was proving to be an asset. His disarming openness about his inexperience, his constant efforts to learn, his intransigence in the face of adversity, all of it compelled people to respond to his requests. Everybody loved to teach young Prakash, or guide him in his operations. Even Chedi found himself boasting that he too had guided Prakash.

That day was momentous. Chedi, dressed in trousers of indeterminate origin and a shirt that had seen better days, left his lodge and visited the RI office. What motivation Chedi had for undertaking that trip could never be understood. There was no money involved. Prakash's detractors said that it was pity for a failed operative that prompted Chedi. But the fact was, he was there, telling Prakash with a deadpan look, 'A killer is staying in my lodge. I think you are the target.'

If Chedi expected panic or excitement, he missed it. Prakash was stoic, he later told someone, as if he expected that another attempt on his life was inevitable.

Prakash's first reaction, as he told Shabnam later, was that his plans always go awry, and now Qasim would escape.

'Well, how do you know that, Chedi Bhai?' Prakash asked calmly as he called for some tea.

Chedi continued, equally calm.

'New boy, maybe not even eighteen. Came from Bombay yesterday carrying just a red bag. Says he's an employee of a courier company. Does not play chess, stupid fellow. Does not even play cards. All courier company boys play cards. He should have known that. How else would they pass the time during their journey?'

Chudasama passed the tea, which was just how Chedi liked it—sugary, milky and strong.

'He was enquiring after your office, and people kept directing him to the Customs office. Finally he came to me, chatting me up to find the location of your office.'

He paused. Then turning towards Chudasama, he said, 'I always told you it was a wise decision to hire this remote bungalow for the office. It's so difficult to keep a watch on this bungalow.'

'What did you tell him?' Chudasama was a little impatient.

'What I tell everyone. That I sit perpetually at the lodge, and if he wants to know the address of any office, he should look it up in the telephone directory. I even gave him the telephone directory, but the guy seems to be illiterate. A courier boy, illiterate!' Chedi said, smiling conspiratorially.

'And?' Prakash prompted.

'I wondered why a courier company boy would be interested in the RI office of Jamnagar.' Chudasama looked askance at Chedi. He continued hurriedly, 'So, when he went out today morning, I rummaged through his cupboard. He is carrying two guns, one Smith & Wesson and one 8" katta. If he is here to sell them, or is a delivery boy, then why should he ask for your office? Also, he is inexperienced. All courier boys carry a return ticket, he does not have one. Thus, check. He is a prime suspect for being a killer.'

'Those are the deductions of a chess player. They can't be challenged,' Prakash said with a laugh. 'What else did you find out, Chedi Bhai, or should I say, what else did you deduce?'

'Just two pairs of clothes in his bag. One red shirt and a blue pair of trousers with a white shirt. With his short height, he can easily pass as a schoolboy,' Chedi replied.

'We will get him, Chedi Bhai. You go back and stay safe,' Prakash said.

'You don't want to know how he looks?' Chedi asked, surprised.

'Short, thin, young, like a schoolboy, wearing a red or white shirt. What more do I want, Chedi Bhai?' Prakash said.

'You know, it's surprising that there is no local support for him. There are rumours that no local boy or gang is ready to take the contract on you because of Kabir ji. But it's time that you develop a reputation, make people believe that you can protect yourself. By the way, this boy seems to be a shooter, not a seasoned killer,' Chedi said on his way out.

Once again, Chedi could say that he had taught the young Prakash a few things.

25

To Die Without a Name

'Should we get him now?' Chudasama asked. He was still unable to fully absorb the enormity of Chedi's visit. Chedi, leaving his lodge! To visit the assistant director of RI in broad daylight! To warn Prakash, knowing well that it was easy for the news to spread! Chudasama grudgingly acknowledged that his boss was gathering followers who were ready to risk their life and livelihood for him.

'No,' replied Prakash after some thought. 'Let's make it a joint police and RI operation. For one, there is no proof that he is out here to kill me. That just seems to be Chedi's deduction, and although he is a good chess player, you can't decide the game with just two moves. In any case, even if we arrest him, we will have to hand him over to the police under the Arms Act.'

Chudasama thought, and finding merit in his reasoning, nodded.

Prakash called up Kabir, revealing little on the phone. Kabir knew better than to probe, and agreed to meet in the RI office after an hour. Chudasama despatched Rathor to Chedi's lodge to keep a watch on the young boy. As an auto driver, he was free to go anywhere, even inside the lodge, purportedly to visit his customers.

Revolvers were cleaned and loaded, and Chudasama and Prakash got ready for battle.

◆

Kabir strode into Prakash's smoke-filled room an hour later. 'When will you quit smoking?' he asked lightly. 'If Salim doesn't get you, these sticks will.'

'Salim is likely to get me today or in the next couple of days, sir,' Prakash said, equally lightly.

'So somebody accepted the contract.' Kabir became serious as he digested the importance of Prakash's statement. He looked at Chudasama questioningly, who nodded imperceptibly.

'Some new Bombay boy, probably trying to make his mark,' Prakash said, and briefed him about Chedi's visit. Kabir knew about Chedi. Like every self-respecting young police officer, he prided himself for knowing everything that happened in the largest lodge that was frequented by nefarious elements.

'Where is the boy now?' Kabir asked.

'Chedi's lodge. Rathor is keeping watch over him,' Chudasama replied.

'So, all the hours of chess with Chedi finally paid off,' he said with a smile. 'This piece of information is worth much more than anything else he could have possibly told you. Let's go and arrest this adventurous boy who has ventured so far from his terrain.'

'No, sir,' interjected Prakash. 'If he's arrested now, he may be convicted under the Arms Act, but not for an attempt to murder. And what happens if he denies that he has been hired to kill me? There is a better strategy.'

'What do you have in mind?' Kabir asked.

'Let him have a shot at me. We now know of him and I will be ready. He is at our mercy. Let us exploit the situation to our advantage. We gain leverage if he is caught after taking a shot. For one, Salim will know that I am not afraid of his henchmen. And maybe, there will be other rewarding ways in which this boy can be used.'

There was silence in the room. Even the smoke seemed to hang, not drifting at all.

'You are ready to risk your life to become a bloody hero? You can bloody well be killed and then there will be just an obituary, and no hero. Rewarding! An attempt on your life can be exploited! Are you out of your bloody mind?' Kabir exploded. Prakash realized that he had a tough task ahead of him.

'There will be no obituary, sir.' Prakash spoke calmly to counter Kabir's anger. 'If we have to take the fight to the lion's lair, then every snake on the way has to be stripped of its venom. We can't afford to let Salim set all the events in motion, leaving us only the luxury of a reaction. I am working on finding this Mandrax factory somewhere in Vapi. There is a person called Qasim in Bombay who knows about it, and he needs to be interrogated and compromised. This boy can help me break Qasim, and once Qasim breaks, the path to Salim will be clearer.'

Chudasama tried to interrupt, concerned that Prakash was sharing confidential details of an operation with Kabir. He did not know that Kabir already knew everything. Kabir, of course, understood the import and guessed correctly that Chudasama was not aware of the source of the information. He played along with Prakash.

'Who is this Qasim? And how do you know that Mandrax was made in Vapi?' he queried innocently, checking his anger.

'Some second-rate movie producer in Bombay who has partnered with another guy called Bhatt to produce Mandrax for Salim. Now we need to get him to talk before Bhatt can destroy the factory and the Mandrax with it,' Prakash replied.

'What is the connection with the killer?'

'None. Except that after this boy is either killed or arrested, we pick up Qasim and implicate him in this conspiracy to kill me, and threaten him with the possibility of an encounter as retribution. I think he will crack under that much pressure.'

Kabir thought about it as his anger dissipated. 'It could work. But I have a better plan. We go and pick up this killer now, stage a fake-firing incident through his gun, release the news that an attempt has been made on your life and send a team to pick up Qasim now.

That way, you won't have to risk your life.'

Chudasama enthusiastically supported this proposal. Prakash thought about it. It was tempting. There would hardly be a dozen people who would know, and he would be safe. But then the cardinal maxim of the intelligence community—the possibility of a leak increases in geometric progression with the addition of each person to an operation—held him back. A dozen complicit officers meant a near certain possibility of a news leak that a fake encounter had been staged by them. He can't let go of one of the mottos of his life. The loss of honour is a fate worse than death.

'Sir, let him have a go. More than anything else, it will send a message across to the underworld that I am not worried about being shot at. We will create a legend, you and I, that we knew of this boy having picked up the contract even before he left Bombay, and we had followed him from Bombay. It is also bound to create a little confusion in Salim's ranks about possible traitors.'

They finally agreed to go ahead with Prakash's plan, but on the condition that he would be wearing a bulletproof jacket at all times.

Before parting, Chudasama handed over a wireless set to Kabir.

'Sir, for secure communication. Only three sets operate on this frequency. Now this is the fourth.'

Kabir was awestruck. He had heard of the resources at the command of RI, but having exclusive wireless frequencies was indeed impressive.

◆

Pandey was detailed to track the boy, and he picked up the boy's trail immediately. He soon realized that the boy was working alone, and surprised at the confidence of the boy, informed Chudasama of his discovery. Chudasama quickly checked with Chedi, who confirmed that nobody had met the boy at the lodge. They followed him for the next forty-eight hours as he tracked Prakash's movements, and by the end of it, they were left wondering if Salim was really running short of resources. The young boy, however courageous he might be, was clearly an amateur.

◆

Chhotu surveyed the RI office first. The big bungalow, surrounded by a big lawn and protected by high walls, did not offer the possibility of rushing in for a shot and quick escape. And Chhotu was not going to sacrifice his life for a paltry ten lakh. He was destined to be Chhaliya Bhai. He also ruled out shooting Prakash as he got into his car after finishing office. The long driveway precluded the possibility of taking a shot.

Caught in that moment of introspection, he was not aware that he was being photographed through a partially open window of the RI office. The photograph was printed, and now he was no longer a ghost. Now, there was a record that he had done a recce of the RI office. The date stamp on the photograph was evidence. And now, his face was also known to the intelligence agencies.

He was also followed by Rathor as he walked past the building where Prakash lived. And then, Prakash spotted him standing at the turn. Chhotu was watching Prakash's Gypsy closely as it waited for the watchman to open the door of the building complex. Chhotu may have progressed in the art of surveillance and of shooting unsuspecting people, but he was, as yet, no match when it came to the experienced RI operatives.

Chhotu was cautious, but his confidence overshadowed his apprehensions. It was the confidence of youth, generated out of a sense of immortality. The young believe that death or failure, when it came, would bypass them for they were destined to conquer the worlds. And he had, after all, been approached by Azim Bhai himself for the contract. A contract carrying rewards normally offered only to seasoned killers who were legends in the underworld. Nobody could stop him, for he was Chhaliya. He was never seen, never heard and he could change his appearance whenever required.

He was mistaken. He was doomed, not because he lacked the capability but because he lacked knowledge about the operatives of the intelligence world.

◆

Chhotu was stuck. This was his first solo operation. He was operating in an alien environment, without any backup or support. Earlier jobs had been simpler. He just shot the target and then the others took over. There would be a getaway car, the crowds invariably panicked and by the time there was some semblance of order, he would vanish in the bylanes of the city that he had researched well.

This job was different. There was no getaway car, no crowds and no traffic signals where he could shoot at a stationary vehicle. Moreover, his intended victim did not seem to follow a fixed schedule. He needed to improvise. After two days of surveillance, Chhotu realized that he had no alternative except to shoot and run. No deception, no camouflage, no make up was going to help him. He decided to shoot Prakash when he was going home in the evening. The long, isolated lane that connected the RI office to the main road rarely had much traffic, but the Gypsy had to stop for at least thirty seconds before turning and joining the traffic on the main road, sufficient time to walk up to the vehicle and take a shot. By the time anybody on the main road would notice, he would have walked away in the dusk.

He worked on his escape route by going to the bus stop to check the schedules. Jamnagar to Dwarka by bus. If everything seemed okay, then a bus to Bhavnagar, and then a taxi to Ahmedabad, from where he would take the train to Bombay. In Bombay, he would no longer be known as Chhotu. He would have taken a big step towards becoming a Bhai. He would have earned the respect of his peers in the underworld. And then he would go back to his village for Holi. This time, when he returned home, he would be rich. And feared.

In Jamnagar he noticed a number of people dressed in white. He had never seen people in his village, or even in Bombay, wearing white clothes from top to bottom. To come across as a local, he bought a pair of white trousers and white shirt from a shop near the bus stop. Then, in that reckless mood to spend his newly gained riches, he went and purchased a pair of white shoes as well.

Back in the lodge, in the final hours before the killing, he lovingly cradled the two guns. He cleaned the country-made gun, which he had fabricated with his own hands in the workshop at Jhansi. He had made his mark with that gun. This was his Annapurna, the Goddess that had provided him with food. Then there was the Smith & Wesson, the trophy, the recognition of his skills. He would have to find a hiding place for both of them. He couldn't bear to part with them. They were the symbols of his victory over his circumstances. But there would be too much checking after the assassination of a government officer. He couldn't carry the guns with him. He decided that he would bury the guns after the shooting and come back to retrieve them later.

Chhotu never noticed Rathor, or Pandey, who had been following him. They watched as he was digging the ditch to bury the guns. As Chhotu scooped dirt nearly half a kilometre away from the office on a side lane that led nowhere, they knew that the countdown had started.

◆

Pandey returned to the office to brief the others after Chhotu had returned to the lodge, leaving Rathor to continue the surveillance, comfortable with the realisation that he had another set of eyes in Chedi. They agreed that the killer intended to carry out the operation that day itself, or possibly the next day. The arguments started at that point. Prakash, confident by now that the killer was an amateur, wanted to face him alone. Chudasama agreed that he could not find the killer on their database, but advocated caution as some of the best killers were not known till they were caught. Kabir agreed with Chudasama.

'I will post a police patrol close by,' Kabir said. 'They will reach you as soon as you give the signal.'

'That may alert him,' argued Prakash. 'He will be watching for any break in pattern.'

'He doesn't know the pattern. He has been here for just two days,' said an irritated Kabir.

'Why take a chance? He doesn't know that I know he is out here to kill me. I will be ready for him, as will be Chudasama,' Prakash countered.

The arguments flew back and forth. Ultimately, Kabir agreed to station a team of shooters a kilometre away at a regular patrol point. When they dispersed, Prakash was confident, Kabir apprehensive and Chudasama in a ruminative mood.

◆

Chedi called Prakash at 4 p.m. Chhotu had left the lodge, and although the bag was still there, the guns were missing. Prakash informed Chudasama, who rechecked his revolver. They knew Chedi would have informed Kabir also. Chudasama decided that Prakash should leave the office around 6.30 p.m. The sun would be setting, leading to at least some loss of visibility, making a long shot difficult for the boy.

Prakash decided to drive himself. He would not risk Manu Bhai's life.

◆

Chhotu watched the Gypsy as it turned left to enter the lane. He had decided to dress in his new clothes: white shirt, white trousers, white shoes. Standing in front of the mirror with his news clothes on, he liked the look.

I should wear whites more often, he thought. *I look like Jeetendra. Maybe it can become my trademark when I am big and feared.*

'Is he watching me or is it just my imagination?' he wondered out loud as he walked towards the Gypsy as it approached the turn. 'Yes, he is definitely watching. He should have been looking at the road but instead his eyes are on me. Why is that? Does he suspect something?' He grew more cautious, gripped the katta in the sling bag a little harder, and moved a little faster to reach the spot where Prakash's Gypsy usually halted. He hoped he looked like a pedestrian trying to cross the road.

As he got closer, he noticed that the target was driving with his left hand and his right hand was on the lap. The Gypsy slowed down a little earlier than expected. There was something in the target's posture, which, instead of being aligned to the road, was aligned towards him, that told him that his victim was watching him instead of the road.

He knows, his mind screamed, just before he heard a loud noise and felt a searing pain in his leg. He thought he even heard the sound of something hitting his leg, but the pain overshadowed every other sense. He could not focus, his hands felt numb, the mouth was dry, and the evening seemed strangely silent. He looked at his leg and saw blood oozing out from the back of his leg.

I have been shot, he thought in wonder as he watched Prakash drop down at the other end of the Gypsy, vanishing out of sight.

◆

There he is, Prakash thought as he saw the killer move towards his Gypsy. *All my planning stops at this stage, and it's just the two of us. I hope he is not very fast. If he is, I will die today.*

Then he chided himself. *I know about him, and he doesn't know that I know he is out there. What was I thinking when I planned this? Does everyone who is likely to be shot at thinks like this? What am I thinking? People never know they will be shot before they are shot. I am lucky that I know! There, he is moving. I am not supposed to stare at him. But I can't take my eyes off him. He looks so young. He must be fast if he is so young. Should I take out my gun now?*

Prakash had taken his eyes off the killer for a moment, worried that he may have left the safety catch on, when he heard a loud noise, followed by another.

'Mayday!' He shouted into the open microphone of the wireless before opening the side door and dropping out on the other side of the road.

Has he pulled the trigger already? But he was still too far to try and take a shot, Prakash said to himself.

Who fired then? He wondered as he crawled towards the back of the Gypsy, ready for the shootout.

He heard the police moving in and moved out of the cover of the Gypsy. He saw Chudasama standing over the fallen shooter, pointing his gun at the sobbing boy. The shooter looked at him, and Prakash recognized that look. He realized that the boy was sobbing not because of the pain of a broken leg but because of the pain of shattered dreams.

◆

Things were a blur for Prakash after that. He was bundled into his Gypsy by Pandey, rushed to his home and a drink was thrust into his hands. Chudasama arrived an hour later to explain that he had decided to take matters into his own hands to keep Prakash safe. He had decided that he would shoot the shooter as he approached the Gypsy. Even then, he informed Prakash, the young killer had been fast. He had managed to let loose a hurried shot from his country-made pistol, but it had not found the intended target.

The boy was taken into custody and rushed to the hospital. They had no intention of letting him die, and Kabir personally oversaw the security arrangements. He did not want the killer to be shot dead by a policeman in a display of loyalty to the force. And, of course, Salim should not have the boy killed either.

The press was called. Chhotu was photographed, details were shared and Prakash was bombarded with questions. He left the reporters to Kabir and Chudasama, the two veterans who knew how to deal with the press. They shared just enough details with the reporters to keep them hooked, looking for more. Around 9 p.m. the reporters rushed out to file their copies.

They all met at Prakash's residence thereafter.

'What about Chedi?' Prakash asked.

'Chedi is capable of taking care of himself,' Kabir said. 'His name is not featuring anywhere. The story that we had been keeping a watch on Chhotu since he left Bombay is holding so far. One enterprising reporter did ask why he had not been arrested earlier, but he was firmly told that operational details would not be divulged, and then everyone else was quiet. Maybe we will still make a hero out of you.' Kabir was on a high. He paced around the room, picking his drink, then keeping it down, walking up to Prakash to pat him on the shoulder, then pumping Chudasama's hand. He couldn't keep still. He had eliminated one high profile criminal, solved a high profile murder and arrested another murderer in the act, all within a month. Prakash was calm, maybe because he had faced death earlier, although not at the end of a gun.

'Still, we need to keep him funded if he has to rush to a quick holiday,' Prakash said.

'We will see later. What next?' Kabir was not finished for the day.

Prakash picked up the phone and dialled a Bombay number.

'Where is he?' he asked Lal.

'Left him as he was entering his Bandra flat with a starlet around half an hour ago. It looked like they were not going anywhere, but I still left Pawar there to keep watch,' Lal replied from the other end.

'I will reach tomorrow morning. Meet me at the airport, please.'

'Qasim is secure,' he told the other two after hanging up. 'He does not seem to suspect anything.'

Chudasama and Kabir stared at Prakash, the cub who was now growing claws. While they were worried about his life, he had been mounting the operation to nab Qasim. He seemed unconcerned about the fact that there had been an attempt on his life just an hour back.

For Prakash, it was just another moment of his life, experienced and lived. At present there was work to be done. Kabir called the Air India station manager, and three confirmed tickets were kept aside, along with the boarding passes to be collected by the PSO to the District Superintendent of Police.

The station manager wondered what he would say to the three irate offloaded passengers tomorrow in their perpetually full flight.

'You don't want to meet the guy who came to kill you?' Kabir asked in the midst of all these arrangements.

'He is just a hired gun, sir. I would, someday, like to meet Salim, the guy who is supposed to have ordered the kill. Look him in the eye alone, mano a mano. This boy is a tool. He may have his own compulsions, but I have none to meet him.'

Kabir looked at Prakash. He seemed to be mercurial, changing with every event, revealing a new facet with every development.

'I talked to him at length. He has a history of violence behind him. This is his first setback, and the guy is shattered. He is ready to talk, but he knows very little. Just that his mentor, Azim Bhai, got him the contract. Azim Bhai, absconding after the Bombay bomb blasts, does not have any overt links with Salim. This boy is not our ticket to Salim.'

'I never expected him to be, sir,' Prakash replied in an offhand manner. 'He is a contract killer, not a confidant. The man who will get us to Salim is Qasim, and that's where we need to concentrate.'

Kabir decided to go with Prakash's instincts. After all, those instincts had proved to be reliable so far. The team sat down to plan the fall of the Lion of Dubai.

26

Roasting the Rooster

Prakash called Singh.

'What's so urgent, Prakash, that it couldn't wait till tomorrow morning,' Singh said irritably.

It's just eleven! I may have disturbed his second drink. Doesn't the guy realize that intelligence operations don't observe office hours? thought Prakash.

'I got shot at, sir,' he said.

'What do you mean you got shot at?' Singh said, perplexed.

'There was an attempt at my life this evening, sir,' Prakash elaborated.

There was a short silence at the other end.

'Have you gotten a tattoo of a bull's eye or something on your body that guys just keep taking potshots at you?' Singh said. It was probably his attempt at humour. He must have also realized that he sounded a bit callous, so he said, 'What I meant was that you must be really irritating people if they are shooting at you.'

Prakash nearly laughed but choked it back. 'Probably, sir,' he said.

Singh was at a loss for words, probably realizing that his indisposition towards Prakash was showing.

'Are you okay?' He asked after a short pause. 'Do you need any help? Should I talk to the DGP?'

He had finally asked the right questions, Prakash thought.

'I am okay, sir. Kabir sir and Chudasama had information about it and they apprehended the killer as he was about to take a shot at me. Things seem to be in control.'

'What did the interrogation reveal? Were there any accomplices? Who hired him? Salim?' It seemed like the importance of the event was finally sinking in.

'They are still interrogating him, sir. Kabir sir is not letting anyone get close to him. He doesn't trust us to keep our temper in control, I guess,' Prakash lied smoothly, and then continued. 'I just wanted your approval to go to Bombay tomorrow. You know, that case about Qasim? The report that I had filed.'

'What's the hurry?' Singh interjected. 'You are safer in Jamnagar. Send a report about today's events to me first, and then let's see.'

Prakash laughed this time; his notoriously cavalier attitude coming to the forefront again. 'File a report about the attempt on my life, sir? What do I write? The bore of the bullet, the name or age of the supposed killer? I think I will let the police do their job here, while I do mine in Bombay.'

There was no reply from the other end. Prakash waited for a few seconds, and then continued, 'If Qasim even gets a whiff that we know of his involvement in the Mandrax case, he may flee; and I am not going to take that chance, sir. Anyway, if the shooter has any accomplices, they will be in Jamnagar, not in Bombay. In any case, they won't be expecting me in the city. Additionally, I can't keep up surveillance on Qasim indefinitely.'

Singh had finally got Prakash on the hook. 'You are using private surveillance, Prakash? This kind of thing can get you into trouble.'

Prakash realized that he had reached a point of no return.

'More trouble than getting shot at, sir?' he retorted. 'I will update you about the developments tomorrow after apprehending Qasim.' He disconnected the phone without giving Singh a chance to say anything else.

Chudasama and Kabir gaped at him, seeing a new side of Prakash, and he rolled his eyes. This time; even Chudasama did not say a word to support Singh.

'To success,' said Kabir, raising his glass of drink and hoping that Prakash's lucky streak would continue.

◆

The last call of the night was to his counterpart in the Bombay branch of RI. He seemed to be more aware than Singh.

'Heard someone took a shot at you today?' He asked. 'Hope you are fine.'

'Yeah, one of Salim's chaps,' Prakash replied, probably sounding a little more carefree than he had intended. 'Listen, I require some logistical support tomorrow. Nothing much, just a car and a couple of people to conduct a search. And we may be arresting someone. Any possibility of a quick hearing for a transit remand, if required?'

'Don't worry. Come in. Is this related to today's case?'

'A little.'

'Call me for anything you need. We can't let them get away with shooting at an RI guy.'

'Will keep you updated,' Prakash said. 'Thanks, man.'

◆

Qatil Qasim. That's what he went by now. He lovingly gazed at the interiors of his new office at Lokhandwala. He was among the first to have moved in the area, buying an expansive office in an upcoming area rather than an expensive one in a swanky location like Juhu or a posh place like Bandra. After all, his new relationship with Salim Bhai would ensure that he would be the producer in demand.

He dreamt of the future as he lazed in his office, leaning back on his plush leather chair, soaking in the luxury—the cool air of his imported Hitachi air-conditioner, the brightness of the imported wallpaper from Italy and the sparkling lights of the chandelier from Belgium. All smuggled, of course. There was no need to pay duty when you could smuggle something. This office would be perfect after he had won a couple of trophies to display on the wall. Now with Nazir's death, he might be able to influence the jury. After all, he could now be the main producer for Salim Bhai. Nazir had been stupid. He could never distinguish between art and glamour. He wanted to create art that could be glamorous. Why should one antagonize Bhai just for creating good art?

Life was good, made better by his ability to exploit young aspiring actresses flocking to Bombay. Now even stars would flock to him for work. And that would be the consummation of his dreams. He would sleep with the stars, not just the aspiring starlets.

It had been a long journey from the bylanes of Lucknow to this posh office in Andheri. He had come to Bombay with dreams of becoming a star. His struggle, like that of countless others, had started from shared one-room tenements of Azad Nagar. All of them had made the obligatory visits to casting agents. The whispers of a rare audition would make them rush to iron their best clothes. As time had passed and his hopes dimmed, he turned to religion, trekking bare feet from Lokhandwala to Haji Ali every Thursday night, reaching the dargah early on Friday to pray to the maula to grant him his wishes. Nothing had worked.

He had done everything they had told him to do. Joined a theatre group, worked as a stage hand, worked as a spot boy, even swept the floor after a shot. 'It showed your dedication to art,' they said. And then they sniggered at him behind his back. 'Another Bhaiya in Bombay who wants to be a star. Why do these Bhaiyas keep coming to Bombay?' But he ignored the sniggers and toiled on, hoping that someday someone would recognize his talent. But no one gave him a chance, and with each passing day, the bitterness accumulated. And then, the offers came. 'We will give you a break, but you will have to sleep with us.' He drew the line at sleeping with men. He just couldn't stomach the idea. And so, he struggled in vain.

Ritu, his second girlfriend, showed him that scruples don't help. She would sleep with the casting director, or the assistant director, or even the casting agent, for a bit role. She was pretty enough for people to tolerate her, and shallow enough to not aspire for anything except the small roles. He became her agent. Some said her pimp. But he got her at least a dozen bit roles a year. Enough for her to remain famous in her small town in Rajasthan, and justify a comfortable existence.

Ritu brought him other girls, and soon he was the 'secretary' for a dozen aspiring actresses. The party organizers called him to fill their glamour quotient, casting directors called him when they needed to cast a girl in small roles, or sometimes, even for the second lead in those 'dirty pictures' that had spilt over from the eighties into the nineties. He became famous for providing the 'qatil' beauties who set the screen on fire. Girls who made sure that the movie would be a hit in small towns and villages. He was Qasim who provided the qatil girls, and he was the prime rooster in their pen. Soon, he abandoned his dreams of becoming a star and, collecting his life's savings, started making small-budget raunchy movies for hinterland audiences.

His luck truly turned when Ritu brought Shabnam to him, who, after struggling for more than a year, was ready to shed her modesty for a role in movies. But she was more canny than the others. She agreed to sleep with the casting director or a director only after the role had been finalized to her satisfaction. She created a buzz, but she did not get meaningful roles. There was no space for a newcomer among a bevy of established beauties. But it was Shabnam who had caught the eye of Bhai.

He had taken her to Dubai to meet Salim Bhai. And for his troubles, he had gained for himself those elusive two minutes with Bhai that every producer in Bollywood craved. Bhai had been generous. Once Shabnam agreed to be with him—*as if she had had a choice*, he thought—Bhai had allocated him his first movie with a budget of two crore rupees. The cast, of course, was decided by Bhai. After that he never looked back. He had to, of course, do some odd jobs for Bhai. Like financing that factory of Bhatt. And hiding that *asla* during the bomb blasts. Transferring a few crore from the extortion money dropped off at his house to Mukul Sheth. Thankfully, the police never got wind of his other activities, and Bhai was happy.

He is bound to give me more movies, and soon I will replace Nazir, Qasim thought. *Life has been good, and it is only going to get better.* He nearly preened as he looked at himself in the mirror.

◆

Lal was waiting at the airport. Prakash quickly introduced Chudasama and Sisodia, and watching the quizzical expression on Lal's face, explained that it needed to be a joint operation involving the RI and the police.

'Sisodia had led the team that killed Ahir, which resulted in the apprehension of Sharma sir's killers. And then yesterday, he led the police team that was detailed to protect me. He is the trusted officer of the SP, and the point man between the RI and the police in Jamnagar,' Prakash said, trying to allay Lal's concerns about sharing sensitive information in the presence of an outsider. 'We plan to threaten Qasim with arrest by police if he doesn't cooperate.'

'He is at his office at Lokhandwala,' Lal said, reassured. Noting the quizzical expression on Prakash's face, he continued, 'It's an upcoming area near Andheri, a favourite with the underworld at the moment.'

Lal seemed to be deeply stirred by whatever he had learnt about Qasim. 'You are after a typical sewer rat of Bombay, sir. Thrives by exploiting the bodies of others. He started off as a struggler, but is now virtually a pimp for a number of aspiring actresses. He is the favoured agent to approach for casting in all smut. You remember Shabnam? You told me about her in Dapoli. That new mistress of Salim? He was her secretary also for a while. I believe that he introduced her to Salim, and Salim in turn financed a few of his films. He is also rumoured to have laundered Salim's money, not substantial amounts but enough to keep Salim happy.'

Lal did not notice Prakash flinching when he mentioned that Qasim had introduced Shabnam to Salim. Prakash was silent for a while. He wondered whether this was just Shabnam's way of getting back at her first pimp, or was it her way of revealing another facet of her life to Prakash? Or was it just another way of severing ties with her old life? He shook himself free of these thoughts and focused on the job.

'Will this be sufficient to turn the screws on him?' he asked Chudasama.

'Is there anything else that we know about his personal life?' Chudasama asked Lal.

'You mean except the fact that he is a philanderer?' Lal asked. He glanced at Prakash, and then with a wry face, stated, 'One of the girls he used to handle is now working as an air hostess. I helped her out of some sticky situations a couple of times. She tells me that he is fond of screwing girls in the ass. Some sort of domination fetish. Will that help?'

'Is he good-looking?' Prakash asked.

'Yes,' Lal replied.

'Then yes...more than you can imagine.'

◆

The three of them—Chudasama, Prakash and a local RI official—entered Qasim's office at 4 p.m., timing it so that if they were to arrest him, they could interrogate Qasim for a full night and the following morning before they were required by law to produce him before the magistrate.

'What are you looking for?' Qasim asked, staring uncomprehendingly at the search warrant served by the local RI officer. 'I am not a smuggler.'

'Okay, let's save time,' the fair one, who seemed to be their leader, said. 'I just need the details of your bank accounts and a copy of your company's balance sheet. And I want to know where Bhatt is, and how much money you gave him to establish the factory for manufacturing Mandrax. Oh, and by the way, it would be helpful if you could take us to that Mandrax factory.'

Qasim blanched at the mention of the Mandrax factory, but recovered quickly.

'I don't know anything about any Mandrax factory, or where Bhatt is. I have not met him since we last produced a movie together, and I paid him his share of the profits more than a year back. I don't have a company, and my bank accounts are with my accountant. I will come with them to your office next week.'

'So you admit knowing Bhatt. Why don't we go and meet him?' The fair one spoke again.

Qasim could guess that they did not know the location of the factory, and without the factory, everything was conjecture. He was safe. He just had to get a message across to Bhatt advising him to escape. He will play for time, he decided.

'I am not in touch with him. Let me trace him and bring him to your office next week when I bring the bank records,' he replied.

'Wrong answer. I want Bhatt's location today.'

'Somebody seems to have given you some wrong information,' he said, just a tad nervously. 'Just give me a couple of days and I will be able to find Bhatt. He will explain everything. I have a very good relationship with many of your colleagues. They can vouch for me. I think we will be able to come to an understanding if you just let me make a couple of calls.'

'Stalling, Qasim Bhai? Not today. Today, you have to give me

Bhatt and the factory.'

'I can't give you something I don't have,' he said.

Qasim watched nervously as one of them left the room. That left the fair guy and the guy with the handlebar moustache in the room. Then, another hefty man, one with a gun strapped on a standard holster, entered the room.

'Are you trying to intimidate me?' he asked. 'I have told you—I know nothing.'

The burly man handed him a paper to read. He tried to control his pacing heart, which became increasingly difficult as he read through the paper.

'What is this? Who is Prakash?' he asked in a trembling voice.

'This is the confession of a killer named Chhotu,' replied the fair one. Qasim had by then identified him as the team leader. 'He admits that you paid him five lakh rupees, on Salim Bhai's instructions, to murder me, Prakash, because I was interfering with the Mandrax smuggling. So, Jamnagar Police wants to take you for interrogation.'

'But it is all false!' blurted Qasim.

'It is only as false as your own claim that you don't know where Bhatt is. Or maybe it is the truth, as much truth as the Nawabi hobbies you enjoy,' Prakash spoke calmly, referring to the universal Indian phrase adopted for anal sex.

This rattled Qasim. They knew too much about him. He was now convinced that this was no random fishing expedition. But Salim would kill him if Qasim betrayed him. He made one last ditch effort.

'I am really telling the truth. I don't know where Bhatt is. And I don't know anything about Mandrax.'

Prakash gave him a wry smile.

'Such a pity, for such a good-looking man. Qatil Qasim they call you. I think you will be the Qatil beauty in prison. They love your kind of good-looking men in jail. No girls in there, you see.'

'And, sir, we should lodge him with the real bad lot. They will ensure he dies a slow death. That way would be better than the quick death he will get if we kill him in an encounter. After all he tried to get you killed,' said the police inspector from Jamnagar in a gruff voice.

Qasim looked at each of them with a hunted look. There was the impassive man with the handlebar moustache. He looked like he was capable of doing anything. Then there was Prakash, the fair guy, sarcastic but full of purpose. And he just could not place the policeman. 'Was he loyal enough to do something illegal?' he wondered.

'If you are wondering about my team, let me introduce them.' Prakash said, seemingly reading his thoughts. 'This is Chudasama. He shot Chhotu Chhaliya yesterday. And he is Sisodia,' he continued, gesturing towards the policeman. 'He recently killed Ahir in an encounter.'

Sisodia went stiff. 'He was, after all, planning to kill you, sir. Just like this pig over here.'

Qasim looked at all of them and decided that he had a better chance of surviving Salim than these guys.

'What happens if I get you Bhatt?' he asked.

'That is not sufficient. I also need to find the Mandrax factory. If that happens, this confession made by Chhotu Chhaliya vanishes. You will no longer be a part of a conspiracy to murder me. You will, of course, go to jail for financing the Mandrax factory for Salim, but you will be in a good jail, with a friendly jailer, and you can try and fight the rap.'

◆

It was easy after that. As Prakash had learnt during his days of high-altitude trekking, fear is a powerful stimulant but panic makes you lose your reasoning. Qasim had been used to the good life for a few years, and once the panic of a slow, painful, humiliating death set in, there was no way he could have staggered back from the precipice. Prakash and Chudasama knew that they just had to keep fuelling that fear with doomsday predictions, and Qasim would not be able to reason.

The only path Qasim could finally see was the one Prakash had chalked out for him, and he stumbled on it, hoping to salvage a reprieve. He gave them Bhatt's number. They forced Qasim, totally cowed down by now, to call Bhatt. They relaxed a little when Bhatt informed Qasim that he had no intention of moving out of Vapi for the next two days. In fact, he was cooking a new batch of methaqualone, which will be used for manufacturing Mandrax tablets. Qasim slumped when Bhatt said that. He was now a conspirator under the dreaded NDPS Act. He was at the mercy of the RI and the police. He tried to strike a final deal.

'What if I show you the factory?' he asked Prakash. 'Will you let me go?'

Prakash let out a sigh of relief. Now there would be no need to break Bhatt. And Qasim, with his knowledge of Salim's operations, could prove to be a valuable ally.

'No,' he said. 'But I will make it soft for you. Maybe record that when you gave the money to Bhatt you didn't know that you were financing a factory to manufacture Mandrax. Maybe mention in the report that you willingly showed us Bhatt's residence. That can possibly help you a little before the judge. And I will make sure that you have all the facilities in jail, although you can create the legend that you are getting those facilities because you are paying for them. Life will not be easy, but it won't be as hard as it can be.'

◆

Vapi was a six-hour drive, and they left Bombay at 10 p.m. Prakash called Singh when they stopped for tea at four o'clock in the morning. Singh received the call calmly. He was getting used to Prakash calling him at odd hours. He listened to the implausible story that Prakash told him, but then stoically accepted that Prakash was in Vapi, an area not in his jurisdiction, trying to find a Mandrax factory and that he had a person from Bombay in illegal custody, meaning they had neither arrested him nor taken any remand, that this person was likely to be arrested over the next forty-eight hours, that this was going to be a joint operation between the RI and the police, that there was a police inspector accompanying Prakash's team and that the Bombay wing of RI was also part of the operation.

He did not know whether to acknowledge or disown the operation. Finally, he decided to ride the proverbial tail of the tiger, hoping to gain a gun sometime in the future. He, accordingly, added one face-saving condition. The local officers from Vapi and Surat should be involved in the operation. Prakash readily agreed. He would call these officers only after he had found the Mandrax factory.

◆

They barged into Bhatt's house at the break of dawn. It was easy to break Bhatt. He was a businessman, just a youngster who had inherited his family's pharmaceutical business and had wanted a good time. He had met Qasim at a small party where he was trying to get friendly with the young starlets, and Qasim had been trying to convince businessmen to finance his film. They forged a mutually beneficial relationship, which blossomed when Bhatt kept getting returns on the money he invested in Qasim's movies. The company of the starlets Qasim managed for him was a bonus. So when Qasim had come with the offer to manufacture Mandrax, he had been quick to accept it, particularly when he had been told that Salim would be investing the money. Like a lot of other businessmen with little contact with the underworld, he believed in Salim's infallibility. Now he was living a dream. Beautiful girls, easy money and delusions of invincibility. After all, he was working for the biggest and richest underworld don of the country.

It did not take much to break him. He capitulated as soon as he saw Sisodia and Chudasama's drawn revolvers as they crashed into his room, rudely waking him up. The fear in Qasim's eyes acted as a catalyst. He immediately agreed to lead them to the factory.

The factory was in the industrial area of Vapi, one of the dozens manufacturing pharmaceuticals and chemicals. As they entered, Prakash casually asked Bhatt about the quantity of methaqualone in there.

'2,100 kg of methaqualone powder, 840 kg of Mandrax tablets, 950 kg of acetic anhydride and about 600 kg of other raw material,' he said in a beaten voice.

Then, looking at the quizzical expression on Prakash's face, he continued. 'It's expensive, and it's drugs. I don't allow any pilferage. I have an account of every gram of raw material and every kilogram of Mandrax that enters or leaves my factory.'

◆

After that, the investigation progressed as per the rule book. Kabir observed that it was rather funny that an investigation goes by the rule book only after the book has been torn and thrown to the winds. There was little to search at the factory. Everything had been immaculately recorded: the raw materials, intermediates and the final product were neatly stacked in separate store rooms, with the daily use and issuance of raw material properly recorded in the books, and the final production logged and stuck on the store room door, duly signed by Bhatt and his production manager Shiv Pratap.

Eyebrows were raised at the impeccable records, and Bhatt admitted that he believed that with Salim's backing, he was invulnerable.

The drugs were inventoried. The supplier of acetic anhydride, the precursor chemical, was named by Bhatt and arrested that day and the factory was sealed. Bhatt accepted that he had met Salim and Hanif in Dubai to explain the manufacturing process of Mandrax, that Hanif had later called him to explain the design of the barrels that had later been seized at Jetpur, that the drivers who had earlier transported the drugs to Porbandar were known only to Hanif, and that he had no record of those trucks. The statements that were recorded were a mixture of truths, half-truths and convenience, and some of the dates were randomly picked from Bhatt's passport to corroborate his confession about his visits to Dubai to meet Salim.

Qasim was, as promised, not mentioned in the confession.

At the first hint of reprieve, Qasim cooperated fully. He admitted that he had given money to Bhatt at Salim's directions, and that this had been done through a convoluted route of purchase and sale of film rights to mask the true nature of the transaction. But he also claimed that he did not know that the money would be used to manufacture drugs, and that Hanif had introduced him to Bhatt. Bhatt blanched upon hearing Qasim, but at this stage they were more afraid of the stoic looks of Chudasama and Sisodia than Salim. He quietly acquiesced to the false confession being made by Qasim.

Qasim's company bank account showed that a sale of overseas rights of the film *Anna* had been made to a Dubai company for three crore rupees, and a transfer of ₹50 lakh had been made immediately thereafter. The trail of transaction was also linked to Bhatt, who had purchased the machinery immediately on receiving fifty lakhs in his account. A *letter rogatory* was sent to Dubai Customs to verify the ownership of the company that had purchased the overseas rights of Qasim's movie to check if it had any links to Salim. Prakash knew that chances of getting a reply were slim, but he was not concerned. He already had Qasim and Bhatt's statement to link Salim to the Mandrax, and the two of them were not likely to retract their confessions, unless both of them stood face to face with Salim. At this stage, there was little possibility of that happening. Salim was not likely to return to India to be incarcerated under the NDPS Act. The team could do what they wanted to, which included going soft on Qasim.

It was a relieved Qasim who left with Prakash for Jamnagar from Vapi under a transit remand for further investigation of his role in financing Salim's activities. Bhatt and the others were arrested and sent to jail in Vapi itself.

It ended up being one of the fastest investigations ever—sources for the raw materials were identified, the manufacturers and financiers were apprehended, and the biggest don of the country had been conclusively implicated in the conspiracy.

It even merited a grudging praise from Singh.

27

Shifting Sands

'I think this operation is over,' Prakash told Kabir.

'What do you mean by over?' Kabir said sardonically. 'Over after just one attempt on your life?' He looked at Prakash with an indulgent smile, and then continued. 'Although, now I do appreciate that letting Chhotu take that shot at you worked brilliantly. Qasim would not have been so cooperative had the news been just another small piece in some corner of the newspapers. A full-page headline across newspapers—*Killer arrested while trying to shoot at Assistant Director, RI*—certainly creates more impact than—*Another Salim hitman arrested with two guns.*

Prakash laughed. The two joint operations by the police and RI, first for catching a killer, and then for identifying the Mandrax manufacturing unit, had been praised in all quarters. The buzz was spreading. The agencies were winning the war against the underworld.

Now, three weeks after the bust of the factory at Vapi, they were sprawled on the floor of Prakash's house, the whisky glasses and the half empty bottle creating kaleidoscopic patterns on the white marble floor. Black Dog was the preferred brew now, especially after they had, in a drunken fit, started to call themselves the 'Howling Hounds'. After all, Prakash had drunkenly stated, we can howl and hone in on our prey at will, with unerring accuracy. Prakash had, apparently in that inebriated state, also stated, 'If a thousand dogs could bark within Amrish Puri's body on seeing a pretty girl, a thousand dogs bark within us when we see a gangster.' The hoots and cheers of the only other one in the party, Kabir, led to a unanimous vote of two, and the name stuck.

'What next?' asked Kabir.

'I should go and meet Shabnam,' said Prakash. 'All this would not have been possible without her.'

'Should you do that now, without putting Qasim in jail?' Kabir seemed wary.

'There is that, of course. I should inform her, at the least, that I can't come for a couple of weeks,' Prakash said despondently.

'You know, it's not over, and will never ever be over. Salim's killers are going to keep coming after you and Shabnam, especially after he comes to know that the two of you are together,' Kabir said gently.

'I know. That is what worries me. I need a sword that can effectively neutralize his thousand arms. Qasim is cooperating, and I think we should milk him dry of all the information he has on Salim before we send him to jail. After all, Vapi may not be the only factory that Salim financed. He must have laundered money for Salim for other operations too. Let us play good cops. Let him have a good time in exchange for information.'

'What are you saying? No bad cop! Only good cop?'

'Just thinking whether we should allow Qasim a little romp with his favourite starlet. It may loosen his tongue some more. Girls seem to be his major weakness.'

'First a bootlegger, now a pimp,' Kabir said with a laugh, taking the sting out of the comment. 'What a quantum jump for a young crusader!'

'One does whatever it takes to survive,' Prakash replied with a straight face.

Kabir laughed and then said, 'Back to sarcasm, I see. The pressure seems to be reducing. No plans to turn this victory into a crusade against Salim?'

'What crusade, Kabir Bhai? The two of us are not Knights of

the Round Table, capable of taking on the horde of armies. And I am just a nincompoop trying to save his sorry ass, and being lucky so far. Maybe there will be no Chedi when the next killer comes.'

'So why not create the round table?' Kabir asked, only half in jest.

'What?' Prakash was confused.

'Why not build an unsanctioned round table?' Kabir repeated.

'I don't know what has come over you in the past few months. You seem to draw pleasure from breaking the rules. I seem to be a bad influence on you,' Prakash said. 'I am going to pump some more information out of Qasim. You sit and drink some more and think of more rules that we can break.'

'And what about milking Shabnam for some information?' Kabir asked. 'She also knows a lot about Salim's world. Arc you not going to milk her for knowledge?'

Prakash was only partly taken aback by the suggestion. Shabnam and Shelley had so far been part of a separate life, away from his work. But the lines were blurring. Shelley had already signed the information sheet, and Shabnam had given him Qasim.

'I am not going to ask her. She will decide what she wants to tell me, and she can decide when. I am not going to force her,' Prakash said.

Kabir was not finished. He had other arrows in his quiver, though they were not meant to hurt.

'That's not what I meant at all. It's time we learnt a few things from Shabnam, Prakash. Babes in the woods, she called us. Unfair, I would say, but not totally wrong. She said that we are irrelevant in the scheme of things. She was right. We are bound by innumerable rules. Just think. When did we succeed? It was when we broke the rules. Let us make ourselves relevant. She is opening the world for us, and you want to leave Shabnam out of this? You really are a nincompoop.'

'Where are you going with this?'

'We have broken rules, traditions and law. At some stage, somebody will come after us for all the wrongs we have done. And then it will be difficult to fight for your life, since then you will also be fighting for your career. That's when nobody will remember why you broke the rules. What they will remember is that I murdered a guy, that you slept with the mistress of a dreaded gang lord and that Chudasama shot a guy, and it will be too easy to pronounce us guilty.'

'We did what was right,' said Prakash. The thought that at some stage he would have to answer for his unsanctioned actions had crossed his mind, but then, with his devil-may-care attitude, he had pushed it to the back of his mind. Kabir, of course, was more analytical and grounded. He had to be, to survive in a job that put him constantly in public eye.

'Yes, you and I do the right thing. It may be because we are inherently decent. We trust everyone, when we should not. The underworld is more ruthless. They don't trust anyone. And that is why they have an edge over us. They are lone rangers who rule by fear. We can't spread fear. But we, with our decency, can have loyal friends. It's time that some of us develop loyalties that the knights shared. Brothers in arms whose first commitment is only to each other. We have information flowing in from Qasim. And Shabnam can add to that. Why can't we have a brotherhood that can effectively use that information?'

It was just an idea, but it stuck with Prakash. He decided that he would talk to Shabnam. But there would be time for that later. At the moment, he wanted to pump Qasim for everything that he had.

'Comrades in arms, sir,' he said flippantly, trying to close the issue. 'I can't call Shelley and Shabnam sisters in arms, and they would be up in arms if I call them brothers in arms. What you are saying is that we create an extra-legal caucus within the larger caucus of the government, I see. But let me get Qasim to talk first, and then we will talk. Another drink?'

Kabir did not reply. He was looking into his glass rather intently. He knew that Prakash was deflecting from the topic. But he himself had mentioned Shelley and Shabnam. *Is he planning something that I do not know of?* he wondered. Kabir was worried. *Is he so secretive now because he is planning to go after Salim alone? He seems so intent on interrogating Qasim. Where was Prakash moving? Does he not realize that he can't take on Salim's organization all by himself?*

Kabir decided that he would talk to Prakash soon after Qasim was arraigned.

◆

In Dubai, Salim was raging. It was just Hanif and him now. Two people who had grown up together, plotted the murders of rival gangs together and had planned the expansion of their empire together. And now, their mistakes were leading to the collapse of their empire. The fawning favour seekers were gone, and his fiery temper did not seem to foment fear in their foes anymore. Their glitzy nights had turned into brooding evenings.

Salim missed his power, but he missed Bombay more than anything else. He had, time and again, to all and sundry, to the powerful and the poor, to the politicians and the people, expressed his desire to return to the city from where he had started his criminal career. He had prospered over there, and he loved it despite the filth and the crowds, the sticky humidity of April and the flooded streets of June, the pot-holed streets and the eternal traffic jams. He loved the sleazy dance bars, the sexcapades of the stars, the joyful celebration of festivals by communities, but above all, he loved the spirit of the people in the city. It was this spirit that could catapult anyone, just like it had catapulted Salim, to the top.

And now, he knew, he would never see the city with the eyes of a free man.

'How did he know? How could he know about Qasim and

Bhatt?' Salim raved. 'Those statements by the truck owner and drivers, those would have been thrown out of the court easily. But this statement by Qasim and Bhatt, and that money transfer… How does one get out of this? This gaandu…this behenchod…this guy you used to call a nincompoop has cooked my goose. I can't risk going to India anymore. Murder was different, one could get away with it, and I had just started to work on the politicians and the policewallahs to convince them that I was not involved in the bomb blasts. But now this! Nobody will help me with this kind of evidence stacked against me. How did he know about Qasim?'

Hanif kept silent throughout the outburst.

The rage eventually subsided, only to be replaced by a searing anger at the betrayal. *But who had betrayed me the most?* he wondered. He looked at Hanif, with his thinning hair and henna-coloured beard, the reddish tinge that told everyone that he was pious and not vain. He was like a brother to him, sometimes more than the three brothers he had from the same mother. They had been friends since the age of six and had planned the takeover of Bombay together. While Salim had strutted on the streets, Hanif had plotted in the dingy rooms that worked as their operations headquarters. The boys saluted Salim but went to Hanif to tell their tales. They knew that Salim had the brains, but Hanif was the executor. And so, they had worked together. In their early days of struggle, Hanif used to land on the streets of Bombay, trying to sniff out, and even kill, traitors. On one occasion he was able to smoke out and kill someone who had been hired to kill Salim. That was when he had earned himself the sobriquet—kutta. Salim hoped that Hanif did not mind the name and had not carried a grudge. *Was it him?* he thought. After all, it was Hanif who had advised him to work with the Pakistanis. *Was it a part of his plan to replace him? After all, Hanif is more comfortable with the Pakistanis.*

'We had some good times, Hanif Bhai,' he said.

'And we are going to have more.'

'Not like those, Hanif Bhai. There is no place like Bombay. Like they say in the movies, it has that fragrance of familiarity. I like Dubai. The house on Naif Street was nice, with all the familiar people from India and Pakistan. The bustle reminded me of Crawford Market. Both of them were so similar, and then our own people were out there. I like this house too. This Deira, with its view of the water. Dubai, in some ways, is better than Bombay. We have Europeans here, Africans and even Americans. It's a cosmopolitan Bombay, everyone is looking for a piece of the action, everybody wants to make some money and just like Bombay, one can get everything for a price here. But one can't cut off one's roots. There is something that dies within you when you are transplanted. I miss the mango orchards of Devgarh, the fish market of Boria, the hilly road to Dabhol.'

'Inshallah, we will be there again,' Hanif said. He too was nostalgic, but his faith dulled his longing.

'No, Hanif Bhai. Now we will never be going to Bombay as free men. Our dream of calling the stars to our home in Bombay will never be fulfilled. This boy, this behenchod…,' he flared again, '…has made sure I can never go back to India. First with that boat that came back from Dabhol, which those Pakis burnt. I had to compromise with the Pakis because of that.'

He suddenly grew silent. After a while he looked at Hanif and said quietly, 'You pushed me to make that deal with them, Hanif Bhai, didn't you? I did not want to go for it.'

Hanif understood that this was a festering wound that needed to be cauterized.

'Yes, Bhai. I did. And that was the right decision at that time.'

'How could it be? I told you that we should not bring religion into business. Now the police is after us, and instead of being considered Robin Hood who avenged the deaths of the poor, we are being branded traitors. Our associates have deserted us—Lambu Raju, Mast Mehendale, Nikka Nitin, Anthony Malabari. We had people from all across the country, from all communities, and now we are being talked of as Muslim terrorists and drug smugglers. We were not a communal gang; we were businessmen who were taking advantage of the stupid economic restrictions imposed by the archaic laws enacted by the countries. How was it right at that time, Hanif Bhai, to use our organization to kill innocent people?' Salim was only repeating what he had said before.

'Bhai, our people were calling out for justice. The blood of innocents had been shed.'

'Who are our people? I thought Indians were our people. Who was crying for that justice that you are talking of?'

'Bhai,' Hanif replied with the dreamy look of the believer, 'in our world, first there is family, and we owe our primary loyalty to the family. The cardinal principle is that no one threatens our family. Then comes my extended family, my relatives. It's my duty to take care of them. My loyalty after that lies with my qaum, my community and my religious brothers who are part of my faith. They come before my country, and if a hand is raised to smite them, it's my duty to defend them. The borders on earth dividing it into countries are artificial, but the blood that flows within my qaum is common. And at that time, their blood had been shed and that had to be avenged.'

'There were boys who owed us loyalty because of faith, and there were people who worked with us for profit,' he continued in a sombre tone. 'Those who were more loyal to money than to our fraternity, moved on. What we have now are the people who are loyal to us, and their number is increasing by the day. They may be silent now, but when the time comes they will all be there for us, standing shoulder to shoulder to defend our families, ready to lay down their lives for you. They have seen your loyalty towards them, and they will show theirs when the time comes. We may have suffered a few setbacks, but we have gained an army of grateful people. What we did was right, Bhai, and we will reap the rewards, in this world, and the other one too.'

Salim was silent. Hanif had spoken passionately, and there was truth in what he had said. One sacrificed so much for the family. He had left one country for his family. Maybe leaving the other for the qaum may not be so bad. But Hanif and Salim, it seemed, had drifted apart. They had chosen their ideologies. They had started as businessmen, but now one of them had become a crusader. Salim knew that he would have to deal with it, but not immediately. Right now he needed Hanif for his dealings with the Pakistanis.

'I hope what you say comes true, Hanif Bhai. But what hurts me the most is that this upstart puppy has, by now, forced my hand twice. Had that boat not returned from Dabhol, that Jatt fellow would not have been able to attack it, and I would have dealt with the Pakis on my terms. I would possibly have given them my routes, my boys, but I would have left it to the boys to decide if they wanted to work with the Pakis. And now, these Pakis know that I have been pushed to a corner again. The channel to move money from India is blocked, and the money that we could have gotten from the Mandrax will not come through. They are watching us, and they will be putting pressure on the sheikhs to call in their debts. And now this. This case under NDPS. Now they also know that there is no possibility of us ever going back to India.'

He paused for a while and then continued, 'They have been circling us like vultures for some time, Hanif Bhai, looking to pick our routes to Africa, so that they can get their heroin into America and Europe using the same route. They don't want just India, they want Africa also. And I guess they will also want the people who manage our money to manage theirs as well. I don't know where they will stop. They are not like us. They don't have a single drop of chivalrous or adventurous blood in them. They are pure mercenaries, heartless. And I may have to compromise with them. All because of that puppy! But how did he know about Qasim?' Salim was having a tough time moving past this one question.

'That is what surprises me,' Hanif said. 'There were only four people who knew about Qasim. You, I, Qasim himself and Bhatt. So either Qasim had a loose tongue, which I doubt, or Bhatt wanted Qasim out of the way to branch out on his own. But since Bhatt has also been implicated, that does not seem like a possibility.

'Think, Hanif Bhai,' Salim urged. 'Use your famous nose to sniff out the traitor. We have never spared a traitor, and we shall not this time either. And then I will kill Prakash.'

◆

Ritu, one of Qasim's girls, had come excitedly to Jamnagar to experience, as she said, bedding a criminal. Some girls have a fetish for uniforms, others have a weakness for the famous. In her case, it was for suave criminals.

'He must have such a devious mind. I never guessed he was so close to Salim. What crazy secrets he must have! I will have so much fun,' she told Prakash happily as she proceeded for her rendezvous with Qasim. Prakash suspected that a considerable portion of Qasim's funds would be transferred in the next few days, and maybe Ritu would report back to Salim, but he was not worried. He had control this time.

With each passing day, Qasim seemed to lose his fear of Salim and was willing to talk. He had guessed that he was not going to die at the hands of Kabir or Prakash. He also realized that he would need their support to survive in jail. He also intended to make the most of the time that was at his disposal before he was shifted to Sabarmati Jail. And he was ready to trade information for those luxuries.

'Yes, I laundered money for Salim Bhai,' he told Prakash, who was now the only person, except Ritu, to have access to Qasim. 'I sold the overseas rights for *Jali Jawani* to Salim Bhai's Dubai company for five crore, and then bought the DVD rights for *Chalu Sanam* for four crore. Salim Bhai's Indian company had bought those rights of *Chalu Sanam* for five lakh just a month back. He bought the *Jal Pari* building in Colaba with that money. Who owns the company? How would I know that? I just know it is Salim Bhai's company. Of course, I am sure of it.'

Ritu stayed for three days and Prakash would be there, interrogating Qasim every time she left for the hotel.

'You will only be able to sleep with her and be fresh for tomorrow if you tell me more.'

More, that became Prakash's mantra. I want more! How is he laundering his money? Who are his main associates? What are his main properties? Which companies have received investments from him? Does he own horses? Who is fixing the races for him? Why is he not interested in running the matka in Bombay? Who were the girls who have slept with him? Was Shabnam involved in any illegal activities for him? He would pester Qasim, threaten him, cajole him, giving him all kinds of incentives and soon, Qasim was remembering long forgotten incidents and events that he had considered insignificant but seemed fascinating to Prakash. Like delivering the .38 to Izaz Miyan, or sending Shivangi to that upcoming politician, or the private show of *Stripper* organized for the senior bureaucrat and his girlfriend. Nothing was recorded and no notes were taken, the incidents were filed in Prakash's very reliable memory.

The jackpot was hit on the third day when Qasim, irritated by lack of sleep and cigarettes after some extremely satisfying times with Ritu, finally blurted out, 'Why are you pestering me? Why don't you go and pester Mukul Sheth? He was the person who told me where to send the money.'

'Where do I find this Mukul Sheth?' Prakash asked.

28
Gossamer Ties

Hanif's inquiries took some time. He wanted to be sure of his facts before going to Salim about the traitor. Meanwhile, Salim had been holding long discussions with the Pakistani agents, trying to understand their workings and calculating the role he would be required to play in their scheme of things. He had aged visibly in just one month. The flamboyance was gone. The cigarette, his style statement, was now a compulsion. The famous moustache was now often unkempt.

They were all changing, and even the warm glow of the setting sun now appeared bloody red to him. *It is an appropriate time to brief Salim*, Hanif thought. *Blood is likely to flow, and soon.*

'I think I know who betrayed Qasim to Prakash.'

Salim looked up with faint interest. There were other things on his mind, and he had always known that Hanif would be able to sniff out the traitor sooner or later.

Another irritant out of the way, he thought. He was moving on to another life, and would not like to leave any debts behind. Even if that debt was the debt of betrayal that someone else owed him.

'Who?' he asked when Hanif stayed mum.

Hanif replied in a low voice, 'Shabnam.'

Salim exhaled slowly. He had always, vaguely, suspected it, but had hoped that his suspicions would turn out to be wrong, and Hanif would come up with a different name. He had also replayed all the events in his mind immediately after Qasim's arrest, and could not find any possible source of leak, except Shabnam.

'She was here the day you asked me to call Qasim to explain the design of the barrels to him.'

'And?' Salim remembered that.

'I asked Poonam, Shabnam's make-up girl, if Shabnam had met any government chaps. She says that there was a government officer staying in the same hotel as theirs during the Kutch shoot about six months ago, and they had to vacate a room for him. She is not sure if Shabnam met him. I found out. Prakash was staying there at the same time.'

Salim looked at Qasim, 'How long was he there?'

'Just one night.'

'That could be a coincidence.'

'Yes, but then, Shabnam went via Jamnagar while going to Bhuj the second time. She gave Poonam a bandhani saree she had brought from Jamnagar.'

'Had she told them that she was going to Jamnagar?'

'Yes. She said that a friend of hers knew about a lovely bandhani saree shop and she wanted to go shopping. She didn't want any publicity. I checked it. Nobody knows of such a friend.'

'And Prakash lives in Jamnagar,' Salim said thoughtfully. 'But that still doesn't tie her to the leak, although it does seem probable that she was the one.'

'We have punished people for less, Bhai,' Hanif said. 'But there is more. She left for Ahmedabad this morning without informing anybody. Only the taxi service that she uses had booked a car in her name for Ahmedabad. I rang up Prakash's office, pretending to be the assistant of a Commissioner, and was informed that Prakash is also in Ahmedabad for two days. And, just for good measure, she was never questioned by the police after the blasts, although everyone knew that she was your girl.'

'Three instances. One could be a co-incidence, two a probability or possibility in the world of traitors, but three! Three, I agree, is a certainty. Your nose never fails you, Hanif Bhai. You can still sniff out traitors. So what should I do? Should I take out a contract for both of them, together? The last one failed.'

'She is in Bombay. Bombay is always easier. She is not like Prakash, vigilant and aware. She would not even know when we kill her.'

'But I want her to know, Hanif Bhai. I want her to know why she is dying. She has betrayed all of us. My reputation is at stake. Salim's mistress ditches him and informs RI about his consignment. We will be the laughing stock of the underworld.'

'She is coming back to Bombay tomorrow. I will ask Liaqat to arrange for a painful death.'

Liaqat was one of the few hitmen still left with the organization.

'I want to talk to her before that. I want her to be afraid. She should be watching over her shoulder for the next twenty-four hours. She should know that she is going to die and that she can do nothing to prevent it.'

'I have a number that she left with the taxi service. She may be available there,' Hanif said.

'Call her,' said Salim.

◆

Shabnam was not alone with Prakash that day. Prakash had called her a week earlier, asking if she was free the next Saturday. She hated peremptory summons and therefore, refused to commit.

'Please come. It is important,' Prakash had said before disconnecting the call.

Shelley called the next morning.

'Well, hellllooo darling,' she said excitedly over the phone. 'I believe you are coming to Ahmedabad on Saturday? I am so excited to meet you again. It would be great if we can travel together. Should I pick you up?'

'Shelley too?' Shabnam wondered. She knew that the excited voice over the phone was a put on, intended to make her comfortable, but even then she was not going to travel with her, however much she liked Shelley. Ten hours together would be interminable if she found out that Shelley had been Prakash's love interest earlier. She politely refused the offer and then pondered over her reaction. *Am I jealous of Shelley? And does that mean that I am falling in love with Prakash? Unthinkable!* She chided herself, pushing the thought out of her mind.

Lal called Shelley the next morning.

'Ma'am, I believe that you are going to Ahmedabad on Saturday. I was told to accompany you, if you want.'

Shabnam, herself and now Lal. Shelley did not know Lal very well, and so naturally refused. But she wondered what Prakash was up to, gathering all his friends and close associates. She was now looking forward to the day.

◆

There were finally six of them in Ahmedabad. Prakash, Kabir, Shabnam, Shelley, Chudasama and Lal, all crowded in a small one-bedroom flat in the Satellite area in Ahmedabad.

'Sorry about the cramped space,' Kabir said apologetically, 'but this is my hideout. I use it when I don't want to be found, and it was furnished to take care of a lone man.'

'Why alone?' Shelley asked, looking meaningfully at Prakash and Shabnam. 'Haven't you taken any tips from your friend so far?'

Chudasama was also staring at the two of them. To say that he was shocked would be an understatement. He was among the first to arrive and had incredulously watched Prakash hug Shabnam when she walked in. He had also hugged Shelley, but it was clear that Shabnam and Prakash were more than friends. Lal was equally surprised, but knowing Prakash from his Pune days, it was easier for him to accept the fact that Prakash could be hugging the mistress of the guy who had been trying to kill him.

Introductions were brief, and everyone felt awkward, feeling confined with strangers in that small space. Prakash took some time out to make tea while Shelley settled for a cold drink and Shabnam had some plain water.

'What, no drinks?' Shelley joked.

Shabnam, feeling a little irritated, said, 'What, no joints?' That gave Chudasama a shock, and Kabir a better comprehension of the aroma back at Prakash's place when he had first met Shabnam.

'Will you two take it seriously?' Prakash said in a slightly admonishing tone, while trying to supress his laughter. He did not mind the careless comments, but there were lives at stake. However, it was better that they knew each other's weaknesses, as well as strengths, at the earliest. He hoped that they would understand that what he was about to ask them would put their lives in danger. He began to speak.

'Welcome to the first meeting of the Howling Hounds.'

'Howling Hounds? What is it, a new rock band? Like the Grateful Dead?' Shelley could not resist and Shabnam collapsed into another fit of giggles.

Lal and Chudasama wondered what they had got themselves into, but their discipline and faith in Prakash kept them there, listening to what was developing around them. Shabnam's presence had already thrown them off, and now the announcement of the 'Howling Hounds' added to the confusion. However, they could sense that something momentous was likely to happen. After all, Prakash would not have made his relationship with Shabnam and Kabir public unless he was planning something big.

'Not a rock band, but a band of rocking stars,' Prakash said, building on Shelley's dialogue, and then continued on a more sombre tone, 'Our lives have been intertwined over the past couple of years, and in myriad ways, all of us have become a part of the fight against Salim. So now...,' he continued dramatically, gesturing to all in the room, '...over here is one who is under a death threat, one who is likely to be under a death threat, two who have broken laws, one who is going to break the law, and Lal, who is, well, just the man who is at the right spot, always. Kabir sir thought that when we were anyway breaking the law to fight the underworld, why not do it in a more planned manner? After all, we trust each other. We will have a better chance of succeeding if we work together.'

'Do we trust each other?' Chudasama asked. He did not know anything about Lal, Shabnam or Shelley. The natural suspicions of an intelligence officer overtook his normally reticent nature.

Prakash gave Lal a wink, reminding him of their discussions on loyalty and trust.

'Okay, we may not trust each other yet, but we are certainly loyal to each other. All of us, Chudasama, have done something dangerous or illegal for the others over the past few weeks—all because of loyalty, if not trust. And now, today, everyone knows everybody's secret. Isn't that the first step towards absolute trust?'

'You are saying that you wouldn't have included me in this motley gang if I had not broken the law? Friendship counts for nothing for you. What a dog!' Shelley tried to lighten the mood.

'I am not the only one who counts here,' Prakash said. 'We are not standing in a line where I am the first point. Everybody has to trust everybody else. Let me finish, please. Otherwise, we will be locked up in here for the next two days.'

'And you want to be locked up with Shabnam alone,' Shelley said with a scoff, but she leaned back against the wall, indicating that she was ready to listen.

'But then, what are the dangerous or illegal acts that have been done? Let me in too, because I thought I had been absolutely irreproachable for the past few weeks. What were the dangerous acts committed by all of you?' Shabnam inquired with a faint smile, but in a challenging tone.

Prakash pondered for a short while, and then looked at Kabir, who gave him a nod. Shelley was absolutely quiet. She was looking at the floor. Besides Shabnam, she faced the maximum risk in exposure. She did not mind. She had grown up in a world full of secrets with the knowledge that secrets would be exposed at some stage. Prakash looked at her, and she smiled. Prakash was relieved. His gamble of getting all of them together seemed to be paying off.

He now needed Chudasama and Lal to believe in Shelley and Shabnam. This group would not be complete without them. They were the foot soldiers, and battles were not just fought by generals. He decided to make them comfortable first. That required telling them the crucial role that both Shabnam and Shelley had played in the operations so far.

'Chudasama first taught me the importance of slush funds for anybody doing undercover operation. He had created more than twenty benami bank accounts over the years, and he trusted me not just with the knowledge of them, but also let me use the slush funds parked in them over the years. Lack of money is the biggest constraint for any organization, and so, I decided to add to the corpus of free cash flow, as Shelley's finance managers would say. Shelley is the informer in the Mandrax case of Vapi, and she will get the reward money. She agreed to put it in these bank accounts for use of Howling Hounds.'

Chudasama went still, while Lal gasped. Both of them, since they met Shabnam that afternoon, had suspected that she had been the source for Prakash's information about Qasim. They never expected Shelley to be the informer. Shelley was again looking at the floor, while Lal was looking at her, thunderstruck. He had seen Shelley and Prakash in Dapoli, and knew that they were close. But even then, he could not have imagined that Shelley could commit to an act that could put her life in danger. Salim would kill her if he thought she was the informer. And she was not even sleeping with Prakash. He was in awe of her.

Prakash looked at Shabnam with a partly challenging, partly encouraging look. Shabnam realized that Prakash was leaving it to her to contradict him, and thus, announce her decision if she wanted to be part of this group. She decided to wait, and instead, asked, 'What money?'

Prakash looked a tad disappointed, as did Kabir.

'The money that an informer gets for giving tips to the government about possible smuggling or tax evasion. I convinced Shelley to reduce the information into writing and sign the sheet. Qasim led us to the drugs that were worth over three crore, and a committee has sanctioned a reward of forty lakh rupees for the informer.'

'Tell me more about the others. The saga seems to be interesting. Maybe I will make a movie out of it.'

'Lal is the backbone of all our surveillance outside Gujarat. He had been keeping an eye on Qasim, and on you as well because he thought that I wanted to interrogate you. I just wanted to ensure that Salim's men were not following you. He thought that he was watching Salim's mistress, and not one of my friends.'

'Sorry, ma'am,' Lal said a little sheepishly.

'And?' she queried.

'Nobody was following you until yesterday. Nobody was watching your house either. Kabir sir, of course, as you know,' he said, addressing Shabnam, 'killed one person in a fake encounter, and then illegally detained a number of others, and Chudasama and I were partners in that, although unknowingly. But it was Chudasama who shot Salim's hired gun at point blank range, somewhat illegally. All of us, as they say in the underworld, have made our bones.'

'And you, what have you done?' Shabnam asked.

'Put his life in danger to get Qasim to confess,' Kabir said in a slightly irritated voice. This questioning was getting to him. *Why couldn't she just trust them?* He thought.

'She doesn't know the granular details, boss,' Prakash said reasonably. 'And she is in equal danger now.'

Shabnam felt slightly chastised. She had, in her own travails, forgotten that it was Prakash who was first threatened by her paramour. She decided to come clean.

'Okay, Prakash is telling a lie. I told him about Qasim, and also about Bhatt and Mukul Sheth, but the rest was all his doing.'

There was little reaction to the announcement. Only Lal and Chudasama had not known the identity of the informer, but the seasoned intelligence officers that they were, they had guessed that Shelley was fronting for somebody. Shabnam was the logical choice. The only response came from Shelley, who got up and gave Shabnam a light hug, welcoming her to the group.

'But why us?' It was now Shelley's turn to voice doubt. 'What is so special about us that makes us capable of fighting the underworld? And why should I, who is having so much fun expanding my business, fight the underworld?'

'Oh, because you are going to have exciting times, rubbing a lot of bad people the wrong way, riling them up.' Prakash looked at her with a mischievous twinkle in his eye.

'Why *us*?' Shabnam repeated the question.

'Because all of us are unique in our own ways, Shabnam. You know more about Salim's gangs, and possibly also about the connections of the underworld with the underworld than any one of us. And Shelley is a wizard at networking and finances. She also knows about the political affiliations of the underworld. Lal and Chudasama have amazing knowledge of the history of the underworld, and are experts when it comes to analysing the changing trends in their activity. Kabir sir, by now, knows most of the bureaucratic connections of the underworld. With the pool of knowledge we have, and the resources that will be at our command, we can make a formidable combat force.'

'And we go and finish them all?' Shelley said sarcastically.

'There is no end to crime, or criminals, ma'am,' Lal said with typical sincerity. 'But a combat force makes a significant difference in the sequence of events when they unfold. We can't finish them all, but we can at least make the fight less unequal. And see, so far we are winning.'

The idea was making a little more sense to him. Chudasama's face still bore its usual inscrutable expression. Prakash knew that a long discussion, on another day, lay ahead of him.

'Ah, a practical guy, finally. Probably the only one among us,' Shelley said. 'Have you seen this group,' she continued indulgently, 'one who has never followed the rules, the other who has possibly never broken one.' She pointed at Lal's stiff figure. 'Another who has no vices...,' she said, gesturing towards Kabir, '...and me, who has no belief in morals. Plus a gangster's moll who is always in the public eye, and another who will never tolerate being in the news. Do you think we can even co-exist, let alone fight together?'

'Ideals and temperaments don't matter, loyalty and trust does.' This time, it was Kabir talking Prakash's language. 'We have a common goal, and all of us now have one binding thread—Prakash. All of us trusted him, now let us trust each other, for at the moment, we have a monster we need to bring down. And then, let's see. Maybe we will have too much fun to disband.'

'I was always in. You don't need to convince me, Mr Kabir,' Shelley said. 'It would be silly to miss all the excitement I am going to get for free. What do you want me to do with the money I get tomorrow?'

'Invest it, unless Shabnam has other ideas,' Prakash said. 'Honestly, it's her information, and thus her money, after all.'

Shabnam looked at each one of them. There was an expectant air about them. She knew that she could, with one sentence, halt the formation of this nascent bunching of rash individuals. They thought that they were playing a game, these people who had come out of nowhere and were now trying to change some of the eternal truths of life. Don't they know that power flows from the barrel of the gun? Do they seriously think that they can counter Salim? She wondered whether it would be better to take the money and vanish forever, maybe somewhere in the hills. She could change her name, her looks and pursue her passion for writing. But was money more important than friends like these? The loyal Lal, the ever supportive Shelley and the braveheart Chudasama. There cannot be a better set of people than these. And then she looked at Prakash, and realized that above it all, she may just be in love with Prakash. She was here for Prakash.

'Nah, invest it,' she said. She was now a part of the group as well.

'Wow! We are now officially a crime chasing spy group,' Shelley said in her typically sarcastic and jovial tone. 'Should I order some Saville Row suits, different wigs and a few pearl-handled revolvers? Am I supposed to take acting lessons from Shabnam so that I can infiltrate criminal gangs? Should I book tickets for exotic locales?'

There was only one way to shut her up. Order some food. Or pass her a joint for the night, which Shabnam, on the sly, did. Chudasama and Lal went out, got some food that all of them shared and left soon thereafter for their hotels. Chudasama was to be a witness when the money would be given to Shelley tomorrow, and Prakash had to be present as well. Kabir decided to go back to Jamnagar. But he had to stay and lock the house first. Shelley informed them that she too had called a late evening meeting in Ahmedabad.

'Which hotel are you staying in?' Prakash asked Shabnam, somehow always unsure of his status with her. They had slept together, and Shabnam had bared her soul to him, but he was still unsure every time he met her. There was still a sheer curtain between them, making their relationship opaque.

'I had no intention of staying at another impersonal hotel room. I am forced to stay in them during shoots, but given a chance, I shun them. A friend who studied here for her fashion degree has a flat. She was nice enough to pass on the key to me for this trip.'

'Should I drop you there?' Prakash asked tentatively.

'Of course, silly,' Shabnam said disarmingly. 'I am not going to hunt for the place all by myself. I have already told the taxi driver to pick me up from here tomorrow. Told him that I am going to be here in a two-day storytelling session. Keeping him with me would have led to the whole industry knowing what I was doing in Ahmedabad on a real-time basis.'

Kabir was watching Shabnam intently during the explanation. She looked quizzically at him.

'It's great that you have joined us. I was sceptical, but Prakash was confident that you would be a part of the Howling Hounds. But why are you doing this?' Kabir asked. 'You do understand that you may lose everything that you have worked for, that you may be throwing away all the gains you made by sleeping with Salim and that your life will now be constantly under threat.'

Shabnam gave Kabir a sweet smile, a smile that Prakash recognized as trouble.

'It's because I have sinned and now I need to atone for my sins,' she said sweetly.

Prakash couldn't choke back his laughter.

'Oh! Be serious, Prakash,' she admonished. 'Here I am, trying to be like Faustus, and you spoil it by laughing.' Then she continued, hurt evident in her voice, 'Why is it that I have to be interrogated at every stage? You didn't question Lal about his motives. And, may I ask? Why are you here? All the others, including me, are connected to Prakash in one way or another. Why are you here? Is it a hunt for glory?' She asked challengingly.

That was the second time Kabir had been challenged by Shabnam, and he was slowly coming to respect that she would ask for an explanation if she was asked to give one.

'Prakash and I come from the same milieu,' he replied. 'Those of us who clear the Civil Services Examination, we consider ourselves the elite, unapologetically. When the need arises, we stand by each other. Initially, I was with Prakash because of this brotherhood. But later, it was the excitement. It was non-stop, and I was also sucked into his whirlpool. I am here because I believe that we can make a difference. I have seen each of us act, and not just wait, for change.'

Shabnam looked a little mollified. This time, when she spoke, it was as if her voice was floating from somewhere far away.

'Imagine living a life of shattered hopes every day. In a world where the normal is considered passé. I came looking for a life that would be extraordinary, but was trapped in a tedious tale of monotony, expected to play the same role that others had played before me, over and over, again and again. It was a time warp. And then I met Prakash, for whom every action was a new adventure, pursued with an intensity that obliterated everything else. It was not for glory, nor for approval. He failed often, just as I did. But even when he failed, he resurrected himself to resume the pursuit. He and I, we died a thousand deaths of disappointment, and then lived again, with a flame of hope that was lit eternally within us. Have you ever noticed how often he had been ridiculed, or how often he had been taken for a ride? But did you ever see him bitter, or shaken? His faith in himself and his friends never wavered. He had the courage to believe that anything that goes wrong will be right again. He had the courage to dream, like me. We have the same psyche. We believe in intensity, passion, hope and loyalty. I am not a gambler, but I have taken my chances in life. And as the dice of life rolls, I would like nobody else but Prakash to stand by me when the chips fall.'

Kabir was speechless. Whatever he had expected, it had certainly not been this.

Shabnam took a long breath, and then continued. 'Death changes you, sir. And unexpected death gives you a close peep at your own mortality. There were too many untimely deaths among people I counted as my friends. Those who died without even getting a chance to try and chase a part of their dreams. There are too many demons dominating my dreams as well. There are choices you make in life. Some haunt you forever. I don't want to relive my life, and probably it's time that I fly with an angel to experience the magic of life.'

'She did that to me too,' Prakash said after a suitable pause, letting it sink into Kabir. 'Makes one feel so inadequate. I never knew that I was all of this. I thought I was just the nincompoop trying to make good in life.'

'Would it have been more appropriate if I had said that I am in this to extract sex, drugs and money from a loser?' Shabnam spoke with a mischievous, impish look. Now that she had chosen her path, Kabir sensed suppressed excitement in her. She seemed liberated and was laughing again, wondering whether she had, maybe, discovered herself. Maybe Prakash was not ready, but she surely was.

'But then, that would be difficult to explain, you know. Prakash is not as good in bed as Salim, and Salim provides me money, while I supply drugs to Prakash…like these four joints I am carrying for him all the way from Bombay. It's all so convoluted, so let me try to put it in Shelley's words,

I love Love—though he has wings,
And like light can flee,
But above all other things,
Spirit, I love thee—'

Thou art love and life! Oh come, Prakash picked up the refrain from where Shabnam had left, narrating in his deep baritone. *Make once more my heart thy home.*

'Shelley?' queried Kabir, bewildered.

'Not our Shelley, sir. This one is by Percy Bysshe Shelley. Although, I am sure our Shelley can write better limericks than Percy,' Shabnam said. 'Leave it sir. We will have more time to understand each other, what with the Howling Hounds set to hound the underworld.'

They left, arm in arm, leaving Kabir to wonder whether the idea to bring them together had been the right one. They seemed like a bunch of Romantics, intent more on dying than living.

He did not see that they were not out there just to fight crime. That was just the spinoff of their attempt at living life.

29

The Price of Freedom

The interiors of the one-bedroom flat off Jamnagar highway were painted in orange, yellow and red. The bedcovers were of Bhuj patchwork, and the bedsheets in the cupboard were straight off the Law Garden market in Ahmedabad.

'I am pathetic when it comes to making beds, even my hostel matrons used to say that. So you make the beds while I will arrange the cold drinks and something to eat.'

'It's going to be a psychedelic nightmare of a night,' Shabnam groaned, looking at all the reds, oranges and yellows on the walls and the bed. 'But who cares?'

They made frantic love after the first joint, Shabnam's prediction of convergence of psychedelic colours proving true and spurring them on.

'Love, sex, money, drugs,' Prakash said. 'All here, and you wanted to speak of intensity. Poor Kabir must be scratching his head.'

'I doubt it. I think he must be scratching his balls, because I know that he has them at least. Head, I don't know.' Shabnam laughed maniacally in that hedonistic mix of hash and sex.

They had the second joint in a leisurely manner.

'What now?' Shabnam asked. 'I am going to be busy with my shoots. I have three films in hand, all big banners.' She was proud. 'With you in Jamnagar, will this nomadic life continue, frenzied sex over clandestine meetings?'

'You make me feel like a boy again,' replied Prakash, the high helping him overcome his insecurity. 'I am scared to admit my feelings for you even to myself, afraid to think of giving you a call just to say I miss you, and then, even after mustering the courage to do it, I won't do that. I thought of sending you a perfume, so normal otherwise, but couldn't do it with you. I can't, simply can't, take decisions where you and I are concerned.'

Shabnam stared at him, the glazed eyes failing to conceal the understanding reflected in them.

'You are not ready to enter a relationship, maybe because you want Shelley, and you are scared of losing her forever. It scares you, taking responsibility for someone else, and now you think that you have to care for me. You flatter me,' she said, kissing him lightly on the forehead.

'Shut up,' Prakash replied. 'You are spoiling my high.'

Inside, he churned. Shabnam was repeating what Shelley had once said to him.

Shabnam cuddled him, and kissed him gently on the lips. The naked bodies fondled each other till they were ready for a more relaxed bout of love making.

'Open your eyes,' Shabnam said.

Prakash stared at her.

'They're kaleidoscopic, because of one star I can see in them.' She laughed as she thrust harder.

After the third joint, they were lolling against each other in a somnolent mood when the phone started ringing.

'It must be the driver,' Shabnam said. 'But why is he calling at night? Fuck it. Let him call tomorrow morning.'

'Could be your friend? Maybe she's trying to find out if you are using or misusing her place. Pick it up.'

'If you say so, but you know, you are such a buzz kill,' she said playfully, reaching for the receiver. He watched her listen for a moment, then saw her face blanch and her body sag. She seemed to crumble, and her frail form seemed to shrink further. It looked like she was trying to transform herself into an insect so that somebody could stomp her.

He took the phone from her, and threw his arms around her.

'Yeah, what is it?' he said on the phone.

'Who are you, *bhadwe*?' The voice over the phone said. 'Give the phone back to Shabnam if you love your life.'

He was riled up. He had never been good at responding to threats. Although he had never heard the voice on the phone, he could immediately guess the identity of the man on the other end. He looked at Shabnam, who trembled slightly in his arms and gave her a reassuring look.

'Not before you tell me who you are. She seems scared of you. She is hardly in a position to talk.'

'It's good that she is scared. Because she is going to lose her life soon, and so are you.' The voice was calmer now. 'This is Salim Bhai from Dubai.'

He had possibly used this introduction a thousand times, making the person at the other end of the line collapse in terror.

'And who are you?'

'Prakash,' he replied simply.

This time there was a pause at the other end, as Salim possibly digested the information. And then Salim continued, anger palpable in his voice, 'So, this whore is sleeping with you now? Good, now both of you can die together.'

Prakash looked at Shabnam. Her eyes seemed so large on her wan face. *What has she gotten herself into?* he thought. She had left her home aspiring for fame, for the adulation of fans and the admiration of her peers. And then, he had landed into her life, although not by his own design, and had changed everything for her. He was possibly her escape from reality, a fantasy chased and a few fleeting moments stored in her memory. But now, her life was under threat. And although she must have thought about it and even anticipated it,

Prakash knew that the first credible threat, even over phone, shatters you. That threat was real. More real than anything else. There would be nothing else she would be able to think of for the next few days. She would be afraid to step out of the house; she would be watching over her shoulder constantly and jumping at any sudden sound on sets. A slow rage burned inside him. Whatever mistakes she may have committed, she did not deserve this.

'Nothing like that is going to happen, Salim Bhai. Or Mukul Sheth will be singing a different song in the lock up for attempting to murder me. And he will have to explain to the public why he is managing the money of a traitor like you.'

There was a period of short silence at the other end.

'Are you trying to threaten me? *Nobody* threatens me. Both of you will be killed before you leave Ahmedabad. Try talking about Mukul Sheth once you are dead. How dare you threaten Salim Bhai? In any case, you cannot touch Mukul Sheth. He is protected.'

'Oh yes. Call him and tell him that. He and I already had a long chat. He did not call you after that? Has he lost confidence in your ability to protect him? I think he may now be more afraid of me than you. Does that tell you something about me? Or about your failing clout? So to continue, neither Shabnam nor I will lose our lives, and maybe, in return, I will not reveal that you own *Jal Pari,* or that you also own *Shreejeet.* Or that you have the majority shareholding in *Scourge,* or that the contract to pick garbage in two major cities has been given to your benami companies.'

The pauses at the other end were getting longer.

'And do you think that this is sufficient for me to spare your lives? It doesn't affect me even if you make it public.'

'You think so? That's just about three hundred crore I am talking about. I guess that will hurt a little at least, having those three hundred crore tied up for a long time, particularly when there is a bit of a financial crisis that you are facing after the Mandrax bust.

Are the sheikhs putting you under pressure? And I do believe that Mehendale is also looking for support to take over your networks. Will you be able to hold him back after losing three hundred crore? Can the Pakistanis really protect you in Dubai? Will these three hundred crore be the catalyst that can bring you down, Salim Bhai?' Prakash gambled desperately, throwing every rumour he had heard over the past few days at Salim.

This time, there was a longer silence at the other end.

Salim wondered how much Prakash knew. Intelligence agencies had known about his operations, but his finances had always remained secret. Those were sacrosanct. Mukul Sheth was the treasurer of a major political party, and it was the ultimate coup that he had pulled. Nobody ever suspected, or even if they suspected it, had the gumption to question the treasurer of a political party. They could not be touched. And so, his money had been safe, mixed with the finances of a political party. And now somebody had gone and questioned his treasurer, and was threatening to expose him.

'I will have you killed in the next two hours,' Salim continued, more rhetoric than conviction evident in his tone.

'You will do nothing of that kind. You think that I am the only one who has this information? If you can have a syndicate, then so can I, and without me, they have no reason to hold back. They will not just go after your properties but also after the bookies who fix the races for you. The jockeys are not so well protected, Salim Bhai. Do you think that they will be able to resist sustained police interrogation? We will also go after every builder who has ever paid you any money. The flow of money is going to dry up. That will finish your run at the top, what with your foot soldiers not being paid. Where will be your reputation as a Bhai then, Salim Bhai?'

Shabnam was now giving him a hopeful look. He gave her a wink, reassuring her. She had probably never heard anyone threaten Salim, but then there were very few people who actually had decided to fight for their lives against him. Most of them had ended up dead before they could even think of fighting back. And Prakash's stint in the government had taken away his capacity to listen to threats. *Not that I used to succumb to them earlier, but now I am more arrogant*, he thought. It may be the result of surviving a killer. And maybe the result of going after a gangster. He held on to Shabnam tightly, hoping desperately that the gamble he was playing worked.

'Doesn't affect me too much,' the voice said, but he could detect a tinge of uncertainty there. He decided to go for the kill.

'But it will, especially when we release the list of your African contacts. You had, after all, transferred money to them through Mukul Sheth. I don't need to arrest them. Just need to give it to the DEA so that they know that they are with you. Just hurt them enough so that they are of no use to the Pakistanis anymore. And revealing the amount of money they paid to the politicians through Mukul Sheth could be the icing on the cake. Will they lose their heads? And if so, what would happen to your reputation as a protector.'

This, he knew, would hurt. Shabnam looked at him quizzically. She had no idea about the amount of work Prakash, Lal and Chudasama had done after the revelations by Qasim, and hearing him, she nursed a faint hope of having a fighting chance. The silence felt interminable.

Then the voice said, a little gruffly this time, 'You seem to know a lot. Where did you come by this information? That whore doesn't know this much.'

'There is more, and there will be people waiting to act on each part of it if either of us here are hurt. I am not fighting a war by laid down rules, Salim Bhai, and I am ready to compromise. Let you live and rebuild, if you let us live. I am already under a death sentence. It is you who have to decide if you can live with that much money blocked and your networks rendered ineffective. Will the Sheikhs and the Pakistanis let you survive then? Maybe they will, but you will lose at least ten years. Will your rivals let you survive till then? Withdraw the contract on me, Salim Bhai, and maybe all of us can live. Tell some reporter that it was given wrongly, or that I had sought your forgiveness, or any such crap. I can live with a loss of face, and it won't matter to me. Think, Salim Bhai, it's just two lives.'

This time, the pause was even longer. Prakash clenched the phone, his knuckles white, while Shabnam nervously played with his nipples.

'Read the Khaleez Times day after tomorrow,' Salim finally said. 'Ask someone to post it to you if you don't get it in India…'

Prakash interrupted him to say, 'Wait, there is more…"

'Don't push it, boy,' Salim said over the phone. 'I am not used to people dictating to me.'

'Nor am I, Salim Bhai,' Prakash said mercilessly, but in a softer tone. There was one more life, besides his, at stake. 'I just want to make sure that this reprieve lasts for some time. After all, I lose all leverage if you sell these properties or surrender these contracts tomorrow. So just a small request. Don't do that for a year.'

Salim heard, and then, without a word, disconnected the phone.

'Yes!' Prakash said exultantly.

30
The Mohajir

Back in Dubai, Hanif looked at Salim, concerned. He had never seen Salim so subdued, not even when he had received death threats.

'What happened?' Hanif asked.

'You should have killed him a long time ago, Hanif Bhai. It's all your fault. You should have killed him when I told you to.'

'We will kill him now. I will make sure that he is killed tomorrow. Even if I have to go to India for it.'

'It's too late. His time will come, but it's not now. I need to talk to that new boy at Khaleez Times. I need to give an interview.'

'What happened? Why do you need to give an interview?' Hanif was concerned now.

'With all the rumours circulating, I think it's the right time to set the records right. I need to tell people that I am not a drug smuggler, despite what Prakash and his team may say, and to publicly state that I had never given a contract to kill Prakash, and whoever acted to kill him, acted under a wrong impression and that anyone who threatens Prakash in future will have to answer to me. I am also going to say that we are not in the business of making films and that we had never had any relationships with anyone in the film world, including Qasim, and Qasim has wrongly implicated me.'

'That will endanger Qasim's life in jail,' Hanif said.

'That is not my concern,' Salim replied curtly. 'And Hanif Bhai, we will shift to Karachi in the next few days. It's time that we explored avenues beyond India. Let us be global players. '

'It's decided then?' Hanif asked.

'Yes, it's time for a change. There is no option, and they are opening the world for us. I will be a Mohajir, as would you be, but then, if I can't go back to India, then it's better I live where some of our people live.'

'Inshallah!'

'Yes, but I wonder is it this what we worked for. But there will be time to wonder, and ponder, Hanif Bhai. For now, let's look forward to the nautch girls of Karachi.'

31

The Journey of Life

Shabnam looked at Prakash expectantly.

'Hope reigns eternal. He has asked me to read the Khaleez Times day after tomorrow, so we are alive at least till then,' he said, trying to lighten the mood.

'Don't be crass, tell me what happened.'

'He listened to me, and I think I was able to convince him of the folly of pursuing a course of action he had probably decided upon in a fit of anger. I think I was able to get through to him that peace and non-violence are the major doctrines by which the world survives.'

Shabnam stared angrily at Prakash.

'Are you feeling light-headed? Do you need a cold shower? Or maybe some appropriately targeted violence that will ensure that you don't ever have a future generation to spew the trash you are currently dishing out?'

'Okay, okay,' Prakash said, relenting. 'One is bound to be a little light-headed when one has won a reprieve of his life. Our lives,' he said, looking fondly at Shabnam.

'He agreed?' she said with a little bit of hope and disbelief.

'It seems like it. And it seems like he has also given up on you. Couldn't handle a firebrand like you, I think.'

Shabnam fell silent. It all seemed so incredible. The journey so far. In the past five years, she had moved from being a small-town girl doing bit roles in movies, to being the concubine of the biggest gangster of the country, and then, the bed mate of his nemesis.

Incidentally, she thought, *she had also achieved stardom in that period.*

'Are you really ready to let him go and let him have those three hundred crore you talked of, for my life?' she asked. The feeling that she was alive despite Salim knowing about both of them dawned on her.

'It's not just your life. I negotiated for mine as well,' he said, continuing softly. 'After all, you are my life as well now.'

'Are you planning to break all barriers in one night? Now you are even talking like a romantic,' Shabnam said, looking at him with bright eyes. With the fear dissipating gradually, she was experiencing the light-headedness of hope.

'Who else knows?' she queried.

'About Salim's assets? Everyone. That I was going to use the information to negotiate for my life? No one. That was impulsive, but now it's done, and I am happy it's over.'

'Happy it's over? How long do you think this reprieve will last? Salim neither forgives, nor forgets. He is known to have stalked his rivals for months, sitting and smiling with them across tables, before killing them ruthlessly. How long do you think you have before he comes for you? And will your friends accept this?'

'I don't think I will have to look over my shoulder for some time now. And I have no scruples about letting go of either Salim or his money. There is a war coming, and we can't fight that war if we are dead. Anyway, do you even know how many consignments of Salim were caught when he was smuggling that silver and gold? He was getting away with smuggling contraband worth over ₹3,000 crore, making more than ₹500 crore a year by exercising his monopoly over the coasts of Bombay and Konkan. What is three hundred crore when he is ready to pay for it with two lives? And it was not as if he would have necessarily lost it. He also knew that. We would have tied him up in the courts for some time, but there was always the possibility that he would have won ultimately. Have you ever seen a major crook losing a case? It was a simple deal of dropping troubles. I dropped the trouble of looking over my shoulder, and he dropped the trouble of getting his assets locked up in court cases for a long time.'

Prakash decided to skip over the second part of Shabnam's question. He would face Lal and Chudasama's indignation later, although he doubted that it would come to that.

Shabnam looked at him. He sounded so convincing that she actually wanted to believe him. She wanted to believe that they were going to live. But more than that, she wanted to believe that what he had done was the right thing.

'Are you happy that you compromised? I thought that you never compromised. And you still have not answered what the Howling Hounds will think,' she said, remembering her first-ever encounter with Prakash. A sense of nostalgia overwhelmed her. *How is he changing so fast?* she wondered.

'One of my friends recently told me that I had graduated from being a bootlegger to being a pimp,' Prakash said seriously. 'It hurts, but see where it got us. Head-to-head with the most dreaded gangster of the country, and he blinked. No, it isn't compromise. It's the reality of death that always wins over the notions of living. So I chart my path to damnation, for there is hardly any redemption, ever. And because of that, I don't mind compromising in life.'

Shabnam wondered if she knew Prakash at all. But then, dropping all her concerns, she buried her head in his arms. 'I am safe for now. I will think about it tomorrow,' she said to herself.

'Although I know that I am safe for now, I can't get it out of my head that he will come for us again.'

'Yes. I expect him to. But not in the near future. And this time, we will be ready. "Howling Hounds" is not as motley a force as you think. We have the motivation, we have the knowledge and now, courtesy you, madam, we also have the intelligence and the resources. And more important than that, we know where his money is. We will be watching it very closely. Yes, he will come for us, but he will be surprised by how well prepared we would be to face him.'

Shabnam desperately wanted to believe all he was saying. She looked at him, searching for any sign of doubt on his face, any indication that he was saying all this just to reassure her. But she saw utter calm and absolute confidence. He looked like the same brash and rash young renegade she had first met by chance at a party in Pune, ready to take on the world.

'And in the interim, what do we do while we wait for him to strike at us again?' she asked tentatively.

'Ah, in the interim. In the interim,' Prakash said, looking romantically at Shabnam, 'we will be looking for...

a World in a Grain of Sand
And a Heaven in a Wild Flower
Hold Infinity in the palm of your hand
And Eternity in an hour...'

'You know that this is a religious poem? William Blake was talking about God here. How can you try to convert a religious poem into a romantic composition?'

'If people can call the *Kamasutra* a religious work, why can't I call Blake's poem a romantic composition?'

'What are we talking about at the moment, romanticism or religion?'

'Is there a difference between the two?'

'Maybe not,' Shabnam said, laughing.

'I thought you would finally see it my way. Pass me another joint, and let us try and achieve a fusion of the two,' he said, feeling content.

In Gratitude

To my father, who was always sure of both his sons' success;

To the school that taught me to never quit;

To my wife Niti, who 'carried the world on her shoulders' to ensure I could chase my dreams;

To Ishan, who had faith in me;

To Ekansh, who is still trying to create the ideal world;

To my college friends—Shantanu, Bhavna and Roshan—who helped shape the book;

And to Dibakar—without your inputs, this book would not have been what it is.